STARS IN DIFFERENT SKIES

Shelby Elizabeth

For my parents.

CONTENTS

Prologue

The whispers rose to shouts that night.

There was always whispering in the alleys of Brooklyn: the people passing by on the sidewalk late at night or, more accurately, in the earliest hours of the morning; the voices carried down from the residents living in the surrounding buildings when their windows were open; the hushed tones of the people who lived in the alleys.

The city was never completely silent. Tony had gotten pretty good at listening to those whispers, sorting through the information, and acting on anything that might be useful. If he heard something bad, he mentioned it to his friend Mack, making sure to keep his head low so he didn't get caught. Not that anyone cared to even try catching him. The only person who even knew his name was Mack, and Tony didn't let the man stay with him for too long at a time.

He didn't want to be taken somewhere, like an orphanage. He was just fine where he was.

But as he listened that night, tucked into the dark corner, the whispers seemed to be much louder. Occasionally there were loud nights, with shouts and sirens. Sometimes things got violent, and Tony had to hunker down for a few hours for safety. But this volume wasn't chaotic like any of those nights. And the whispers seemed to be about one thing, though it took him a few minutes to catch it.

The parallel world. That was what they were all saying. The whispers weren't fearful. If anything they sounded hopeful, incredulous but amazed. Tony poked his head out a little further, so his ear was closer to one conversation that was drifting towards him.

"Upstate, that's what I heard. What's that place with the racing horses again? Sarah-something?"

"Saratoga?"

"That's the one. There's people flooding there, 'parently. Says they can make new lives in the parallel world."

Tony clung on to these words. Parallel world. Saratoga. New life.

Can it be real, he wondered? He'd never heard the whispers be this loud and not seen something happen. It had to be real! He felt energy rush through him, and knew he wouldn't be sleeping anytime soon. He wanted to check this out.

He ducked as far back into the shadows as he could, hoping to disappear from sight. Not that anyone even knew he was there; they ignored each other. He was thankful of his dark skin and clothes, and the late hour, and once he was confident he hadn't been seen by anyone he Shifted.

No one batted an eye at the bluebird as it flew over their heads. Tony could've laughed at how easy it was to get away like this. If only those people knew what he could do. But he knew none of them were Shifters, or Elementalists. He didn't actually know any others, though he knew some of the animals in the city had to be Shifters in disguise.

Tony expanded his wings and flew higher, level with the tops of the buildings. The sky was its usual gray-black, lit up by the lights of New York City and the pollution in the air. He flew to an alley a few streets down, landing on the railing closest to it. Nothing suspicious about a bird landing on a railing. There were a few people around a fire, eating and talking. He listened for what seemed a long time before he heard it, but they definitely said parallel world. This group didn't know where it was, but just the fact that they talked about it had to mean something.

Didn't it?

His stomach rumbled, and he looked hopefully at the food they had. He hadn't eaten in hours. Maybe they would toss him a piece of crust. He hopped to the ground and chirped at them, catching their attention. Most of them completely ignored him, but there was a teenage girl who stopped to look at him. He took a small hop closer, doing his best to look cute. That got her. She broke off a piece of the bun and tossed it to him. Tony jumped on it and took off. It was always easier to get food as a bird. People were always nicer to animals.

He gulped down the crust and flew to a few more whispering alleys, collecting as much information on the parallel world as he could. No one seemed to know much. That first group, in the alley he had originally been in, definitely knew the most.

He flew back there, hoping they were still talking about it. But they'd moved on to a different topic.

He flew to a tree and settled in there, deciding to sleep as a bird that night. It was probably safer than being in that alley, and he didn't want to listen to those people. Tony could count the number of people he trusted even minimally on one hand, and there was only one person could he call a friend. That person was Mack, a thirty-something police officer with a serious face and a loud voice. At first he'd scared Tony, but Mack was the kindest person he knew. He was just loud and didn't smile much.

Tony decided to go see him the next morning. Maybe his friend would know something about the parallel world, or find something out.

The night passed quickly. Tony snoozed. He didn't pass out, but he was definitely comfortable, safe in the branches of a tree. When he dropped down from the tree the next morning, back in his human body, he felt very rested.

He knew Mack liked to check in on him, and walked to the spot Mack usually waited. The officer told Tony he would go to that spot every day, for a few minutes, so he could have help if he needed it. He'd also told Tony his usual route, so Tony had a way to find him. Today Tony went to the meeting spot. Mack usually drank his morning coffee there, near the pastry shop.

"Morning, stranger," Tony said when Mack arrived a few minutes after he did.

Mack smiled one of his rare smiles. "Good to see ya, kid. Hungry?"

"Starving."

"Let's get some breakfast, huh? You look like you got something to talk about."

Man it was easy to be with Mack. Sometimes

Tony wished he could live with the guy. Mack had offered more than once to take him in. But he couldn't accept. He couldn't take advantage of the man like that. He was completely fine with letting Mack buy him a few meals a week, though. It kept Mack from worrying too much, and made sure Tony had at least one solid meal that day. And Mack liked to buy something for himself that he didn't end up eating, so Tony had a little something for later, though neither of them acknowledged this obvious trick.

Once they had coffee and a few fruity pastries they walked back outside. Tony licked a speck of cherry off his finger, savoring the last morsel. "Thanks for the food."

"You always have a meal with me," Mack said seriously. "So what's up?"

"Have you heard anything about the parallel world?"

Mack sighed. "That nonsense again. What about it?"

"Is it real?" Tony looked hard at Mack. "What do you know?"

"It's some scam. No such thing as a parallel world. You shouldn't waste time thinking on it."

"There's not a chance it's real?" Tony pressed. He told Mack all the conversations he'd over-heard. "I've never heard it that loud for a good thing before. Seems real to me."

Mack looked almost sad. "You want a fresh start, don't ya?"

Tony looked at his feet. "Not too much, but this might be my chance for something better. I don't think I'll get many."

"Tony, why don't you come and stay with me? I got plenty of space and—"

"Mack, you know I can't," Tony interrupted.

"But why not?" Mack demanded. Tony hadn't seen him so agitated in some time. "You need a home, and I've got one!"

"Because you'll get sick of me," Tony said bitterly. It had happened before. He'd tried staying with a friend that had an apartment, and he'd seen how miserable they got after he lived there a few weeks. So he'd run away, back to the streets. He hadn't seen Craig since. He couldn't let the same thing happen with Mack.

"I'll decide what I feel," Mack said. "And that won't happen."

Tony looked away, stone-faced. He knew Mack was trying to look out for him. It didn't change anything. Mack made an exasperated sound and started to walk away, but turned around. "At least promise me you won't do anything stupid."

"You know me," Tony said.

Mack sighed again. "Yeah," he said. "I do."

"See ya." Tony walked the opposite direction, sticking his hands in his pockets. He hated making Mack upset, but he couldn't promise that he wouldn't at least look for the parallel world. If it really did exist, it was worth checking out. He had to try. And he had to do it before the opportunity was gone. He looked at Mack's retreating figure and silently apologized to the officer, and thanked him again. Then he Shifted and flew up, to the north, towards upstate.

He stopped a few times to rest, including overnight, but by that time the next day he was in Saratoga Springs. Flying overhead, there seemed to be a lot of people in one of the parks, moving along a trail. He flew lower and faltered when a family passed through a glowing rock wall. That had to be the parallel world!

He flew closer and watched another person walk through, and waited for the guards to look at the next person. Then he flew past them, and into the parallel world.

Into a new life.

CHAPTER 1

The Kingdom of Astrum

Demetrius had been called the Prince of Shadows for as long as he could remember, but he hadn't expected the title to be so literal. In this world, he was living the role of a prince. Christopher had named himself King, and Demetrius Prince, of the Kingdom of Astrum as soon as they had enough of a population to merit it. As strange as it had been initially, Demetrius had grown used to the responsibilities associated with the position. With the rigorous education and etiquette lessons his father had put him through since pre-adolescence, he was thoroughly prepared for the position. There was always something nagging at his consciousness each night, though. Something he couldn't figure out, which left him in a near constant state of dissatisfaction.

He felt muddled.

Demetrius didn't think he'd ever felt muddled, but that was the only word he could identify to describe it: as though he were forgetting something, or that information was glossing over his mind without being absorbed—but he didn't know what. This unknown, muddled feeling assaulted him every night as he lay down to sleep.

It was better in the mornings. All day, really. He had tea with his father and went out into the kingdom, checking in with the citizens and attending to tasks Christopher assigned. It was fulfilling work, and he was pleased to do it— yet once evening struck, and especially closer to when he went to sleep, the placid contentment faded.

His father had been preparing him for this life for as long as he could remember. Demetrius knew something was wrong.

This life was shadowed.

He just didn't know why, and by the time he realized anything felt off he passed out from exhaustion, and the morning reset everything.

He only ever realized it at night, but this cycle continued for a long, long time.

Nine months.

Christopher may not have been able to *control*

a dragon, but he'd proven more than capable of keeping one *contained*, Tristan thought bitterly, marking another day on his log. Today marked nine months since he, Riley, Wyatt, Allyssa, and Demetrius entered the parallel world—nine months since Christopher had taken over.

Tristan looked out the window of his room in the castle. The trees were filling up with leaves again, branches becoming overwhelmed with green. Spring had arrived in full force. Could the others see the change in seasons?

He had no idea where the others were. He assumed they were imprisoned, as he was. Sure, he wasn't in an actual cell. He had a comfortable bed, and access to clean clothes. He had a decent view. He was brought two good meals a day, and provided books and writing materials whenever he requested them. He was still a prisoner. Tristan wasn't allowed outside his room without multiple guards present. He wasn't allowed to see anyone. The isolation was taking a toll, forcing him to find ways to occupy himself.

He'd thought those depictions in novels and movies, of people in prison focusing on physical exercise, were unrealistic. He understood now. There was only so much reading he could do before he needed to move, and with minimal space, exercises like sit-ups and push-ups satisfied that need. It was something to do to keep from going mad or becoming lost in despair. Something to center himself, help him stay sharp.

He warred with himself inside, vacillating between rage at himself for opening the portal and confidence that he had done what the Celestials wanted. He knew they'd wanted it, from the dreams they'd been getting. He'd thought it made sense to open the portal as an attempt to stop, or at least lessen, the war. He'd just also underestimated how quickly Christopher would move to control the situation for his own benefit. He'd thought they would have time to speak with the Celestials privately before they rejoined Christopher, so everyone would be ready for the inevitable betrayal.

He'd been wrong.

Every day brought another opportunity for escape. He just had to be ready for it. That he'd tried dozens of times didn't matter. He had to believe next time, he would break through their defenses.

It had been two months since his last escape attempt, and a great effort on his part to act defeated. He hoped Christopher would take the lack of resistance as a sign Tristan was giving up. Tristan just needed the man to lower his guard a bit more, and he could fight his way through the men Christopher sent.

Rage soared within Tristan at the thought of Christopher, an emerald aura blazing into existence around him. The man had stolen nine months of his life. Had kept him from his family, put his friends in danger.

Today would be the day Tristan would break through his defenses. It had to be. He would make it. *Now,* he told himself, *before I decide to wait again.*

He took a steadying breath that focused his power, strode to the door, seized the handle, and pulled with all his might. The door shuddered against the pressure and then popped off its hinges. Tristan threw the slab of wood to the side and ran out, arm already up to block the attack of the first guard permanently stationed outside. The second guard landed a hit on Tristan's back, but Tristan barely felt it. Rage and determination surged in his veins. He would not fail again.

He had to get past these two quickly. It was usually the sounds of the struggle, and these two guards' calls for attention, that drew more people to the scene, and ultimately overwhelmed Tristan. He slammed the first guard into the wall and immediately spun and did the same with the second. He must have used more force with the second guard, whose head struck the wall with a sickening force that immediately rendered him unconscious. Tristan turned back to the first guard and struck him with a precise blow, making the guard's eyes roll up in his head.

Tristan didn't wait to see the first guard fall to the floor. He turned and ran. No sounds captured his ear, giving him hope that he'd taken those two out quickly enough to avoid their call for reinforcements. As soon as Tristan rounded the corner of that hallway he slowed to a brisk walk. Running flat out might attract attention he didn't want.

He forced himself to drop his Shift in another effort to go unnoticed, and moved through the halls of the castle. He knew he had to find a staircase at some point; the view from his window told him he was at least one floor above the ground. Tristan passed a few servants who were so focused on their tasks they didn't notice him, and walked by quickly.

He stopped when he saw a familiar figure. He'd just seen the stairs he was searching for, but the figure in his periphery made him stop. Demetrius, he realized after a slight delay. His back was to Tristan, but though Demetrius and Christopher strongly resembled each other, Demetrius had a very different body type. This was Demetrius. Tristan threw a look at the stairs and then partially Shifted and strode over to him.

"Demetrius!" he said in a loud whisper.

The boy turned, saw Tristan, and frowned.

"Surprised to see me out of my cell?" Tristan pushed him against the wall. "How can you live with yourself, knowing we're prisoners? How can you let us sit in cells?"

Demetrius had his mouth open and searched Tristan's face with a strange expression. "What are you talking about?"

Some of Tristan's indignation ebbed. The look in Demetrius' eyes, and the alarm in his voice . . . it was the same as that day. "You don't know, do you?" Tristan asked slowly.

"Don't know what? What are you doing here?"

Something like horror moved Tristan, and he let go of Demetrius. All this time he'd wondered how Demetrius, who had seemed so much like a friend, could stand to have Tristan and the others held prisoner. He'd begun to think the worst of Demetrius. Now, if possible, he thought worse of Christopher than he had before.

"He used his powers on you," Tristan said.

Demetrius' brow ridged in confusion, and Tristan figured out what else was strange about his expression. It was pained—as if concentrating on Tristan were difficult. It was definitely horror Tristan was feeling as he looked at the young man in front of him. Not only had Christopher used his powers on Demetrius, but he'd also drugged him. Tristan didn't have proof, but he believed it absolutely. Demetrius was just another prisoner.

"Come with me," Tristan said, looking over his shoulder. They'd been in one place too long, and guards would surely be looking for him soon. "I'll explain everything, but we need to get somewhere safer."

He could see the hesitation and confusion swirling in Demetrius' eyes, and grabbed Demetrius' wrist, pulling him toward the stairs. "Wait —"

"We don't have time to wait!"

They were halfway down the stairs when Tristan heard them—the sounds he'd been waiting for since breaking down his door. Sounds of pursuit. Shouts of, "Where's the dragon?", "He's this way!", "I see him!", "Stop!", echoed in the stone corridors, overlapping. Demetrius stopped. Tristan started running.

He would have to come back for everyone, including Demetrius. If he had to guess, he would place himself somewhere in the middle of the castle. He vaulted from the bottom step and sprinted to the right. There was a large space this way, and an immense wooden door. That had to be the main entrance, and Tristan adjusted his course to reach it.

A wall of fire stopped him. Tristan was confident Riley's fire couldn't hurt him since they were both Celestials. Random fire users? He was pretty sure those could burn him easily. Especially when he only had a partial Shift. If he could fully Shift this would be so much easier!

He moved to skirt around the wall of fire and felt his arms pull behind his back, one with a whip of water, the other a tendril of hard-packed earth. By the time Tristan broke free of the elemental restraints the fire user had moved the wall of fire all around Tristan, trapping him in a circle of flame.

Tristan looked around frantically. Five guards stood outside the circle of fire, at least three of them Elementalists. Tristan felt something inside him start to break, and roared to keep it together. The guards flinched. The flames lowered. Tristan took the opportunity and jumped as high as he could, over the flames and onto the floor beyond. At this point it was a desperate gamble, but he had to keep trying.

The Elementalists caught him again. Water whips restricted his movement until stone encased his body up to his chest. Tristan couldn't move.

"Easy, Dragon," one of the guards said.

Tristan glared at the woman who had spoken, and for a fleeting moment, almost felt better when she cowered. The green aura still burned around him, his partial Shift giving him strength. He could probably break through the stone surrounding him if he flared his energy.

A bucket's worth of water poured over Tristan, as if the guards knew his thoughts and wanted to distract him. Tristan didn't have time to flare his energy and try to break the stone. The water was definitely a distraction.

He didn't see the punch coming.

It wasn't enough to knock him out, but his ears rang and he dropped his partial Shift. The guards closed in on him, and Tristan cast his gaze to the floor.

Demetrius stood on the landing between the two sections of the staircase, watching Tristan fly down the remaining steps with more than a trace of confusion. What was Tristan doing here? What had he been talking about when he mentioned being a prisoner?

Demetrius found himself moving automatically back up the stairs. Several guards raced past him near the top of the staircase. Demetrius walked without seeing much, and stopped when he realized he was standing in front of his chambers. He opened the door and walked to the bed, sitting down on the edge, and placed his head in his hands. He needed to figure out what was going on, but his thoughts seemed so slow.

Start at the beginning, he told himself. *Tristan.*

Tristan, Riley, Wyatt, and Allyssa had gone

back to their world after opening the doorway to this one. They'd tried convincing the Celestials to come with them, to help the Shifters and Elementalists end their foolish war, and when the Celestials refused, the Shifters and Allyssa had gone home, back to their normal lives.

That was what Demetrius remembered. Except that didn't seem to be the case. Tristan was here. Did that mean the others were as well?

Hours passed with Demetrius lost in thought and memory. As the day progressed and all his energy remained fixated on memory, his confusion lessened more and more. He didn't remember the others leaving. He had no visual or verbal memory to corroborate that version of events. All he had was a vague, comforting belief that they had gone home. He didn't remember entering this world at all when he thought of it like this. Again, he had no visual or verbal memory of that significant day. Only vague recollections.

As though he had been told a story and made to believe it.

Demetrius stared at his door at twilight and stood with purpose. He'd been fed lies. The muddled feeling he now remembered experiencing every evening made sense. Everything had a new, horrible clarity.

It was time to face his father. Now, before Demetrius forgot something else. Before he let fear stop him.

Christopher's chambers, which he shared with Madaleine, were on the opposite side of Demetrius'. Demetrius walked to the pace of his thrumming pulse, and arrived quickly. He didn't knock on the door, but pounded, and opened it himself immediately after. Christopher's chambers were almost identical to Demetrius', though this space was larger with its king bed, full worktable, and sitting area. Christopher and Madaleine sat in armchairs near the window when Demetrius entered, reading.

Christopher stood, dropping his book. "Demetrius, what is the meaning of this?"

Demetrius met the spark of anger in Christopher's eyes without flinching. "We need to discuss something, Father. Our entrance into this world. The Celestials. I need to know the truth."

Christopher adopted a confused expression. "You already know the truth. You were there." He stepped closer to Demetrius. "What has you so worked up?"

They stood two feet apart. "I saw Tristan today," Demetrius said firmly. "I know he never returned to Earth. I know you used your powers to make me believe he and the others did."

Christopher studied him, his face still conveying concern. He abruptly let the façade fade, and his face became expressionless. "Pity."

Demetrius felt a wave of exhaustion tug at him, lulling him into complacency. He dug his feet into the ground and threw his shoulders back. "No!" he shouted, casting out his father's attack. The exhaustion vanished. "You were only able to manipulate me before because I wasn't expecting it. I never believed you would alter my memories, which gave you a way in. You don't have that now!"

Christopher couldn't hide the shock in his eyes. The man had liberal streaks of silver in his dark hair: a massive change from their months in this world. Using his powers so much was taxing him, aging his appearance beyond his years. His powers were still at their full strength, though. Demetrius was sure of that. And Demetrius had never tried to resist them before.

"Tell me the truth," Demetrius said forcefully.

"You'll only forget it again."

Demetrius felt his eyes narrow. He didn't need Christopher to tell him; he could find out on his own. He felt Christopher using his powers again and focused his own on penetrating Christopher's memories. As if he held a mental shield aloft, Christopher's attack didn't land. Demetrius' did.

Suddenly Demetrius found himself in his father's mind, both a spectator as the memories flashed across his mind and an active participant, as he experienced them from Christopher's perspective.

Christopher stepped onto the grass on the other side of the portal and immediately smiled in open-mouthed wonder. The parallel world was a mirror to their own, with one crucial difference: this world was untouched by humans. As a result, it was unravaged by pollution and not depleted of its resources. It was a fresh, vibrant world, and simply breathing the air and standing in the grass left Christopher practically giddy.

He could see the children nearby, spread out and looking around with some of the wonder he was feeling himself. It was the dragon's Shifter who spotted him first.

"I'm sorry," Christopher lied, before the boy could ask what he was doing. The others whirled at his voice. "I couldn't resist stepping through."

It was clear at least one of them wanted to say something to him, but Riley captured their attention. "Look!"

Christopher followed her gaze and sucked in a breath. On the horizon was visible a shape resembling rippling flame, brilliant red and orange demanding attention. The phoenix, coming to greet the Shifters. No doubt all of the Celestials had felt the portal between the worlds open, and already the first was appearing!

The bird landed in front of them with its wings

spread, and Christopher immediately set to work. At first he was subtle, extending his influence on the Celestial's mind without it noticing as it greeted the humans. Once he had several hooks in place he abandoned subtlety and fully extended his powers, effectively bewitching the phoenix. It cried out once before settling, looking to Christopher expectantly.

In the same instant Christopher flared his powers out to reach the children and knock them unconscious. Riley, Wyatt, and Allyssa dropped to the ground. The dragon's Shifter was immune to Christopher's power, unfortunately, and watched his friends fall with more than a trace of concern.

Demetrius turned on Christopher with a look of betrayal.

"Father, what are you doing?"

An emerald outline appeared around the dragon's Shifter, after he checked Riley's pulse and realized she was alive. As if Christopher would kill them, and create a hassle for himself when other Shifters eventually took their place as Celestials. Christopher saw the confusion in the boy's eyes when he couldn't do more than partially Shift. "There can only be one dragon, phoenix, and griffin in a given space," Christopher said. "You won't be able to take on their forms in this world."

The boy was vibrating in his fury. "I knew we couldn't trust you."

Demetrius walked over to Christopher. "The

plan was to speak with the Celestials, to tell them what we wanted to build. Why are you doing this?"

Christopher studied his son and sighed. "You've gone soft on me, Demetrius. That was never the plan, but I can see you won't cooperate with the real one." He fixated his powers on Demetrius, and the boy dropped to the ground in the same way the others had.

The dragon's Shifter surprised Christopher with the intensity of his attack. Christopher actually didn't see him coming, and staggered. Then he smiled. He enjoyed a good physical confrontation. Though he took a few more blows than he expected, the dragon's Shifter fell. Christopher surveyed the area, looking at the sleeping children and docile phoenix, and straightened his cuff when he saw another shape in the distance. The griffin.

How perfect.

Demetrius left that memory and skipped through others, aware that his father was trying to push him out of his mind and desperate to gain every bit of information he could before that happened. He could sense Christopher blocking one memory with a ferocity that momentarily distracted him, and before he could stop himself he was breaking through Christopher's blockade to view it. His breath caught immediately.

It was a memory of his mother.

CHAPTER 2

In Darkest Night

Demetrius entered the memory with force.

Christopher turned at Layla's voice. "Darling, I've found something!"

"I don't care." She walked up to him with a fire in her otherwise gentle eyes. "You haven't spoken to our son in over a week. You've barely spent any time with either of us."

"Because I'm so close to a breakthrough! This research I'm doing, it's for all of us! Surely you understand that?"

"No," she said. "I understand that you're missing out on the life Demetrius and I are living." She took a shaky breath. "And I'm tired of it. I'm leaving."

He looked at her searchingly. "What do you mean?"

"Demetrius needs his parents. If you're not going

to be a father to him, it's better for you to not be here, so he doesn't get hurt every time he sees you walk by. If you decide to actually be the man I married, you'll come for us."

"But where are you going?"

"I don't know exactly—"

"You have to stay here!"

Layla turned away. "This is already one of the hardest things I've ever done," she said, and he heard the wavering in her voice—grief. "Please don't make it any harder." She started to walk out of the room, and Christopher realized that she was serious. She'd approached him once before, telling him she was leaving, but that had been quickly smoothed over with his powers—his powers.

He couldn't afford to lose her. Last time she was this upset, he erased her memory of it, and they'd gone on happy for months. He just had to do it again, that was all, so he didn't lose her. So he stopped her movement and sought out those unhappy thoughts and feelings she was having, making them fade like smoke from a fire. He didn't expect such strong emotions, though. Her love for their son was pure, but the primary emotion towards himself was anger, and betrayal. That couldn't stay put.

He became so desperate to make everything right, and do it in haste, that he slipped. His powers gave a surge, amplifying the task he was currently *performing: erasing. Her memories began to slip away, all of them, in a horrible flash. Her personality leaked away, and then her basic skills were lost; he watched as she fell to the ground when her body forgot how to stand, and when her chest ceased rising and falling when she forgot how to breathe.*

He was next to her in an instant, touching her face, trying to understand what had happened. He felt the last pulse of her heart as he gripped her wrist, and saw her vacant stare from his lap. He shook his head, trying to reverse what he had done, to give her back her memories, her life. But it settled over him that he was too late.

He had erased her completely. His cheeks were wet with tears, the first he had shed in many years, and he couldn't restrain the guttural cry of loss that sounded from him as he held onto his precious Layla, rocking her slightly and murmuring her name. He was dimly aware of his son running in, but he couldn't take care of him then, not with this wound so fresh . . .

Demetrius flew back to his own mind. He was frozen, his mouth parted and his eyes blind as he saw those images again. It wasn't registering. He had been told it was an accident, that she had lost control of her powers . . .

"Son," Christopher said.

Demetrius looked to him slowly, numb, barely remembering why he'd come here in the first place.

"It was an accident," Christopher said, and Demetrius saw his father had unshed tears in his eyes. "I only wanted her to stay with us."

"With you," he said, barely a whisper. "She would have taken me with her. You would have been alone, but she would . . ." She would probably still be alive, he realized. "You—you took her from me. It was you."

There was a strange detachment when he spoke, his tone lacking any inflection. But he was feeling now, so much so that he couldn't express it through tone. Fresh grief poured out of him, and the only thing more powerful than that was his anger. He recalled his reason for being in Christopher's chambers, and although he felt he couldn't take anymore, he renewed his search of Christopher's memories, knowing he had to see the rest of what had been done to him. He saw Christopher exert his influence over the griffin. Once he had the two Celestials under his control, he turned his efforts to building the kingdom he'd been planning for decades. Demetrius found the other memory he'd been searching for most.

"You still want him to act as prince?" Madaleine asked. She stood in the newly constructed castle, next to a bed. Demetrius lay on the bed, in a deep sleep. Christopher sat next to him, thinking. "You could do what you did with the others," she con-

tinued, "and give him a new life."

"He is still my son," Christopher told her. "Eventually, he'll come around and appreciate what I've built for us. For now, we simply need time." He placed a hand to Demetrius' forehead and put a gloss over the memories from recent days. Their entrance to the parallel world he now knew the Celestials thought of as Terraria. That bond Demetrius was forming with the wind user. Once those memories were shrouded, and the narrative Christopher desired implanted, Christopher withdrew his hand and looked to Madaleine.

"That's it?" she asked. "He'll just do what you say now?"

Christopher stood. "He should behave as he did before, but to be certain . . ." He thought of the greenhouse back in their world. Demetrius' problem was thinking too much. Christopher believed him to be a loyal boy, on the whole. There were natural ways to keep him from overthinking—especially with the assistance of their powers. "I need to make a final trip through the portal," he told Madaleine, picturing the flowers in the section only he had tended: the more useful of the flowers he'd enhanced. A mixture of several varieties should serve his purpose well. "I have something that will help him stay focused and happy."

The words echoed in Demetrius' head as he exited the memories and retreated from his father's mind.

"Demetrius—"

Demetrius silenced him with a look as his emotions got the better of his control. His powers surged. Madaleine and Christopher fell.

Tristan set his pen down when he heard a muffled noise outside his door. He jumped to his feet when the doorknob turned, partially Shifting, and tensed as a figure opened his door and stepped just inside. The candleholder near the door cast a weak illumination, but Tristan recognized him quickly enough.

"Demetrius?"

The boy stepped closer. "Let's go."

Tristan dropped his Shift. "Go where?"

"You were trying to escape earlier. We're actually doing it now."

His words were sharper than they'd been that morning, and everything about Demetrius screamed that he was in a state of extreme agitation; he seemed shaken. "Where's Christopher?" Tristan asked.

"Asleep, but I don't know how long he'll stay that way."

They'd had a confrontation, then. Maybe Tristan had gotten through to Demetrius earlier after all. He didn't hesitate any longer, grabbing up the lantern from his desk and walking from the room at a fast pace. He wanted to run, to make sure he could reach the door. His pulse hammered inside him, his legs twitching in their urge to move faster. No one seemed to know they were escaping, though. No one even realized the Prince of Shadows was going against Christopher's wishes yet, Tristan thought. Those few individuals who did cast them looks adopted vacant expressions as they walked by, and Tristan was tempted to smile. It was wonderful to have that power as an ally.

Demetrius led Tristan out a side entrance of the castle so they emerged in a stable. The sturdy wooden beams seemed much warmer to Tristan than the stone walls and floors that made up most of the castle. The glow from Tristan's candle showed at least a dozen wooden stalls as Tristan and Demetrius walked along the center aisle, each stall housing a horse. Demetrius stopped at one of the last stalls and opened the gated section.

"This is my horse," he told Tristan. Holding the candle up a bit higher, Tristan saw that the horse had a black body, with a large white patch on its face that ran from between its eyes to its nostrils. "Perseus has been my companion since we came here," Demetrius continued. "I'll ride him out. You should pick out a horse as well."

A jittery sensation entered Tristan's heart, and he swallowed it down as best he could while he looked at the horses in neighboring stalls. Did it matter which one he chose? He knew nothing about horses, and looked at the one next to Perseus—a slightly smaller horse with a brown body and matching brown mane. The animal pawed at the gate of its stall, apparently itching to run. "What's this one's name?" Tristan asked. "And how do I ride it?"

Demetrius helped him get the brown stallion —Roman—saddled, and gave Tristan the briefest of instructions on mounting and urging the horse forward. Tristan hadn't realized Demetrius had a satchel on his person until the boy took it from his shoulder and tied it to Perseus' saddle. "Just a few things I grabbed on the way to your cell," he explained at Tristan's look.

Tristan nodded, once again forcing down that jittery sensation as it made a second attempt to unnerve him. "Where should we go?"

"I know a place nearby where we can stop and make a plan. It's hidden in plain sight." Demetrius clicked his tongue and started forward. Tristan gripped Roman's reins and pressed his feet against the horse's sides, and Roman seemed to know what to do as he followed Demetrius and Perseus.

Tristan had blown out his candle once both

he and Demetrius were astride their horses, and it was difficult to see much as they left the stables and emerged into the open night air. The moon was bright enough for Tristan to see a worn path in front of them, and to clearly see Demetrius just ahead. Otherwise, he couldn't have begun to say where they were going, or even what they were leaving behind. That would have to be observed in daylight.

Demetrius slowed and stopped, Tristan slightly delayed in doing the same, and then dismounted Perseus and led the horse off the small trail. It was definitely worn less than the path immediately outside the stables, smaller and not completely smoothed by feet. Tristan slid off Roman's back, stumbling a bit, and followed Demetrius off the trail and into what looked like a forest.

"Here," Demetrius said. Tristan peered around him and saw a fallen tree blocking the way. It was massive, its trunk wide and its branches sticking up straight; the tree almost reached Tristan's head just in circumference while lying flat. Demetrius climbed over the tree and then pushed from the other side, and Tristan realized the tree wasn't fully intact. Where Demetrius pushed on it was a crack that, with a bit of force, made an opening large enough for the horses to step through. Once they were all on the other side Demetrius pulled the broken section of the tree back into place, and turned to look at Tristan with a hesitant smile. "It's not perfect, but here we're slightly protected from anyone pursuing us, and not too far from town."

He sounded so calm as he sat down with his back against the fallen tree. He looked at the horses and Tristan watched as they lowered themselves to the ground, no doubt influenced by his power. Tristan wanted to keep moving. He had to keep moving, to keep doing something, to keep that feeling at bay. He realized with a shock that it was too late; he was already feeling it again, much more strongly than before. Maybe it couldn't be denied any longer.

Tristan's body began to shake. He drew in shallow breath after shallow breath, too quickly and forcefully to properly breathe, and he couldn't get enough air. A horrible acid in his throat told him he was close to throwing up, and his heart seemed to be twisting painfully inside his chest. What the hell was happening?

"It's okay," said Demetrius, leaning forward. "You've been wanting this for so long, and your emotions are so strong, you're having a physical reaction."

This was because he was finally free? Tristan fell to his hands and knees and closed his eyes, willing himself not to vomit. He just had to breathe. There was plenty of air—fresh, clean air, unrestricted by walls. There was no reason for this reaction. He had things to do.

Gradually, he recovered himself, his panicked bodily reaction fading. He stared at the green grass and clutched a few strands between his fingers, anchoring himself, and sat up to look at Demetrius. The other boy was sitting nearby, purple eyes somehow bright in the moonlight.

"How are you?" Tristan asked him. He didn't ask if Demetrius was okay. He already knew that answer.

"Almost back to my normal self," Demetrius responded. "The spell I was under was reinforced every morning, and mostly wore off by nightfall. Since my father won't be able to reinforce it tomorrow morning, I'll be completely normal by then. I may never drink tea again, though."

Tristan let the topic drop. That was good enough for him. They did have something else to discuss, though, that couldn't wait. "Where are Riley, Wyatt, and Allyssa?"

Demetrius breathed out low. "My father gave them new identities. They remember nothing of their true lives."

Tristan reacted as though struck, whipping to fully face Demetrius. For a long moment he was speechless in his fury, too overcome with words to utter any and too conscious of the fact that they would only increase Demetrius' guilt

—which aggravated him even more. "That bastard!" Tristan finally said, breaking his eyes from Demetrius. "I thought he put them in a cell, like he did with me. Why would he give them new identities? What does that even mean?"

"It probably seemed easier to give them new identities," said Demetrius in a low voice. "You have an innate protection the others lack, being the dragon. Your sense of reality can't be challenged by our powers. The others' can. My father blocked their real memories and replaced them with fabricated ones. They believe they came to this world with their families for new lives."

Tristan's head shot back up. "You said their real memories were blocked. They can get them back, right? We can fix them?"

"It takes a lot more energy to erase than to hide, and my father has to use a lot of energy to keep the control he has. He's more concerned with keeping an absolute grip over the Celestials than their chosen Shifters. I'm sure he only hid their true memories, overlaying them with the false ones. I can set things right."

"Okay, good."

"We still need to find them. I have no idea where they'll be."

Tristan looked up at the calm night sky. "We'll find them."

CHAPTER 3

To Turn Back Time

Ash loved superhero stories. He had pictures from his favorite comic books, cartoons, and movies on his bedroom wall. In recent months he'd begun looking at them with more than a geeky pride; he'd begun looking at them with jealousy.

He knew it didn't make sense to be jealous of the heroes that decorated his walls, but he felt he had a good reason. Even if some of his favorites didn't have the right powers, circumstances often allowed them to break a rule Ash desperately wanted to: they could travel back in time, and prevent bad things from happening. Ash couldn't.

He would love to go back to the day Tristan, Riley, and Allyssa had gone to Christopher's house to train, to stop them and convince them to stay at the Temple. That wasn't the day they disappeared, but it was the reason. If they hadn't gone back there, none of this would have happened.

Ash remembered discovering his brother's absence vividly. He recalled how Emily had become increasingly more concerned as the day drew toward its end and Riley didn't reach out to her—as soon as Riley called or texted each day, Ash felt like he could breathe, knowing nothing bad had happened, and the girl was like clockwork in her communication with her mother—until she snapped into action just past nightfall. She'd wanted to go to Christopher's alone, to race out the door and make sure they were safe, but Derek and Noah had refused to let her. She'd absolutely forbidden Ash or Alice from coming, though, waiting for Derek and Noah to follow her to the car with an impatience that reminded Ash painfully of Jordan.

He, Alice, and, once he'd returned from his friend's house, Matt, had sat in the entryway for two hours before the others returned, and Emily's expression had turned Ash's stomach. They were gone, Emily had told them. Left without a trace.

Ash marked off another day on his calendar. They knew more now. Within a month of Tristan, Riley, and Allyssa vanishing, something strange happened. People began disappearing. Shifters and Elementalists, mainly, but even non-powered humans. When enough cars were left abandoned in the parking lot, it became clear where they were disappearing from—Spa Park.

Ash just didn't know what it meant. As he looked at the calendar, thinking of the months of crossed-off days, his resolve deepened. Alice had been trying to get him to do this for weeks, and he finally agreed that they had to try.

He walked to her room and knocked twice before entering. Alice was shrugging on a jean jacket as Ash walked in. Her hair reached about her shoulders now, her natural curls emerging as her hair lengthened again. She flicked her hair out as she settled the collar of her jacket and turned to face Ash, brown eyes sharp.

"I want to do it," he told her.

Her eyebrows went up just a tick, and then she dipped her head. "Let's go."

"Now?"

"Yes."

Ash didn't argue. He hoped they could walk out without seeing Emily. The woman was too adept at reading Ash's intentions on his face, and would surely stop them if she knew what they planned to do. "We'll get into trouble," was all Ash said, in a low voice.

Alice responded just as quietly. "Tristan could

be in trouble right now."

They walked down the hall, and Ash glanced at the gym as they passed, out of habit. Noah had always been the one to use the gym most, but it had almost become an obsession in the last few months. Ash didn't stop as they passed the gym, but the door was open, and through it he caught a glimpse of Noah standing by a punching bag. Ash looked forward again as they walked down the stairs. Noah would probably love to come with them, and actually be upset they hadn't asked for his help. Ash felt he was lucky Alice had asked *him*. She was the one with the best chance of getting through without being detected, being the smallest.

Ash looked around when they hopped off the last step, and tensed when he saw the door to Jordan's—Emily's—office tightly shut. She'd been going through a lot of paperwork lately, spending hours in that room. This was their window. Alice reached the door first and soundlessly drew it open, and Ash rushed to close it behind them. He and Alice ran down the Temple steps and maintained a jog when they hit the street.

"How long do you think we have before she starts looking for us?" Ash asked.

Alice jogged with her head held high. "She usually checks on everyone around lunchtime. I'd guess we have at least an hour."

Considering it would take them probably a quarter of that time to even reach Spa Park, Ash was glad to hear it. He didn't want to make Emily worry about them any more than she already did. Although Ash had never traveled to Spa Park on foot, he and Alice had planned their route several weeks ago, when she'd first had this idea. The walking/jogging commute actually wasn't bad.

It was the looks they got when they first left the Temple that bothered Ash the most, though he did his best to let it go. Shifters and Elementalists weren't a secret anymore. With the war between them raging, there had been no way to keep the general population ignorant of their existence any longer. Many of the people were indifferent to the knowledge that people with special abilities lived among them. Some were amazed and accepting. Some looked at Shifters and Elementalists with fear and anger, mostly from the damages the war was incurring. Ash didn't think the couple walking their dog a few minutes ago had seemed angry, but he'd caught a glimpse of the fear in the taller man's eyes. It definitely didn't make Ash feel any better.

"Let's Shift over there," Ash said, pointing near a sign to enter the park. Alice could Shift anywhere and fly into the park without receiving much attention. Ash, as a wolf, needed to Shift much closer to the interior of the park. He really did not want to wind up in a zoo.

Alice made a sound of agreement, and they walked closer, breaking into a sprint for the final stretch. In their attempt to enter the park unnoticed they trampled fresh shoots of flowers, but Ash was pretty sure the officers stationed at the nearest entrance didn't see them. They Shifted as they ran, Alice taking to the air on owl's wings, Ash bounding forward on four paws.

He looked up at Alice, opening his mouth in a smile when they reached the interior of the park. She issued a brief sound Ash took as a warning to stay alert, and they began their search. It was hard searching for something when they had no idea what it was. A tunnel? A wormhole? Ash looked for any abnormality in the somewhat familiar park. He'd been there several times, but he knew Congress Park much better.

He slowed to a walk on one of the paths, noticing how slick it was. One of the natural springs rose in a mound, water trickling down and across the path before rejoining the stream. Alice flew around it. Ash walked carefully, picking up the pace again once he'd passed the slippery section.

Well, he picked up the pace for a minute. Then he skidded to a stop. Two people stood on the path, leaning against the rocky wall and facing opposite directions. The one facing Ash and Alice saw them and immediately alerted the other.

Alice made a louder sound. Ash didn't need to be an owl to know she was telling him to run. He turned but found his way blocked by a wall of water.

"Relax!" the nearest person said. She had a commanding tone of voice. "We don't want to hurt you!"

"We just need to talk to you!" the other person called, his voice quieter. Alice swooped toward the ground and landed, hopping close to Ash.

"Please Shift back," the woman said.

Alice looked up at Ash, hopped a few feet in front of him, and dropped her Shift. She stood in front of him, staring at the man and woman. "Who are you?"

"Officers Rhine and Davis," the woman said. The man grabbed a radio from a strap on his shoulder and walked away, speaking into it. The woman reached toward her belt and showed them a police badge. "I'm an Elementalist. He's a Shifter. We're on guard duty here, part of a joint task force. Now who are you?"

Alice didn't answer.

"Okay, how about this. Why are you here?"

Ash could tell Alice was debating answering. He stepped up next to her, brushing against her leg in the process, and dropped his Shift. "We're trying to figure out what happened to our family. They disappeared from here months ago."

The woman's stern expression softened by a degree, and the wall of water dropped back to the stream. "I understand wanting to try to find them, but you aren't allowed in here."

"Why not?" Alice demanded.

"The doorway might open," the man said. "We can't have anyone else disappearing."

Ash locked onto the word *doorway*. If he'd still been Shifted, his ears would have pricked. "What kind of doorway?"

The woman glared at the man, then sighed. "Have you ever heard of the parallel world where the Celestials are said to live? Apparently it's real. That's where people disappeared to."

Alice had her eyes trained on the wall behind the officers. Ash studied it and saw that it had a huge crack. It looked ordinary, but if the officers were stationed in front of it . . . "Don't you want the doorway to open?" Alice asked. "We need to get them back!"

"We can't open it," the man told them. "It's sealed, somehow."

Ash stepped forward. "Then why are you guarding it?"

"Because someone might come by who knows how to open it," the woman said, "and no one's allowed until our investigation is finished."

"Sorry," the man said. "Believe me, we're trying as hard as we can, but we also need to keep others safe."

It was clear Alice wanted to argue. Ash kind of did too. He knew they both saw that it wouldn't do any good, though. He believed the officers when they said they didn't know how to open the doorway, and that they were trying to figure it out. It didn't stop him from wanting to rush at the stone and try to make the doorway open, but he resisted the impulse.

Ash turned his head when he heard feet on the stones behind them. Another adult jogged over.

"Tripp, take my post," the woman said. "I'm going to make sure these two get home."

"Are you writing a report?" the newcomer asked.

The woman looked at Ash and Alice for a long moment. "No, I don't think that'll be necessary. Come on, you two."

She let Ash and Alice walk in front of her. They were silent as they made their way back to the park entrance, to a sedan in the parking lot. The woman watched them get into the backseat before getting in herself.

"Where do you live?" she asked, starting the

car.

"The Temple," Ash told her.

She drove them home, and whatever small hope Ash had that she would just drop them off and leave faded when she undid her seatbelt. She followed them up the steps and knocked on the door.

Ash could tell the second Emily opened it that something was wrong. Emily almost always looked worried these days, but she had crinkles around her eyes that made it clear something new was bothering her. When her pale blue eyes fixed on Ash and Alice, and the officer just behind them, she opened her mouth in speechless confusion.

"Are you the Guardian of this Temple?" the officer asked.

Emily nodded. "Yes. Emily Madison. What's going on?"

"I just wanted to let you know that these two Shifted and snuck into Spa Park. We had a little chat, and nothing serious needs to happen, but I wanted to make sure you heard. They know that area is off-limits now. I'll leave you to it."

She turned and strode down the steps. "Thank you for bringing them back," Emily called after her. Emily set her gaze on the twins, seeming speechless again. "You went to the park?" she finally said. "What were you thinking?"

"Mrs. Madison?"

Ash's eyebrows shot up at the unfamiliar voice. Emily startled and stepped back, motioning for Ash and Alice to come inside. The unfamiliar voice belonged to a middle-aged man in a long overcoat. Derek, Matt, and Noah were also in the entryway, all seeming tense. The man smiled when he saw the twins.

"You must be Ash and Alice. Perfect. Now everyone's accounted for."

Alice looked at everyone. "What's going on?"

Emily swallowed. "Apparently your father's trial is in two weeks, in Washington, D.C., and we need to be there to testify."

The man put his hands in the pockets of his overcoat. "But don't worry. We have time to talk and pack before we leave!"

CHAPTER 4

Search and Rescue

"I was careless."

Tristan looked up at Demetrius' words, surprised. "What do you mean?"

Demetrius stared at the grass. "I had complete control, in my father's room. I could have gone through his thoughts, or Madaleine's, and discovered where Riley, Wyatt, and Allyssa are. I'm sure they both know."

Tristan stood and stretched his arms above his head. They'd gone to sleep soon after Tristan calmed down from whatever that attack had been, Tristan relishing in the feeling of the grass beneath his hands. After so long deprived of nature, the soft grass felt wonderful. Tristan hadn't even minded the cold. It was early morning now, the sky lit with a soft blend of pink, purple, gray, and hints of orange. The sun hadn't even cleared the horizon yet. "You can't beat yourself up over that," he told Demetrius. "We'd both still be stuck in the castle if you hadn't confronted Christopher."

"But I had a perfect opportunity—"

"No one can think of everything in the heat of the moment. You got us a few supplies, and most importantly you got us out of there. We can figure out the rest." He'd thought Demetrius was quieter than usual, and wondered if this was the only reason.

Demetrius brought gentle eyes up to Tristan's and nodded. "I'm sure there are already guards looking for us in town. My father will probably send guards near wherever the others are, knowing we'll go after them."

"Then we should get moving. Maybe we can get to the others before the guards. If not, we use guards as clues. If we see a bunch, we'll know we're getting close."

Demetrius seemed close to smiling for a second. "I can see why the dragon chose you as its Shifter."

Tristan extended a hand and helped Demetrius up. As much as he didn't want to, he thought it best if they split up. Everyone knew what Demetrius looked like. On his own, he could search for Riley, Wyatt, and Allyssa without anyone questioning his motives. Tristan had one thing going for him, in that no one outside the castle had ever seen him. He could pretend he was from one of the other settlements, looking for a friend. Demetrius had told him there were at least two others, with smaller ones forming each day. He ran this by Demetrius and both agreed it made sense.

"Meet back here," Demetrius told him. "Assume something's gone wrong if the other isn't back by midday."

"And if something is wrong?"

Demetrius looked at him with solemn eyes. "Find the others and keep going."

Tristan shook his head. "That won't work. We need each other if we're gonna fix things. You have to give the others their real memories back. Let's just plan for nothing to go wrong."

"You can't exactly plan for that."

The corners of Tristan's mouth twitched up. "We'll see."

He didn't dare waste any more time. He climbed onto Roman's back and left their temporary shelter, heading back the way they had run last night. Now that it was daylight and he could actually see his surroundings, Tristan had to appreciate how established everything looked. Christopher must have been preparing for this for years, and it showed in how organized everything was. No signs of construction. No signs that the castle and surrounding village hadn't been here for years.

Maybe it was too big to be called a village, but that was the feeling Tristan got from the small houses and huts, and the wooden stands for trading goods. The market space was closest to the path Tristan came from. There were plenty of people about, setting up stands of clothing, food, and other supplies. Tristan slid off Roman's back and walked the horse forward as he scanned the market space. He started when a flash of bright color caught his eye, but sighed immediately. That orange was nowhere near the dark, autumnal red of Riley's hair.

"You'll need to move your horse," a man in a nearby stall said. "Market opens in a few minutes, and we don't have room for horses."

"Sorry," Tristan said. "I'm new here. Looking for a friend from the old world. Have you seen her? She's about my age, with red hair and blue eyes."

The man set down the fabric he was holding. "I might know who you're talking about. She's always got a horse, too. Try the stable. Just down that way."

Tristan looked the way the man pointed, thanked him, and walked forward with more energy than before. He kept scanning any faces he saw, searching for his friends. The stable was in the direction the man pointed, but Tristan had to pass many houses before he got there. He thought he recognized one building as a schoolhouse, and thought for a fleeting moment of how much work Jordan would assign him—he jerked and stopped, his heart twisting painfully. He hadn't slipped up in so long. Why did he think of her now?

Roman turned his head to look at Tristan, and Tristan managed to start walking again. Wasn't that what he'd always heard about grief? That sometimes, little things triggered it? Not for the first time that morning, Tristan found his thoughts turning to his siblings. This time it was with more than just missing them, though. How were they adjusting to life without Jordan? *Were* they adjusting?

Don't go down that road, he told himself. He had to stay alert. He reached the stable, one of the biggest buildings in sight, and peered inside the open entryway. There had been a fair number of horses in the stable connected to the castle. This building housed even more. At least twenty horses were in stalls in this structure, several of them very young. One slender figure stood in the stable, with very familiar shaggy, dirty blond hair. When he turned to face Tristan, dark hazel eyes confirmed it.

Figured Tristan would find Wyatt first.

Demetrius let Tristan have a few minutes of a head start. He should have told Tristan to meet back here by nightfall. He doubted he would be back by midday. Then again, his plan might not work at all, so maybe it was better for Tristan to get the others to safety.

He'd never tried this before. Not on himself. He mounted Perseus and let the horse lead them back to the castle, knowing Perseus knew the route well enough, while he turned his powers to his own mind. They could search the village, but there was no way of knowing if the others were in this one at all. Demetrius could find out where they were in an instant if he searched his father's or Madaleine's memories.

So he constructed a mental block over his memories of the past day, specifically formed to keep Christopher out. In front of the block he placed false memories. If Christopher searched Demetrius' mind, which Demetrius knew he would, hopefully it would be enough to fool him. That, and the immediacy of Demetrius' return.

He reached the stable connected to the castle, put Perseus in his stall, and walked inside. A guard stationed near the entrance from the stable rushed after him, seeming startled.

"I need to see my father," Demetrius told the guard without stopping.

"Sir, we're supposed to escort you if you come back."

"Then escort me." It was early enough that Demetrius thought his father would either be in his chambers or in the dining room, sitting for breakfast. He hoped to find him in his chambers, and walked there first with the flustered guard at his heels. He let the guard knock on the door, so the man wouldn't get in trouble.

The door opened with a rapidity that made the guard jump. "The Prince of Shadows has returned, Highness," the guard reported.

Christopher didn't even glance at the guard, his eyes snapping immediately to Demetrius. "Father," Demetrius said. "I'm sorry I—"

Christopher pushed into Demetrius' mind with a crashing force. Demetrius flinched but didn't resist while Christopher reached for the memories from the past day. He felt a trill of satisfaction when Christopher latched onto the false memories.

"The dragon betrayed you?" Christopher mused, stopping the flow of his powers.

It took a moment for Demetrius' vision to clear from the pain, and then he set his gaze on Christopher, just below the man's eyes. "I was confused, Father. I never should have released him. I'm sorry."

"Do you know where the dragon went?"

Again Christopher searched his mind, and again he latched onto a false memory. "He went into the woods," Demetrius said. "I couldn't stop him."

This last comment was easy to believe. Not only was Tristan immune from Demetrius' powers, but he was physically stronger than Demetrius even without partially Shifting. Demetrius had never been particularly strong, physically. His father had always insisted that his focus remain on his mental abilities rather than physical training. As a result, his mental prowess was unrivaled, his physical prowess . . . debatable. The past nine months had altered his slim form, giving him more definition in his arms and torso, but this minimal growth still left him much weaker than Tristan.

"No matter," Christopher said. "I have guards patrolling near the other Celestials. If he goes after them, they'll catch him."

Christopher had always been an arrogant man, and his arrogance worked in Demetrius' favor in this instance.

"I told Madaleine you'd eventually come to see things our way. If it took the dragon to make it happen, so be it." He placed a hand on Demetrius' shoulder. "It's time The Prince of Shadows knowingly embraced his role."

Demetrius swallowed. "I'll do my best to make you proud."

"Let me bring you up to date on our expansion. Astrum is growing nicely . . . ."

Christopher kept Demetrius busy all morning, working alongside him as they consulted the most recent maps of the kingdom. Inspecting the hand-drawn maps, Demetrius realized he had visited several of the settlements. While memorizing the main map, he was certain he'd been to the settlement near the lake. He could dimly recall standing beside a frozen expanse of water, what had to be several months ago, mesmerized by the wisps of fog stretching up from the ice and surrounded by guards. He had been there. Had he fully realized what he was doing at the time? Had the guards known about the drug-induced stupor in which he'd existed? Demetrius realized that outwardly, he would have seemed normal. It was deep thought that had been inhibited. He could still think on the surface, following directives from his father. It made sense for Christopher to send him with a cohort of soldiers, to keep him busy and keep him useful in the eyes of the citizens yet ensure he was looked after.

Select details seemed to come back to Demetrius while memorizing the map and conversing with Christopher, slightly hazy but meaningful. He remembered the numerous trips he and the cohort of soldiers had taken to add detail to this map and pave the way for different settlements. Most importantly, he remembered the terrain. Paired with the memorized map, he knew the best way for them to travel and avoid detection once they'd found everyone.

It was so tempting to reach out with his powers and search Christopher's mind, to claim the information he sought and leave. Demetrius didn't dare risk it. Although Christopher seemed to believe him, Demetrius suspected his father had his mental defenses on high.

Being so near him, pretending to be the obedient son Christopher still believed him to be, was one of the most difficult things Demetrius had ever done. Every time he looked at Christopher he relived that horrible memory Christopher had hidden above all others. The truth of how Layla had died. The reason Christopher never tolerated even mentioning her name.

"How far we've come," Christopher murmured when they finally put away the maps. "I know you weren't as involved in it as either of us first imagined, but we've made our dream a reality. Now that you've come to your senses, you can appreciate that fact. Things will be better from now on, *filium meum*."

Demetrius forced himself to smile at the words. *Filium meum. My son*, in Latin. It was a rare term of endearment, coming from Christopher. One which would almost always elicit a sense of pride inside Demetrius. In this instance he felt nothing.

"Madaleine should be waiting for us for lunch," Christopher continued. "I'm sure word has spread that you've returned."

Demetrius forced himself to half-listen to his father and Madaleine when they sat down for lunch. He had to be ready to answer any questions or respond immediately, or Christopher would know what he was doing. He remained fully focused on the conversation as they started eating, realizing once the food was in front of him how ravenous he felt. He didn't drink anything. Once he'd sated his immediate hunger, and apologized to both Christopher and Madaleine for the night before, he set to work.

It was easy to enter Madaleine's mind. The challenging part was doing it undetected as she kept up a conversation. Demetrius carefully moved over her thoughts, focusing on memories. He flashed an image of the Celestials in the front of her subconscious, and let her mind automatically bring the most recent related memories to his attention, careful not to let them fully surface.

"Do you think the boy will find them?"

Wyatt, walking by the school in the village.

"No, but even if he does, they won't believe

58

him."

Riley, brushing a horse's mane in the stable.

"And you're determined to imprison him again instead of something more drastic?"

Tristan, being thrown back into his room just yesterday.

"Demetrius, what do you think?"

Demetrius focused on Christopher and answered without pause. "I see no reason to harm him. Once he's back in our custody, he won't escape again. I'll make sure of it."

Christopher nodded approvingly, and Demetrius delved back into Madaleine's memories. Wyatt and Riley were in the village, then, but what about Allyssa? He brought her image before Madaleine's mind and latched onto the first memory that appeared: Allyssa, bent down on a cold stone floor with a rag and scrubbing at dirty footprints. The room seemed familiar, and in seconds Demetrius recognized it as the entrance of the castle. His grip on his fork tightened involuntarily, his pulse thundering. She'd been right under Demetrius' nose this whole time. Christopher had made her a servant.

Madaleine was commenting on the usefulness of having royal guards. Demetrius glimpsed another brief memory of Allyssa. She was standing inside a cottage, looking at an old woman as the woman shut the door and sealed them inside. Again, the setting was familiar. That was one of the cottages closest to the castle. Demetrius must have walked by it hundreds of times without sparing it a glance.

He lingered on memories of Allyssa too long. Just as he had begun his search for the locations of the phoenix, dragon, and griffin, the meal ended. Demetrius carefully stopped the flow of his powers and set down the fork he'd been gripping too tightly.

"The guards are very efficient," Demetrius said, picking up where Madaleine left off. "Everything about our little kingdom is." He smiled. "I'm glad to be able to see it clearly."

Madaleine seemed to be studying him. Christopher nodded. "We still have much to do."

"What would you like me to do?" Demetrius asked, straightening his shoulders. He wanted to suggest something outdoors but knew he had to appear completely obedient to whatever Christopher said.

"Come with me for now. We finished going over the maps of our populations, but I could use another set of eyes to organize the planting schedule."

Demetrius nodded and strode after his father, asking about the irrigation procedures they had in place, half-paying attention. It could be useful.

The focus of his thoughts remained on what he had to do next. At some point he would be able to slip away. This would be the final break from his father. As soon as he fled with Allyssa and the Celestials, Christopher would know he had lost him. It was with a strange eagerness that Demetrius realized it.

Demetrius kept his destination firmly in mind while he followed Christopher back to the study, imagining every step bringing him closer to the door behind which Allyssa had been hidden.

CHAPTER 5

Best of Intentions

Emily thought she was sure to get gray hair soon, with all the stress the past year had brought her. After the Official came, and the officer escorted Ash and Alice back home, she thought she might have gotten gray hair just in that hour. There had to be some sort of outward sign of the way her chest kept tightening, her insides clenching with anxiety.

But apparently she was good at hiding her stress in front of the kids, or so her husband said. She took a calming breath and looked at Ash and Alice, who watched her as if expecting a rebuke but also wanting an explanation.

"Let's go sit down in the common room," she said, touching their backs to guide them forward. "We have a lot to talk about."

Derek directed the Official to the room. Matt

and Noah walked close behind, leaving Emily and the twins to follow.

"How long has he been here?" Alice whispered.

"Not long," Emily murmured back. She patted their shoulders. "We'll talk about your trespassing later."

Ash gave a nervous chuckle. They walked into the common room and sat down at the table, Emily placing herself immediately across from the Official. He took off his overcoat and placed it over the back of his chair.

"Ash, Alice, my name is Mr. Mathers," the Official said. "I haven't even told Mrs. Madison everything yet, so no worries about missing anything, okay?" He'd been here for all of ten minutes, and Emily already liked him. He had a horrible mustache and smiled easily, and spoke to the kids like he valued them. Her shoulders relaxed ever so slightly.

"You haven't heard anything about Michael Dawes since last year?" Mr. Mathers continued.

"Since he kidnapped his kids and his friends killed our mother?" Noah asked. "No."

Mr. Mathers' smile faltered. "Right. I'm sorry about that. He's being charged with kidnapping, aggravated assault, and accessory to murder. And I know what you're thinking," he said, holding up a hand. "Why is he just being put on trial now, when it's been the better part of a year?"

Emily had definitely been thinking along those lines. "Is there a reason, other than the system being slower than usual because of the war?"

Mr. Mathers nodded. "The war has definitely demanded a lot of the Nation's attention. The Elemental and non-powered governments' as well, actually. But Michael Dawes' trial was also postponed until his recovery was almost complete. He suffered extensive injuries the night of the incident."

Noah's hand tightened into a fist on the table's edge, and it was clear he was remembering attacking Michael. From the slight upturn to his lips, it was also clear he wasn't sorry in the least. Given everything Michael had done, Emily was okay with that.

"He was in a medically induced coma for several weeks," Mr. Mathers said. "He had a broken jaw, collarbone, several ribs. When he woke up he had memory issues. He was sent to a rehabilitation center down South, where he is still being housed, though he's as healed as he'll ever be. His memory came back to him on its own, and physical therapy helped him regain motion. He's fully deaf in one ear, though, and has mild scarring."

No one around the table betrayed any sympathy. Alice was expressionless, as Emily had noticed she tended to become when dealing with sensitive subjects. Matt stared at the table. Noah was fuming silently, a shimmer in the air around him. Ash looked at Emily, his expression thoughtful. Derek, next to Emily, rubbed a hand on her leg, and she felt his gaze on her as well. Emily herself looked at Mr. Mathers.

"Where is he now?"

"He's being held in a hotel in Washington, D.C. until the trial is over, with a guard stationed outside his door at all hours."

"Living it up with fine dining and entertainment?" Noah asked.

Mr. Mathers shook his head. "He hasn't been allowed to leave his room since he was brought there. He has a rigid meal schedule, and limited television time."

The shimmer around Noah faded, and he looked at Mr. Mathers with open shock.

"The Nation knows he's guilty of trespassing and assault, and for that he'll definitely be put in prison. It's the other charges that are more unknown. He should already be in prison, but I hope you'll find some comfort knowing he hasn't been living it up."

"So you need us to go to the trial, to make sure he's found guilty of the other charges?" Ash asked. "Because he is guilty of all of it."

Mr. Mathers gave him an understanding smile. "You and your sister witnessed everything from the start. Your testimony will convince the jury that Dawes is guilty. Noah, you and Mrs. Madison also played a critical role that night, so you'll be called to the stand as well. We're leaving today so you can have plenty of time to get comfortable and meet with the prosecutors and other relevant personnel."

Other relevant personnel? Emily wanted to ask what that meant, but Derek was already speaking. "How long will we be gone?"

Mr. Mathers looked at Derek and Matt, his mustache quivering as his smile reversed. "Unfortunately the two of you will need to stay here."

Derek's eyes narrowed behind his glasses. "You can't really expect me to stay behind." Emily touched his arm, but he brushed it off. "Em, there's no way I'm letting you do this alone."

"I'm sorry, but I've been told to bring Noah Gants, Emily Madison, Ashton Dawes, and Alice Dawes. No others, no exceptions."

It was clear Derek wanted to fight. Emily was surprised to see that Matt simply nodded.

Mr. Mathers spoke before Derek could. "We should leave as soon as possible. It'll take about six and a half hours to drive there, not counting evening traffic. Trust me, the traffic can be insane. If you'll go pack bags, please, then we can get going."

Noah stood from the table, sending his chair back with the motion. He righted it and strode from the room, looking like he was . . . excited was the wrong word. Eager? Relieved? Being called for this trial would give him something he could do to make a difference. She knew he'd been itching for something to do. This would definitely be a hassle, and she worried there would be more emotional strife, but it would also give everyone something to keep them busy.

Ash and Alice both looked at Emily by the door. She gave them an encouraging nod and watched them walk out as well, then stood herself. "You don't mind waiting in here?" she asked Mr. Mathers.

He shook his head. "Not at all."

"I'll stay with him," Matt said.

Emily walked upstairs with Derek, and once their door was closed, he turned on her. "How are you okay with going without me?"

She grabbed her suitcase from under the bed and set it on her comforter, opening it. "Derek, it's not like I don't want you to come. But there's a crucial reason for you to stay."

He paused, and his shoulders sagged. "Right."

Emily placed a few folded articles of clothing into the suitcase. "One of us needs to be here. Riley, Tristan, and Allyssa could come back any day. If they come home while I'm in Washington, you need to be here to make sure they're safe."

"As if you wouldn't hop on a plane the second you heard they were back."

The tension broke with Derek's slight smile, and Emily almost laughed. Derek went to her dresser and handed her more clothes to pack. "I'll be fine," Emily said in a low voice.

"I know. I just hate that you have to do it alone. When we were contacted about Forte's case we were able to record videos and send them in. Why do you have to go in-person for this one? And why do you have to go so long before the actual trial?"

"Forte wasn't a high-ranking Official in the Nation," Emily said. "And honestly, I'm thinking they want to talk about more than just the trial. The way Mr. Mathers said other relevant personnel . . . ."

"Just keep me updated," Derek said.

"That goes for you too, you know," she pointed out. "See if Matt will talk to you. He seems a little off. And if you hear anything about the kids, tell me immediately."

Derek stood behind her and wrapped her in

his arms. "That I can do."

Emily leaned into him, closing her eyes. "I love you."

He kissed her temple, then helped her finish packing. He grabbed the suitcase from the bed. "I'll bring this down."

Emily went to check on Noah first. She knocked, and he opened the door with a very-full duffel bag slung over his shoulder. "All set?"

He studied her. "What do you think of this?"

She didn't lie to him. "It'll give everyone a little closure, I think, by the end. It might be hard, but it's important."

He shook his head, dark eyes solemn. "I mean that we have to go early. That we're being brought there with no warning."

"I don't know, Noah. It's definitely weird, but I'm guessing we'll be told more when we get there."

He held her gaze and then dipped his head. "Okay."

She wanted to hug him, but knew Noah wasn't a huge fan of hugging. Every once in a while he permitted it, and even more rarely, sought it, but for the most part, he preferred to be given his own space. Still, she wanted to do something to reassure him, and ended up reaching out and rubbing his upper arm. "I'm going to get the twins. We'll be right down."

She thought she'd made the right move, because the solemnity in his expression lightened with her touch. He headed toward the stairs. She knocked on the room the twins sometimes still shared. Ash opened it, Alice visible behind him.

"I thought you might be together. Just about finished packing?"

"Are we supposed to have formal outfits?" Ash asked.

"I'd bring a few nicer outfits, but bring casual stuff too. You might want to bring your pillows; the ones in hotels can be dirty, and we'll be there long enough to mind."

Ash snatched a pillow from the nearest bed. Alice chuckled and grabbed another. "We're good now," she told Emily.

Emily forced a wider smile than she felt. "Then let's go."

Mr. Mathers was right about D.C. traffic. They barely moved for an hour because there was so much congestion on the road, when they were fifteen minutes from their destination. Apparently a fender bender contributed to the delay, but still. Walking would have been faster. It was a relief to pull into the hotel parking lot and get out of the car in which they'd spent much of the day. Even when they had to wait twenty minutes to gain access to their room, at least they could wander around the hotel lobby.

"Dang," Noah said when they were finally shown to their room.

"This is huge!" Ash said.

It wasn't a room, as Emily had expected, but an entire suite, with a living room, kitchenette, one full and one half-bathroom, and two spacious bedrooms. She, Noah, and the twins walked around, and the foul mood that had settled over them in traffic dissipated completely. It was the nicest hotel accommodations Emily had ever had. Ash jumped onto the couch and gave them an approving thumbs-up.

"You should be comfortable here," Mr. Mathers said through a chuckle. "Someone will be stationed in the hallway at all times, so if you need anything, talk to them. You'll see an itinerary on the kitchen table." He pointed to the small, circular table. "It has the basic schedule you'll follow until the trial. Any time that isn't specified is free, and you can do anything you'd like. Please let someone know where you go if you leave the hotel, though. Other than that, we're all set. Sleep well!"

He left them, and Emily walked to the table. The itinerary was a stapled packet of crisp white paper. Emily would have to read that carefully, but another item on the table caught her attention: a cream-colored envelope with her name handwritten on it, propped up against the decorative vase. In her initial inspection of the room she'd assumed it was a welcome sheet from the hotel. When she saw her name, she knew that wasn't the case. She tore the envelope and pulled out a note, also handwritten.

"What's that?" Alice asked.

Emily's eyes went to the bottom of the note before she began reading. The signature belonged to President Aiden Match. "A letter from President Match," she said.

Ash sat up straighter on the couch. Noah, who had been reaching for the TV remote, stood. "What's it say?" Noah asked.

Emily read it to herself first, and clutched the table's rim before bringing her eyes back to the top and reading it aloud. *"Dear Mrs. Madison. I would like to apologize for the surprise this must have been. I know you probably have many questions, and I promise I will do my best to answer them. You'll see in the itinerary that we have plans to meet for dinner tomorrow night, and I invite you to ask any questions then. I would like to provide one answer right now, though. I'm sure you're wondering why you've been kept in the dark about Michael Dawes' condition, and the trial preparations. The war is only partly to blame. I made a decision to do as much as possible without you, to spare you and the children from pain and hassle. With the loss of the Celestials, I felt you needed time to yourselves. Unfortunately, time is running short now, and your involvement is necessary. I hope you can understand my decision. Sincerely, President Aiden Match.*"

Emily tightened the hand that clamped the table's rim, willing it not to shake. She fought back the hot, sticky feeling rising in her throat. "It was nice of him to write it by hand," Emily managed to say. Her voice didn't sound right even to her own ears, but it was as steady as she could make it. "I'll study the itinerary and we can go over it at breakfast, okay?"

Alice was closest to her, and stared at the letter in Emily's hand for a moment before nodding. "Yeah."

Emily turned to the boys. "Do you want to watch a movie or something?"

"Sure," Noah said.

"Why don't we take fifteen minutes, get comfy, and start then?" Emily suggested.

The others agreed. Emily waited until they had all moved, Noah and Ash to the one bedroom, Alice to the half-bath, before dropping the letter on the table and walking to the other bedroom, shutting the door behind her. She sat on the edge of the bed and leaned down with her head on her legs, and only then, knowing the sound would be muffled, did she let herself cry.

With the loss of the Celestials . . .

The words pierced her. They made it sound so final. Like they were gone forever.

Emily gave herself five minutes to release her emotions. Then she washed her face, changed into pajamas, and washed her face again, to hide any signs of crying. By the time she walked back into the living room, she didn't have to fight to keep a normal expression. She didn't have to fight to contain a sob, or control a shaking hand.

She curled in close with Noah, Ash, and Alice on the couch and found a comedy to watch, and by the midpoint of the movie, didn't have to fight to laugh. That letter made it sound like she'd lost her daughter for good. Maybe President Match thought that was the case.

Emily Madison wasn't about to give up so easily.

CHAPTER 6

What's in a Name?

"Can I help you?"

Tristan stared at Wyatt, thinking quickly. He'd really expected to find Riley first. "Uh . . ." he muttered lamely. He gripped Roman's lead more tightly. "I'm new here. Looking for a friend I knew on Earth. I thought she might be here."

It was strange seeing Wyatt look at him without a trace of hostility or competitiveness. At most he seemed politely interested. "What's her name?"

Tristan internally groaned. She definitely had a new name, and Tristan had no clue what it might be. "About that," Tristan started. "I never knew her real name. We were friends at school, and I always called her Red."

"You were friends but you didn't know her

name?"

Roman sniffed and moved closer to the nearest stall. "I'm a little socially awkward. Not very good with names. By the time we started hanging out, it was way too late to ask what her name was. So I stuck with the nickname."

The best lies were based partly in truth, and it was very true that Tristan was socially awkward—with people his own age, anyway. Put him in a room with adults and he was perfectly fine. He thought Wyatt believed him. It seemed like Wyatt was judging him, actually; the narrowing of his eyes was familiar and, for once, welcome. Wyatt wordlessly took Roman's lead from Tristan and let the horse enter the stall, pulling out hay to feed him. "Red hair, blue eyes?" Wyatt asked once Roman was happily eating.

"That's her," Tristan agreed.

The politeness vanished from Wyatt's features, and he drew himself up to his full height. "Why are you really looking for her?"

Maybe he hadn't believed him. Tristan sighed. "I know this is going to sound crazy, but I do know her from Earth. I know you too. You just don't remember it. I'm going to help you get your real memories back."

The truth caught Wyatt off guard. There wasn't time to see his full reaction, though. Tristan heard commotion outside and turned to look, tensing.

"Check the stable," a nearby voice called.

Had he attracted too much attention at the market, or was this Christopher's guards just being thorough? Tristan plastered himself against the wooden wall, hoping the jutting beam that framed the doorway blocked him from view. Wyatt remained in place but looked at the entryway, his expression closed-off. Tristan could see the tips of a guard's slate gray boots, immediately outside the stable.

"Did someone just come in here?" the guard asked. Tristan recognized the voice of the fire user he'd fought the day before.

"A boy looked in, but he left without saying anything," Wyatt lied, pointing in the direction from which Tristan had come.

Tristan heard the guard leave and looked at Wyatt. "You didn't turn me in."

Wyatt looked at him carefully. "I haven't decided if you're trustworthy yet. I'd like to make up my own mind before anyone does anything drastic."

Tristan stepped forward. "This is the smartest thing you've ever done. I want to help you get your mind back, Wyatt. Yours and Riley's and Allyssa's."

"Why are the guards looking for you?"

"Because I'm a Celestial." Tristan partially Shifted, watching Wyatt's eyes rake over him and take in the green aura. "I'm the dragon. And until last night, I was imprisoned just because of that." He stepped forward again. "We need to find Riley. I'll explain everything to the two of you, but we need to do it now."

He couldn't tell what Wyatt was thinking, but found it encouraging when the boy nodded. Wyatt looked out and said the coast was clear, and led Tristan from the stable to a series of small houses. Tristan saw the guard that had questioned Wyatt minutes before as they walked. The fire user was talking to an older woman a few doors down from the one to which they walked. Tristan stood with Wyatt between him and the fire user, hoping the woman kept the man talking until they were inside. Wyatt knocked on the door, and a little boy with carrot-colored hair opened it. "Tyler!" the boy cried.

"Hey John," Wyatt said. "Can we come in?"

The little boy pulled the door open and Tristan, with a glance behind him, followed Wyatt inside. "I thought you and Jane were going for a ride later?" John asked.

"Change of plans," Wyatt said with a motion at Tristan.

"Is Tyler here?" Riley called. Tristan turned toward the sound and saw her come into the room. His mouth tugged up in a smile at the sight of her, and he had to force himself not to say her name. Her hair was loose over her shoulders, and her dark blue eyes lit first on Wyatt, then on Tristan. He'd expected it, but it still made his heart constrict when he saw that she didn't recognize him in the slightest, and his smile faltered. "Who are you?"

"Tristan," he said.

"Okay," Wyatt said, standing next to Riley and facing Tristan. "We're both here. Start talking."

Riley looked between them in confusion. "John, go help Mom and Dad in the garden." She looked meaningfully at the little boy when he stood in defiance, and he sighed under her stern gaze and did as she asked. Riley touched him on the shoulder as he walked by, and then turned back to Tristan and Wyatt.

Tristan wasted no time. He told them everything. Riley paled as he spoke, while Wyatt seemed to grow bolder. "That's quite a story," Riley murmured.

"I could tell you were lying earlier," Wyatt said, "but I brought you here because you seemed to start telling the truth when I called you on the lie. You believe you're telling the truth, at any rate. There's one big problem in your story. We're not Shifters."

"Yes, you are. You're the griffin," Tristan repeated. "And Riley, you're the phoenix."

Wyatt looked at Riley and stood partly in front of her. "I didn't want to get you in trouble with the guards earlier, but you need to leave."

"Not without you," Tristan said.

"How can we have false memories?" Riley asked.

"We don't," Wyatt said firmly. "He's delusional."

Tristan had a sudden inspiration. "What's your name here, Wyatt? Tyler? Boy, Christopher really did a number on you. I thought for a second he made you smarter. Turns out he left you the same pigheaded fool you've always been. He might've actually made you worse."

Tristan had always been able to get under Wyatt's skin with ease. Apparently it worked even if Wyatt didn't remember him. His goading succeeded, and Wyatt started forward with rage in his eyes. Riley extended a hand to keep him back, opening her mouth to say something, but Tristan spoke over her. "You're a pathetic fool," he spat, staring hard at Wyatt. "And when I'm done kicking your ass, you'll kick *yourself* for believing this could ever be your life."

Wyatt shrugged off Riley's hand and sprang forward. Tristan blocked his fist, almost smiling.

There was a shimmer in the air around Wyatt. "Not a Shifter? What do you call that?"

Wyatt shoved Tristan against the door, and the shimmer became a brown, yellow, and white light that rippled around him.

"Tyler, don't!" Riley cried.

Wyatt stopped with his fist drawn back and looked at the hand that gripped Tristan's shirt. His eyes traveled to his fist and over his body, and he let Tristan go and retreated several steps. "What the . . . ?"

Tristan rubbed the back of his head where it had collided with the door. "I had to make you Shift, to prove it to you. I'm sorry I said those things, but I had to get you really angry." *And it isn't hard, considering you're such a hothead,* Tristan added silently. Christopher clearly hadn't changed that.

Wyatt's partial Shift faded as he calmed. "The king really gave us false memories?"

"Demetrius can fix everything," Tristan said. "I just need you to come with me." He looked at Riley, who had been silent for most of the time he'd been here. He hated that there was so much fear in her eyes. "I promise I'll help get everything back the way it should be."

She gave a tiny nod, and Tristan relaxed for the first time that day. He walked to the window and peeked outside. He guessed he'd spent about half an hour talking to Riley and Wyatt. The sun wasn't near where it would be for midday, so he couldn't take them back to the meeting spot yet. They should stay here until it was closer.

"We're actually too early to leave," Tristan told them. "Demetrius is trying to get information from Christopher and said to meet back midday. With guards looking for me, we should stay inside, either here or the stable."

"When Demetrius fixes our memories," Wyatt said, "then what? Where do we go?"

"We need supplies," Tristan realized, seeing where Wyatt was going with this. Maybe he *had* gotten smarter . . . "Once the two of you and Allyssa are back, we need to work together to make a plan. We'll have to do that away from the village, so we'll need supplies."

"Jane and I—*Riley,* and I, can go get some things from the market," Wyatt said. "No one is looking for us."

Tristan didn't like the idea of sitting and waiting while they went out, but it was true that they wouldn't attract any special attention on their own. He also thought Riley might need something to keep her mind off the fact that the life she remembered was fictional. Wyatt was coping by jumping into action. If Tristan were in their position, he would probably want to do something too, to find even a small sense of control. "That'd be great," he said.

Riley was staring at the floor, apparently lost in thought. Wyatt reached his hand out, brushing a curled finger beneath her chin to tilt her head up. "Hey," he said softly. "Agonizing over it won't change anything."

The smallest spark entered her eyes. "Right." She looked at Tristan. "We'll be back soon."

They each retrieved a bag, and Tristan watched them walk out with difficulty, an uncomfortable feeling in his chest again. Fear, he realized. He didn't want to be alone again. But they would be back in no time. He just had to wait.

Riley walked out of the house with a tight grip on the empty bag slung over her shoulder. This morning she'd woken up relaxed as could be, sure of who she was. Jane Grant. One of the first settlers of Terraria. The thought almost made her laugh now, even as the back of her throat burned. She wasn't Jane Grant at all, but Riley Madison. The phoenix, apparently. Her little brother John, her parents—all had been strangers until nine months ago, when they'd had their memories hijacked and replaced. Her real family lived on Earth, yet she couldn't place them. She couldn't remember the names Tristan had said, or picture their faces. They didn't seem real, compared to the family she'd known here.

Yet Tyler—*Wyatt*, had partially Shifted.

It didn't take long to reach the market. With the maelstrom of thoughts in Riley's head, the short walk felt like miles, and each step made the confidence she'd feebly shown in the house weaken.

"You're awfully quiet."

She looked up and saw Wyatt glancing back at her. "I've always been quiet." She paused. Was that true? Tristan would know.

The corner of his mouth twitched with amusement. "You know that's not what I mean."

"I'm just thinking."

"I can tell. What I don't know is what you're thinking about."

Riley looked ahead of them. They would reach the first stall in seconds if they didn't stop moving, and it wasn't safe to discuss it there. It was barely safe to say anything outside of the house, but she couldn't help it. Wyatt seemed to read her thoughts and drew her to the side, and she voiced her concerns. "I know we need to act like nothing's changed, so we don't attract attention. But everything's changed! How are you acting so calm?"

He took his time answering. "Honestly? I'm

doing everything in my power to not think about it. I'm telling myself to look forward, to take actionable steps, and think later. Because if I don't do that, if I think about it, I won't be able to do what needs to be done to get our memories back, because guards will catch us." He studied her with conflicted hazel eyes. "We need to pretend we're getting supplies for our families. Just like we've done plenty of times. Okay?"

Riley swallowed and murmured agreement. *Focus on actionable steps*, she told herself. The burning in the back of her throat lessened. "We need foods that will keep," she said.

Wyatt smiled approvingly. "All right. Let's find some supplies."

They went to several stalls and selected items they thought would help the most. Wyatt chatted with the vendors as he usually did, and when they walked by a pair of guards near a vegetable stand, he put his arm around Riley and made a joke that, despite her nerves, triggered a smile. The guards didn't give them a second look. They tried not to take more than their fair share. Luckily, as Wyatt had reminded her, they had shopped for their 'families' before, so it was easy to grab five or so portions of everything for each bag and not arouse suspicion. In no time the bags that had been empty bulged with wares, and Riley and Wyatt made to go back to Riley's house. Wyatt stopped near a station they had never visited before: knives.

He looked at the weapons with an intensity Riley couldn't decide if she liked or not, his expression solemn. The woman who owned the knives sat on the edge of a blanket, next to the variety of knives she had spread upon it. They ranged from hilted daggers to paring knives, in a range of materials.

"Looking for anything in particular?" the woman asked.

"Something for protection," Wyatt stated. "My dad will be traveling soon, and mom wants him to have something to keep him safe. I told him I'd find him one."

The woman perked up and motioned to the left side of the blanket. "I have a few fine daggers right here." Four daggers were placed close together, each about four inches long, barring the pommels. Two resembled daggers like Riley had seen on the belts of guards, with metallic blades. One had a blade of a lighter, shiny color, which Riley thought was made of marble. The fourth had a blade of a dull black material Riley didn't immediately recognize. The woman noticed Riley's gaze and smiled. "You have a keen eye. That's my last obsidian blade from Earth. Sharp and strong."

Riley looked at Wyatt. "He really wants a knife?"

Wyatt studied the four daggers. "I don't think he wants one, but he understands that he might need it. Can I hold one?" he asked the woman.

She allowed him to grip each blade in turn, commenting on the best qualities of each. Wyatt held the obsidian blade the longest, and the woman nodded. "Seems like you've made your choice."

"This one feels best in my hand," he said. He held it out to Riley, but she shook her head, and he returned his attention to the woman. "Do you have a scabbard for it?"

They left the woman a few minutes later, Wyatt with a sheathed dagger tied to his belt. Riley found she kept glancing at the weapon.

"It's just a precaution," Wyatt said when Riley's house was in sight.

"I know." Riley opened the door and walked inside, Wyatt close behind. Tristan sat near the door, dozing, breathing through an open mouth. John and his parents stood across the room.

"Why'd you leave him here?" John asked.

Tristan startled awake and scrabbled upright, eyes traveling around the room. Riley set down her bag and approached her foster family. "I know you're probably a little confused right now. Tristan is a friend, and he needed a place to rest for a little while."

"Sorry," Tristan said.

"It's fine," Riley's foster mother said. Her tone made it clear she still had questions, but she wouldn't demand answers now. Riley was tempted to tell them the truth, until she saw that both boys thought that would be a mistake. Wyatt had a serious expression again. Tristan ever so slightly shook his head.

"Would you mind if we talked privately?" Riley asked, gesturing between herself, Tristan, and Wyatt.

Her foster father studied them and reluctantly agreed, prompting his wife and son to follow him back into the garden. Once the back door shut, Wyatt emptied his bag, setting everything out. Riley did the same. It seemed much more impressive when everything they'd collected was laid out. Bundles of vibrant leafy vegetables, round potatoes and sweet potatoes, pouches of assorted nuts and dried berries, dried strips of meat, rolls of hearty wheat bread, whole carrots . . . these supplies could definitely last them several days.

"Did you attract special attention?" Tristan asked.

"No," Wyatt said immediately.

Tristan almost smiled. "This is great. Hopefully Demetrius can grab some stuff too, and we'll be set for a little while. We'll have to focus on putting distance between ourselves and Christopher until we come up with a more specific plan. Once you have your memories back."

Wyatt looked out the window. "You said we're supposed to meet around noon. We should probably wait a little longer before leaving." He repacked his bag and put it over his shoulder. "I'll bring this back to my house and stay there for a while. It'll look less suspicious. We should pack some clothes. Meet at the stable in two hours or so?"

Tristan and Riley nodded, and Wyatt walked out. Riley put everything back into her bag. "I'll go grab a few things," she said.

Tristan held out a hand in a *wait* motion. "Riley, I know it seems mean to leave those people in the dark, but they'll be in danger if you tell them the truth. When Christopher realizes you're gone, he'll question them. The less they know, the better." His gaze was steady. "We'll fix their memories before we go back home."

How had he known she was stressing about that? His words assuaged most of her misgivings regarding her foster family, and Riley went to her room to pack, suddenly more eager to find the others.

CHAPTER 7

I Trust You

Christopher only kept Demetrius with him for a little over an hour after lunch, and then he looked at his son carefully. "You had a rough night. Take some time to get a clean change of clothes and walk around. We can continue later."

"Yes, Father."

Demetrius walked to his chambers with a burgeoning smile. He'd been instructed to change and walk around. He could pack a few materials easily in his chambers, and walking around was exactly what he needed to do. He forced himself not to rush his steps. When the door to his chambers shut securely behind him, he allowed himself to move quickly. He did change, and threw a few more garments into his satchel. He left the most room in the satchel for two of the blankets that covered his bed. With the cold castle walls, he had several layers of blankets. No one would notice two of the inner layers missing. That being done he strode from his chambers, assuming an air of casual observation as he began his search for Allyssa.

He didn't search blindly. He passed several servants in his wanderings and slowed his walk as they passed, going through their recent memories. One had been doing laundry with Allyssa just moments before, spurring Demetrius to walk toward the washroom. This was the only room in the castle that lacked a proper door. With the large baskets of laundry servants had to carry, Christopher had thought it made more sense to hang a curtain over the entryway instead. Demetrius brushed past the thin curtain and raked his eyes over the room.

Two people stood inside: an older gentleman and a girl with brown hair. The girl was singing as she worked, her back to the door. Her voice was high and sweet. "Allyssa?" he asked.

She spun at his voice, and Demetrius' heart stuttered. She looked at him with wide brown eyes, her hands pausing over the tub of soapy water in which she was washing something. "Your name is Allyssa, right?"

She nodded. "How can I help you, Your Highness?"

Demetrius looked at the older gentleman.

"Give us a moment, please. I apologize for disrupting your work."

"I can finish folding that, Stephen," Allyssa offered. "You should take your break."

The gentleman smiled at Allyssa, gave a slight bow to Demetrius, and swept past the curtain. Demetrius looked at Allyssa, unsure of how to start. It would be simplest to use his powers and make Allyssa follow him somewhere safer, where he could restore her memories, but he refused to entertain the thought. He'd promised not to use his powers on her, and other than restoring her memories, he intended to honor that promise. He could order her to come with him, but that thought was almost as repulsive as using his powers. He had no right to order anyone to do anything.

He walked closer and assumed the gentleman's post, reaching for a towel to fold. "You shouldn't do that," Allyssa said.

He ignored the comment. "Do you like it here?"

The question seemed to catch her off-guard. "This world is nice. It was strange to start working as a servant, but it's a small price for this experience." Her cheeks flushed. "Not that it's a bad thing. I appreciate being allowed to work here."

A low-burning anger sped Demetrius' pulse. "You were made to work here, Allyssa. There was very little choice." He saw the confusion set in her countenance, and continued. "Are there any gaps in your memory? Any times that are indistinct?"

She looked down at her soapy hands and picked up the cloth she'd been washing. "Doesn't everyone have times that are indistinct in memory?"

He felt tempted to smile. That was true enough. "What were you singing when I walked in?"

"*The Nightingale*. It's one of my favorites. My chorus teacher taught it to me in middle school."

Demetrius knew the shock he felt wasn't hidden, but Allyssa was focused on her task and didn't look at him. How could she have such a specific memory of her life on Earth? How could she remember her true life on Earth at all, when the others had been given completely new identities and blurs of memories? Unless . . .

Her mind worked differently than the others. Christopher had said as much when he'd abducted her last year. Her brain was able to recognize when it had been influenced, and eventually break that influence down. Maybe Christopher hadn't even tried to completely change her identity, instead focusing on more recent years and glossing over memories with Riley.

"This might sound crazy, but please listen. I

asked you about any hazy periods of time because your memories have been altered. Not completely, but enough to make you forget why you really came here." He stepped closer. "Allyssa, you have a very special mind. You can tell when powers like I have, like my father has, have been used on you. I'm sure you've noticed memories surfacing in the time we've been in Terraria. Memories you can't explain."

She set the cloth on a drying table with very precise movements, and took her time to respond. "I don't know about memories, but every so often my guardian says I get confused, and sends me to the castle. She says extra labor eases the mind, and when I go back to her the next day, I always feel better." Her back was to him, her voice low. "I can't think of what I actually do on those nights."

Demetrius gentled his tone. "I would guess my father met with you and put a fresh film over your mind." He was fairly certain that was what had happened, actually. Christopher had probably taken a special pleasure each time, knowing he was renewing the division between Demetrius and Allyssa right under their noses. Demetrius set down the last towel he'd been folding and approached her. "We came here together, with Riley, Wyatt, and Tristan. I can fix what my father did to you. But I can't do it here. We have to be away from the castle, out of my father's reach."

She angled herself so she could see him, standing close as they were, and he could see her considering his words. He wanted to place his hand over hers to reassure her, but quelled the impulse. He tried to convey it in his voice.

"You know me, Allyssa. Let me give you back your identity so you can realize it."

His stomach did a backflip when she awarded him a timid smile. "I guess we better get going."

His lips curved up in a reciprocal smile he felt through his body. "Follow me."

He motioned for her to wait an extra second after he walked through the curtain, to make sure Christopher wasn't nearby, and then the two made their way through the castle, toward the stable. Allyssa walked just a step behind Demetrius, following close enough for him not to worry he'd lost her. They arrived at the stable entrance without encountering anyone in the castle, and when Demetrius opened the door, he realized why. At least six guards stood in the stable, one standing straight in the middle of the room.

"Looks like the king was right to doubt," the head guard, Tobias, said.

Demetrius cast his powers out in a wave to knock out all of the guards. They remained upright, unfazed.

Tobias leered at Demetrius. "He was also right to give us mental shields."

The rest of Tobias' squadron moved to attention, creeping forward. "Allyssa, I need your help," Demetrius whispered. "You're a wind user."

He didn't take his eyes off the approaching guards, but in his periphery he saw Allyssa look at her hands. "The king erased that too?" He heard a trace of anger in her voice.

Tobias pushed them against the door, reaching for Demetrius' arms to restrain him. Demetrius moved to stand in front of Allyssa and attempted to shove Tobias back. The head guard expected it, and deflected the blow with ease. He grasped Demetrius and threw him behind him, into two others who immediately grabbed his arms and twisted them behind his back.

Demetrius heard air whistle past his ears and saw Allyssa holding her hands out. Her brows pressed close in fear, yet her eyes also contained a spark of rage, her mouth set in determination. Another rush of air wound around Demetrius' legs. Tobias reached out for Allyssa, and something in the way she held her hands changed. She had been twisting them experimentally, moving them at her sides. When Tobias reached for her, she thrust her hands straight out in a forceful gesture. A torrent of wind crashed into the guards, and Demetrius. He stumbled backward along with the guards that gripped his arms, partially falling when one tripped.

"I'm sorry!" Allyssa cried, her eyes locking on Demetrius. The wind weakened.

"Keep doing it!"

He turned and did something he'd never done in his life: strike someone. His knuckles stung when they collided with the man's jaw. His adrenaline surged and he scrambled upright, fighting against the rush of wind. Allyssa ran to his side and kicked a guard that was starting to stand, then grabbed Demetrius' hand. The wind stopped pushing against him, though he could feel it pressing against the others.

"Make it stronger," Demetrius urged. He led her to Perseus, pulled the horse from his stall, and swung himself on the horse's back. By the time he reached to help Allyssa up she had jumped, and seated herself in front of him. They didn't waste time getting comfortable. On the contrary, as soon as Allyssa was on the horse Demetrius spurred Perseus forward, wrapping an arm around Allyssa to keep her secure as the horse rocketed from the stable. The satchel bounced against Demetrius' leg, starting to slip from his shoulder, and Allyssa grabbed it before it could fall.

She looked over Demetrius' shoulder, placing one hand there to steady herself. "They aren't following," she said.

"They will," he said, and clicked for Perseus to run at his fastest speed. Demetrius' thoughts raced. He could reach the rendezvous point quickly, but if Tristan and the others were already there, the space really wasn't sufficient to hide them. Especially if guards were only moments behind. "We're going to go past the place we need to meet the others. I know another spot not far off where we can hide for a few minutes, and watch for the guards."

They were approaching the fallen tree that served as the rendezvous point, and Demetrius made a mental message as it appeared in his line of sight. He formed the message to find Wyatt's mind if he was in the vicinity—after several years knowing the boy, Demetrius was familiar with his mind's signature—and threw the message when they galloped past. He had no idea if the move worked, but he'd tried. He'd thought he felt a few consciousnesses near the tree, though he couldn't be sure. Allyssa kept a firm hold on the arm he held around her, and were it not for the adrenaline coursing through him and keeping him hyper-focused on reaching safety, Demetrius felt certain he would enjoy it.

The second spot he knew wasn't as hidden as the fallen tree, but with just the two of them it should suffice. It was a minor cliff at the beginning of the forest, where trees had been excavated to build the village. Demetrius slowed Perseus and slid off before the horse fully stopped. Again, Allyssa moved with him. He wordlessly led her to the minor cliff's edge, knelt, and lowered himself down. Allyssa dropped lightly beside him, looking up. There was a curved edge here, and Demetrius suspected someone in the village had worked on this spot. When he placed his back to the cliff he did see a beautiful view of the forest. More importantly, the recess should keep them from immediate view of the path above.

Demetrius clicked for Perseus to come, reaching up so the horse could see him. "Let me help," Allyssa said. She held out her hands and moved them straight up, a look of fierce concentration on her face. Perseus knickered uneasily as his feet left the ground. Demetrius looked from the horse to Allyssa and back, and felt a wave of relief when Perseus' hooves returned to solid ground—right next to them.

Allyssa swayed, and Demetrius moved to support her. "That was fantastic," he told her.

"Figured it wasn't much of a hiding spot if your horse was standing above us."

Demetrius pulled Perseus closer by the reins and ran a finger down the length of Perseus' head, signaling the horse to lie down. The horse trainer Christopher had recruited had definitely taught him some useful tricks. Then he leaned back himself, fully resting against the grassy cliff. Sounds of pursuit reached his ears in the ensuing seconds: pounding hooves, heavy breathing. Demetrius felt the earth tremble under the sudden weight rushing above them, and drew Allyssa closer to him. Neither of them moved for several minutes.

"I think we're safe," Allyssa whispered.

Demetrius took his first full breath since they'd heard the guards run by. "I think you're right." He turned to look at her. "We should go find the others."

She put a hand on his chest. "Fix my memories first. I want to be myself when we see them." She must have seen the flash of trepidation that ran through him, because her expression softened. "I trust you."

He sucked in a breath, remembering their first meeting, and with a nod he set to work undoing what his father had done. He lost sight of their surroundings as he focused on her mind. He slowed her thoughts and found the tinted ones that Christopher had placed there—those false recollections of volunteering to come to this world and being assigned a guardian, among other things—and dissociated them from actual memory. Then he found her actual memories, buried beneath a glossy veneer. He broke the glaze containing the memories and set them free, feeling the lightness that accompanied their ascent as if they were a collection of helium balloons escaping their cart. He scanned over her mind once more, quickly, to make sure all traces of modification by Christopher were gone, and retreated, letting her thoughts return to normal.

His eyes began to take in his actual surroundings again. Allyssa regarded him with dull eyes before beginning to fall. Demetrius lunged forward and slid to the ground with her, wrapping his arms around her. He looked down, his heart beating frantically, to find her turning her head to look up at him. Her eyes were no longer dull.

"Demetrius," she murmured with a smile.

He felt her warm breath on his neck. All of his anxiety fled. "Welcome back," he said through a laugh.

He knew she was close to sleep. She needed rest, especially after her mind had been shuffled and she'd tired herself using her powers so suddenly and forcefully. She seemed to be fighting it, though. She lifted one hand and framed his cheek with it, gazing at him with half-closed eyes. Demetrius reached out and brushed a strand of hair from her face. She sighed and rested her head against his chest. He only knew she surrendered to rest when her hand fell from his face, curling on his chest. He held her more tightly for a few seconds, comforted by her even breathing, and allowed himself to close his eyes for a moment.

"I'm so glad you're safe."

Tristan sat against the fallen tree and tried not to jump up to throttle Wyatt. "You have to stop pacing," he said for what felt like the tenth time. "Someone could walk by at any time and see you."

Wyatt stopped and dropped into a sitting position with a huff, crossing his legs. "Aren't we supposed to be meeting Demetrius now?" he demanded. "What if something's wrong?"

"He's probably just being careful, and that's what's holding him up. Maybe he's having a hard time finding Allyssa."

Riley looked up at them, one hand still stroking her horse's mane. "You're sure we shouldn't go look for them?"

Part of Tristan definitely wanted to, but he shook his head. "They could be here any minute, and we could keep missing each other. There are probably a lot more guards out by now, too." He remembered how anxious the walk from Riley's house to the stable had made him, and how paranoid he'd felt walking from the stable with his horse. Riley and Wyatt had followed him from a distance, acting as if they were going for a ride —something they apparently did frequently—so he supposed it hadn't been overly suspicious, but he'd still felt himself tense every time he passed a guard. Arriving at the tree had felt like reaching a safe point in a video game: a dangerous game he had to win. It was the first step to fixing things and getting home.

That was at least an hour ago. And they'd waited until just after midday to come to the safe spot.

"I just hate wai—"

Wyatt cut off abruptly, his eyebrows rising almost comically.

Riley leaned forward. "What's wrong?"

It sounded like a horse ran by the opposite side of the fallen tree, moving swiftly. Wyatt's eyebrows remained up behind his bangs. "I just got an email. In my head."

Tristan blinked. "What?"

"Demetrius," Wyatt explained. "That must be his voice. It's like an email in my head." He put his hand to his temple and looked like he was listening. "So weird. He said he found Allyssa, but they couldn't stop, because guards are after them. They're going to another hiding spot nearby."

So that horse had been Demetrius and Allyssa speeding by. Tristan hadn't known Demetrius could send mental emails. "Did you have a notification that you had mail?"

Wyatt's eyebrows moved back to their natural position. "Kind of. He said my name first."

"So more like a voicemail."

"Not important!" Riley cut in. "Are we supposed to go find them?"

Wyatt held out his hands in a *quiet* motion, looking at the fallen tree as if listening intently, and a heartbeat later Tristan heard it: thundering hooves on the path. Much louder than when Demetrius and Allyssa had ridden by. They waited until it had been silent again for several seconds before Wyatt let his hands fall to his sides. "I think he was just letting us know he and Allyssa are safe."

Tristan took in the tension in Wyatt's posture, and the apprehension in Riley's. "He's leaving it up to us to follow or not," Tristan said. It was a guess, but he didn't share that. "If we stay here, he'll come back to get us when he thinks it's safe. If we go find them, we might run into guards."

"Or we might be able to leave right away and put some distance between ourselves and Christopher," Wyatt said.

Tristan nodded. "I think it's worth the risk. The guards have to come back at some point, but it could be hours before they give up the search."

Riley looked between Tristan and Wyatt and squared her shoulders. "Let's go."

They stood and reached for the horses' reins. "Did your voicemail leave you any hints about their hiding spot?" Tristan asked.

"No, but I'm sure it's not too far."

Tristan moved the thick branch that gave them access while Riley and Wyatt led their horses to the path, and nudged his horse through before following and letting the branch rest. Riley and Wyatt mounted their horses with smooth, practiced motions. Tristan clambered onto Roman, trying and failing to not feel self-conscious. When Wyatt snickered, it became a flicker of annoyance.

They rode silently, all very aware of their sur-roundings as they left the village and the fallen tree behind. They took it in turns to quietly call out Demetrius' and Allyssa's names every few feet, after scanning for signs of guards, and were near a thicker section of trees Tristan thought marked deeper woodlands when Wyatt turned his head swiftly. "Demetrius?" he asked in a stage whisper.

"Wyatt?"

Wyatt really did have good hearing. "It's us," Tristan called, looking toward the sound. He realized there was a minor cliff where they stood, and scrabbled off of Roman's back to go look. Perseus the horse was visible resting on the ground below. Demetrius appeared from beneath the lip of the cliff and smiled.

"You did get my message."

"We need to talk about that after," Wyatt said.

Riley hadn't moved closer, and sat rigidly atop her horse. "We should keep moving."

Demetrius motioned for them to come down. Tristan watched Wyatt and Riley lead their horses to the jump before doing it himself. Demetrius had his back to them, crouching and looking at a stirring Allyssa. He helped her to her feet, and Tristan saw that she clung to him with familiarity. His suspicion was confirmed when she looked over at them and her face broke out in a grin. She'd definitely had her memories fixed.

"Riley!"

Tristan glanced at Riley, wondering if the sight of her best friend would jog something of her real life. Riley gave Allyssa a small smile that was more polite than genuine. Her hands fidgeted with the reins of her horse and Tristan redirected the conversation. "Which way are we going?"

Demetrius held out a steadying hand while Allyssa got onto Perseus and then seated himself behind her. "Follow me."

Tristan again waited to bring up the rear. Riley looked at him before starting forward, and he thought she was saying *thank you*. He partially smiled.

They traveled in silence, well aware that the guards they needed to elude could be ahead of them. They moved at a steady pace, wending through the trees and bushes until dusk made it difficult to see. Demetrius stopped near a large oak. Tristan balanced on his toes to stretch his legs and noticed Wyatt looking at him.

"It takes a while to get used to riding," Wyatt said.

"Are you ready to get your memories back?" Demetrius asked, walking over. Allyssa walked beside him, fully alert. "We can stay here for the night. You'll need to rest after I finish."

He instructed them to sit and sat down across from them, and began. He must have started with Wyatt, because Wyatt remained still while Riley looked around, her arms drawn around her knees. Tristan and Allyssa stood nearby, watching. "How long does it take?" Tristan asked in a whisper.

"I don't know. It didn't seem to take long with me, but Demetrius said they probably have more false memories than I did."

Tristan turned to her. "You didn't have a different identity?"

"I was still Allyssa. I just had a few blanks and fakes."

"Huh." The light around them was fading fast. It had gotten chilly the night before. Would it be stupid to try to light a fire? Probably. He remembered they had packed blankets and grabbed the bags they had, digging through them and pulling out every blanket they had. He also pulled out some of the food and one of the canteens of water. He handed Allyssa a blanket and then held up the bag of assorted nuts he'd grabbed. "Hungry?"

"Starving."

They ate about half the bag before Wyatt slumped over. "Guess Demetrius is done," Allyssa said.

Tristan chuckled. Riley had moved to look at Wyatt but turned to look at Demetrius immediately and then stilled, her shoulders relaxing. Tristan grabbed a blanket and placed it behind her. He threw one over Wyatt as well. When Demetrius finished with Riley minutes later, Tristan lunged to catch her and ease her onto the blanket, glad Wyatt had gone first so he'd known what would happen. He spread another blanket over her before looking up to find Demetrius and

Allyssa staring at him.

"Thank you," he said.

"They'll probably sleep through the night. We should get some sleep too, to start moving early."

Tristan leaned against a tree, propped his blanket partially behind his head as a cushion, and stayed awake for several hours, his mind moving too quickly to sleep. He kept a casual watch in the darkness, ears tuned for sounds of guards until his busy thoughts tired themselves out and sleep claimed him.

CHAPTER 8

Questions and Answers

Ash and Alice slept on the two beds in one of the rooms. Emily offered to take one of them, to have the twins take the biggest bed in the other room and Noah use the other mattress in her room, but no one took her up on it. Noah gave Ash a look immediately after Emily made the offer, telling him not to accept—as if Ash would have. He knew Emily had been upset, right before the movie. He wanted her to have her own space while they were here. It seemed like an unspoken rule that the parental figure deserved the single room.

The beds were all huge anyway. He and Alice had each taken one last night, but they could easily share a bed so Noah could take the third.

"We slept late," Ash said, looking at the alarm clock on the stand between the beds.

Alice murmured an incoherent response. When Ash walked into the kitchenette just outside his room, he found Emily sitting at the table, reading the itinerary by lamplight. She looked up when he entered. "Morning."

Ash looked over at the couch and saw that Noah was still asleep. He'd passed out before they finished the movie, something Ash was sure Alice would tease Noah about later.

"Are we going to a big breakfast?" Ash asked.

"If Alice and Noah get up in the next few minutes we can go to the breakfast buffet. We should just have time before Mr. Mathers comes to get us."

Ash looked at Noah again. Did he dare to poke the bear? His stomach was rumbling. Noah might not punch him if he knew he was being woken for food . . .

Alice walked into the room rubbing sleep-filled eyes. "What are we doing?" she asked.

"Getting food!" Ash said loudly. Emily and Alice both raised their eyebrows at him. Noah groaned, waking up, and Ash smiled.

Ten minutes later they walked into the breakfast buffet room, and Ash loaded his plate, devouring scrambled eggs and home fries. He decided he would have to try everything at some point in their stay. He had a pretty massive plate, but he ended up going back for a giant blueberry muffin that he munched on during the walk back to the room, and was very glad he did. They reached their door the same time Mr. Mathers did, coming from the opposite direction.

"Good morning!" he greeted. "What did you think of the hotel breakfast?"

"Delicious!" Ash said around his muffin.

Mr. Mathers' mustache seemed to be alive, with how frequently he smiled and made it move. "Did you get a chance to review the itinerary?"

"I did, but we haven't fully discussed it together," Emily said. She'd told them about the dinner they were supposed to have that night, but not much else. Noah had barely been awake until he had food in front of him, which didn't leave much time for discussion.

"Well you'll see that you don't have anything until tonight, so I thought you might want a tour this morning. All the popular attractions, to start: the Lincoln and Washington monuments, the Smithsonian, the Kennedy Center."

Emily looked at Ash, Alice, and Noah, waiting for their input. Noah shrugged. Ash nodded, excited by the prospect. "That sounds great," Emily told Mr. Mathers.

Matt had to go to work shortly after his mom and the others left with the Official. His part time job at the grocery store had been ideal these last few months. It kept him busy, and let him add to his savings account, but it also gave him an excuse to leave the Temple without questions. Once a week he said he had a shift when he didn't, grabbed his laptop, and spent time doing a job he found much more important: trying to find his little sister.

He had to actually work at the grocery store the day they left, but the next day let him continue where'd he'd left off in his search the week before. He parked the old, beat-up Corolla he'd bought last summer, climbed into the backseat, and opened up his laptop. Some days he went inside a coffee shop with all the other people glued to their laptops. Some days he didn't feel like being asked how his novel was coming. As if even half the people in there were really writing novels . . . stupid stereotype. So he stayed in his car. On those days, he drove to other locations, for a different parking lot view. Several times he'd gone to the student lot at the college he was supposed to be attending, thinking the academic site might inspire him to do his research.

He'd decided not to go to college this year. He didn't want to be busy taking classes he didn't care about, when he could be busy working (in both capacities). He'd only agreed to go because his parents wanted him to get a two-year degree, since he had no idea what he wanted to do with his life, but he absolutely refused to go after Riley and the others went missing. Maybe next year.

He pulled up the master document on his laptop and reviewed what he'd added last week: *Garcia, June. An architect. No family, skilled in her field. Disappeared nine months ago.*

Dozens of other names littered this document. He'd painstakingly looked them up, combing through results when more than one person with a name popped up, until he confirmed that he had the right individual. He knew he did when he saw a sudden disappearance from social media eight to nine months ago. Not everyone had social media, but for those that didn't, more web searching about their occupations helped him piece things together.

He remembered his first attempts to find out if the people on the list had disappeared. He'd tried going to some of their houses. It hadn't gone well.

After flying overhead, Matt dropped to the ground as a human and pulled the paper out of his pocket, looking at the address on it. 129 Heartwood Place. He looked around to see where he'd landed and sighed. There were street signs showing different Places and Ways and Avenues, but none of them were Heartwood.

After twenty minutes, Matt decided Luther Forest was the Labyrinth. He swore he went back the way he had come before, but when he reached the end of one street he found himself outside the developments, looking at the traffic circles. Unfortunately, the area was active enough that he couldn't Shift again to search for the house. An eagle would attract attention, flying low over the houses. He walked back the way he had come.

He didn't know how long it was before he found the right street, but eventually he stood in front of 129 Heartwood Place. It was one of the shared buildings that made up a lot of the developments here, cut in half so two families shared a driveway. Matt banged on the door for 129, hoping he didn't wake up the people in the other half, 131. When three minutes passed without a response he tried opening the door. No surprise it was locked. He looked behind him. No car in the driveway on this side. He knocked on the door again. It wasn't that late, probably only seven or eight. It was just getting really dark.

When the door didn't open, Matt took it as a sign Dean Lawson wasn't home. He didn't have proof, but he guessed Dean Lawson hadn't been home in about two months. He was about to leave when he decided to look inside. He had to know for sure. If Lawson was just out for a movie, it would change what Matt was thinking. He started jiggling the handle of the door, trying to make it give. He even partially Shifted, throwing some force against it.

"What are you doing?" a voice demanded.

Matt looked over to see the neighbor standing outside his door. "Does Dean Lawson still live here?" he asked.

"Who's asking?" the neighbor demanded.

"A concerned citizen," Matt said in a rush. "Has he been home at all in the last few days?"

It was clear the man thought he was unstable. He whipped out a phone and pressed three numbers on the keypad.

"No, wait!" Matt cried, running towards the man. The guy backed up quickly, raising his phone to his ear. Matt looked at him for a second. What could he do, hit him over the head? He sprinted off the driveway, ignoring the man's shout to stay put. As soon as he reached the street he Shifted, vaulting into the air and flying up into the clouds, where he couldn't be seen.

Not Matt's finest moment, but he'd never claimed to be the smartest, and he'd been a little reckless those first weeks of searching.

The names came from a list he'd found in Christopher's house. He wasn't finished going through it, but by now, it was clear that the people on this list weren't here anymore. They were wherever Christopher had taken Riley and the others. Matt had made a copy of the list when he'd flown back to Christopher's house the day they'd lost everyone. There hadn't been any physical documents that seemed valuable, but apparently Christopher hadn't thought anyone would dare to look at his computer. He hadn't even locked it with a password. Stupid man.

Since then, Matt had been running his own investigation, with the copies of Christopher's documents as his guide. He wasn't any closer to knowing where they'd gone, but he knew this was something Christopher had been planning for years. All of the people on the list had specific skillsets: carpentry, architecture, agriculture, weaponry. Matt hadn't found evidence, but he was sure plenty of them were Shifters or Elementalists. It was clear Christopher had found the people he would need to build and sustain something substantial. A town, or something.

Matt turned his attention from the list. He didn't need to go through more of the names. He opened up another document from Christopher's computer, titled *Research*. He'd glanced at this one before. It wasn't really one source of information, but an annotated bibliography. (Matt hated that he now knew an example of someone using that in real life, because he now owed Mrs. Hanes a dollar.) All of the websites and books referenced in the fifty-page document related to the Celestials.

He sighed and read the first entry, pulling out

his notepad. It was boring, tedious work, and when he stopped several hours later, his eyes burned in a way they never did after hours of playing video games. It had been so long since he'd played video games for hours on end.

Another reason to hate Christopher Thrane.

Matt marked the spot he'd stopped reading, shut the laptop, and scrambled back to the driver's seat. Time to pretend he was just getting out of work. His head swam with the information he'd just read, and he blared rock music to drown it out. He'd get there eventually. For today, he was happy with the little progress he'd made.

Besides. With his mom out of town, he would have more freedom to conduct his investigation. He could work from within the Temple while his dad went to work. The idea of not having to hide at all—being able to sit in a comfy chair in the library, laptop open, bag of chips in hand—was wonderful, and he found himself eager for work the next day.

Emily was glad Mr. Mathers had planned a distraction for them. The kids seemed to enjoy the tour. Mr. Mathers said he would bring them to the Smithsonian again later in the week, because there was just so much to see. Noah seemed particularly interested in the museum. Emily had been once before, when she and Derek were first married, but she'd forgotten a lot. It was a nice distraction for her as well.

It was almost easy to pretend they were on a family vacation, but a voice in the back of Emily's head reminded her of every hour that drew them closer to dinner with President Match. The hour finally drew near, and Emily looked at the kids as they waited in their hotel suite, inspecting them.

It was strange seeing Noah in anything but T-shirts and sweatshirts, and Emily could see the change the past months had wrought in him now, as he wore a short-sleeve polo shirt. It was almost too tight around his arms. All the time he'd been spending in the gym had made him noticeably stronger. Ash and Alice had changed too, but mostly in height. She swore Ash was shooting up every day, like Matt had done at that age. He was starting to be taller than Alice, and they'd been head-to-head for years. His khakis were getting a bit short for him. Emily made a note to herself to get everyone new clothes for the fall. She smoothed her own skirt and blouse, suddenly nervous.

"Emily?" Alice asked, playing with the cuff of her cardigan. "He said in the letter that we could ask him any questions we had. Can we really?"

So young to worry about playing the game, but so wise to know there was a game involved. "What did you want to ask?"

"How about what he's done to search for our family?" Noah asked.

"We don't know what he's done," Emily said, trying to give him the benefit of the doubt. "Just try not to say anything rash. Trust me, I have questions for him."

They may not have trusted Match, but Emily thought they trusted her to ask the questions that burned in all their minds.

Mr. Mathers came to escort them to the restaurant where they were meeting President Match. The man that had been stationed in the hallway also accompanied them. They went to a small Italian restaurant, and were led to a private room in the back. Match was already seated at the head of the table. His vice president, Madame Neer, sat to his right. A woman in a dark suit stood in the corner, her hands clasped in front of her. The president's personal security, Emily guessed.

Match stood. "Mrs. Madison, children. Thank you for joining us." He gestured at the table, and they seated themselves around it. Match took his seat again. "We have a lot to discuss, but before we start, why don't we choose our meals? Gianni's has a wonderful mushroom ravioli."

Ash whispered something to Alice behind his menu, and she grinned. Once they placed their orders, Match leaned back in his seat. "How are you liking D.C. so far?"

"It's nice," Alice said.

"You'll have plenty of time to explore it more thoroughly," Neer said. The woman's shrewd gaze seemed softer than it had the last time they'd met, which Emily took as a good thing. "I understand you like to go to your local park at home. There's a nice one here."

"Um, President Match?" Ash asked. "If you don't mind, sir, why did we need to come so early, when the trial isn't for two weeks? Sir?"

His cheeks flushed. Emily gave him a soft smile.

"I brought you here now partially because of my own schedule," Match said. "I wanted to meet with you, but I'll be busy for the next week and several days after, and after that, you'll be meeting with the attorney. I wanted to make sure we had an opportunity to talk before the trial."

"What did you want to talk about?" Noah asked.

Match raised his eyebrows. "I thought you would like to ask more questions about your father, but I guess there's time for that with the attorney. I want to discuss the Celestials, young man." He looked at Emily. "You filed a report when they went missing nine months ago, and when there were more disappearances, both

Shifter and Elemental forces began conducting an investigation. I'd like to hear everything you know, and then I'll share what the Nation has uncovered."

Emily saw the shock in Noah's eyes, fast replaced with approval. She told Match and Neer everything. Ash, Alice, and Noah chimed in, but allowed her to share the big details herself. They had steaming plates of food in front of them before she'd finished. No one touched their plates until she was done, and she was very aware of how intently both Match and Neer listened. The last thing she told them was Ash and Alice's excursion the day before, and how they learned about the doorway in the park.

Match regarded her for several tense seconds after she finished, his face inscrutable. Then he picked up his fork, signaling everyone to eat. "You weren't told about the doorway in the park until yesterday?" he asked.

Ash shook his head. "We knew people disappeared from the park, but we didn't know how."

"We still don't really know how," Neer said. "Beyond identifying it as the doorway to the parallel world where the spirit animals took refuge, we aren't sure about anything. We have no idea how to open it. Still, you should have been told months ago."

They ate while their food was still hot, and

when they were mostly done, Match restarted the conversation, sharing everything he knew about the disappearances.

"We first heard about it when you filed your initial report, and then when you filed the official missing person report to your local police 48 hours later. Since the Celestials were involved, Neer and I were informed by the Nation Police immediately, and have been communicating regularly with the officers and detectives closest to Saratoga. We discovered that Christopher Thrane is a rare form of Elementalist, which you already knew. A search of his house was conducted and his property was seized and examined. Reports of people disappearing from the area became more frequent, and even people who didn't live nearby seemed to have gone from Spa Park. We closed it to the public, and scouring through Thrane's notes, realized that his theory that the entrance to a parallel world is in the park must have been accurate. There was no other way for so many people to disappear without a trace. We even found the doorway, but by the time we prepared a task force to go through it, it had been closed. That was about three months after Thrane and the Celestials went through."

Match sighed. "Unfortunately, our investigation hasn't given us anything fruitful in months. You don't know how they got through the doorway?"

SHELBY ELIZABETH

Emily shook her head. "Not at all."

It obviously wasn't the answer he'd been hoping for, but he nodded. "I suppose that's that, then. Unless you have any other questions, we can leave this for now."

Emily glanced at the kids and didn't think they had any other questions. She returned her gaze to Match and Neer. "I have one request," she said. Match motioned for her to continue. "Don't make Noah, Ash, and Alice go to the trial. I know they're needed to testify, but when they aren't needed, keep them from the courtroom."

She could feel their eyes snap onto her with an energy of indignation.

"Emily—" Noah started.

"I want to—" Alice began.

"Why?" Ash asked.

"I don't want you to experience it," Emily told them. "It could get very ugly."

Noah's face hardened. "Keep Ash and Alice away if you want to. I'm going."

Emily looked to Match and Neer appealingly. "I can set up a nearby room for them to go into when they're not needed," Neer said, "but you should decide for yourselves whether or not to use it."

They were silent, Noah and Alice's eyes still

turned on Emily, and then Emily dipped her head. "We'll discuss it later. Thank you."

Everyone stood, and Match extended a hand to Emily. "Until our next meeting, Mrs. Madison."

Emily felt a slip of paper hit her palm, and tried not to show her surprise. She shook his hand, then moved hers to her purse, using the motion to surreptitiously drop the paper into the bag.

The kids stayed quiet as they walked out of the restaurant, though once they reached the car they told her very plainly that they wanted to be present for the trial. Emily listened to them with 95 percent of her attention, and agreed to leave the decision up to them. The other part of her attention remained on the note in her bag. Mr. Mathers and their hall monitor walked them to their suite, and they separated right away, Emily going to her room. As soon as the door shut she withdrew the small paper from her bag and opened it to read. The message was short:

Meet me at noon tomorrow, by the reflecting pool near the Washington Monument. Come alone.

CHAPTER 9

Kin Woods

A yelp from Tristan jerked Riley fully awake. She shot upright, thinking they'd been found, and saw Wyatt, Demetrius, and Allyssa also jump. Tristan leaned against a tree, his eyes fixed on a chipmunk standing on his thigh.

There were several animals around them. Another chipmunk scampered away from behind Wyatt. The tip of a deer's small tail marked its passage as it fled between the trees. Several birds rested on branches above them.

"Sorry," Tristan said. "Didn't expect to wake up with a chipmunk on my chest."

The chipmunk studied him and turned to look at the others, calm as could be. "I don't think anyone expects that," Wyatt said.

Demetrius yawned. "The Celestials' power

must have drawn the animals to you, since you're their chosen Shifters. That would be my guess, anyway."

Tristan studied the chipmunk. "The others left. Why is this one staying?"

"Maybe it's deranged," Wyatt said.

The chipmunk climbed down from Tristan's leg. "He's so cute!" Allyssa crooned.

The sound of her best friend's voice brought Riley back to her senses, and she turned and tackled Allyssa with a hug. Allyssa seemed surprised for an instant, and then returned the embrace. "I'm so sorry," Riley said. She hadn't recognized Allyssa yesterday. She hadn't recognized any of them yesterday aside from Wyatt, and even then it hadn't really been Wyatt she remembered, but his false identity.

They'd lost so much time. Riley's seventeenth birthday had come and gone in the fall. Allyssa's as well, in early winter.

"Why are you apologizing?" Allyssa demanded.

"I—"

"No one here has any blame," Allyssa said in a firm voice. "Got it?"

Riley was tempted to smile. "Got it." She inspected her friend for subtle differences but didn't really see any. She seemed comparatively normal. Yet she hadn't had the same experience Riley and Wyatt had. "Why did Christopher keep you away from us? I never saw you."

Allyssa's gaze darkened. "He made me a servant and had this old lady keep watch over me. I didn't get out much."

"My father was very careful to keep us contained to the roles he wanted," Demetrius said, his voice rigid. "He'll do anything to keep control of this world. Since he knows that we can stop him, he won't stop searching for us, wherever we are. We're still very close. We should keep moving."

"I get why we aren't just going home, but where exactly are we going?" Allyssa asked.

Everyone stopped and looked at Demetrius. "We need to set things right here. To free the Celestials from my father's control. I wasn't able to find out their locations, so for now, we should focus on putting as much distance between ourselves and my father as possible. We can make a more specific plan then."

They took a few minutes to eat and pack their blankets. Riley approached her horse with small steps. The gray mare was completely familiar to her; she'd been taking care of this horse since she was only a few months old. She'd ridden her countless times—as Jane. She combed her fingers through her mane. "Hi Athena. I'm Riley."

Athena snorted and stepped closer, apparently eager to be pet.

"It's no different now," Wyatt said, suddenly beside Riley. She felt her eyes widen in surprise, and he offered a crooked smile. "I figured you might be stressing about the different identity thing." He swung himself onto his horse Hermes' back. "I know there's more to it, but look at it this way. We're ourselves again, but now we have more skills that can help us."

Riley got onto Athena's back and noticed Tristan awkwardly climb onto his horse. "I guess that's true." She wasn't sure about his claim that things were no different now. She'd spent the last nine months getting to know Wyatt as a friend. Before they'd come through the portal, they had started to move into something beyond friendship. Where did they fall now? It wasn't the time to think about it, but it was one of the first thoughts she had as they started riding, which cemented her belief that things were different for all of them. How could they not be? They'd lived different lives. Even Demetrius, in a way.

Except Tristan. He'd been isolated and imprisoned. Just thinking about it made her stomach twist into knots. He traveled just behind Riley, to the right, and when she glanced back she realized the little chipmunk was on Tristan's shoulder.

Tristan caught her eye and gestured at the chipmunk. "He wanted to come for a ride."

Wyatt narrowed his eyes. "We're sure it's just a chipmunk? Not a Shifter in disguise?"

Demetrius shook his head. "It's not a Shifter."

"Just a chipmunk with a very low IQ," Wyatt muttered.

"Or a very high one!" Allyssa said.

"The important thing is he's not Peter Pettigrew," Tristan said.

"Who?" Demetrius asked.

"Riley, you're the expert here," Allyssa said. "Let's teach the Prince about Harry Potter."

Riley let the others go slightly in front of her so her voice would reach them more clearly, took a deep breath, and began. She hadn't had a proper geek-out session in ages (even discounting the last few months), so it was easy to eat up the time giving them a detailed summary of her favorite book series. It was also a wonderful distraction from her worries, which she realized was probably Allyssa's goal. She didn't know how much Wyatt and Tristan heard, being farther away, but Demetrius and Allyssa seemed to enjoy the conversation.

They weren't pushing the horses, traveling at slightly above a standard walking pace, but they stopped to give the horses a break around midday, and Demetrius told them they might reach the next settlement by nightfall. It was at the natural edge of the forest, by a lake. He said that was part of the reason he wanted to wait to discuss their next step; the locals might have knowledge about the location of the Celestials. Rumors, at least, which would give them a starting point.

They did reach the forest's edge by nightfall, though it was darker than Riley thought it would be by the time they saw the settlement. They moved in a tighter cluster as they left the thick trees behind, quiet. The ease that had settled over them for much of the day faded, wariness taking its place. Riley gripped Athena's reins more securely when they reached the first pool of light from the lanterns lining the smooth dirt road.

"There should be a barn somewhere around here," Demetrius said. "We can drop off the horses, find some warm food, and make a plan."

It actually went smoothly. Since horses and wagons made up the only transportation other than walking, each settlement had at least one place to house horses. They found a spot for their horses, gave them hay and water, and went to one of the largest buildings in sight, which had a sign in front naming it a bed and breakfast. After a whispered urge from Wyatt, Demetrius made the man behind the desk believe they had arrived separately, and had reservations for two rooms. The man went to bed after, and the five gathered around a fire in the empty dining area.

Tristan started cooking immediately, using some of their supplies and some of the leftovers from the dinner the inn had made. He boiled vegetables in a shallow pot held on a spit and heated the fish fillets in a pan he held over the fire.

Demetrius stared at the crackling fire, his face expressionless. "My father has control over the minds of the phoenix and griffin. He can't control the dragon, but since he has the other two Celestials, the dragon isn't a threat to him. Their powers are balanced, meaning any two can overpower the third."

Riley looked at Tristan. "Do you have any idea where the dragon is?"

The chipmunk that had been traveling with them remained close by; Allyssa kept inching closer to the tiny animal.

Tristan stirred the pot. "No. Radio silence since we got here."

"We can't go for the dragon first anyway," Wyatt said. "We need either the phoenix or the griffin, then the dragon. That way we can take the third easily."

"You can free them from Christopher's control?" Allyssa asked Demetrius, momentarily distracted from the chipmunk.

His eyes traveled from the flames to Allyssa, and he nodded. Allyssa's eyes narrowed minutely, studying him, and Riley realized she wasn't the only one to think Demetrius was acting unusually. It was almost like he was in some kind of pain.

"So we just have to figure out where they are," Wyatt said.

Riley moved to help Tristan when he reached for plates, and once everyone had a plate they devoured the meal. After, sitting in front of the warm fire, full and relaxed, Riley found herself blinking much slower, and fighting back yawns. She'd never been a night owl. She saw Allyssa next to the chipmunk, carefully extending a hand toward him. Everyone was watching her, but Riley doubted Allyssa was even aware of them. Her attention was completely on the chipmunk, and she made a soft coaxing noise.

The chipmunk considered her, quivered, and then stepped onto her hand. Allyssa beamed but remained silent, moving the chipmunk to her lap and, with one finger, stroking the creature's head. The chipmunk seemed to sigh and relaxed in her hand, and Allyssa couldn't contain her squeal of joy.

"How'd you do that?" Tristan asked.

"She's great with animals," Riley said.

"We have to figure out a good name for him," Allyssa said, still stroking the chipmunk.

"We have to figure out what to do tomorrow," Wyatt said, "and I think we should split up." He raised his hands before anyone could object. "Just for the morning, and in two groups. If we split up, we can ask more people about the Celestials, and be less conspicuous."

It was Allyssa that responded first, and to Riley's surprise, she agreed with Wyatt. "The people here don't know we're . . . what would we be, here? Criminals? Delinquents?" She shook her head. "Whatever Christopher labels us, the people here shouldn't recognize us. There's no way any guards beat us here."

Riley turned to Tristan and Demetrius. She would rather stay together, but if they agreed about splitting up, she wouldn't be the one to dissent. After all, it was only for a short time.

"I'm fine with it," Tristan said, "as long as we're not gone for long."

Demetrius dipped his head. "Agreed. We'll leave first thing in the morning. It wouldn't be a bad idea to get more supplies while we're here, which will also help us stay inconspicuous. One group can question people doing morning shopping, while the other goes to other public spaces."

Riley tried to stifle a yawn and failed, and her cheeks warmed when she saw the looks the others gave her.

Wyatt had a half-smile, looking at her. "Since we're leaving early again, we should get some sleep. You guys go. I'll do clean up."

"I'll help," Demetrius said.

Riley, Tristan, and Allyssa walked up the stairs, to the two rooms they would be using. Allyssa walked right into one. Riley hesitated. She stopped Tristan with a light touch before he went into the boys' room, and he looked at her questioningly. She hadn't noticed before, but of everyone, he had changed the most visibly. There had been a softness to his face before, a boyish youthfulness which was now mostly gone. His features were more mature now, with a sharper jawline. He'd grown taller, and though he had leaned out slightly, his shoulders seemed broader.

She caught herself and spoke. "I realized I didn't say thank you, earlier. If you hadn't found us . . ." She hugged him. "Thank you."

He tensed, and then his arms wrapped around her with urgency, holding her securely. It took Riley a moment to realize he was fighting back tears, but that had to be why his shoulders seemed to be shaking. She tightened her grip and didn't break away until he started to, about a minute later. He let her go and she saw that his eyelashes were wet; some of his tears had broken through. He didn't meet her eyes, and his voice was low and warm. "Sorry. I just . . . that was the first hug I've had in a long time." He swallowed heavily. "Goodnight."

Riley had her mouth open, caught between overwhelming sympathy and a desire to say something, though she had no idea what. It didn't matter. Tristan ducked into the room he was sharing with the other boys. She knew he'd been imprisoned, and alone, but she realized now she hadn't fully appreciated what that meant. To go so long without any true human contact, other than the fights he'd gotten into in his escape attempts . . . . Riley gripped one arm, shuddering to even think of it. She partially Shifted, and once the red and orange aura rippled around her, she reached out to Tristan as delicately as she could. *I'm sorry you had to go through all that time alone. I won't let it happen again.*

And she dropped her Shift and went into her room with Allyssa.

"You really think the glasses are necessary?" Demetrius asked.

Allyssa smiled, leading him forward by their linked arms. "You may not have spent much time here recently, but if people see your purple eyes, they'll probably recognize you. Now no one can see your eyes. This makes it look like you're blind."

"I feel like that's a pop culture thing."

Her arm tightened over his. "Maybe. But it won't hurt anything, and this way I have an excuse to stay right by your side."

"That does sound nice," he admitted.

After last night, Allyssa had told everyone what their groups would be. Something was bothering Demetrius, and she thought maybe she could convince him to tell her if they had time alone. Boys were oblivious, so sending Demetrius with Wyatt—even though she knew they were close—might not result in the conversation she wanted Demetrius to have.

He looked so different in the dark sunglasses they'd procured from the innkeeper. It had been a whim to ask for the pair when she'd seen them on the man's desk, but now she was glad she'd done it. The shades, paired with the clothing they'd made him change into (less formal than what he'd been wearing before) would make it difficult to tell he was the prince, unless someone was trying to identify him.

"What kind of supplies do you think we should look for? Other than more food."

"A tent would be good," he said. "It's bound to

rain sooner or later, and if we're not in a settlement, we'll want a bit of shelter."

Allyssa scanned the surrounding stalls in the marketplace that was very similar to the one near the castle, though slightly bigger and already more crowded than the other typically became. This settlement, Kin Woods, was actually larger. There were more families here. Christopher had kept mostly single residents in his immediate area. Demetrius had told her it was because when he'd been looking for skilled workers, he'd purposely found individuals with no strong ties to anyone or anything on Earth, to more easily entice them to move to Terraria.

"I'm not seeing any sporting goods shops," Allyssa said.

Demetrius made as if to move his head to look around and sighed, keeping his head still. "We can make the tent ourselves once we have the pieces. Just look for a large piece of material."

"Got it."

She didn't press him while they walked around. They did have something important to do. She struck up conversations with several vendors and others doing their shopping, asking about the Celestials. Most people didn't know anything that could help them, but a few mentioned rumors that the phoenix was near a volcano.

Allyssa gave it about an hour wandering through the main commercial section of Kin Woods, casually grabbing supplies and starting conversations before Demetrius whispered that they should get going. There were definitely more people out, so Allyssa agreed. She hoped the others had more luck in hearing useful information, because she and Demetrius struck out. It wasn't a total bust, though. When they reached the far edge of Kin Woods—the agreed upon rendezvous point—she decided she'd given Demetrius enough time. Plus, she was tired of waiting to really talk to him. It wasn't like the forest on the other side, but there were still plenty of trees as the lake came closer in view. They retrieved Demetrius' horse from the stable and walked a short stretch beyond the settlement, then sat down by a large tree, letting the horse meander nearby.

"You've been acting different," she said without preamble.

He took off the dark sunglasses and blinked at her. "How so?"

"You're not blaming yourself for all of this, are you?" she asked in a quieter voice. "I wouldn't let Riley take the blame yesterday, and I'm not letting you take any either."

Something in his gentle eyes shifted, and she moved to her knees in front of him. "Demetrius, Christopher is the one who brainwashed the phoenix and griffin, locked Tristan in a room, and gave me, Wyatt, and Riley fake memories. He used his powers on you, too. He drugged you! His own son! He's the monster. We all know you acted as soon as you could."

He seemed tempted to smile. "I appreciate that, Allyssa, truly. That's not what's bothering me." He took a deep breath, as if to steady himself. "I learned something about my father, right before I helped Tristan escape. I went into his memories to see what had really happened the day we came to this world, and in the process I saw a memory he'd kept locked inside him. He . . ." Demetrius' jaw clenched. "He killed my mother."

Allyssa rocked backward, moving off of her knees. "He killed your mom?"

"It was an accident," Demetrius said, "but he took her from me." He told her what he'd seen in Christopher's mind, his usually smooth voice roughened in grief, and Allyssa couldn't tear her eyes from him even after he'd gone silent.

"Demetrius," she said in a hushed tone.

He reached for her hand, resting on her lap, and some of the fragility faded from his eyes.

She moved closer to him and leaned her head on his shoulder. That hadn't been what she'd expected, but she was grateful he didn't have to carry it alone anymore.

Riley was really glad Tristan and Wyatt weren't bad conversationalists, because she was about as awkward as could be when it came to starting conversations with people. She could participate well enough, but initiating conversation? She let her nerves get to her too much to do that well most of the time. The boys didn't have that issue. Tristan gravitated more toward the adults; Wyatt was fine talking to anyone. Riley chimed in as necessary.

They steered clear of the market, focusing on other social areas like the well, the sports field, and the schoolhouse. They managed to speak to a good number of people, despite the early hour, yet Riley could tell by the boys' faces that they agreed the information wasn't very promising.

"Thanks," Wyatt said to the last teen they were talking to, right outside the school. A teacher stood in the doorway, calling kids inside, and the boy slumped as he moved in that direction. Wyatt looked around. "Let's go before they charge us with truancy."

They started walking back toward the stable, Wyatt in front.

"Did you guys go to school?" Tristan asked.

"Yep," Riley said. "It was basically independent study, though. There weren't a lot of kids our age in the village. And we had afternoons off to take care of our horses."

Wyatt stopped them by holding one arm out, tense. "Turn around," he said quickly.

Four guards stood in front of them, talking to a woman on horseback, also in the uniform of the guards. The woman had a piece of paper in her hands. Riley reached for Tristan and Wyatt's wrists and made sure they moved with her, spinning around and striding back toward the edge of Kin Woods.

"Not too fast," Tristan murmured. "We don't want to look like we're running. They might not have seen us at all."

"I don't think she's been here long," Wyatt said. "She's probably the first one to get here, which is why she's meeting the local guards to show them our wanted poster."

It made sense, but Riley's stomach still flip-flopped anxiously. "Are they looking?"

Tristan glanced behind them. "No."

"Here." Wyatt walked to the side of the inn, so the building sheltered them from view of the guards even if they did look this way. Wyatt had his hands tightened into fists at his side. "How could I be so stupid? We should have left right away!"

"It was a good idea to ask around," Tristan told him. "I'll look around back and see if we can sneak by."

Tristan ducked behind the inn. Wyatt watched him move, looked up at Riley, and glared through the building, in the direction of the guards. "Stay behind me if it comes to a fight."

"Wyatt—"

Someone walked on the dirt road immediately in front of them. Wyatt looked ready to pounce, the air around him shimmering, but it was just an old woman. She didn't even look at them, her gaze fixed on the quilt she held in a basket. Wyatt was clearly agitated, though. The shimmer around him burst into a partial Shift.

Riley reached to touch his arm. Wyatt stiffened before she could reach him. He turned, and looked at Riley with a blank expression. For a moment, when he met Riley's eyes, she saw that his hazel irises were ringed in glowing gold.

In the next she felt her balance slip.

His eyes began to swirl, black and gold and silver and brown blurring together in a kaleidoscope. The question that had been rising in her mind whirled away in the sea of color, as did every other thought. All that existed was Wyatt, staring at her so intently, and she felt her breath enter and leave her in a rush as his kaleidoscopic eyes drew her in. He held out his hand and she reached for it immediately, feeling their warm palms brush each other as their eyes remained locked. He turned slightly, gripping her hand more securely to pull her after him, and she moved with him, following his lead.

"What are you doing?"

The voice seemed to come from far away. Wyatt's eyes left hers to glance behind them. An afterimage of swirling black and gold and silver and brown muddied Riley's vision, blurring their surroundings, but she felt Wyatt's hand securely linked with hers.

"Drop your Shift," the voice said, a bit closer this time. Riley turned her head to see who the voice belonged to. Wyatt tensed and snapped his attention back to her, and the kaleidoscope spun faster than before. All thoughts of the other voice vanished, and a euphoric feeling made her feel weightless, as if Wyatt's hand were the only thing keeping her standing.

"Drop your Shift!" the voice insisted, and Wyatt's hand ripped from Riley's. The second the direct contact ended Riley became aware of her surroundings again. The blurring whirl of colors vanished from her sight, and her feet were steady on the ground. She stood on the edge of the road, facing the forest, and hastily stepped back so the building blocked her from the guards again. Her heart started beating faster as she realized Tristan and Wyatt were struggling against each other. "Dammit, drop your Shift!" Tristan said, obviously trying to be quiet but louder than before. He shoved Wyatt to the ground.

The impact jarred the boy, and the rippling aura around him flickered and went out. Wyatt looked around with confusion in the set of his brows, first at himself on the ground, then at Tristan, standing near him and breathing heavily, and finally at Riley, standing several feet away.

"What happened?" he asked.

Tristan had been giving him a hard look, but faltered. "You don't remember what you just did?"

Wyatt shook his head and stood.

"You used the griffin's gift," Riley said in a small voice. She glanced up to see his eyes. No ring of gold. No swirling colors. Her heart started to settle.

Wyatt visibly paled. "On you. Again."

Riley dipped her head. Tristan turned to her. "Again?"

"When Wyatt was just starting to practice with Shifting, he tried to do it too fast. He got lost in the flow of his powers, and acted on instinct. That instinct was to gain control of the situation."

"To control *you*," Wyatt said. His voice took on a desperate note. "It's one of the griffin's gifts. I can control people through either fear or attraction if I make direct eye contact. But I learned how to control it! I worked with Demetrius so that wouldn't happen again!"

"This wasn't your fault," Riley said immediately. She strengthened her voice and met his eyes with confidence, willing him to believe her. "There was something different with your eyes this time. And it started right when you Shifted."

Wyatt looked between them for an answer, looking about as vulnerable as Riley had ever seen him.

"Your eyes had a golden ring," Tristan said. "You said you don't remember anything? Maybe it wasn't you that was doing it. Maybe it was the griffin, acting through you."

The weight of this statement momentarily silenced them. "I didn't know that was possible," Wyatt said quietly.

"But it makes sense. You used the griffin's gift on Riley to make her follow you. You were leading her back toward the forest."

"Back to Christopher," Wyatt realized.

Tristan nodded. "Shifting is different here.

Christopher has the phoenix and griffin under his control. They have connections to you. He must be using those connections to try to get you back."

"If they can sense when we Shift, and take control . . ." Wyatt trailed off. "Riley and I can't Shift. It's too dangerous."

Riley bit her lip. Maybe Demetrius would have a solution that would allow them to Shift. She hadn't Shifted in months, aside from that moment last night, but had been comforted since having her identity given back to her, knowing she could call on the phoenix's powers if she needed to. There had to be a way. They *needed* there to be a way.

"We can ask him about it later," Tristan said. "We need to get out of here."

He motioned for them to follow, and Riley made a point to keep a lookout behind them. Wyatt seemed lost in his own mind, his head angled down. They made it to the stable, retrieved their horses, and rode to the opposite end of town at a jog. It wasn't long before they found Allyssa and Demetrius, and they rode in silence for what had to be several miles. They left Kin Woods behind and reached the massive lake, and wordlessly began traveling alongside it.

Allyssa was the one to break the silence, stopping the horse she and Demetrius rode. She got off and turned to them. "Okay, what happened?"

Riley almost smiled at the brusque question. The impulse faded when she saw Wyatt slide off his horse, still staring at the ground so his hair covered his eyes. "The griffin took over."

They listened with rapt attention as Tristan explained. The horses drank from the lake as they spoke, and Athena and Hermes started playing together. Demetrius looked graver than Riley had ever seen, squashing her hope that he would have a solution to allow them to Shift.

"I didn't imagine the Celestials could control you," he murmured. "They must feel when you Shift, in this world. My father has probably ordered them to take control whenever they feel you Shift."

"So he's desperate," Allyssa said.

"He finally has everything he's dreamed of for decades," Demetrius said. "He won't let that go without a fight."

They didn't have a clue which direction to travel, so they continued their path along the wide lake. Allyssa couldn't help but marvel at the landscape. The water was clear and inviting. There were animals everywhere, though their chipmunk remained her favorite. He'd been missing when they woke that morning, but he'd found them in the woods. Apparently Riley, Tristan, and Wyatt were like magnets, and the chipmunk was especially sensitive to them. He rode on Tristan's shoulder like a parrot.

The air fascinated her. She knew the feel of it from training since she was a little girl. It was different here. Stronger. Wilder. She looked forward to stopping for the night and being able to properly train, to test it out. Especially knowing that Riley and Wyatt couldn't Shift. She would have to be at the top of her game, to defend them if they got into a fight.

A light rain seemed to ruin that plan. The sun was noticeably low in the horizon when they stopped, but it had been gray for at least an hour. Raindrops started falling, prompting them to call it a day. Allyssa helped Demetrius put up the thick sheet they'd found, making a canopy above them. The plinking sound of the rain on the sheet was muted, but welcome, background noise. Riley brought fire to her hand, and Tristan and Wyatt found some sticks to keep it going on the ground, under their canopy. It was actually kind of cozy, resting near the fire, eating more leftovers they'd packed from the inn. Cozy, but as the sun truly dipped below the skyline, the damp and dark made it chilly.

Allyssa reached into one of the bags, intent to find the sweater she'd gotten earlier, and paused when she felt something solid in the bottom. Her hand closed around it and she pulled out a surprisingly heavy object. She turned it over in her hand and saw a glassy surface reflecting her face back to her. "Hey guys?" she asked.

They turned to look at her, and she held up the mirror.

"Is that . . .?" Wyatt asked.

"My father's mirror," Demetrius said. Allyssa handed it to him and delighted to see him smile in open-mouthed amazement. "I must have grabbed it the night we escaped, without realizing it."

"How do you not realize that?" Wyatt asked.

"I went on autopilot for several minutes after confronting my father. I didn't process much of what I was doing until I reached Tristan's door," Demetrius said, and though his smile faltered, it didn't fade. "Do you know what this means? We might be able to see where the Celestials are."

Riley stared at the mirror. "How does it work?"

Demetrius set the mirror down in front of him. "It was a gift from the Celestials to the first Shifters. When the phoenix, dragon, and griffin closed the portal between our worlds, they wanted to create a way for people to learn about them. Shavings from the griffin's claw, a tear drop from the phoenix, and a ground-up scale from the dragon were added to the reflective surface, imbibing it with a trace of their combined power. Their act made it so the mirror can show people information about the Celestials, and by extension, their chosen Shifters. Whenever a Shifter or Elementalist touches it they're able to will the mirror to show them something."

"So why did it show us things unprompted?" Riley asked.

"You're Celestials," Demetrius said simply. "The samples the dragon, phoenix, and griffin had built into the mirror are naturally connected to you, so when you touch the mirror, it recognizes their signature."

Tristan leaned forward. "So if any of us pick up the mirror and think about finding them, it might show us where they are?"

Demetrius nodded.

"Let's see!" Wyatt said, darting forward to snatch the mirror before Tristan could.

Allyssa chuckled when she saw Tristan's light scowl, but they all grew serious as they watched Wyatt. Allyssa could feel the static tension in the air. Wyatt stared at the glassy surface for what felt like an eternity but was probably half a minute, and when he looked back up at the group, the tension dissipated in an instant as they took in his victorious smile.

"Ladies and gentlemen, we have a location."

CHAPTER 10

Peace In Our Time

Madame Neer arranged for Emily and the kids to see the park the next day. Apparently the grassy sections they'd seen the day before, between some of the monuments and buildings, were actually part of a park called National Mall. Mr. Mathers dropped them off there that morning (basically afternoon, once Noah finally got up).

Ash was surprised the Official left them unsupervised, until he realized there was a woman watching them from a distance. She had a book in hand, and seemed to blend in very well, but Alice helped Ash spot her, about half an hour into their park day.

"They must be really worried someone will try to hurt us, to have us monitored so closely," Alice said.

"It might not be all because of the trial," Emily

said. "The Guild and Temple here are pretty large, and a number of fights have broken out."

"That's reassuring," Alice muttered.

"So what should we do?" Ash asked.

Emily looked around. "Want to go for a walk?"

No one had any objections, so they meandered. It was a nice park, but Ash still felt homesick for Congress Park. This one was too crowded, and just wasn't familiar. When they circled back to where they'd started, Noah slid his backpack to the ground. "Who's up for a game of catch?"

"You brought your disc?" Emily asked with a slight chuckle.

"Noah always brings his disc," Alice said, very matter-of-fact.

"Do you want to play?" Ash asked Emily.

"No thanks, sweetie. I'm just gonna walk around a bit more."

Ash, Alice, and Noah spread out and started throwing Noah's disc. Noah took the first swing, and when he let it go Ash heard him say, "whoa." Whoa was right; the disc went flying with force. It was going to go over Ash's head. Ash started to run back, arm stretched up to catch it, and when he realized it was too high he jumped, touching it with his fingertips and snatching it before it could fall. He landed, grinning at the successful catch, but the grin faded when he saw the looks on the others' faces.

"What?" he asked. "I caught it!"

"And you Shifted!" Alice said with a laugh.

Ash looked down at himself, but there wasn't an outline around him. "I did?"

"Yeah. Unless you normally jump that high, in which case you need to start basketball right now."

Ash hadn't meant to Shift at all. He hadn't even realized it when it happened.

"It's okay," Alice said, taking a step closer. "You just got excited to be here. We've been pretty low recently." She looked at him reassuringly. "There's nothing wrong with it."

He nodded and tossed her the disc. He wasn't scared, but he was definitely more alert now. He thought the others were too. The next time the disc came his way, again too high, he let it fall behind him and went to retrieve it. The following throw was perfect, and he clapped his hands on it gratefully. Ash let himself relax more and actually have fun, mixing it up and throwing the disc back to Noah. He forgot to worry about unintentionally Shifting and let himself be happy, laughing when Alice fell over backwards reaching up for a catch, and when he wasn't paying enough attention and the disc hit his shoulder. He almost forgot everything that was bothering him, just for a few moments.

Noah reminded him, catching a disc that coasted about an inch of the ground and saying, "Tristan would try to catch this one with his foot."

Alice's easy smile faltered. Ash hurried to give her a reason to keep it, wanting to keep the fun going. He had a feeling things would be serious for a lot of this trip. "Remember when he tried to do that last year, and sent the disc flying up at his face?" Ash asked.

"It hit him in the chin," Alice said with a hint of a chuckle.

"Jordan thought I'd punched him when we got back," Noah said. "It took half an hour to convince her he was really just that clumsy." He had a bittersweet expression on his face, no doubt remembering that day. Ash understood completely. He'd gotten to the point where thinking of Jordan wasn't absolutely devastating every time, and he could smile or even laugh about many memories, but it was still sad. He had a feeling it always would be.

Alice looked around. "Hey, have you seen Emily?"

Ash scanned their surroundings and realized he hadn't seen Emily in several minutes. It wasn't like her to disappear without warning.

Noah frowned. "I guess she just wanted to walk the loop again."

Ash caught the disc when Noah sent it to him, but he didn't want to get lost in fun anymore. He made sure to look around as they continued tossing the disc, and kept a count in his head. It had taken them several minutes to walk the route they'd taken before. If Emily wasn't back in that time, Ash was going to look for her.

Emily hated to just leave the kids, but they were so absorbed in their fun that she decided to jog to her meeting with Match. She wouldn't be gone long. She preferred not telling them about the meeting anyway. They had enough to worry about. They were very close to the reflecting pool near the Washington Monument, so she reached it in no time.

She'd seriously debated coming, but it wasn't clear if the note was a plea for a casual meeting, or a secret summons. She also really wanted to know why Match was being so secretive. Did he have more information about the entrance to the parallel world, or the Celestials, that he didn't want to share with the kids? There was only one way to find out.

Match stood near the pool, peering into the water. A blonde woman stood close to him, and as Emily approached, she saw that the two were having a hushed conversation. They stopped talking when Emily came within earshot, and Match smiled. "Mrs. Madison. So glad you came."

Emily inclined her head. Did he need her to leave so he could finish speaking with the woman? He seemed to notice her indecision, because he gestured at the woman.

"This is Katya. My protector. She has the same abilities that Christopher Thrane and his son possess. She's an Elementalist of Shadows, as she describes."

Emily automatically took a step backward, then recovered herself. She'd assumed there were more with Christopher's abilities. She hadn't expected to meet another today. "Christopher called himself a Dark Elementalist," she said, more in an attempt to hide her wariness than to contest the term.

"My abilities are neither light nor dark," Katya said. "They may be used for either purpose, depending on the Elementalist, as can any power with any individual. But my abilities are often used in the background, in subtle ways, which prompts me to refer to myself as a Shadow Elementalist."

"Katya has worked with me for many years," Match said firmly. "She has my complete trust."

"I thought you were surprised when you

found out Christopher was an Elementalist?"

Match smiled. "I didn't know about Thrane, but did you really believe the president of the Nation wouldn't know about Shadow Elementalists? How do you think we kept our world secret for so long? Elementalists like Katya alter the memories of any humans involved in or witness to Shifter/Elemental actions. They did until recently, at any rate. Now there's too much to hide."

Derek would be fascinated to learn about this apparent cooperation of Shifters and Elementalists, but Emily didn't dwell on it. She had to get back to the kids. "Why did you want to meet with me privately?"

"I told you she's very practical," Match said to Katya. "She handles each piece of information she's presented, in exactly the manner needed. She's the voice we need."

Emily strove to hide her agitation. "You need my voice?"

Match regarded her with solemn eyes. "This is the other reason I had you and the children come so long before the trial. I'm meeting with the president of the Elementalists, Elaine Summers. We're each bringing three people. I need you to be one of mine."

Emily hadn't known what to expect, but that certainly wasn't something she'd considered. "Is this a meeting to discuss ending the war?"

Match nodded. "A very important meeting. Summers and I haven't met in-person in over a year. We're both tired of the fighting, and all of the innocent lives it's cost. We want to discuss changes to be made, to satisfy both sides enough for the fighting to stop."

"Then why choose me? If you can only choose three people, there are so many others who are more qualified, and more experienced in meetings like this."

She thought she knew the answer, and Match confirmed her suspicions. "You will represent the Celestials. In their absence, who better to speak for them than you, who know them so well?"

"I'd rather let them speak for themselves, when we figure out to how bring them home."

Match's jaw tensed, though he smoothed over his features in the next heartbeat. "Of course it would be best if the Celestials could be here, but we have to do what we can without them. You do want to stop the fighting, don't you?"

Emily didn't hesitate. "Of course I do." She'd seen too many news reports in recent months detailing casualties and fatalities caused by feuding Shifters and Elementalists. They were lucky to live in an area where the nearby Shifters and Elementalists got along fine. It let her worry only minimally about the kids' safety at home. If she could do something to enable other people to feel the same way, to only worry in the way a parent always worries about their child, and nothing more, she absolutely wanted to help. Still, something felt off. "But what do you expect me to say that you can't?"

Match's eyebrows raised in mild surprise. "Why, the reason the Celestials went to the parallel world in the first place. To find the phoenix, griffin, and dragon, and bring them back here. To force the Elementalists to admit that the majority of the blame for our decades of animosity, for this war, lies with them. Once the assembly hears of the Celestials' intentions, they'll accept responsibility and concede, ending the war."

Emily was shaking her head. "Riley didn't tell me why they went to that world, President Match. If she went willingly, it was for a good reason. She would never find the Celestials and use them to threaten Elementalists. Neither would Tristan."

Match was looking at her like she was a misguided child. "Oh, but Mrs. Madison, that's exactly what they went to do. Don't you remember?"

Emily realized what he wanted to do too late. She tensed to run, willing the outline of the snow leopard to surround her to aid her sprint. Katya was faster. *Calm*, the woman said, in a surprisingly soft voice Emily found impossible to ignore. *Please don't be afraid.*

"Don't worry, Mrs. Madison," Match said, as Emily stared at him, wanting to run but unable to muster the adrenaline, or even really feel the fear she knew she'd felt seconds before. "Katya will only change the memory associated with the day the Celestials disappeared. And this one, of course. I know you might judge me, but it's the only way we can do what needs to be done to restore peace."

And to let you get revenge, Emily thought. His goal may have been purely peace at one point, but the murder of his wife had clearly changed that. He wanted Elementalists to pay.

His rage is understandable, Katya said. *I know you can see that. This course of action will save lives. Still, I'm sorry to have to do this.*

"I have to step out for a few hours," Emily said. "Throw on a movie, go for a swim, play a game—just don't leave the hotel, okay?"

Ash paused his Gameboy and looked up. Emily was dressed up like she'd been when they went to the dinner their second night, in a skirt and blouse. She'd been wearing jeans in the few days they'd had without any scheduled meetings. Ash had looked at the schedule and knew there was nothing on it today.

"Are you meeting with President Match again?" he asked.

Emily stopped with her hand on the door handle. "I am meeting with him, yes."

"Don't go alone."

The words rushed out. Emily turned to look at him with an amused smile. "I'm not meeting him alone, sweetie. There will be a group of people there."

Ash held her gaze. "When you met with him by the pool, did you think it would just be you and him?"

"How did you know—?"

"I went looking for you," he confessed. He'd convinced Alice and Noah to walk around a few minutes after they'd noticed Emily was gone, and he'd seen Emily by the reflecting pool, talking to Match and another woman. Right when they'd seen Emily they'd gone back to the section where they'd been playing catch, but the secret meeting had stuck in Ash's thoughts since. "But did you know he'd have that woman with him?"

She took a step closer. "What woman? I met with him for a few minutes, privately. I knew going into it that it would just be the two of us, because he gave me a note. That was when he asked me to come to this larger meeting, today. There should only be eight people at the one today. He's been honest, Ash. I'm sorry I didn't tell you, but I didn't want you to worry."

"How do you know you'll be safe?"

She walked over and wrapped her arms around him. "It's a diplomatic meeting about ending the war," she told him. She flattened the back of his hair. "I was surprised when he said he wanted me to come, but his reasoning makes sense. I think I can help." She walked back to the door. "I'll be back in a few hours."

Ash nodded and watched her walk out, and looked at the game he'd paused. He didn't really feel like playing anymore, and was still staring at the screen when Alice came out from the shower a minute later. Noah continued his nap in the other room, but Ash told his twin what Emily had said.

"Isn't it weird?" he asked when he finished relaying the conversation.

Alice continued toweling her hair dry. "Why are you so worried about it?"

"Because last time someone we care about did something Match asked, Match abused their trust. If he hadn't edited that video and sent it to all the Guilds, Riley and Tristan wouldn't have been kidnapped. What if he's asking Emily to be part of something that will get her in trouble?"

Alice sat down next to him, scrunching up

the towel in her lap. "Emily was the one who warned us to be wary, the first time we met Match. If she's helping him right now, she must trust that what he's doing is right."

Ash picked up the Gameboy. "Okay."

Alice went to raid the fridge. Mr. Mathers had taken them to a grocery store and let them pick out whatever they wanted, to keep in the suite. Ash turned off the Gameboy, watching the screen go dark. One thing was still bothering him.

He didn't know how good Emily was at lying. He didn't think she'd really lied to him before, so he didn't know her tells. She could have been lying about knowing who would be at the meetings with Match. Or, the more concerning possibility: that she didn't remember meeting with the woman back at the reflecting pool.

Even in the less-than-minute Ash had seen the three meeting a few days before, it had been clear the blonde woman was involved in the conversation with Emily and Match. Emily had been looking right at her. Emily had seemed genuinely confused when Ash mentioned the woman. His gut instinct said Emily hadn't lied. But why wouldn't she remember? Something was definitely off.

Ash couldn't shake the unease that had settled in his stomach when he'd seen them, and knew it would only get worse waiting here, doing nothing. He couldn't do anything, but someone else could.

"Alice, I need you to do something for me. Right now."

CHAPTER 11

A Brusque Meeting

President Match had told Emily he would have a car pick her up immediately outside the hotel. She waited there somewhat anxiously, and then rode in the taxi to a nondescript building. She was searched when she arrived, and then led to a room with a long rectangular table in the middle, with eight chairs arranged around the edges. Two people were already seated. Emily found the card with her name on it and sat down in the corresponding seat.

She fiddled with her hands under the table as the rest of the participants gradually entered and found their seats. Match walked in second-to-last. His eyes scanned the table, and his lips quirked when he saw Emily. He walked to one of the ends of the table. The last person to enter, a woman, walked to the other end: Elaine Summers, president of the Elemental government. Emily had never seen her before, and her first impression was that the woman seemed so young. She had to be around Emily's age, but there was something more youthful about her dark features.

"Thank you all for coming here today," Summers said. "I won't waste any of your time. I want to have an open, honest discussion, so we can figure out the best way to resolve our differences."

"We should start by going over the most recent news from our respective populations," Match said.

So began a summary from both presidents of recent attacks, propaganda, and the results of surveys sent to the general public that allowed citizens to record their opinions on the war. It seemed to be a little less than half of each side that wanted to continue fighting, while the other, larger halves were either indifferent to Shifter/Elemental tensions or actively wanted peace. One of the guests each president had brought was an analyst, and both explained the statistics when Match or Summers asked.

"I think it's fair to say that the majority want us to push for a peaceful resolution," Summers said. "Even those who don't care either way about the other group. Peace suits them more than war. The real issue, and the primary reason for calling this meeting, is to determine how to best approach calling for that peace."

"We have important information you should be aware of, relating to that. This is Emily Madison," Match said, gesturing to her. "She'll speak on behalf of the Celestials."

Summers looked at her appraisingly. "You know the Celestials well?"

"My daughter is the phoenix," Emily said. "And I'm now the legal guardian of the dragon and his siblings."

"Now?" one of the Elementalist representatives, Ying, asked.

Emily looked down at the table for a second. "My sister was their legal guardian, but she was killed last year."

"My apologies," Ying said.

Emily returned her gaze to Summers. "I'm sure everyone here is aware of the entrance to the parallel world in which the phoenix, dragon, and griffin are said to reside. My daughter opened the doorway between the worlds. I haven't seen her in the better part of a year, because she went to the parallel world with the dragon and griffin, with a very important goal. They were devastated when war was declared. They went to find the true Celestials, to convince them to return. And they went to convince the Celestials to fight, if necessary."

The Elementalists stiffened. Summers narrowed her eyes. "What do you mean, if necessary?"

"If you don't accept most of the responsibility for everything."

Multiple people started to speak, but Summers raised a hand and they silenced immediately. She still seemed perfectly calm. "Your daughter told you she, and the other Celestials, blame Elementalists for everything?"

"Yes."

The woman kept her gaze trained on Emily, and it was so scrutinous that Emily had to look down at the table. Why did she feel so wrong, saying that?

"She's biased!" one of the Elementalist representatives said.

"Riley's best friend is a wind user!" Emily retorted. "Allyssa went with them to the parallel world."

"Your daughter probably forced the wind user to go with her."

"Riley doesn't force Allyssa to do anything. She hates confrontations, and settles things as equitably and peacefully as she can."

Summers' calm voice rose over the others.

"Yet in this case, she's using the threat of an attack by the Celestials to force us to surrender?"

The woman still had her eyes set on Emily, and Emily faltered in the process of saying yes. Defending Riley had helped her push the unease she felt back, but it surfaced again now. Hearing it out loud, it didn't seem like something Riley would do. But Emily remembered the conversation they'd had over the phone. Didn't she?

"If you'll remember, a group of Elementalists kidnapped the phoenix and the dragon and tortured them for sport," Match said. Emily looked away from Summers to find Match leaning forward in his seat.

Ying looked at Match. "And two months later a group of Shifters set fire to a Guild in California, after blocking the exits. There have been unforgivable acts of violence on both sides."

"Exactly why we need to do something to stop it, now."

"Ending the war isn't as simple as making statements to the people to cease fighting," Summers said. "Something has to change if Shifters and Elementalists are to stop seeing each other as enemies. If I thought taking responsibility would be a solution, I might humor you."

A shimmer formed in the air around Match. He took a slow breath, and the shimmer disappeared. "I can see you need more time to consider. Let's pause here for now, and reconvene at a later date."

Summers studied him for a long moment before nodding. She seemed disappointed. "Very well. Forty-eight hours should be sufficient time."

She and Match stood, and Summers was the first to leave. The Elementalist representatives went next, and the other two Shifter representatives. Emily started to walk to the door but paused when Match said her name, and turned to face him.

He had a tight grip on the back of his chair, and there was a shimmer around him again. "What was that?" he asked.

"What do you mean?"

"I needed you to be a strong voice. You sounded hesitant, which undermines everything. You know the Celestials went to find the phoenix, dragon, and griffin. You know they're going to make them act as our allies in this war. So why did you let her confuse you?"

Emily's heart started racing. Had she let Summers confuse her, or had she been confused all along? It didn't feel right to say that Riley was trying to get revenge for being kidnapped. It also didn't make sense that Tristan would go on a mission like this without at least talking to his siblings, and Emily didn't remember him saying a word. What was going on?

Something flashed in Match's eyes, and he strode across the room and gripped her arms. "Elaine Summers is a strategist, Mrs. Madison. A master chess player. She uses anything she can to her advantage, and right now, she's using your motherly instinct to wiggle out of accepting responsibility. You know people can change. Maybe your daughter wouldn't have made this plan a year ago, but after everything she and the dragon went through at the hands of Elementalists? Including the loss of your sister? She changed, Mrs. Madison. Realize it, and stay firm. You know she's doing the right thing. It's our job to convince Summers."

Emily stared into the wide face and reluctantly nodded, once. Match dropped his hands. "I'll have a car collect you for the next meeting, in two days."

Alice had never stayed Shifted for so long, but she didn't dare Shift back in her current position. She knew there were lookouts around the building she was watching, and she really didn't want to be seen as a potential threat. She was well-hidden like this, perched behind a flowerpot on the window-ledge of the building across the street. It was a large flowerpot, filled with sunflowers. She could give a little hop straight up and still feel completely hidden.

It was an effective spot, but not very comfortable. She kept her eyes trained on the door of the building she'd seen Emily walk into, an hour earlier. It had surprised her when Ash asked her to Shift and fly out from the balcony, but he'd been so worried it was impossible to tell him no. She hadn't expected to see Emily, having left a few minutes after the woman, but Emily had still been standing just outside the hotel when Alice flew by. The taxi took a minute or two to arrive after Alice spotted Emily.

Alice did understand Ash's worry. If she was honest with herself, she felt it too. She felt like stationing herself outside the building was something of a useless gesture, though. She couldn't hear or see anything inside.

She perked up when she saw someone leave the building. She watched several people walk out, and stepped out from behind the flowerpot a bit more when they'd all gone. No more movement. No sign of Emily either. She kept her eyes on the door, not blinking, and felt her feathers start to ruffle as her nerves climbed. After about two minutes the door of the building opened, and Match walked out and got into a waiting black car. Roughly thirty seconds after that, Emily emerged.

Alice thought she would wait for a taxi. Instead, Emily paused by the door and then got into the same car Match had.

Alice swooped down, not caring if she was spotted, and flew to Match's vehicle, trying to see into the car windows. She fluttered her wings to stay aloft, leaning close. The windows were tinted, but she could hear, and she was sure she heard Emily say her name, sounding surprised and concerned.

The door whipped open. The window slammed into her and she was thrown back with a burst of pain. She landed on the ground in a heap, stars popping before her eyes. Distantly, she heard a sound like a car pulling away. She couldn't seem to move yet. Those stars wouldn't go away.

"Whoa, you really took a hit," a masculine voice said. Alice strained her eyes, trying to see who it was. What had she been doing? "We need to get you checked out, birdie."

She saw a face, peering down at her. "Don't try to Shift back yet," the boy said. "It's not safe here. We'll move faster if you let me carry you like this."

Hands tenderly reached beneath her and lifted her, and the boy cradled her against his chest. She could feel him walking, but she couldn't look around. She was too dizzy. The stars finally started to fade, which made her feel a little better, but she couldn't figure out what had happened.

"Stay awake," the boy said.

She turned her head to look at him. He was definitely a teen, probably a little older than her. Latino. His cheeks were really round. She noticed because he smiled when he saw her move.

"Maybe you aren't hurt too bad, birdie. I'm still bringing you to get checked out." He studied her. "Can you communicate?"

She made a low hoot, and he nodded.

"All right. Are you a girl or a boy?" He chuckled, and his curly black hair bobbled when he dipped his head. "One hoot for girl, two for boy."

One hoot. Alice tried looking around again. Still dizzy, but not as bad.

The boy didn't ask any more questions. Several minutes later she felt him stop. He reached out and opened a door, walked again for about a minute, and stopped again. Alice moved to see where he was looking, and saw a man walking closer. "What do we have here?" the man asked.

"She's a Shifter, Pat. Took a really hard hit from a car door and was stunned. I thought you should check for a concussion."

The boy set her down on a medical bed in what looked like a hospital room, though it was long and had multiple beds. Alice got to her feet, spread her wings to steady herself, and looked between the boy and Pat. They studied her in silence for a minute, and she made a noise to ask what they were doing. They seemed to understand. Pat seemed encouraged by it.

"You can Shift back now," Pat said. "I need you to be able to answer questions."

Alice closed her eyes and breathed out to focus herself, and opened her eyes seconds later as a human.

"I guess you could have Shifted back on the street, chica," the boy said. "You're tiny enough to carry either way."

Alice narrowed her eyes.

"It's better that you waited. What's your name?" Pat asked.

"Alice Dawes."

"Do you remember what happened?"

The boy had said she'd been hit by a car door, but she didn't remember it happening, so she shook her head.

"Do you remember what you were doing before Havier found you?"

Alice looked down at her lap. "No."

Pat moved right in front of her and put his hand on her chin. Alice stiffened and tried to back up, and Pat held up his hands. "I just need to check for signs of a concussion. I'm the doctor for this Temple."

"You have your own doctor?"

Pat went to tilt her chin up again. "It's quite the sizable Temple. Many Shifters visit us. Before the general public knew about Shifters and Elementalists, having doctors staffed at large Temples and Guilds made sense, for secrecy. How's your vision?"

"Fine now."

He inspected her eyes and asked her to walk around, and once she was seated on the bed again, he sat himself down as well, on the bed next to hers. "Tell me exactly what you felt when Havier found you." She did. "And what's the last thing you remember?"

Alice brought her gaze down again, and felt her eyebrows press closer together. She knew they were in Washington, D.C., for the trial, and that it wasn't their first day there, but the specifics . . . she couldn't recall. They had a hotel room . . . . She didn't even know where they were staying. What had she been doing, Shifted? Why had she been alone? "We're visiting," she told Pat and Havier. "We have a trial to go to, but we got here early. I can't remember how long we've been here, or what we've done."

"Who's *we*?" Havier asked.

"My family. Emily. Ash. Noah."

"Did you see anyone else around?" Pat asked Havier.

The boy shrugged. "There are always people around, but birdie here is the only one that caught my attention. And no one went to help her." He looked at her. "You really went for that car, like you wanted something."

Pat drew her attention by sighing. "You don't have any of the lasting physical signs of a concussion beyond the bruise forming on your forehead, but based on your memory issues and the initial physical symptoms you described, I do think you have one. You need to stay here for a while."

"I need to find—"

"Not really a suggestion, chica," Havier said.

"What do you expect me to do here?" Alice asked Pat.

"Rest," he said simply. "Give your brain time to heal. Even if you did remember where you were staying, I would insist you stay here for a little while."

Havier sat down on the bed on her other side. "I'll keep you company so you don't get bored. And to make sure you don't die, but mostly the bored part."

"You're not going to die," Pat said, giving Havier a look. Havier flashed him a grin. "It's only a mild concussion. Try not to worry," Pat continued, looking back at Alice. "You should be just fine within a day or so."

Alice nodded. Pat left, saying he would return soon. Alice sighed, willing her brain to give her back the information she needed. It didn't.

"You know a lot of people don't look like their spirit animals, but you look like yours."

Alice turned to glance at Havier. "Meaning?"

"Just an observation. It's not just your size, either. Do I look like mine?"

He was waiting for her to look at him, a hint of a challenge in his eyes. Alice honestly had no idea what his spirit animal was. "Are you a stallion or something?"

She regretted the guess immediately, because she could see his cockiness increase when he sat a little straighter. A coppery outline appeared around him, and then he fully Shifted. A fox regarded her from where he'd just been sitting as a human. He stayed Shifted for several seconds, apparently waiting for her to react, and then Shifted back. "You're hard to read. It's annoying."

"You would know what's annoying."

One corner of his mouth tugged up. "Whatever you say, chica."

"Stop calling me that."

He chuckled and reclined on his bed. Alice swore in her head. She'd let him know his nickname bothered her. She fought back a wave of frustration. She couldn't remember what she'd been doing, or where her family was, and she was stuck with Havier for company.

Fan-freaking-tastic.

CHAPTER 12

Around the Lake

"The griffin's den is at the top of a waterfall?"

Wyatt raised an eyebrow at Tristan's tone. "Something wrong with that?"

Tristan shook his head, staying silent, but Wyatt was pretty sure he was judging. It could be seen as a bit ostentatious, but Wyatt thought it sounded awesome. It was a strategic location, offering vantage and protection, and it was beautiful. The spray of the water against the rocks could make rainbows in the right light. It might be just as attractive in moonlight, though he'd seen it in daylight in the mirror.

He could have looked for any of the Celestials' locations, but he'd had a reason for searching for the griffin. The incident that morning had reminded him how dangerous the griffin could be. If they found the phoenix first, but encountered the griffin before the dragon, the griffin could use its gift to hypnotize the phoenix. Then everything would have been a waste. If they restored the griffin first, they could use that power to help themselves.

"Any idea where the waterfall is?" Allyssa asked.

She took her answer from their expressions. Wyatt tried to remember more of what he'd seen in the mirror, but he hadn't seen anything beyond the waterfall itself, with the cave near the top where the griffin kept its nest. He had no idea what the surrounding area was like. Except that it had flowing water.

"Flowing water," he said aloud. "If we find a river, we might be able to follow it to the waterfall, walking opposite the current."

"There should be another settlement nearby," Demetrius said. "There are several around this lake. We can find one and orient ourselves from there."

"There's no way for Christopher to let anyone ahead of us know he's looking for us, right?" Riley asked.

"We saw the guards right behind us," Wyatt reassured her. "As long as we stay ahead of them, we'll be fine."

He caught Demetrius' eye and subtly shook

his head. He knew there was a way they could be walking toward a trap, but if the others hadn't thought of it, he didn't want to add to their worries. Christopher could have made the phoenix or griffin spread word, but it was only a possibility. It was equally plausible that Christopher had told them to stay in their dens, in an attempt to hide them while he let his human guards try to capture the group. Demetrius seemed to understand. He was good like that.

"We have another big decision to make," Allyssa said. "We need to name our chipmunk!"

Wyatt glanced at the creature, which was curled up near Tristan. It still seemed weird that it was near them. What kind of chipmunk rode on someone's shoulder? The others all thought he was cute. Wyatt supposed he was, but was it right to get attached to him?

"I've been thinking about that," Tristan said. He touched the chipmunk, prompting him to startle awake and make a noise. "We should call him Chitter."

That was the noise. Wyatt had heard the chipmunk do it a few times . . . he could see the others considering the name, and Riley and Allyssa smiled. "I like it," Riley said.

And they officially adopted a chipmunk named Chitter.

Allyssa decided not to let the rain keep her from training. It wasn't very heavy. Besides, she would only feel it if her plan didn't work. Before rising from their canopied shelter, she closed her eyes and felt the air around them. She pushed the air nearest to the ground up, condensing it into a sheet about as high as the middle of the nearest trees. She stepped outside, waited several seconds, and smiled. Not a drop of rain got through.

She reached out her senses, feeling the natural wind before trying to manipulate it more finely. The protective sheet had been one of the first things she learned to do, and required very little actual shaping of the air. The next thing she wanted to do required a lot. Once she had a sense of how strong the air was she started gathering it closer to her, intensifying it by trying to contain it in a smaller space.

The wind always had a certain feel to it. She was familiar with the pull of it as it strove to go back to its natural state, its push as it obeyed her will. She was accustomed to the tug in her chest that accompanied the wind strengthening in her realm, building in amount and power. It was always tricky to handle.

This wind had a different feel. Its pull was greater than the wind back home, and when she felt that tug in her chest after accumulating some, it was more like a jerk. She dropped the accumulation and started again, this time with more precision and focus. The feeling was still different, but she could handle it much better this time. She molded the wind into a sphere, making it keep its shape as it grew, extending her hands out. They shook slightly, but she tried to ignore it. A few days of training should make it stop. She was just extremely out of practice.

She had to know how far she could go. She built it up, up to a height far greater than her, and felt the jerk in her chest turn into a punch. She breathed through her nose, ignoring the pressure inside and focusing on the sphere of air. She had to let it go, without losing it. She could let it escape slowly. Or she could try something a little more fun.

She decided to go for the more fun option, and focused completely on the sphere. She exhaled, then moved her hands in a slicing motion, imagining the sphere cutting into three sections. She felt the connection cut, the freed sections rushing back to their natural place via the currents she directed them toward.

"What are you doing?"

Allyssa turned at Tristan's question. The fire still crackled reliably under the canopy, illuminating the others inside. Allyssa wondered how clearly they could see her. "Training."

Riley stood, brought a new flame to her hand, and walked out. "You shouldn't train in the dark."

Allyssa moved her hand in a whooshing motion, using the air around the fire to pluck it from Riley's hand. She kept it buoyed in the air between them, and saw Riley's eyes narrow. The fire started pulling back toward Riley, and Allyssa smiled. Game on.

She'd been planning to train with Riley the next day, when they stopped midday to let the horses rest, but she'd do it now, too. They kept pulling the fireball between them, warring air and fire in a test of strength. Things got more interesting when the fireball grew. It had been about the size of an apple. It expanded to volleyball dimensions.

"The size doesn't matter," Allyssa said. "I can still control it."

"What about the heat?" Riley countered. She lifted both hands in front of her and locked her eyes on the fireball. It had been burning a steady orange, with red at the tips of the crackling flames. When Riley moved her hands, the fire transitioned to a bright yellow, bordering on green, and progressed to blue. The center of the flame burned blue, spreading to the edge, and then the center changed once more, fading to palest blue before becoming white.

Allyssa recoiled from the wave of heat, dropping her hands and surrendering control of the fireball. Riley grinned, called the fireball back to her hand, and extinguished it by making a fist. She took in a staggered breath, obviously winded but pleased. "It's been a while."

"Felt good, right?"

Riley nodded.

"More tomorrow, in daylight," Allyssa promised.

Allyssa thought Riley might voice a desire to do more tonight, from the excitement in her eyes, but her friend merely nodded again and turned back to the canopy. Allyssa didn't want her to try to do too much too fast. That was usually Allyssa's job.

"You done for the night?" Tristan asked Allyssa.

"Nope."

Tristan held up a hand, looking at Riley. "Tag me in."

Riley slapped his hand on her way back under the canopy. Tristan partially Shifted and shook his arms out, walking over to Allyssa. Then he charged at her.

Allyssa called up a wall of air in front of her, bearing it like a shield. He hit it and couldn't get past. While he tried to find a way around it, she sent a tendril of air snaking along the ground, which wrapped around his ankle and hoisted him upside down. He kicked through the tendril with his free foot and dropped to the ground, rolling onto his knees in a crouch. The outline seemed brighter around him, and Allyssa tried to keep the threat coming, as it would in a real fight. She sent wind whips after him in quick succession, keeping him light on his feet. She also sent the occasional burst on him from above, which he dove under after being tossed back by the first one. He ran around, dodging her attacks and searching for a way to get closer. Allyssa was so focused on her flurry of whips and snares that she didn't notice how close he had gotten to her; not until he ran against her shield again. And this time, he let out a yell as he hit the wind shield, striking it with both his fist and body.

Allyssa felt her hold on the shield snap as he broke through it, splintering it like glass. Of course he couldn't see it, but that was what it felt like. The destruction felt like a blow to the sternum, and she sucked in air as it felt like all of it left her lungs. Then Tristan rammed into her, and she literally flew back. She landed on the ground, now really struggling for air, and when she could breathe again, looked at him. "How was that?" she wheezed, half smiling.

He helped her up, the outline no longer around him. "Sorry. I hit you too hard."

"No harm done."

"You should get some rest now," Demetrius advised. "We get up early, remember?"

So protective. "I remember."

Two days of traveling brought them to another settlement: a sleepy little collection of cabins, with several people fishing in the early morning. They didn't spend much time there, collecting more food supplies and asking about a waterfall before continuing. Several of the people fishing along the banks of the lake had told them that they had to move in a different direction to reach the nearest river, and helpfully pointed them north.

When they traveled in that direction for about an hour and found a collection of guards waiting for them, Tristan cursed. "They set us up."

"Run!" Demetrius said, already steering Perseus to turn around. But they were already surrounded.

"Look what we've got here," one of the women said. "A bunch of outlaws, neat as presents."

"He went with outlaws?" Allyssa murmured.

"Are you going to come willingly?" the same woman asked.

Tristan looked at the others, as if checking.

Allyssa sliced her hands in front of her. Tristan and Wyatt jumped from their horses in the next instant, as Allyssa's gust of wind buffeted the circle of guards. Riley moved a second behind.

Several of the guards dropped to the ground, unconscious. "The rest have mental shields," Demetrius said, sliding off Perseus' back. Tristan didn't like how nervous Demetrius sounded.

Tristan partially Shifted, and with the fresh wave of strength and energy the rippling aura gave him, ran forward. Three of the guards still standing were Shifters, and the one Tristan reached first fully Shifted to become a moose. His transformation was so quick that Tristan ducked out of the way, slightly scared of being hit by the massive antlers.

The fight spread everyone out, and he saw Allyssa standing in front of Demetrius, fending off a fox Shifter and an earth user. Wyatt was acting like the karate kid or something, spinning and kicking in a whirlwind. And Riley was facing the third Shifter: a dog. A golden retriever.

He was only able to glance at the others before the moose demanded Tristan's attention. It rushed him, and Tristan again jumped to the side to evade it. He had a feeling that trick wouldn't work a third time, and ran toward the moose before it could face him again. He focused his strength on his shoulder and rammed into the moose. It staggered slightly. Tristan's shoulder throbbed.

He'd never seen a moose before. He hadn't appreciated how massive they were. He didn't appreciate finding out this way.

He risked another look away from it, his eyes fastening on Riley. Why did that Shifter have to be a dog? It was hard to fight any animal, even knowing it was a Shifter, but when the animal looked like a friendly pet? He would have a difficult time doing it. Riley wasn't. He could see her retreating, calling fire to her hands and sending it out to try to scare the dog back.

Tristan looked away too long. The moose tossed him aside like a rag doll, making him collide with a tree. The moose raced toward him, too fast for him to do more than stand. Wyatt saved him from being trampled. He appeared in Tristan's line of sight, diving from behind the moose, grabbing it around the neck, and making it turn with his own momentum. The moose stumbled, one leg giving out. Wyatt jumped up and looked at Tristan.

"Thanks," Tristan said.

"Don't mention it. How do you knock out a moose?"

"If I knew that I wouldn't have needed your help!"

Tristan charged the moose from one side, Wyatt from the other. When it went toward Wyatt, the boy dove and rolled out of the way, and Tristan slammed into the moose's side. It would take forever if they had to keep bashing into it like this. It would also leave them seriously bruised.

"Allyssa!" Tristan called, looking over to her. His voice caught in his throat. Riley had backed into one of the guards Wyatt had left when he came to Tristan's aid. She sent out another wave of flame to keep the dog back, and jumped when she bumped into the guard. The dog jumped over the flames, growling with its teeth bared.

That was when she partially Shifted. Tristan looked at Wyatt, saw that he had his full attention on the moose, and decided he could handle it. The dog wasn't growling at Riley anymore. She straightened, red and orange light around her, and ran after the guard, to a horse.

"Riley, don't!" Tristan called.

She swung onto the horse behind the guard and cast him the briefest of looks, and he saw in her eyes the same golden light he'd seen in Wyatt's eyes back in Kin Woods. Riley wasn't hearing him at all.

Tristan ran to the closest horse of theirs, jumped onto its back, and yelled for it to chase after Riley and the guard. He realized it was

Riley's horse, Athena. They moved through the sparse trees, leaving the fighting behind. He spurred the horse to move faster, seeing Riley and the guard a short distance ahead of him. They were going back toward the forest now. He had to catch up. "Come on!" he yelled at the horse. Athena seemed to understand his urgency, moving into a full-on sprint. He leaned his head down, clinging onto the horse's neck, and when he reached level with Riley he sat up a little bit.

"Riley!" he yelled to her. "You have to drop your Shift!"

She didn't even look at him, staring ahead with those golden-hued eyes. He was losing time. And he felt a breeze start around him that he realized wasn't all natural. The guard was a wind user. With the guard pressing a force of wind on him, Tristan was starting to lag behind them. He looked around, thinking as fast as he could, and one of the most reckless ideas ever occurred to him.

He sighed when he thought of it, but didn't think of anything better, so prepared himself as best he could. He moved his legs up to the top of the horse's back, holding on even tighter with his hands while he did so. It was extremely shaky, trying to stand on a moving animal. Once his feet were up on the horse he turned his body to the other horse, let go of Athena's neck, and jumped.

The few seconds during which he was in the air between the horses were slightly terrifying, especially when the guard looked back at him. He thought the guard would swat him away with a stiff breeze. There wasn't time for that before he reached their horse. And apparently Tristan had shoved off his horse with a little too much force, because he didn't land on the other horse; he basically jumped over it. As soon as he realized he had miscalculated he did the only sensible thing left, and grabbed Riley as he flew past. His objective was getting her, right? Well, this was one way.

He wrapped his arms around her and they fell to the ground painfully, with a full body impact. Tristan groaned but didn't give his body a second to recover. He rolled over, placing his hands on Riley's wrists to keep her from rising. He cast a glance at the guard, who had stopped a few feet ahead. Something in his look must have been scary, or maybe the guard realized he didn't stand a chance, because he started sprinting away. Riley tried to tear her arms free, and Tristan fixed his gaze back on her. "Phoenix, stop. It's over."

She kept trying to rise, her legs kicking at him, and he climbed on top of her, pinning her down. She lay flat under him, her arms pinned on either side of her head. He knelt above her, his knees on either side of her body. He saw the rage in her expression as she continued to try to tear free of his grip, rage that didn't belong on her face, but his hands were like iron.

"I'm not letting go."

When he said this she stopped fighting. She looked at him, eyes tinged gold, and breathed heavily, letting her head rest on the ground. He kept his eyes on her, willing Riley to retake control. It took a few seconds, but he saw that golden glow start to dissolve. The aura around her faded. When the last flecks of gold disappeared he smiled and dropped his own Shift.

She looked at him searchingly, her eyes wide and confused. "Tristan, what's going on?" she asked.

"You're back," he said. "You don't remember what just happened?"

She squinted her eyes a little, then shook her head. "I Shifted to get away from that guard, and then . . ." She looked around in growing comprehension. "Why are you pinning me down?"

He realized he was in fact still on top of her and quickly scrambled off. "I kind of tackled you off a moving horse. Sorry."

He reached out a hand to help her stand. "Thanks for stopping me," she said. "I was trying not to Shift—"

"It was an instinct," he said over her. "That

guard snuck up on you."

Riley walked over to Athena, who was anxiously pawing the ground nearby. She stroked the horse's face, and Athena calmed.

"The moose," Tristan said. "We need to get back."

They rode back toward the others at a fast pace, but Tristan's concern was unfounded. Allyssa, Wyatt, and Demetrius were fine, and had finished fighting. The guards and their horses were gone.

"You're okay!" Allyssa cried, running over.

"What happened?" Wyatt demanded.

"I Shifted, and Tristan stopped me."

"How'd you take out the moose?" Tristan asked.

Allyssa smiled. "I thinned the air around it until the Shifter went back to human form, and Wyatt knocked him out."

"Sorry I left you to it," Tristan said.

Wyatt's hands twitched, but he didn't say anything. Tristan slid off Athena's back. "We should get away from here. Think those fishermen lied about the river being north?"

"We're past the lake," Demetrius said. "Let's keep going this way."

They climbed back onto their horses. Chitter hesitantly crept out of the bag on Tristan's saddle, going back onto Tristan's leg when they started riding in silence. Tristan stroked the chipmunk with one finger. "Believe me, buddy, none of us wanted that to happen."

Riley didn't speak much as they traveled that day. She'd failed in every way when those guards attacked. She could have used her fire to *fight* them, instead of trying to scare them back. She could have tried to throw a punch, or kick, or do anything physical. But what did she do? Let herself get cornered, Shift in fear, and allow the phoenix to take over. She truly had no memory of the time she spent with a partial Shift. It seemed like one second she'd been surrounded by fighting guards and friends, and the next Tristan had been kneeling over her, pinning her to the ground.

She had to be able to defend herself. They'd fought guards today, heading away from Christopher. When they found the Celestials they would have to go back to the castle to confront Christopher, and they were sure to run into more fights when they did.

Demetrius motioned for them to stop late in the afternoon. Riley had barely realized, but they'd skipped their usual break around midday. They decided to make up for it by stopping for the night. Riley guessed they had several hours before nightfall, and decided to use the daylight to do some serious training, similar to what she'd done at Christopher's house in the days before their entry into Terraria.

She slid off Athena's back, took the blanket and lead off the mare, and let her drink water from cupped hands before she walked several feet away. Then she called fire to her hands and started going through the motions Christopher had shown her as a control exercise, all those months ago. She'd been practicing with her fire the last few days, but mostly in mock sparring matches with Allyssa, in which she'd been too worried about losing control and hurting her friend to truly test herself.

It felt good to wield her flame, and as she practiced, some of the shame that had weighed her down all day dissipated. She stopped when she felt her energy start to dip substantially. She hadn't eaten since that morning.

"You were doing some serious training," Allyssa noted when Riley walked over. "Everything okay?"

Riley just nodded.

Tristan went to the bags and started looking through them. "I'll make some dinner."

Allyssa coaxed Chitter onto her lap, and stroked the chipmunk as Riley started a fire and

Tristan put some of their meat over it to warm. Riley offered the chipmunk a dried berry, tossing it on the ground near him, and watched with a trace of amusement as he took the berry, ran several paces away, and cautiously ate it.

They paired the fish they'd taken that day with white bread and cheese, entertaining themselves as they ate by throwing Chitter more dried berries. "Thank you for cooking," Demetrius told Tristan. "That was delicious."

Tristan smiled wistfully. "I wish I had some of the spices I have at home. I could make it so much more interesting. But the smoke does give it a decent flavor."

Allyssa stared at the small fire. "Now if we only had the stuff for s'mores."

Demetrius turned to her. "What are those again?"

Everyone gave him an incredulous look, but Allyssa seemed almost offended. "You've never had a s'more?"

"It's graham crackers, chocolate, and a marshmallow, like a little sandwich," Wyatt informed Demetrius. "You roast the marshmallows over the fire."

"You've really never had one?" Tristan asked.

Demetrius shook his head.

"We'll have to fix that," Riley said.

"When we get home, s'mores galore," Wyatt said. "We'll make all kinds."

"There are multiple kinds?" Demetrius asked.

Allyssa and Tristan started telling him about the kinds of s'mores they'd had. Riley hoped Allyssa kept the combinations they hadn't liked off of her list, for Demetrius' sake. Those Sweet Tart s'mores had been horrendous. Riley wanted to relax and enjoy the cozy conversation by the fire, but they still had daylight. Wyatt had already stood, and was giving the horses some attention.

Riley stood and walked up to Wyatt, helping him give all of the horses more to drink. That done, she turned to him and asked something she really hoped he would agree to. "Can you teach me how to fight?"

He frowned at her. "Sure, but why?"

She blinked. "You saw me earlier. I'm useless in a fight if I can't Shift or fully use my fire."

His jawline tensed. "I won't let anything happen to you, Riley."

"I know you won't, but I want to feel like I can handle myself in a fight, without Shifting or fire. You're a great fighter." She looked him full-on. "Please."

Wyatt stared right back at her, strands of hair falling into his eyes in that way she loved, but somehow failing to soften their intensity this time, and nodded. "Okay." He motioned her forward. "Attack me."

She blinked. "How?"

"Don't think about it. Just pretend I'm one of those guards."

She breathed out to focus herself and ran towards him, bringing her arm back as she approached to swing. Wyatt waited calmly and ducked to the side, dodging her blow. His hand came up and grabbed her arm, and he pressed down, jerking her backwards and driving her into the ground. She looked at him with an open mouth from the ground. "That was less than ten seconds."

He grabbed her hand and helped her up. "This is serious. Again. Try not to go for the direct attack."

Three attacks and falls to the ground later, Riley jumped up, her breath shorter but her determination stronger. He had all the advantages here. Height, strength, experience. She had to expect guards to have those advantages too. Since she couldn't trust her Shifting, or fully count on her fire, the strength she had now would be the only thing on which she had to rely. Unless she found a way to not use her strength . . . .

Her mind started working on alternate possibilities as she rushed Wyatt again. Even when he trapped her hands behind her and forced her to her knees she was thinking of any pieces of information that could help her, tiny things that could give her an edge. He released her and she turned to face him again, this time with an idea. She kept her approach the same, keeping her eyes focused on his face and raising her fist behind her as though to strike. She saw the cocky light in his eyes as he prepared to sidestep her again. She turned herself and kicked out her leg, wrapping it around his ankle and pulling back. It made her lose her balance, but it also made Wyatt lose his. The difference? She was prepared for it.

Wyatt stumbled forward, and she righted herself behind him, grabbing at his arm and twisting it behind his back while leaning onto him, forcing him to take a knee on the grass. She paused, catching her breath. "How was that?" she asked.

He was still, and she felt him shake beneath her fingers. Alarmed, she let go, walking around so she could see his face. "Did I hurt you?"

Wyatt looked up at her, and she realized he was laughing. "Why are you laughing?" she asked. Her concern was trickling away, replaced by minor annoyance.

He managed to stop and smiled at her. "You surprised me."

"You told me to."

He chuckled again. Then he reached out and kicked her feet out from under her, sweeping her to the ground. She hit with a grunt and turned to look at him, irritated. "You didn't finish the job," he scolded with a playful glint in his eyes.

Riley jumped to her feet, narrowing her eyes. "Then let's go again." She needed to get that cockiness out of his system before he got himself hurt. Plus, he'd knocked her flat quite a few times that night. It was about time she returned the favor.

Tristan walked over then. "Can I get in on this practice?" he asked.

Wyatt gave him a terse nod.

Wyatt helped them pack the most power into their punches by showing them more efficient ways of doing it. He made them practice moving light on their feet, and dodging. After doing this for some time they started to spar, all of them at once, every man for himself.

Tristan and Wyatt clashed first, Wyatt moving low to the ground and relying on speed. Riley tried to sneak behind them, but after Tristan blocked a blow from Wyatt he grabbed Riley's wrist, pulling her in front of him. Riley tore her arm free by jerking towards Tristan's thumb, forcing his hand to open. Wyatt had shown her that. Freed, she turned to block the blow from Wyatt that she had seen coming in her peripheral vision. Tristan kicked out at her feet as she blocked Wyatt, but she grabbed onto both boys' arms as she fell, either taking them with her or using them to stay upright. They were sturdy enough and close enough together that she was able to use them to bounce back up, and she kicked out as she jumped, catching one of them in the leg.

They progressed in this fashion for a while, one of them almost going down and then making a comeback and starting the struggle anew. It was an almost steady ebb and flow, the tide slamming against the shore and sinking back to sea, over and over, until finally Riley couldn't do anymore. She put her hands up in mock surrender and leaned over, trying to recover her breath. "I can't do anymore," she panted. Every muscle screamed at her that it had had enough, and she was covered in sweat. But she was smiling. She hated workouts, but this had been a successful exercise; even if she felt like her whole body was bruised. She saw the boys stop and look at her, and sank down onto the grass. "You can keep going if you want. I'm done."

She knew they were both smiling at her without looking, Wyatt with his almost impish grin and Tristan with his soft, confident smile. She glanced up just to check her accuracy, and felt a rush of triumph when she was proven right.

"It's really dark out," Tristan said.

It certainly had gotten dark. The day was gone, fading when they had started training and sparring. The moon was up now, and it was by that glow that Riley could dimly see their faces. She lay back against the grass, looking up at the clear night sky.

"I'm going to bed," Tristan said.

Riley closed her eyes. "Me too. But I'm not moving."

They laughed, and she heard them settle on the grass around her.

"Goodnight."

Demetrius sat on a blanket near the remnants of their tiny fire and watched Wyatt, Tristan, and Riley practice in the waning daylight.

"She's beating herself up over the fight this morning," Allyssa said, her eyes on her best friend. "It's scary that if they Shift, the Celestials can take over. I wish she didn't blame herself for Shifting out of instinct, but if this helps her feel better . . . ."

"I should join them," Demetrius said. "I'm no good in a fight if my powers don't work."

Allyssa turned to look at him. "You dropped some of those guards in seconds. You did your part. Besides, the only one of us who's really good in a fight without powers is Wyatt."

Demetrius almost smiled. "He is quite the warrior. He's still wary from his incident with Shifting, back in Kin Woods, so this will hopefully help him regain his confidence."

Wyatt had never seemed to be lacking confidence to Allyssa, but she realized he had been quieter the last few days.

"Riley and Tristan are turning to Wyatt for instruction in a fight," Demetrius said. "Maybe I should turn to you."

She leaned back, stretching her hands on the blanket behind her to balance. "The prince wants the servant to tutor him?"

"You're not a servant," he said tersely. He knew she was joking, but he still felt a rush of resentment whenever he remembered the roles Christopher had assigned them. He softened his tone. "You never were. And I'm not a prince. Not really."

"I've never seen Christopher as a king, but I've always thought you would make a great prince. And not just because you're called the Prince of Shadows. Actually, you kind of remind me of Prince Er—," she cut off, looking mortified.

"Who?" Demetrius asked.

"Not important."

"Come on," he insisted.

She blushed. "Prince Eric, from *The Little Mer-*

maid. It was Riley's favorite when we were little. You look like him."

"That's a Disney movie, right?"

Allyssa nodded, her cheeks still tinged pink.

Demetrius looked up at the calm sky, struggling to remember. "My mother showed me a few when I was very young, but I barely remember them. Father didn't want me living in a fantasy world. Not one he didn't organize, at any rate."

Allyssa sat up straight. "Another reason to hate him. He stole your childhood from you."

He didn't have a rebuttal. It was a fair statement. Christopher had groomed Demetrius all his life, and after Demetrius' mother died, Christopher had been able to take complete control of his son's upbringing. Demetrius could see the anger in Allyssa's tense shoulders, as she thought of Christopher. Demetrius felt it whenever he thought of the man, but he hated seeing Allyssa so angry, and didn't want to feel this rage himself, right now. He wanted more of the lighthearted conversation they'd had earlier, and found a way to bring it back. "You said *The Little Mermaid* was Riley's favorite. So what was yours?"

"*Beauty and the Beast.*"

He didn't know much about that one either.

"I can show you," she offered. "Look at my

thoughts."

He wanted to protest, but recognized her stubborn expression and hesitantly brushed his consciousness with hers. She seemed satisfied as she brought images of the characters to mind, naming them for him. He was surprised at how relieved he was to retreat back into his own mind, and realized he was still scared of his powers affecting her without conscious will. "You're too trusting of me," he said before he could stop himself.

He saw her open her mouth to say something immediately, most likely to brush off his comment, but she stopped and studied him in silence. "I trust people who deserve it," she said. "You have done nothing wrong, Demetrius. I know you're more worried about your powers now because of what you learned about your mom, but that was Christopher's mistake. Not yours. Don't you dare compare yourself to him, when you and I both know you will never be like that monster." She placed one hand over his. "In all the years he tried to mold you, to make you just like him, you stayed yourself. You stayed gentle and compassionate and strong in so many ways. That's why I trust you."

Her intense brown eyes demanded his gaze, and Demetrius felt a slight ache in the back of his throat. Allyssa applied pressure to the hand she covered, and they turned their attention back to their friends, sparring beneath a darkening sky.

CHAPTER 13

Making Friends

It was so much more comfortable to pace as a wolf than as a human. Ash didn't have to think about how to move his hands as he walked, because he moved on four paws. He was also much faster, letting him burn more of his nervous energy.

Noah had given up trying to get him to stop, and was doing a workout routine on the floor of the living room. Whatever he said, Ash knew Noah was full of nervous energy too.

When Ash heard the door start to open he stopped and whirled to face it, dropping his Shift rapidly. Emily walked in and seemed surprised to find Ash and Noah standing and facing her, but laughed. "Doing some light training?"

"Just a little," Ash said quickly. "How was the meeting?"

Emily set her purse on the table. "I'm cautiously optimistic that a peace treaty is in sight, and beyond that, actions to actually help resolve the differences between Shifters and Elementalists." She looked around. "Where's Alice?"

Ash tried to look casual as he walked toward the balcony window.

It wasn't casual enough. "Ash?" Emily asked. He could tell she was moving closer to him. "Did Alice go somewhere?"

"Play it cool," Noah murmured.

"I asked her to Shift and follow you," Ash said.

"Or not," Noah said, and went back to doing arm rotations, watching Ash and Emily.

Emily seemed stunned. "You . . . you asked her to what?"

Ash squirmed. The alarm Emily was showing was making him think it hadn't been a good idea. "We wanted to make sure you were safe. Alice Shifted and flew from the balcony. She had to have seen you, because she didn't come right back. She should be here any second." He looked at the balcony again.

Emily strode to the balcony, opening the door and stepping onto it. "Do you have any idea how dangerous that is?" she demanded.

"We had to make sure you were okay," Ash admitted. "Something isn't right with Match, whatever you think, and we're not losing you too!"

Some of the anger seemed to abandon Emily. Her mouth opened and closed, and then she stepped closer to Ash. "I appreciate that you're so protective of me, but you shouldn't have done this. Alice shouldn't have gone out." She looked at the congested streets. "With this traffic, Alice should have been able to keep pace with my cab. She should be back by now."

Ash gripped the edge of the balcony and scanned the sky, his heart in his throat. "I didn't think," he managed. How could he have been so stupid?

Emily rubbed a hand on his back, briskly but still soothingly. "Let's give it a few more minutes before we really start to worry. I'm sure she's just taking her time flying back."

Alice made it an hour listening to Havier talk incessantly before she realized it didn't matter if she couldn't remember the hotel where her family was staying. "Do you have a phone I can borrow?" she asked, interrupting him in the middle of a story about his sister.

"Sure thing."

He rose in a fluid motion and walked out, and returned about a minute later with a cell phone in hand. He tossed it to her.

Alice dialed Emily's number and put the phone to her ear with energy. They had to be worried sick by now. How could she have been so stupid?

"Hello?"

"Emily, it's Alice."

"Alice, honey!" Alice winced at the increase in volume, and heard Ash and Noah's voices in the background, asking what was going on. "You're on speaker phone. Alice, where are you? What happened?"

"I don't know what happened, but I'm at a Temple."

Emily paused for a second. "We can figure out exactly what happened after. Do you know where the Temple is?"

Alice looked at Havier, who was surprisingly giving her space, standing by the door of the room. "Can you give my family directions here?" she asked.

He was beside her in a heartbeat, plucking the phone from her hands and telling them where to go. Then he listened for a second and handed the phone back to her.

"Alice, we're leaving right now," Emily said. "We'll be there as fast as we can."

"Okay."

Alice tossed the phone back to Havier. He slipped it into his back pocket and studied her. "Pretty smart, chica," he said. "You're definitely an owl."

There was no teasing in the comment, and Alice softened toward him by a degree. "You were saying your sister started a fight at a bowling alley?"

His round cheeks stood out when he chuckled. "Yeah, Maribel likes to fight. When the person next to her bowled at her turn and cost her the game, she got into a fight with them. She dumped a pitcher of water over the guy. She didn't realize the person was an Elementalist until he made the water fly onto her too. It was labeled as an attack relating to the war, but really Maribel just has anger issues. She'll fight anyone that crosses her." He perched on the bed next to her. "There was this one time she really screwed up and picked a fight with our instructor. Helen taught her a lesson that day!"

"My brother Noah tends to pick fights too," Alice said.

"Let's hope he and Maribel don't meet, then. She'd kick his butt."

Alice scoffed. "If you were smart you wouldn't say that until you'd met him."

Emily, Ash, and Noah arrived shortly after that, led by Pat. Emily ran to Alice's side, embracing her. Noah walked just behind her, stopped on the opposite side of Alice's bed, and put a hand on her arm. Ash walked about halfway into the room and stopped, his eyes wide and searching.

"I'm fine," Alice told him.

Her voice seemed to jolt him, and he rushed over and took Emily's place hugging her. "We were so worried when you didn't come back."

"You have a bruise," Emily said motheringly, her hand hovering near it.

"It doesn't hurt anymore," Alice said.

"Time to figure some things out," Havier said. He'd stepped back when the others entered, but came closer now. "Alice has a concussion and doesn't remember what she was doing before she got hit."

Three sets of eyes snapped to Alice, two surprised and one angry. "You got hit?" Noah asked.

"You don't remember?" Ash and Emily asked at the same time.

Havier explained how he had seen her. Alice told them she didn't remember. "I didn't think about calling you for a little while," she admitted.

Emily shook her head. "Don't worry about that. The important thing is that you did call, and that you're all right."

Alice looked at the three of them, glad to

see them but still incredibly frustrated with her faulty memory. "What were we doing earlier? How did we get separated?"

Ash flinched and shifted his feet. "It was my idea, and you agreed. You went to follow Emily to make sure she was safe." He explained the concerns they'd both admitted having that morning, and the plan for Alice to follow her.

Havier held out a hand that loosely pointed to Emily, apparently lost in thought. He kept his hand pointed at Emily but directed his eyes to Alice. "I saw you go after that car like you had a mission. You wanted to get someone's attention." His eyes slid back to Emily. "You must have been the one to get into that car."

Emily was shaking her head. "I didn't see Alice after my meeting."

"She saw you, or at least thought she did," Havier insisted. "Maybe she went to the wrong car. There were a few that looked almost identical."

"And then someone slammed the door in her face," Noah growled.

"And that's where I enter the story," Havier said. "There you go. Now you know what you forgot."

Except she still didn't. Not really. "My brain better work right tomorrow," she muttered.

Emily covered one of Alice's hands comfortingly.

Noah walked around Alice's bed and right up to Havier, looking at him with narrowed eyes. Havier was taller. Noah was stronger. Alice noticed Havier tense when Noah stood immediately across from him, and wondered if she'd made Noah sound like he was always looking for a fight. He wasn't. Alice really wasn't sure what he was doing right now, though. He did seem a little worked up . . . . Everyone was silent while they looked at each other, and then Noah held out his hand. "Thank you for helping my sister."

Havier's eyebrows shot up. He half-smiled and shook the proffered hand. He glanced at Alice, and she thought she understood his quick look well enough to know he wouldn't be placing any bets on a fight between Noah and Maribel. She was tempted to smile.

"So what happens now?" Ash asked.

"I'd like Alice to stay here for the next twenty-four hours, so I can make sure she fully recovers." Pat stepped forward. He'd been over by the desk in the far corner, and Alice had forgotten he was here. "Pat Michaels. I'm the doctor for this Temple." He looked at Emily. "You're welcome to stay here as well, given the circumstances. We have plenty of rooms."

"Thank you," Emily said. "We'll take you up on it."

"Do I have to stay awake for the next day?" Alice asked Pat.

He smiled sympathetically. "Unfortunately."

Havier tutted. "You underestimate how entertaining I can be. The next twenty-four hours will fly by."

Being a captive audience, Alice wasn't sure how likely that was. The others seemed amused though, and at the very least she was sure she wouldn't be left alone.

Havier was the only one to stay awake the entire time. Emily, Ash, and Noah claimed bunks in the med-bay, and Alice could tell they wanted to stay awake, but one by one they fell asleep that night. Noah was the last to drop off, still sitting up against the wall with his arms crossed. When his head lolled onto his shoulder Alice knew he was asleep. She'd known with Ash when he suddenly stopped talking, mid-sentence. Emily had just gotten quieter, and her breathing had evened.

"It's funny how even the way a person falls asleep tells you something about them," Havier said in a low voice. He'd kept the bunk immediately to Alice's right that he'd used earlier. "Like your twin. He puts his full energy into whatever he's doing, right? So much so that when he crashes, he crashes hard."

"I wonder what I'll learn about you when you fall asleep."

He chuckled. "I've been where you are now. Know how annoying it is for people to try to stay up with you and fail. We'll both take a siesta when Pat clears you."

Alice glanced at him. "When did you have a concussion?"

"I played soccer as a kid. This game I played goalie and dove for a ball. The other player didn't have time to stop and kicked me in the head. No lasting damage, but I had to stay up for a while too."

She lowered her voice. "Did you have memory troubles too?"

"Nah, but I was so dizzy I couldn't walk straight. It faded as the day went on, and when I was finally able to sleep, I woke up with just a tiny headache, but otherwise normal."

Alice loosened her arms, which she'd involuntarily tightened around her legs. "I don't mind if you go to sleep," she said quietly.

"I won't sleep till you can, chica."

His response was immediate and calm, and surprisingly kind, and Alice found she was glad he would be staying awake.

"I'm sorry we fell asleep, honey," Emily said.

"It was nighttime. It's been daytime for hours. You're good," Alice said.

It was mid-afternoon, so Emily knew Alice was right. They'd all been awake for hours. Still, she felt a lingering sense of guilt about the rested feeling she had, seeing how tired Alice was.

"It's been about a day since you came here," Pat said. "And nothing's changed with your condition, right?"

"Nothing's gotten worse," Alice told him. "My brain is starting to work right again." Emily remembered how thrilled Alice had been to name their hotel, and to tell Ash she recalled their conversation the day before.

"That's a great sign," Pat said. "Okay, then, I say you're good to go! A little well-deserved sleep, and hopefully your brain will finish accessing those memories while you're powered down, and you'll wake up back to normal."

Alice smiled and leaned back, burrowing into her pillow. "You don't have to tell me twice."

Havier laid back and closed his eyes as well. Emily looked at Pat and thanked him again, and the man nodded. "Not a problem. If you'd like, I can give you a tour of the Temple now."

Ash and Noah had been getting antsy, and seemed happy to follow Pat out the door. He kept them out of the med-bay for the better part of an hour, and Emily could tell they'd been to the gym when they returned.

"This Temple is huge!" Ash exclaimed when Emily met his eyes as he walked in. Alice tensed and opened her eyes. Ash saw her move and winced. "Sorry," he whispered.

"Just a few more minutes," Alice murmured, closing her eyes again.

Ash walked over and sat next to Emily and continued in a whisper, telling her about the tour while Alice got a bit more rest. She woke not long after, and everyone turned to her with anticipation.

Her eyes were brighter than before. "I remember what happened." She stared at Emily. "I did see you. You followed Match into his car after your meeting. I'm pretty sure you saw me, too."

Emily's relief at Alice's restored memory faltered at this. Again, the kids contradicted what she seemed to remember. Was it possible . . .?

Ash, Alice, and Noah were adamant that she not go to the second meeting with Match and Summers. Even Havier was against it. They had him convinced President Match couldn't be trusted. Honestly, Emily mostly agreed with them. She also knew she had to see it through, though.

So the four teens escorted her to the meeting the next day, and waited for her right outside. President Summers was already in her seat when Emily walked into the room, as were several of the others. Summers looked at Emily when she took her seat and dipped her head in greeting.

Emily sucked in a breath in the next instant, as it felt like part of her snapped back into place. Several memories flooded her mind. She saw her conversation with Match and Katya by the reflecting pool, and then, more disturbing, she saw herself get into a car after Match after the first meeting.

She was set to walk away and hail a cab when she found herself following Match. Once inside the car she saw both Match and Katya. She started to ask what was going on. Then there was commotion by the car window. A tiny owl, knocking its wings against the window with urgency. She recognized that owl! "Alice!" Emily cried.

Katya whipped the door open, and Emily tried to rush out to help. Sit, Katya ordered.

"What did you do that for?" Match asked, as Emily internally fumed and worried but found herself unable to react externally.

Katya raised an eyebrow. "She's questioning things. This will keep her mind occupied with worries about the children, and keep her from unraveling what I've done. The owl will likely need med-

ical attention." Katya turned to Emily. "Now to get things back on track."

Emily took a staggered breath when the memory returned to her, her heart racing. Everyone was staring at her, but only one person seemed unsurprised.

"Judging from your reaction, you had memories manipulated by a Shadow Elementalist," Summers said, looking directly at Emily with her intense stare.

Emily forced herself to take a few regular breaths. "How did you—what did you do?"

"I thought your behavior at our last meeting seemed odd. You were questioning what you were saying. I asked one of my team members, a Shadow Elementalist, to cast a simple net over everyone who enters this room today, to filter out any unwelcome influences. With you, Mrs. Madison, there was clearly something caught in that net."

Emily stared at her for several heartbeats. "Your team member didn't do anything else?" she clarified.

Summers' eyes softened. "I understand your wariness, Mrs. Madison. On my honor, whatever memories and beliefs you possess right now are fully your own, without tampering or manipulation."

Emily believed her. There was just something about the woman—Emily suspected it was the power in her eyes, that earnest desire for the truth—that reassured her. "Riley didn't go to the parallel world for revenge," Emily said. "I don't even know if she went to that world willingly, or if Christopher took her, but I do know she would never threaten Elementalists in order to win the war." Emily shook her head, still horrified by how completely Katya had changed those memories.

The door opened again and Match walked in. Emily stood and saw a white and gray aura appear around her as her emotions climbed. Match saw her, paused mid-step, and sighed.

Summers stood. "Aiden, do you have anything to say for yourself?"

His jaw clenched.

"How could you?" Emily demanded before he could speak. She stalked closer. "I would have been happy to come to this meeting and honestly help figure out how to approach peace, and you made me part of your revenge agenda!"

He didn't meet her eyes. "I need Elementalists to take responsibility."

"You need to accept that while some Elementalists killed your wife, it doesn't mean they're all to blame," Emily countered in a snarl. "You've let your pain ruin you, and your pride."

"Just a minute—"

"No, she's right," Summers said. "You approached a meeting intended to promote peace with underhanded tricks and a closed mind. There will be an investigation regarding your recent actions, and I assume I can speak for everyone here when I say your services at this meeting are no longer required. Vice President Neer will have to represent the Nation, assuming the two of you haven't been working together on this. Please leave."

Match looked at each face, as if waiting for someone to defend him, and then gave a stiff nod and walked out of the room. Emily dropped her partial Shift once he was out of sight.

"An official meeting will have to wait until an elected member of the Nation can join us," Summers said, turning back to everyone. "I understand if anyone here doesn't want to continue, but hope you'll all stay on this committee."

The meeting ended there. Emily stayed behind while the Shifter and Elementalist representatives left, and faced Summers. "Are you a Shadow Elementalist?"

Summers gave her a small smile, held out one hand, and as Emily watched, brought a flame to her hand. The action made Emily think suddenly and painfully about Riley, as she remembered seeing her daughter wield a flame like that for the first time in Match's safehouse.

"Mrs. Madison," Summers said, extinguishing the flame and dropping her hand, "I plan to move forward with this committee, as quickly as possible, but political actions like this can drag out into long processes. I'd like to take some action in the present, while the official peace talks occur. I'd be honored if you would consent to be my Shifter advisor."

Emily blinked. "You want me to work with you?"

Summers' gaze was clear. "Ultimately, I'm going to propose that we create a new form of government with both Shifters and Elementalists, to handle Shifter and Elemental issues together. I think that will decrease the divisions between the groups. Like I said, this is something that will probably take more time than we can imagine to put to action. It isn't just large shifts like this that make a difference, though. Small steps in the right direction. I hope Vice President Neer will consider appointing an Elementalist advisor as well, but I'll leave that to her."

Emotions and negative thoughts about Match still swirled in Emily's mind, keeping her full attention from the current conversation. "I live in upstate New York," Emily managed to say.

"If you become my Shifter advisor, location won't be an issue the majority of the time. Please don't feel like you have to answer me now. I can see that you're still reeling from all of this, and understandably so. I hope you'll give my offer some thought, and let me know in the near future." Summers smiled. "Enjoy the rest of your day, Mrs. Madison."

Emily returned the sentiment and left. The kids were waiting for her just outside.

"We saw Match leave a few minutes ago," Noah said. "What happened?"

"I found out you were absolutely right not to trust Match." The bright afternoon sunshine seemed especially enticing, and Emily started walking. "Let's go to the park for a bit. I'll explain on the way, and then I think we could all use some fun."

CHAPTER 14

Enemy or Ally

The weather seemed to be improving by the day. Flowers began shooting up in full, petals spread wide. Early mornings didn't seem as cold. Spring had finally won its annual battle with winter, banishing the last of the chill.

The land showed gradual signs of change as they progressed. The grass shrank to lower, coarser blades, between increasingly rocky terrain. Trees sparsely dotted the landscape. But what made them stop moving was the faint sound they heard over the wind and the trotting of the horses. They paused the horses to listen, and Riley realized it was a trickling sound.

"A river," Wyatt said with a smile. He started his horse forward, and with a click of her tongue Riley made Athena follow. The trickling sound became louder as they got closer, and eventually a river came into view, just as it started to rain.

"I guess I don't need a bath anymore," Tristan said as they reached the water, sliding off the horse. The rain had come on quickly and was now pouring down. Poor Chitter had been so disgruntled by it that he'd crawled into Tristan's bag. Riley jumped off of Athena and tried to shelter her under the nearest tree, with minimal success. Abandoning the effort, Riley stepped out into the rain, letting the drops fall on her uplifted face. She wanted it to help wash away her memory. Her dream the night before had been absolutely awful. Nightmare would be more accurate. She'd woken with tears leaking from the corners of her eyes, and had to hastily rub them to hide it from the others. The nightmares were getting worse each night, making her sleep restless. She breathed out now as the rain washed over her, pushing the memory away.

"We should set up camp here for now," Demetrius said. "I'll scout ahead to see if there's actual shelter, but this is probably as good a spot as any."

"Hey," Allyssa said from right next to Riley. "We should do something."

Riley opened her eyes. "Train?"

"Rinse off. I know it's raining, but that stream looks pretty inviting."

"You girls going swimming?" Tristan asked.

"I guess you could say that." Allyssa smiled. "We're soaked anyway. We may as well have some fun."

"I could use some of that." Wyatt ran to the edge of the river and jumped in. He leaped out just as quickly. "It's freezing!"

Tristan laughed lowly, and Wyatt cast him a dirty look as he shook his hair out of his eyes. Allyssa faced Riley. "You can warm up the water with your fire."

"I can boil it, but that's too hot."

"Trust me," Allyssa said. "Bring out your fire. A good amount."

Riley was skeptical but did as Allyssa asked. She had to keep replenishing it as the rain weakened it, almost as fast as she made it, but she made it a steady orange flame. Abruptly the fire roared in her hand as the rain vanished. The fire was popping with a loud, healthy crackling sound, as if it were a much larger flame.

Allyssa had her hand held out. "Told you to trust me."

"Why'd you wait to make a cover for it?" Riley asked.

"I wanted to see if your fire was more powerful than rain. Fires need no water and plenty of oxygen, right? That's the 'no water' part. Now for the 'plenty of oxygen.'" She bent one finger towards herself and the fire left Riley's hand, still contained in its air bubble. Allyssa sent it down into the water.

"You're heating it." Tristan shook his head in amazement. "I never would have thought of that."

"Make a few more," Allyssa told Riley. "The water will be warm enough for us to get in if we put in a few more flames."

Riley almost smiled at her friend's cleverness. She made three more fires and watched Allyssa send them into the water. "You're holding them there. Keeping a fire going underwater."

"Yeah. It won't last long. They'll die soon because the oxygen will run out, and some drops of water will break through, but Jacob taught me to make an air bubble in the water ages ago."

Wyatt reached a hand into the water. "It's definitely warmer."

Allyssa unhooked the purple shawl around her shoulders and set it carefully on the ground. Then she jumped into the river. "We might need a little more fire." She looked at Wyatt accusingly. "You said it was warm."

"Warmer," he corrected with a smug smile. "Water a bit nippy for you?"

Allyssa smiled back in a dangerous way, and before Riley could call out warning Wyatt was falling back into the river, pushed by Allyssa's wind. She laughed at Allyssa's gloating expression as Wyatt shook his head again, flicking water everywhere like a dog.

"You going in?" Tristan asked Riley. He was still right next to her, a few feet away.

She looked at him and nodded, and they walked to the edge. Tristan jumped. Riley slid down from the bank. She'd never been a big jumper. If she swam at the park with Allyssa, she would get in step by step, acclimating to the temperature while Allyssa waited impatiently and threatened to splash her. The water wasn't as cold as she'd been expecting. It was only a little colder than the rain, about as deep as her neck in the middle. The flames had already disappeared.

A splash of water to the back of her head made her shriek in surprise, but she was smiling not even a second later. So it was a water war, huh? She'd done this before. She whirled around, arms fully extended, sending a tall wave to— Tristan.

She saw his eyebrows shoot up right before it washed over him, and bit her lip. She'd thought it was Allyssa that had splashed her. Wyatt started laughing uproariously, and Tristan was laughing too.

"Didn't think you'd strike back," he said.

"I plan on doing more than that!" Riley waded

closer, chasing him down the stream. They hopped/swam after each other, playfully splashing and dodging and diving. Riley was laughing whenever she wasn't hit with water, and even some of the times she was. She glanced back at Allyssa and Wyatt and saw Wyatt send a wave towards her friend. Allyssa flicked her hand, making the water bend in the air and flick right back in Wyatt's face.

"Not fair," Wyatt spluttered.

Allyssa stopped a wave from Riley and sent it at her. "We never specified rules."

"No powers!" Riley, Wyatt, and Tristan said in unison.

Allyssa shrugged. "Fine. I can beat you without them."

"Good luck!" Wyatt cried, spinning with his arms spread wide and sending water everywhere.

"Got ya!" Tristan yelled as he sent a strong wave at Riley, knocking her down. She surfaced and tried to glare at him. The effect was somewhat lost because of her giggling, but she tried anyway, taking what she imagined was a menacing step towards him. This was becoming an all-out water war.

"You're going down," she threatened, chasing after him as he laughed and swam farther down the river. They went so far down that they saw Demetrius walking back, though Wyatt and Allyssa were still easily in view. "How far did you go?" Riley asked Demetrius.

"Apparently not far enough. There's no shelter here." He looked at them with amusement. "Aren't you cold?"

"Riley and Allyssa warmed it before we got in. And now we're fine."

"I'm going back to the horses, but you guys keep doing . . . whatever you're doing."

"You should join us!" Tristan called.

Demetrius held up a hand as he walked by, politely refusing. Tristan looked after him. "He needs to loosen up."

"I don't know how much he's ever been allowed to," Riley said quietly.

Tristan was still looking at his receding figure. "Well he's allowed to now."

Riley wanted to call back the playfulness they had had, but she'd never been good at that. Something on the river's edge caught her eye. "Where are you going?" Tristan asked as she went to the edge. She didn't answer, studying the thing that had caught her attention. It was stuck in the ground, dipping into the water. The part that fed into the water extended into a basket. "Is that a trap?" Tristan asked from next to her.

"I think so."

He touched it with one hand and quickly drew it away. "There's a fish in there. It wriggled." He explained.

Riley looked around quickly. "Where's the person who set it?" Demetrius had gone past this point and said he'd seen no shelter. They hadn't passed any people in a long time. Was there another town not too far?

"We should head back to the others."

They swam back more slowly than they had come, not in a rush to chase each other. Wyatt and Allyssa were standing on the bank, Wyatt holding his arms out while Allyssa moved her hands around. Riley could see Wyatt's shirt moving as the air buffeted it and smiled. Allyssa was being a human dryer.

"You two went far," Allyssa said. "Wyatt couldn't catch up."

"I think you mean *you* couldn't."

"Okay, *I* couldn't, and he didn't want to leave me behind." She let her hands fall to her side. "You guys want to be dried off too?"

Tristan shrugged. It was still raining, but not as hard as it had been. A breeze started pushing against Riley, drying her dripping clothes. "We found something down the river," she said. "A trap for fish."

The mood of the others shifted noticeably. "Is there another town being built here?" Allyssa asked.

"Not that I'm aware," Demetrius said.

"Maybe it's just one person," Wyatt said. "Someone trying to escape Christopher's reach. They probably don't want trouble."

"I hope that's the case," Tristan said. "But maybe we should scout along the other direction, see if we find a camp."

"What if we watch the trap?" Riley said. "They have to come get that fish eventually."

"Question: what do we do when we find them?" Allyssa asked. "Shouldn't we just stay here and keep moving in the morning?"

Riley understood Allyssa's stance. She was tempted to just stay in this spot too. But curiosity about the maker of that trap was too strong for her to let it go. She had to at least try to find out if they were friendly. Otherwise she would worry about them sneaking up on their group the whole night. "I think we should try to see them."

"Just to be safe," Demetrius said, looking at Allyssa. "We'll find out how many there are and see where they go. But don't engage with them."

"I'll go that way," Allyssa said, pointing the direction they hadn't investigated yet.

"No one's going alone," Tristan said.

"We're an odd number," Wyatt pointed out. "Unless we leave the horses and supplies alone, someone is on their own."

"I can go on my own," Demetrius said. "If I'm spotted I can make them forget they even saw me."

Riley looked at the others. Allyssa had already said she would go along the river. Should she go with her and leave the boys to watch the camp? Probably. Though it made her nervous to go scouting for people, it might make her feel better than just waiting with the horses and worrying about the others. And it was the right thing to do. "I'm coming with you," she said, looking at her friend.

Wyatt looked at her, silently asking if she was sure. She knew he would go in her place, because she would be more comfortable in the camp. But she shook her head minutely. She wanted to go with Allyssa.

"It's still hours before nightfall," Wyatt said. He looked at Demetrius. "If they don't show up by then, come back here. Or I'm coming after you."

Demetrius nodded and started walking in the direction of the fish trap.

"You think we can take the fish if the guy

doesn't come for it?" Wyatt asked.

"We wouldn't want it to die for nothing," Tristan said.

Allyssa mouthed *boys* to her as they walked in the opposite direction, and Riley smiled at her. They were quiet until the boys were out of sight, and then Allyssa spoke. "So you were really playing. It's been a while."

"And you finally got a decent challenge in a water fight, with Wyatt." Riley chuckled. "He's just as competitive as you are. I'm glad you suggested swimming. It was great to relax and have fun."

"We all needed it," Allyssa said. They walked several feet without comment, and then Allyssa glanced at Riley out of the corner of her eye. "You and Tristan seem pretty close now."

Riley just looked at her, waiting for her to continue. She knew there was more coming.

"It seems like there might be something there," Allyssa said gently, turning to look at her fully.

Riley's voice was quieter than she would have liked. "I've wondered if there was something there myself. But I won't risk losing anyone, and I definitely don't want to hurt anyone."

She hadn't known what she and Wyatt were to each other right before they'd come to Terraria. It had seemed like they were blurred between being friends and being in a romantic relationship. They hadn't had enough time together to make it clear which they really were. In the months they'd spent here as Tyler and Jane, they'd been best friends, and nothing more, and they'd been perfectly happy. Even though they'd had false identities, their personalities had been the same. Riley felt like she knew him better than she ever had before. And that, maybe, she liked it better this way.

As for Tristan . . . it didn't seem as complicated. He was *Tristan*. She felt her cheeks warm slightly.

"Maybe you have to take a risk to find something great," Allyssa said softly.

Riley glanced at her friend, letting her advice sink in. She stared at the reflected sunlight in the rippling water of the river. "When did you and Demetrius become a thing?"

Allyssa got a bounce in her step. "You did notice. I met him before we came here."

"When we were planning and training," Riley said, nodding. "I know he helped you with your wind powers."

"He definitely did. But we met before that. Those three Shifters you told me about that day at the Temple? They kind of kidnapped me."

Riley listened in a combination of horror and shock as Allyssa told her everything that had happened with hers and Demetrius' story. When Allyssa finished Riley hugged her tightly. "I'm sorry Christopher did all that, 'llyss."

They were quiet for a few more minutes as they looked around for signs of a camp, aware that they had just been a bit loud. There were trees every so often, small clumps of them and a few isolated ones. After walking for half an hour Allyssa went and cupped some water from the river, drinking it from her hands. Riley realized she was thirsty too and mimicked her. "How far do you think we should go?" she asked as they stood back up.

Allyssa looked into the distance. "Maybe past that next clump of trees?" she suggested.

"Sounds good. This does seem pretty far to walk for a fish. I haven't noticed any other traps." Riley had scanned the riverbank of every stretch they walked, and there had been no woven trap like the first one she'd found with Tristan.

They reached the clump of trees and carefully skirted between them, looking for signs of human life. Allyssa, being taller, looked in the trees while Riley looked around the trunks. She didn't see any bags or anything, but the grass around one tree looked different. Maybe it was flatter? A scan of the tree revealed a bluebird sitting on a branch. Riley tapped Allyssa's arm, gestured to the ruffled grass, and felt a sharp breeze shoot up the tree. The bluebird launched off the branch, flying away.

Allyssa looked in the direction the bird had flown. "Have you seen other birds outside their nests today?"

Riley hadn't. She'd also never paid much attention to birds. "Don't some birds like the rain?"

"I guess so."

They started walking back, very alert. Riley knew they both agreed that bluebird might be a Shifter. The question was, if it was a Shifter, was it someone Christopher had sent after them? There was a rustling sound behind them and they whirled around. Riley tensed and brought her hands up defensively. Was the bluebird closer than before?

"Someone's teasing us," Allyssa murmured as they turned around. Riley was on high alert now. She kept flicking her eyes around as they walked.

A few feet later Riley felt Allyssa tense next to her, and jumped as she heard the voice. "You girls are new at this, aren't y—aaah!" The Shifter was just touching the ground when Allyssa whirled around and pinned him to a tree, holding him there. Riley felt the wind start pushing against him as well.

"Was that better?" Allyssa asked in a cold voice. Riley stepped closer and looked at the boy they had pinned. He had black skin and was short and thin. He didn't look intimidating. He didn't look intimidated, either.

"So you're the wind Elementalist. I knew it was one of you." His accent made Riley guess he was from downstate, probably somewhere around New York City.

"Why did you follow us?" Allyssa asked, pressing him a little harder against the tree.

The boy looked at her questioningly. "Why were you looking for me? Are you from the Kingdom?"

Riley was taken aback. "No, we're not. Are you?"

"No." Allyssa moved fractionally and the boy sighed. "I get it. You don't trust me. My name's Tony. I don't have anything to do with the Kingdom."

"Then why are you here?"

"Fresh start. Nothing for me in the old world."

"You set a fish trap in the river?" Allyssa asked.

He had a little reaction to that, squirming. "Don't take my fish! I need that trap!"

Allyssa cast Riley a look. "Is this kid for real?"

"I'll show you how to make a trap; just leave me mine," Tony said, looking between them. "Can I go now?"

Allyssa hesitated. They hadn't even been supposed to talk to the kid, and now he was pinned to a tree, staring at them.

"Where are you staying?" Riley asked him.

He shrugged. "Don't have a place."

He looked much younger than them, and he was so skinny. He didn't seem to have anyone. "You should come with us and meet our friends," she said, softening her voice.

"As a prisoner or something?" he asked warily.

"As a friend," Riley said. She glanced at Allyssa, and the wind user stopped pinning Tony to the tree.

Tony shook himself. "How many of you are there? Are you all Elementalists?"

"Five. And yes, we're all Elementalists." Allyssa looked at Riley, silently warning her not to correct her.

"So what kind are you?" Tony asked Riley.

"Fire." It was true in a sense. She wasn't an Elementalist, but she definitely counted as a fire user.

"Sick!" Tony started a string of conversation

as they walked, and when he paused for a breath Riley chuckled. He sure made himself comfortable quickly. She wondered how the boys would react when they brought him back to the camp.

She hoped they didn't freak out.

Tristan hadn't been alone with Wyatt in a long time.

He could tell neither of them were particularly pleased with the arrangement. But Riley and Allyssa needed time to catch up, and if anyone was safe to go somewhere alone, it was Demetrius. Which left he and Wyatt to keep watch over the horses and their supplies.

"How are you doing?" Tristan asked, after several tense minutes of silence.

Wyatt couldn't hide his surprise. "Fine. You?"

"Swell."

Tristan rocked back on his heels.

"Have you been having any dreams from the dragon lately?"

Tristan's turn to be surprised. He thought back to the last few nights. "Nothing really. Are you having dreams from the griffin?"

Wyatt's shoulders tensed. "Some, since the day I lost control. Nightmares." He blinked hard. "Nothing I can use to help us find it any faster."

"We must be getting close to the waterfall. We found the river, and the terrain is changing to what I'd imagine it's like around a waterfall."

"Thanks for that useless pep talk."

Tristan clamped his jaw to keep from uttering an insult. They couldn't go more than a few sentences without turning on each other, when they were alone. He remembered Riley asking him why they didn't get along, ages ago, and telling her that either they were too similar, or too different.

Wyatt's sarcastic expression faded. "Sorry."

Tristan sat down. Wyatt followed suit, a few feet away. "Why did you leave the Temple?"

The question burst from Tristan, charged, before he could stop it. Wyatt looked at him evenly. "Jordan had a lot to handle, running it by herself and raising you and the others."

Tristan stared at him. "That can't be the only reason."

He remembered when Wyatt had trained with him. The boy hadn't lived in the Temple, but he'd come every weekday for lessons, for years. They'd sparred together, eaten meals together, studied together. They'd argued. But it had never felt like it did now. That change happened when Wyatt decided he didn't want to train at the Temple.

"I wanted more of a challenge," Wyatt said.

"Jordan could have given you more challenging practice, if you'd just asked. She would have found someone to teach you the martial arts you loved. She would've worked to learn them herself, just so she could keep working with you."

"Why does it bother you so much?"

"Because it hurt her!" Tristan cried. He had bits of grass and coarse soil in his fists, and flexed his hands to drop the debris. "She cared about you as more than a student, and it felt like a betrayal when you left us!"

He sucked in a breath. All these years he'd never realized why he seemed to hate Wyatt so much. And in one moment . . . *you left us* . . .

Wyatt seemed as stunned as Tristan, his mouth open. "I didn't mean it like that," he whispered.

Tristan swallowed and set his eyes on the ground.

"I'm sorry."

The apology was more sincere than most of what Wyatt had said to him in the last year. It made it harder to fight back the burning behind his eyes that talking about Jordan had started. "Thanks," he managed.

Neither of them seemed to know what to do next, but the silence wasn't tense this time.

Wyatt took the offensive when Riley and Allyssa walked back into view with a boy they didn't know keeping pace between them. Wyatt stood as if ready to fight. Tristan figured their companion wasn't looking for an altercation, and stood calmly. "You made a friend," he greeted.

Riley spoke first. "Tristan, this is Tony. Tony, Tristan. And that's Wyatt." She faced Tristan and Wyatt. "Tony is a Shifter. A bluebird. He's here alone, and doesn't want attention from the Kingdom."

Allyssa looked in the direction they'd seen Demetrius go earlier. "I'll get Demetrius."

Wyatt stared at Tony. "What'd you do to not want attention?"

"I never belonged to the Kingdom," Tony said. "What about you?"

"It's complicated," Wyatt said.

"How old are you?" Tristan asked.

"Fourteen, thank you very much," Tony said.

"You're fourteen?" Tristan had been thinking twelve or thirteen maybe, but he was so small. It wasn't like the twins, who genuinely looked much younger. Tony was skinny as a rail, with a short, stunted look. Tristan wondered what his life had been like before coming here, and when the last time he'd had a nice meal had been. "Are you hungry?"

"Starving."

Riley opened their food bag and pulled out a piece of fruit, throwing it to him.

"You can help us make traps after," Wyatt told him.

Tony shrugged, inhaled the food, and walked over to the horses. "Where'd you get these? They're so cool! I've never been this close to a horse before!"

"He's excitable, isn't he?" Tristan asked Riley.

"He barely stopped talking the whole walk here. He talks so fast." Riley was watching him pet Hermes with Wyatt. "I think we can trust him. And he could use some help."

"We'll see what Demetrius says." Part of Tristan—the part that was comparing Tony to the twins—wanted to make Tony stay with them, so he wouldn't be alone. Another part realized that it would be dangerous for him to do so. He would be safer on his own. He also seemed to like his independence, and might not want to accompany them.

"Oh, we told him we're Elementalists," Riley said in an even quieter voice. "So go along with it."

"Clever."

"It was Allyssa's idea."

Tony was talking to Wyatt now, and Tristan noticed with amusement that Wyatt's cold front had dissipated. He was grinning as Tony told him something about himself, gesticulating wildly. Allyssa and Demetrius came back, and Tony had only just turned to face them when he stopped, his expression frozen. Demetrius walked closer to him, looking at him intently.

"So?" Allyssa asked. "Can we trust him?"

Demetrius was quiet for a few more seconds and then nodded. "He doesn't have any plan to betray us. He has no idea who we are." He looked back at Allyssa and Tony reanimated, as if nothing had happened. Tristan fought to keep his expression neutral, once again amazed at the extent of what Demetrius could do. Tony had no idea what had just happened. He was freaking out over the fact that Demetrius had purple eyes. Demetrius held up the trap. "So this belongs to you."

"Sick! Dinner time!" Tony grabbed the trap and opened it, looking inside.

"Not quite yet," Wyatt said. "First you need to teach us how to make one of those. Who's the best at weaving?"

Tony walked by each of them, looking at their hands. "Wyatt and Allyssa have the longest fingers. Anyone made a trap before?" Everyone shook their heads. "Then you two should try it first. I'll show you where I got the material."

"Any chance you know how to make a trap for something besides fish?" Wyatt asked.

Tristan heard Tony say, "nope," as he led Wyatt and Allyssa off. He wouldn't mind eating meat other than fish either, but he didn't look forward to having to prep any meat they got from now on. They'd finished what they took from the market, which was already sliced and ready to be cooked. He thought he'd be able to stomach preparing a fish to be eaten better than something like a rabbit. He could probably handle a bird.

"What are you thinking about?"

Tristan jarred from his musing at Demetrius' question. "Food."

Demetrius exhaled a laugh. "Understandable. We've been traveling by the river for several days; having a trap or two that we can set out when we stop each day might help us have some fresh meat regularly."

"What do you think of asking Tony to stay with us?"

"I think, on a temporary basis, it's a good idea. Until we find another settlement and can try to convince him to stay there."

Tristan could see that Riley agreed. He

thought again of Ash and Alice, and then of Noah. He couldn't get back to them yet, but he could look after Tony for a little while.

CHAPTER 15

Try, Try, Try

Ash kind of missed their hotel suite. Kind of. He liked staying at the Temple, too, so it was hard to decide which he liked more. Though the hotel had had a pool . . . .

Emily had asked Pat and the Guardian of this Temple, Lori, if they could stay until the trial was over, and they'd gone to the hotel suite the day they'd played in the park to retrieve their stuff. Ash thought maybe Emily was a little scared Match would reach out to her if they stayed in the suite, since Match had arranged it for them. Maybe she felt safer staying somewhere else.

Ash was just glad Emily was okay. And Alice. He wasn't keen to let anyone out of his sight for the remainder of their stay in D.C., but he knew that was too much to ask. It was a relief knowing they were all in the Temple, though. Noah was thrilled to have access to a full gym again, and a computer lab.

Ash was pretty amused in the Temple too. Their library had a decent comic book collection in addition to the Shifting novels and standard library fare, and Ash made it a personal goal to read as much of it as possible. He had plenty of time in the early mornings and evenings, so in the remaining days leading up to the trial, he got through a good number of them. With Noah going back to his gym routine, and Alice spending so much time with Havier, Ash had to do something to keep himself entertained.

They met with the prosecuting attorney, Amelia, very briefly, in the Temple. She asked them to go over what happened, and after hearing their stories, told them that if they said it just like that during the trial, it would be over quickly. She seemed nice enough.

Ash clutched one of the borrowed comic books close that night. Tomorrow they would go the courtroom. Tomorrow they would see their father. It was strange feeling so apprehensive. The odds were he wouldn't even have to speak to his father. Even the thought of seeing him made Ash's stomach turn, and he hated it. Noah wouldn't be feeling like this. He seemed to be anticipating the trial. Alice was somewhere in the middle, as was Emily. It was only Ash that felt weak about it. That feared going and seeing the man that had led to so much loss, and reliving everything.

This issue featured one of his favorite heroes being put on trial. It seemed like they would wrongly convict, and then everything worked out. In this case, there was no chance it would be bad. Michael was already set to do jail time. This trial would just determine how long that would be.

Ash opened the comic book and settled into bed, trying to take comfort in the pages. When he turned out the light and went to sleep, he still couldn't tell if it had worked.

Ash decided to stay in the adjacent room when he wasn't needed during the trial. It was a last minute decision. Alice could tell he wanted her to stay with him, but she needed to see it.

Really, she needed to see *him*. Michael Dawes.

Ash would be fine. An Official was assigned to protect him, and Pat had offered to stay with him as well. Alice walked into the main courtroom behind Emily and Noah, her eyes scanning the room. There were more people than she'd expected, on both sides of the audience. Many began whispering when people saw Emily, Noah, and Alice walk in. Apparently they'd heard Dawes' family would be testifying against him.

The prosecuting attorney they'd met the day before sat behind one long table in the front section. Two men sat behind the other, and when the audience quieted and then started whispering, the men turned in their direction.

Alice saw Noah tense. She tensed herself, and felt an overwhelming wave of hatred inside. One of the men was clearly Michael. He had a long, thick scar down one side of his face, from Noah's claws. There was a scar near his lip on that same side, slightly pulling at his mouth. He seemed thinner than he'd been last year. Otherwise, sitting at that table, he looked fine. Alice raged when his eyes landed on her, but didn't look away. She made him be the one to do that.

Emily's gentle hand settled on Alice's shoulder, as she wordlessly drew Alice toward a bench. They would be in the audience until they were needed on the stand. Alice sat on the firm bench, her eyes locked on the back of Michael's head.

"Relax, chica," Havier murmured next to her.

"It's his fault my mother died," she responded.

He lost his partial smile in an instant. "Sorry. I didn't know."

She glanced at him. He really didn't know. Their meeting with the prosecuting attorney had been in private, and all they'd told Havier and the other residents of the Temple was that they were helping in a trial against their father. She tried to lessen the intensity of her scowl. "You'll hear everything in a few minutes."

Alice had never been to a trial. She'd only seen the inside of a courtroom on TV shows and movies. In those cases, a lot of the proceedings were skipped. Alice wished she could skip through most of the trial. She kept fidgeting, moving her feet and holding her hands in her lap. She had too much pent up adrenaline and rage to stay still. She marveled at the fact that Emily barely moved. It seemed like the woman became a statue, actually, sitting perfectly straight with her eyes locked forward. Apparently it was a family trait, because Alice remembered Jordan being so rigid a few times, under extreme stress.

Opening statements were made, through which Michael remained silent. Emily was called to the stand as the first witness, and questioned by prosecution and defense. Then Brigs, the officer who'd first arrived at the scene last year. Then Noah.

Alice couldn't see Noah's hands when he sat next to the judge, but she knew he was holding fistfuls of his pant legs from the way his arms were strained. He was trying incredibly hard not to partially Shift. It seemed like it took all of his willpower, but he did manage it. That part didn't shock her. What shocked her was the pain that was evident in his voice, beneath the anger. Others in the room might not have heard it. Alice certainly did. She thought Emily did as well, because her statuesque posture faltered.

"Do you want me to get your brother?" Havier asked when they told Noah he could take his seat.

Alice nodded, and Havier slipped away.

Noah scooted past Alice and sat down. Emily leaned toward him and murmured that he'd done a good job. Noah merely nodded. Alice heard motion on her other side and turned to see Havier sitting back down on the bench. "They said they would send someone to retrieve him when the prosecution needs him," he said quickly. "I didn't want to make him come early."

Amelia turned to look at Alice, and raised her eyebrows questioningly. Alice squared her shoulders and dipped her head. She could do this.

"The prosecution calls Alice Dawes to the stand."

"Stay focused," Noah said in a low voice.

As if she could be anything else right now. She moved past Havier and into the aisle, then up toward the front of the courtroom. She slowed for a moment, when she walked by her father, extremely aware of his gaze on her. Then she sped up and walked to the stand. She swore to tell the truth and sat down.

"She's a minor," the defense attorney said.

"Well spotted," the prosecutor said. "Her legal guardian is present. And Miss Dawes is my most reliable witness, next to her twin."

"Proceed," the judge said.

Amelia turned to face Alice. "Miss Dawes, please tell the jury your relationship to the defendant."

"He's my father," Alice said. "But I only met him last year."

"If you would, explain to the jury the circumstances around Michael Dawes' appearance in your life."

Exactly as she'd done the day before, Alice stated everything from Michael's arrival at the Temple to him drugging she and Ash, kidnapping them, and setting a trap for Tristan that resulted in Jordan's death. Her throat threatened to close up once, when she described how the fire user had killed Jordan. It took several seconds for her to be able to finish that statement, and she could only do so by looking at the floor by Amelia's feet. She glanced at Michael and saw him staring at her, and the renewed grief trying to block her words was banished by a wave of fury so strong she partially Shifted.

She forced herself to look directly at the man, focusing on the scars across the side of his face.

"He came into our lives because my brother is the dragon, and because of his quest for power, he ruined everything."

Michael finally looked down, and Alice let herself peek at her family. Emily seemed to be close to tears. Noah was staring daggers at Michael's back. Alice's gaze flitted to Havier, and the absolute rage she saw there caught her off guard.

"No further questions," Amelia said.

"Defense?" the judge asked.

The defense attorney stood. "Miss Dawes, you admitted that prior to last year you hadn't met your father?"

"I mean, I guess he saw me as an infant, but last summer was the first time I remember meeting him."

"Would you say you were angry with him from the start?"

Alice felt her eyes narrow. "He was never a father to us."

"That doesn't answer my question."

"Yes, I was angry with him from the start. He clearly only showed up because he knew Tristan is a Celestial."

The defense attorney paused. "Would you say your anger toward your father colored your perception of events? Is it possible that the fight at the Maine residence, and the death of your legal guardian, wasn't his fault?"

Alice had been close to dropping her Shift, but these words ignited the aura around her with an even fiercer energy. "It was absolutely his fault! You've heard multiple witnesses tell you everything he did!" She glared at the scars on Michael's face. "He may not have killed Jordan himself, but his actions led to her death. They enabled my brother and Riley to be kidnapped and tortured by those same Elementalists Michael worked with."

"Enough," Michael said.

Alice had been leaning forward in her seat, more words ready to fly from her mouth. It was the first thing she'd heard Michael say all day. His attorney looked at him and seemed to frown, then nodded. "Very well. The defense rests."

Alice turned to the judge. "Don't make Ash testify," she pleaded. "He doesn't have anything different to tell the jury."

The judge looked at Amelia. "I see no reason to call him in," Amelia said.

"Do you have any other witnesses?" the judge asked.

Amelia looked at Michael. "I'd like to question the defendant now."

The judge waved a hand to signal for Michael to get up. He took several seconds to rise and walked with a slow, deliberate pace. Maybe he did have more than the scarring and being deaf in one ear. Alice walked by him as quickly as she could, and was back on her bench before Michael reached the stand. He swore to remain honest and sat next to the judge, and Amelia asked him a question immediately.

"Mr. Dawes, do you have any explanation for your actions last summer?"

"None that hasn't already been stated."

The defense attorney made a choked sound. Alice turned to Emily. He'd just admitted to everything, right?

"You knowingly kidnapped two of your children, helped Elementalists trespass on Nation property, and encouraged a battle between Elementalists and Shifters at the site?"

Michael looked at Alice again, expressionless. "I did."

The defense attorney put his head in his hands. The judge looked at Michael critically. "You were pleading not guilty at the beginning of the trial."

"Oh, I'm definitely guilty," Michael said. His voice lowered. "I can't pretend I'm not, after hearing all of that. Maybe this will help make up for some of what I've done."

Havier launched to his feet. "Pleading guilty doesn't mean a damn!" he yelled. His round cheeks flushed. "You're still acting in your own best interest, probably hoping to get a better sentence! It doesn't make it up to them!"

The audience started murmuring, and several of the jurors moved as if to talk to each other. The judge banged her gavel once. "Order! Young man, sit down. If the defendant is changing his plea to guilty, there's no reason to continue with the questioning." She looked at a man who'd been sitting in the audience, and the man walked over to Michael and grabbed his wrist. "Michael Dawes, you are hereby guilty of two counts of kidnapping, trespassing, assault, and accessory to the murder of Jordan Raines, which Enid Hospes was found guilty of earlier this week. You will be escorted immediately to a transfer vehicle and taken to a penitentiary, where you will serve out your sentence. This trial is officially concluded."

Alice's palms were slick with sweat. Her ears seemed to be ringing. It was over, just like that? He'd looked right at her when he confessed. She'd wanted to react like Havier had, but had been too shocked to outwardly react at all.

"I hope he rots in there," Noah said, standing.

"He'll be in jail for the rest of his life," Emily

told them. She touched Noah and Alice's shoulders. "I know how difficult this was for you, and I'm extremely proud of how well you did."

"For once I wasn't the one to lose my temper," Noah said, a bit of levity entering his voice.

Alice almost smiled. She'd taken care of that. Well, she and Havier. The teen was standing at the end of their bench, waiting for them. "Let's go get Ash," Alice said. "I'm sure he's anxious for news."

"Then back to the Temple?" Noah asked.

Emily put her purse over her shoulder and reached inside, pulling out her phone. "Unless you want to go to the park again, to de-stress." She frowned at her phone. "Matt called me."

They walked out of the courtroom and found Ash just leaving the adjacent room. Alice, Noah, and Havier filled him in while Emily listened to a voicemail from Matt, and everyone turned to look at Emily when she put her phone away.

"Is something wrong?" Ash asked.

Emily's eyebrows were close together. "No, but I need to call Matt back. He said he thinks he has a lead on how to get Riley, Tristan, and Allyssa back."

CHAPTER 16

The Griffin's Den

Wyatt's nightmares were getting worse.

The griffin was plaguing his sleep with memories and imagined scenarios that were equally convincing. He kept seeing himself with a partial Shift, using his gift to control Riley and make her follow him. He also saw himself using the gift against the others, freezing them in fear before attacking. Insecurities and fears played before his closed eyes each night in incredible detail, and he woke with a start multiple times. He knew the others were starting to notice. When he woke up from a particularly bad dream the night before with a muffled shout, he knew Tristan heard him, though the boy didn't say anything.

There were bags forming under Wyatt's eyes, apparent even in glances at his reflection in the river. He felt his temper get just a bit shorter. They had to find the griffin soon.

Riley was having nightmares as well. He hadn't been able to tell if Demetrius and Allyssa woke after his muffled shout last night, but both Tristan and Riley had heard it. He'd seen Tristan jerk awake. Riley had already been sitting up, her arms wrapped tight around her legs and her head down. He couldn't be sure, but Wyatt thought he heard a hitch in her breath like she was trying not to cry.

He'd wanted to go over to her and comfort her, but worried she would get the wrong idea. The conversation they'd had a few days before played over in his mind.

"Wyatt," Riley said in a timid voice. "We should talk."

"Sounds like I'm in trouble," he said, trying to make her laugh. Her mouth twitched in a smile that faded quickly, and he shook his head. "You don't have to say anything. I know."

Those dark blue eyes widened. "You're thinking the same thing?"

He hesitated for only a second. So short a time he wasn't sure she picked up on it. "I hate that Christopher erased our real lives for all those months, but getting to spend them with you is one positive that came from it. I got to know you, to bond with you, in a real, meaningful way that we never had before. As a friend." He reached out to take her hand, as he'd done so many times when they'd lived as Jane and Tyler. "We don't need to feel pressured or obligated to be anything more."

She looked at him searchingly. "I didn't know how to bring it up without hurting you, but if you've been thinking it too—"

He squeezed her hand. "I've been thinking I like being your friend," he said in a clear voice. "We never got much past that step before anyway, and there's no need to go past that step now."

She partially smiled. Wyatt thought there was a tinge of sadness to it, but maybe that was wishful thinking. He knew she cared about him, for him. He also knew it wasn't the same way he cared about her, for her. Maybe it would be different if they hadn't spent those months as best friends, but he doubted it. He'd seen the way she acted with Tristan when they'd come to train at Christopher's house. He'd noticed how easily she smiled with Tristan, while Wyatt had to try for a blushing smile. He couldn't even be mad at Tristan, because Tristan wasn't doing anything wrong. He was clearly falling for Riley, just like Wyatt was, though Tristan was doing nothing to act on it.

Since Demetrius had restored their memories, he'd seen the question in her eyes concerning what they were to each other. She had no poker face. She didn't want to hurt him. He decided to tell a little white lie, so she wouldn't have to worry about it anymore.

Did he really just want to be friends?

No.

Did he really want her to be happy?

Definitely.

Honestly, if he'd gone to comfort her he might have given himself the wrong idea.

If he'd known Christopher would make the Celestials give them nightmares, he would have tried looking for the phoenix first, to spare Riley. Once it was free of Christopher's influence it wouldn't send her nightmares. They'd come this far, though, and he felt something in his chest when they started moving that morning. Something like a cord inside him.

"We're close," he said.

The others looked at him questioningly. "You can feel it, can't you?" Demetrius guessed, and Wyatt nodded. It wasn't a feeling like he had to move forward. It wasn't controlling. But he could sense the power of the griffin, relatively close.

"Close to what? Whadda you feel?" Tony asked around a mouth full of food. Wyatt didn't think Tony had gone more than two hours without eating at least a bite of something. No wonder he was a bluebird.

It was time to tell him what they were really doing. He hadn't asked any questions about their progress since he'd started traveling with them, and they hadn't offered any answers. Wyatt had thought Tony would demand to know everything about their lives, but the kid didn't search for sensitive information. He did however ask all about their hobbies. And their food preferences, and their talents, and just about anything else that popped into his head. When he wasn't flying near them in his bluebird form, he kept up a general chatter that made Wyatt kind of miss the quiet they had when he Shifted. Though having him around did add a new energy to the group, which was a welcome change.

"We've been looking for the griffin."

Tony's expression seemed stuck between interest and disbelief. "One of the Celestials? Why?"

"It's a long story," Riley said.

Tristan climbed onto his horse. "We'll tell it as we ride."

Tony Shifted and flew very close to them while they explained. Chitter the chipmunk kept looking at Tony whenever he flew near Tristan, quizzically. It was impossible to tell Tony's reaction like this, but Wyatt thought he took it well enough. He didn't fly off or anything.

They'd only just finished telling Tony the

truth when the waterfall came into view. A massive mountain of gray stone with water gushing from its peak, the waterfall was as beautiful as when Wyatt had seen it in the mirror. He could hear the roar from where they stood. Everyone seemed as entranced as he felt. The spray from the water on the rocks made a mist that shimmered in the morning sun. The pure force of the water that ran from the top . . . it was quite the spot for a nest.

"Okay," Tristan said. "I get the griffin having its nest here."

Allyssa stood tense. "There aren't any guards."

"My father might have told guards living in this region to steer clear. No one seemed to know where the griffin kept its nest. Perhaps that's because it's hidden in plain sight. Guards stationed around it would be a red flag."

"We might still have a lead on the guards behind us," Riley said. "We should take advantage of it."

Wyatt was already looking for the best way to approach. He could tell the griffin was in its den, at the top. It was agile enough to scale the waterfall with ease. Wyatt doubted they would be able to climb it very quickly. "Any chance you could boost us up?" he asked Allyssa.

She studied the waterfall. "Not all at once, but

yeah."

Both Riley and Demetrius started to object. "She can do it," Wyatt said.

"I know you *can*, I just don't know if you *should*," Riley said. "It's really high."

Allyssa half-smiled. "That's the challenge. I've got this, Ry. So who's in the first group?"

"One more second," Tristan said. He turned to Tony. "I'm sorry we lied about who we are, but now that you know the truth, you realize how dangerous this is. The griffin can probably sense Wyatt, the same way he can sense it. It knows we're coming, and it's waiting for us. I want you to stay down here."

Tony glared at him, and then at everyone else when they nodded in agreement. "I'm not a little kid."

"No, but you don't need to be put in danger like this," Tristan said. "Plus, we really do need someone to keep watch over the horses, and make sure guards don't sneak up on us. You can Shift and come warn us if anyone's coming."

Wyatt could see Tony reasoning through what Tristan had said, trying to determine if he was being genuine or making an excuse. Even Wyatt couldn't tell, though he suspected Tristan was more concerned with Tony being safe than being a sentry. Tony didn't look happy about it, but he plopped down and set his gaze in the direction they'd come.

Tristan returned his attention to Allyssa. "Demetrius needs to be in the first group, to start undoing Christopher's spell. I'm going too, to defend him."

It occurred to Wyatt that this arrangement left him in the second group. He tensed. "I need to go first."

"Too risky," Tristan said. "You can't Shift yet."

Wyatt bristled and opened his mouth to retort, but Demetrius was faster. "I don't know how being so close to the griffin will impact you. It might be able to control you." He put a hand on Wyatt's shoulder. "Let Tristan come with me first. You'll only be seconds behind, but it'll be enough for me to start freeing the griffin."

Wyatt clenched his jaw and nodded tersely, and watched Allyssa, Tristan, and Demetrius rise into the air. They hovered for several seconds before they ascended, moving steadily up the side of the waterfall.

"He isn't trying to take your place or anything," Riley whispered. "If the Celestials can control us when we get close, and you went first, we could end up fighting both you and the griffin."

"I get it," Wyatt said. "I just want to be up

there."

The three neared the top of the waterfall and landed on a tiny ledge. Wyatt watched Demetrius and Tristan climb the remaining feet to the cave entrance. Allyssa waited until they disappeared before gliding back to ground level. "Ready?" she asked. She didn't really wait for an answer, buoying herself, Riley, and Wyatt up. It was strange feeling the air pressing against his feet, but also exciting. This was as close to flying as he would ever get, since the griffin didn't have wings.

They kind of fell onto the ledge. Allyssa stumbled, breathing heavily. Riley moved to her side in concern. Wyatt scrambled up the rocks and stepped into the cave. Cave? Cavern? He wasn't sure exactly what to call it, because it wasn't very deep. He also wasn't worried about the terminology.

He was more concerned with Tristan and Demetrius, standing frozen before the griffin as it rushed them.

Tristan partially Shifted and walked in front of Demetrius, bracing himself to fend off an attack. They walked in without issue, though. The griffin stood near the back of its den. Its tufted ears were pricked. Intimidating talons tensed on the rocky floor. Its lion tail swished once.

That was all Tristan had time to notice before the griffin moved. It took a step closer and snapped its eyes on Demetrius. They seemed to swirl, with multiple colors, and Demetrius made a choked sound and drew back. Tristan ran forward, raising his arm to strike. That was when the griffin turned its eyes on him. Tristan paid it no mind, continuing forward.

At least, he tried.

When the griffin's eyes locked on his, he staggered to a stop. Its eyes did swirl. He dimly recalled how Wyatt's had looked back in Kin Woods. One beat of his hammering pulse banished the memory and brought him back to the present. He couldn't look away, and he was staring into a nightmare. He dropped his Shift faster than he ever had. His throat felt dry, and it was hard to keep his knees from shaking. How could he have been charging the griffin a moment before? He didn't have the strength to defeat a Celestial. He couldn't bring himself to take another step closer, knowing if he tried to move he would curl into a fetal position.

The griffin stalked closer, and Tristan felt his body start trembling.

Something collided with his side and almost knocked him over. The moment he stumbled, placing a hand to the floor to stay standing, the paralyzing fear and doubt vanished. He looked over to see Wyatt facing the griffin. Tristan breathed in, feeling strength flow back through him.

"You okay?" Wyatt asked.

Tristan focused on Wyatt, not daring to look at the griffin again. "Fine."

He saw Demetrius move in his periphery, straightening. The griffin moved insanely quickly, forcefully stopping its staring match with Wyatt and lunging toward Demetrius. Tristan just had time to move into its path. He managed to keep it from reaching Demetrius. He failed to do anything to defend himself, and cried out when the griffin's talons slashed across his skin.

"Leave them alone!" Wyatt roared.

The griffin spun to face Wyatt again. *Stand down, little one.*

Wyatt glared at it and partially Shifted. At first it was mostly yellow, and then other colors appeared, and the gold and brown and white aura burned around him. His eyes swirled so intensely, his features so forceful, that Tristan was surprised the griffin didn't take a step back.

"Demetrius, now!" Tristan urged.

"You won't hurt anyone else," Wyatt said.

They seemed to be at a standstill for several tense heartbeats, and then the griffin flinched.

Leave my mind alone!

It went to move, but Wyatt stayed directly in front of it. A snake charmer keeping the danger just contained enough, Wyatt had the griffin cornered. It couldn't stop its defense, or Wyatt would influence it, but in focusing on Wyatt, Demetrius had an easier time getting into its head. Tristan had been a fool to think he would be enough to protect Demetrius. He was sure if Wyatt hadn't come bursting in, he would be as good as dead.

One of the griffin's front legs gave out. Wyatt stepped closer, and the griffin's other front leg went down, so it looked like it was bowing. It lowered itself so it was lying on the floor and rested its head over its front legs.

Wyatt stood in the same position for a few more seconds before dropping his partial Shift.

"That was incredible," Tristan said.

Wyatt continued looking at the griffin. "I didn't know the griffin's gift worked on you. You're impervious to Christopher and Demetrius' power."

Tristan hadn't known it would work on him either. "It must be different with the Celestials' power. Having a thick skull doesn't protect me from the griffin's gift, because the Celestials are all connected." He remembered the total loss of control, and how weak and terrified he'd felt.

"That power . . . it's really something. The way you stared the griffin down—I felt that power, even though it wasn't directed at me." He swallowed. "It was something to see."

"I've hated that gift since I found out I'm the griffin, but you make it sound like it's a good thing."

Tristan tenderly touched his chest where the griffin had scratched him, inspecting his hand to see how much blood came away. "I don't think it's something to hate. Just something to be careful with. The same goes for all of our powers. It doesn't take much action in the wrong direction to make a power seem like a curse. But a few actions in the right direction, and a power can change everything for the better."

Tristan hadn't liked the griffin's gift when he first learned about it. Seeing Riley so completely under Wyatt's thrall hadn't sat right. He definitely didn't like experiencing it, feeling the terror it inspired. But he could kind of appreciate it, now. The griffin was resourceful. It was calculating. That gift was its way of keeping things under control, and in certain situations, that was invaluable.

Wyatt walked over to him. "How badly did it get you?"

Tristan dropped his hand. "I'm fine." He felt like he might have been starting to convince

Wyatt that the gift could be a good thing, and pointing out that his chest was searing where the griffin's talons had slashed him probably wouldn't help his efforts. He needed to wash out the cuts when they were done. The sting would fade in time.

"Are you okay in there?" Allyssa called.

"We're good," Wyatt called back. "Demetrius is working on it now."

The girls appeared at the entrance of the den. "Wow," Allyssa said, looking at the griffin. "It's so weird that it isn't that weird!"

Wyatt's eyebrows pressed together. "What?"

"You know. It's an eagle and a lion mashed together. Seems like it would look weird, but it just looks cool."

"I think you're becoming Tony."

Riley walked over to them, and after inspecting the griffin and Demetrius, looked at Wyatt and Tristan. Tristan crossed his arms over his chest, trying to hide the scratches. "We heard Wyatt yell," Riley said, "but we didn't want to distract you by coming in. What happened?"

"Wyatt had a stare-down with the griffin, and won," Tristan said.

"He saved us both."

Everyone turned at Demetrius' voice.

"I removed my father's influence over its mind," he continued. "Once I started, it didn't fight me. It actually supported me, realizing it had been under a spell. The griffin hates to be controlled."

Wyatt walked up and clapped a hand on Demetrius' back. "You got through to it just in time. It couldn't touch me when I Shifted because it was too busy fighting you."

Tristan hadn't realized the risk Wyatt had taken to Shift. He also hadn't appreciated that the first time Wyatt stared the griffin down, he did it without his powers.

"Allyssa, are you okay now?" Wyatt asked.

She rolled her eyes. "I needed a minute or two to get some energy back. No worries."

Wyatt partially Shifted, and softly smiled, looking at the aura around him. "I've missed this."

The griffin was getting to its feet, stretching forward. *I'm sorry for the pain I caused. And I thank you for freeing me.*

A triumphant energy surged inside Tristan. For so many days they'd been traveling, wondering if they were even on the right track, and now . . . the scales had been tipped. "Griffin, where are the others?"

I no longer have a connection to Christopher

Thrane. When I sensed you coming I warned him, and he put the dragon under watch. The phoenix is near. It was trying to come to me, but you were closer than we expected.

"Christopher probably felt his control over the griffin break," Riley said. "He might have wanted the phoenix to help the griffin, knowing we couldn't face two at once. When he felt his control break, he probably told the phoenix to stop. He'll make it stay away from us."

We have to find it and give it control over its own mind, the griffin said.

"Of course we're going to free it," Tristan said, "but if we blindly try to find it, we could stumble around for weeks. Meanwhile, Christopher can send every guard he has after us, and then we're trapped."

"We need to find the dragon," Wyatt said. "And I have a feeling Christopher has it near the castle."

You continue with your plan. I will continue with mine. I will find the phoenix, and we will reconvene at the castle. Shadow user, you must be ready to erase your father's mark from the phoenix.

"Shouldn't we stay together?" Allyssa asked. "What if something happens to you?"

The griffin didn't use its gift, but its stare was intimidating even without it. *I am stronger than you believe, wind user.* It walked to the entrance of the den. *I will meet you at the castle, with the phoenix.*

Its legs tensed and the griffin sprang from the den. Tristan rushed forward to see it scaling the waterfall's edge, lithely jumping between cracks on the slick rocks. Wyatt ran after it.

"Wait!" Riley called.

"You can't just leave like that!" Wyatt yelled to the griffin. He slipped and had to use his hands to keep himself from falling, then continued. He was definitely agile, but the griffin had practice scaling the side of the waterfall. Wyatt seemed to be barely controlling himself, more aiming short falls than jumping. Tristan could feel the spray of the water here, and knew it would be treacherously slippery where Wyatt was.

"Allyssa, please get him before he gets hurt!" Riley said.

"On it."

Allyssa jumped from the mouth of the den and made a breeze carry her to Wyatt, and the boy was buoyed in the air before she began lowering them both to the ground.

Tristan turned to look at Riley. "See? Everything's fine."

Of course he didn't actually finish saying it, because while he was turning to face her his foot slipped. He lost his balance, his body leaning backwards. Riley reached for his hand, but he was much too heavy for her to lift up on her own. He was already falling. Only now, he was pulling her with him. He saw Demetrius' stunned expression, and his extended hand, too far away to reach.

He fell down the waterfall, Riley falling beside him. He heard Allyssa cry out when they passed her in the air, and saw Wyatt's shock for an instant. Tristan was screaming, mostly in surprise at the rushing sensation of falling. Riley was screaming in absolute terror. However scary this was for him, it wasn't a deep-seated fear like it was for Riley. He couldn't let her fall alone, and mastered himself for an instant.

Just long enough to wrap his arms around her as they plummeted toward the water, holding her tightly as she screamed.

CHAPTER 17

Apply Yourself

Emily convinced the kids that they should all go to the park before returning to the Temple. Even if they left now, they had to find a car, and with traffic they wouldn't get back to Saratoga until extremely late. If they went straight back to the local Temple, she had a feeling they would all be tense and uncomfortable. The late afternoon sunshine would do them good.

It was doing her some good. She was forcing herself not to call Matt and Derek yet. To stay in the moment, walking around with Ash, Alice, Noah, and Havier.

It didn't last long, though. She couldn't get her mind off of Matt's message. Noah was the one to call her out on it. "You're not going to enjoy yourself until you call him back," he said.

She almost smiled. "You're right. Do you want

to stay here for a little longer, though?"

"He might know how to get Tristan and Riley back," Ash said. "We can go to a park anytime. Let's go find out what he has to say!"

Emily went straight to the room she'd stayed in the last few nights when they reached the Temple. She'd promised to tell the kids whatever she learned from the call right after, but she wanted a little privacy. Her first priority was Matt's message, but she also needed to talk to Derek. She hadn't told him everything that had really happened with Match, and the resulting discussion with President Summers.

She tried Matt's cell first, then Derek's. Derek answered. "Hi Em."

Warmth rushed through her. "Oh man, I miss you and Matt."

"We miss you too. How was the trial? It's done, right?"

"Yeah, it's done, but before I tell you about it, is Matt there?"

"He's passed out in the common room. He's been picking up shifts like crazy lately, and crashing hard whenever he's home."

"Have you talked to him about the portal?"

Derek paused. "No. Why? Did you learn something?"

Emily tried to hide her disappointment. "No. Matt might have a lead on how to open it. I'll just have to talk to him tomorrow. We're coming home in the morning."

"So the trial is done, then. Completely."

Emily sat down on the bed and grinned. "Completely finished." She told him everything about the trial. Then she told him everything about Match.

She could hear Derek seething on the other side of the phone. "This is why I didn't want you to go alone!"

"I'm pretty sure it would have happened whether you came with us or not," she said. "And you and I both know you had an important reason to stay."

He wouldn't calm about this for some time, she knew, but she heard him take a slow, deep breath and knew he was trying to process it later. "You're okay now?"

"I'm absolutely fine," she said. "It was just those two memories that were altered, and they're fixed now. I trust President Summers." She hesitated. "Which is why I'm thinking of accepting an offer she made me."

"What offer?"

"To be her Shifter advisor. She really wants peace, Derek. She wants to work to make the gradual changes that will help Shifters and Elementalists, and thinks this is a great first step. And she asked me. She promised it's a job that can be done remotely most of the time."

He was quiet. "That's a big decision. It doesn't mean it's not a good one." He was quiet again. Emily let him think. She'd had days to consider, and she'd only just decided she wanted to do it that morning. She needed to know what Derek thought, though. This did concern their family.

"I think it's the right call," she said in a quiet voice.

"Then you need to do it," he said immediately. "I needed to hear you say it. As long as you think it's the right thing, I'm behind you one hundred percent."

Emily found herself smiling. "I love you."

Alice, Ash, and Noah waited in the kitchen while Emily went to call Matt. Havier had gone to run an errand with Pat, and Noah was currently scouring the refrigerator for a snack.

"Hope they're getting groceries," Noah grumbled. "There's nothing good in here."

Alice had her arms on the countertop, and glanced at Ash when he touched her hand. He drew a circle on the back of her hand in a gesture they'd decided a long time ago would mean *are you okay?* He looked at her with solemn blue-green eyes, and she tapped her fingers against his palm: *don't worry.*

"You two need to talk out loud," Noah said, leaning on the other side of the counter.

"That defeats the point of having a nonverbal code," Ash said.

"I thought you were trying to give her a cootie shot or something. Isn't it a circle, a circle, and two dots?"

Alice frowned at him. "Did you regress to age five? Cooties?"

"You have been spending a lot of time with Havier."

She hated that she felt her cheeks warm slightly, and hoped it didn't show. "He's been spending time with all of us. He lives here."

Both boys were studying her, and she sighed. Boys could be so stupid.

"If you think that's why I'm quiet, you're wrong. I've been thinking a little about the trial, and a lot about the portal."

Noah blinked. "Why are you still thinking about the trial?"

She wasn't thinking about the trial itself, but her father. The way he'd looked at her in the courtroom, and then changed his plea to guilty . . . she was surprisingly hollow about it all. She hated him. She doubted that would ever change. But she thought she would feel more about the event than the dull satisfaction that he was sentenced.

"It might take some time to sink in," Ash said.

"I don't need time," Noah said. "I'm thrilled."

He actually did look happy, Alice realized. Some of the heaviness that had been clear in the set of his shoulders since coming to Washington D.C. was gone. His eyebrows weren't pressed down in a scowl.

"I get thinking about the portal, though," Noah continued. "It's crazy to think it's been so long since we've seen them."

Alice reached absently for her hair, running a few strands between her fingers. She loved being able to do that again, and looked forward to having her curls come back full force. Her hair had still been in its pixie cut the last time they'd seen Tristan and Riley. She'd gotten taller since then as well, as had Ash, and Noah looked like he could be on the cusp of entering college. How had Tristan changed in all this time? Was his hair long? Did he have new scars? What had he been experiencing?

"Think Matt's idea will work?" Ash asked.

"Since we have no clue what his idea is, I don't

know," Alice said. She put her hand back in her lap. "Whatever it is, I really hope so."

They stayed in the kitchen for what felt like a long time, and before Emily came, Havier and Pat returned with a feast.

"Time to celebrate," Havier said, setting his bags down on the counter. Pat did the same with his. "What do you like?"

Pat started taking things out of the bags he'd carried: foil-wrapped items, plastic to-go containers.

"How much food did you get?" Ash asked. "And what kind?"

"None of us like the same kind of takeout," Pat said, "so we have a tradition here. We rotate which type we get for general eating-out occasions. But special occasions, we go all out. We get a little of everything."

Havier began laying out the contents of his bags, and soon they had subs and burgers and tacos and pizza and fried chicken, not to mention sides. "This is enough to feed a small army," Alice said.

"Watch and learn, chica," Havier said. "We don't do this often, so when we do, we eat like champs. And with you four here, we might not even have enough."

"The food carts down the way make it easier

than you'd think to get a variety, too," Pat said.

Noah and Ash were staring at the food. "Dig in," Havier said.

Alice had never eaten from a food truck before. She absolutely wanted to eat from a food truck again. Everything was delicious. The blend of smells should have been awful, but wasn't. Emily joined them a few minutes after they started. Havier's sister Maribel and their tutor, Helen showed up too, along with the Guardian, Lori, and Alice saw that Havier was right. With everyone there, they reduced the meals to scraps (plus, packaging took up more space than actual food, so it wasn't as much as Alice had initially thought).

Emily reluctantly told them she didn't know about Matt's idea, but that they would leave first thing in the morning. Alice listened as Pat, Lori, and Helen helped Emily figure out transportation, and decided to loan them a car. They sat around the dining room table and ate and talked late into the night.

"We'll leave first thing in the morning," Emily said.

"When you say first thing . . ." Ash started.

Emily smiled. "My definition of first thing. By eight o'clock at the latest. Preferably seven."

Noah groaned and went upstairs. Emily

thanked everyone and followed him, walking up with Pat, Helen, Lori, and Maribel. Ash hesitated on the bottom step, looking to Alice. She moved to walk up with him, but stopped when Havier touched her arm.

"Can we talk for a minute?" he asked.

Alice looked at Ash and silently said she'd be right up, and watched him climb the stairs before turning to face Havier.

"Right. I should thank you again. You've done a lot for us, and especially for me."

His eyebrows pressed together. "I didn't need you to thank me. I just wanted to make sure you're okay."

She fought to keep the surprise from showing on her face. "I'm fine."

He scrutinized her and then exhaled a tiny laugh. "Yeah, you are. I don't like how we met," he said, "but I'm glad we did. I'll miss you, Alice."

It was the first time he'd called her by her name, and it took her a few seconds to process beyond opening her mouth. At least, it would have taken her a few seconds to process. She was distracted from it when a spark of steel entered Havier's eyes, and he stepped up close and kissed her. She was distracted from pretty much everything when Havier kissed her, as she'd never been kissed before.

His lips were strong against hers, pushing and pulling at the same time, and it could only have lasted seconds before he backed away, out of reach. Alice felt her breath coming faster than normal, and couldn't tell if she was more angry or pleased. If she should hit him or pull him back and kiss him again.

From his expression, and how much he'd backed away, Havier couldn't tell what she was feeling either. Or maybe he knew she was feeling both. He was watching her closely.

"Was that your way of saying goodbye?" she managed to ask.

His rounded cheeks became more emphasized when he gave her a warm half-smile. "If you're asking if I say goodbye to other people that way, the answer's no. And I guess you could say that was a goodbye just for you. Maybe it's not a goodbye at all."

She studied him, then betrayed the smallest smile, while inwardly beaming. "Good."

"Which?"

She walked past him, heading to her room. "I haven't decided yet."

She could feel his gaze on her, but didn't let herself look over her shoulder. She felt like she was humming with energy. A positive outcome in the court case, the renewed potential to find

Tristan and Riley, her first kiss . . . she wouldn't be able to sleep for a long time.

Matt was at work when Emily and the kids got back to the Temple the following afternoon. He got back from his shift about two hours after they returned. Emily had sent the kids to the park with Derek, for two reasons. First, they had a lot of built up energy from the drive home and the prospect of being home, and needed a way to burn it off. Second, she wanted to talk to Matt privately. No point in getting everyone's hopes up about Matt's idea if it wouldn't work.

She stood in the entryway, mildly pacing, in the minutes immediately before he was due home. She hugged him right when he walked in, and then perched on one of the chairs to hear his theory.

He didn't need an invitation to start. "I've been combing through Christopher's documents since Riles and the others disappeared. I went and found some people he mentioned, and talked to them. Piecing it all together, I know how to open the portal. We need to use the powers of both Shifters and Elementalists at the portal site."

There was a sharp focus about Matt, and she realized that was what had been different about him the last few months. She knew he'd taken Riley being missing hard, as they all had, but thought that was the undefinable something she'd noticed about him: a hardened kind of grief. He'd always been a smart boy, though he rarely fully applied himself. That was the change. He'd focused so much on finding his little sister, doing research and conducting his own investigation. He'd matured, suddenly and wonderfully, and Emily felt a rush of shame for not picking up on it sooner, countered by a fierce pride.

"It says fire is the key," he insisted. "Three Shifters and a fire user, together, will work."

Emily studied him. "Three Shifters?"

"A lion, an eagle, and a dragon of some sort. Bearded, Komodo. I don't think the exact type will matter. With these three Shifters, the same animal types that make up the Celestials will be present. Two of them have fire, so having a fire user send in their own flames will be important. If the Shifters all partially Shift and touch the portal site at the same time as the fire user sends their flames against it, it might be close enough to the energy of the actual Celestials to make the portal open."

Emily hugged him again. "Honey, I love that you've put so much effort into this, but I don't know if it will work. You said fire is the key, and you're probably right. But Riley has her own fire.

She can create and manipulate flames when she isn't Shifted, just like a fire user. It's a gift from the phoenix."

Matt stared at her. "She has her own fire? Why the hell didn't she tell me?" He shook his head. "Doesn't matter. I'm still trying it. I'll ask one of the fire users at the local Guild. I'll be the eagle. Now I just need to find a dragon and a lion."

Could it work? Matt certainly seemed to think so. There was no harm in trying, especially when if it did work, they would get Riley and the others back. "Okay. I'll look for the Shifters. You go to the Guild."

Something changed in his expression. His defiance faded. "Thanks, Mom."

He ran out the front door. Emily wished she knew a place to run and find the Shifters they needed. For now, she had to make a phone call. He'd said she could call with anything she needed, after she'd indirectly helped him become a police sergeant. Luckily, North Carolina wasn't in a different time zone. He picked up just before it went to voicemail.

"Hi, Sergeant Spades? It's Emily Madison. I'd like to ask you a big favor."

"Emily! Nice to hear from you," Spades said in his reedy voice. "What's up?"

"You've heard about the portal here in New

York, right? The one to the parallel world where the Celestials retreated?"

"And your daughter and so many others went through it. Sure."

"We might have a way to open the portal." She told him Matt's idea. "You're the only lion Shifter I know. Of course there are probably some much closer, but the time it would take to find them . . . plus, I was hoping you might know of a dragon Shifter."

She waited in silence, heard him say something indistinct from a short distance, and then heard a jostling sound, likely from him picking up the phone again. "Have you told anyone else about this theory?"

"No. I only just heard it myself."

"Okay, here's what I want you to do," Spades said. "It'll take me a day or two to get up there. In the meantime, you need to contact your local officers. Give them all the information you gave me, and give them my contact information. We need this to be as official as can be, so everyone's sure it's done right."

Emily felt herself smile. "You're really coming?"

She heard him give a dry chuckle. "I'm coming, and I'll do everything I can to bring a dragon with me. Someone I work with is bound to know one, and I'll run a search of my own."

Emily thanked him and hung up, practically trembling. Then she raced from the Temple. Now she had a destination to run: the local police barracks.

CHAPTER 18

Free Falling

Riley was falling.

Falling, at first down a waterfall, with Allyssa's cry of fear fresh in her ears and Tristan's strong arms wrapped tight around her, then in a room with an earth Elementalist as he stole the floor from under her feet, and finally into a pit so dark and cold she couldn't see anything, just knew she was falling: falling fast and hard and unstoppably.

She was screaming, and she knew it but couldn't stop. She felt how Tristan held her so close to his body. That alone told her this wasn't a dream, because in her dreams she always fell alone. But she couldn't sort out her actual fall from the nightmare until just before she hit the water. She saw the river coming up under her feet and knew this fall was completely real. And then she broke through the surface.

Her eyes closed automatically when her head went under the water, and she started panicking all over again, though she still felt like she was falling. Tristan let go of her and she kicked out, hoping she was facing the surface and not the bottom as she propelled herself. A hand grasped hers firmly, pulling her up. When her head came out of the water she gasped and opened her eyes, searching around her. She was panting, and when she realized Tristan was still holding her wrist and saying her name, she fixed her eyes on him.

He looked at her with complete tenderness and concern, green eyes steady as ever, though some part of her realized that from the way he was breathing, he was shaken as well. He led her out of the water, and once they were on solid ground near the others Riley threw herself against him, almost knocking him down. He staggered in surprise but caught her and stayed upright, wrapping his arms around her as he had just moments before, when they were falling . . . .

She shivered against the memory, pushing it away. They were on ground level. The fall was over.

"Riley! Ry, are you okay?" Allyssa's anxious voice cut through Riley, making her turn to face her friend. "Riley, I tried to catch you but I hadn't even gotten us down yet—I can't hold us all up from that high—I'm so sorry!"

Allyssa's panic made it hard for Riley to continue working to steady her pulse. Part of her wanted to curl into a ball. She felt Tristan's hand, warm and steady on her back, and let the calm he so often seemed to exude seep into her, willing her breathing to regulate. "I'm okay."

"That's good. The king wants you captured with as little damage as possible."

Riley spun on her heels to see at least ten people staring at them. They moved to surround the group. "Grab 'em," the front guard said.

Riley steeled herself to fight. She felt anything but strong at the moment, but challenges rarely present themselves at the most opportune moments. She saw Wyatt partially Shift, the multi-hued outline surrounding him with a fierce glow. Tristan did the same, and in an instant they were charging forward to fight. A stiff breeze flew out from just behind Riley, knocking some of the guards down. One went for Riley, and she thought back to her practice battle with Tristan and Wyatt. She couldn't Shift, but she could defend herself without that power.

She ducked past the guard and went low to the ground, sweeping her leg out and tripping the woman. The guard stumbled and Riley elbowed her in the back, then pushed her flat to the ground, kneeling on her and bringing her hand up to strike the woman again. A hand grabbed her wrist and she spun around to kick their legs out from under them.

It was only when she saw a fire user in the fight that she remembered her own fire, and kicked the first guard with a fiery foot. The second guard she had to focus on dodging. The man was an excellent fighter. He was a Shifter, and had a partial Shift around him.

Roughly half the guards were Shifters, she realized, though none of them had fully Shifted. They had partial Shifts, so they could use the strength and agility of their spirit animals but fight as humans, and it was an effective move. Riley turned to Demetrius after jabbing and missing her guard. Why wasn't he knocking them out? But he wasn't even in sight. She went to look for him and felt an awful punch to the stomach; she had ignored the guard for too long. As her eyes watered from the pain she felt another blow, this one much sharper, to the center of her back. She looked up from the ground and saw the first guard sneering at her and pointing to her elbow. So that had been the sharp pain.

"Demetrius!" Wyatt called.

Riley saw Demetrius being escorted away by a pair of guards. Wyatt was trying to run to him but struggling to get past his own opponent. Tristan and Allyssa were too busy fending off multiple guards to try to help. Riley jumped up, calling fire to her hands and aiming one hand at each of the two guards. She surprised them by moving so quickly. She surprised herself, really. She felt the ache from the blows but ignored it as she blasted them with fire. She hadn't aimed for specific parts of their bodies, so one guard took the fire in the stomach. The other was less fortunate. He fell backwards, howling as he clutched at his face. Riley felt awful but moved past them. There wasn't time to dwell on casualties. Her fire was at its weakest strength right now, so it would only be superficial wounds anyway: just enough to make them stand down.

Demetrius wasn't in sight anymore. Everyone else was actively fighting. Riley was partly glad that she wasn't viewed as that big a threat. She usually wasn't, but it meant that now, she had a window to go help wherever she was needed. It was tiny, but it was a window.

Unfortunately, that window closed when she collided with one of the guards Allyssa had been fighting. The guard was being thrown towards the water by a strong gale, and jerked into Riley as she went to pass him. They landed on the ground and the guard kneeled on top of her, pinning her hands together. She willed fire to them and the guard put pressure on her left wrist, making Riley hiss in pain.

"A good try," the guard said, "but if you try it again I'll snap your wrist."

The pressure on her back eased as the guard stood and pulled her upright in front of him. She saw that Tristan was pinned a few feet away. Allyssa was trapped in a huge bubble of water, kicking and frantically cutting with her arms, but her wind powers weren't freeing her. And from the panicked look in her eyes and the bubbles coming from her mouth, she couldn't breathe.

"Let her go!" Riley yelled. Allyssa kicked and flailed. "She's drowning!"

"Make your friend stand down," the water user said.

Wyatt was still fighting. It made sense that he would still be fighting, since he had practiced combat for years. And now that he could use the griffin's powers, he was twice as effective. He glanced at Riley and then at Allyssa, apparently weighing the consequences of not surrendering. When Allyssa's movements slowed Riley screamed for him to stop. She couldn't watch her best friend drown. She couldn't, when the other part of her nightmare was watching her loved ones die, in different ways each time.

Wyatt dropped his Shift and held up his hands, and two guards practically tackled him in their haste to grab him.

The water user let the water bubble fall apart. Allyssa landed on the ground coughing and wheezing. "The king wants you all alive." She forced Allyssa to stand. "Especially this one."

Riley looked anxiously at Allyssa as they were all led away from the river. She seemed all right physically, though she was breathing roughly. She must have inhaled some water. Her steps were uneven too. Riley knew she needed to sit down to recover.

They were led to a stone building not far from the river and thrust inside after a guard bound all of their wrists with twine. Demetrius was inside, as was Tony. Allyssa sank to the floor immediately, and Riley went to her knees next to her. She burned away the twine around her own wrists, and then Allyssa's.

"What happened?" Demetrius asked, kneeling at Allyssa's other side.

"A water user trapped her in a bubble," Tristan said.

"I'm okay," Allyssa said in a roughened voice.

Riley didn't believe her, but could tell she needed a bit of time before she answered any questions. Demetrius moved to sit next to her, so Riley freed his hands, stood, and walked away. Allyssa would be fine with him for a few minutes.

Wyatt followed Riley and touched her arm. "Are *you* okay?"

"Why are you and Tristan soaked too?" Tony asked. "Did that water user get the three of you? Were there a ton of water users? Are you just really bad at dodging?"

Wyatt turned to stare at him. "Which question do you want answered first?"

Tony grinned. "How about one I didn't ask? What happened? I got grabbed before you guys came out of the cave."

"We got through to the griffin," Tristan said. "And then Riley and I fell down the waterfall."

Riley burned away the twine around their wrists, focusing her eyes on it. She could feel Tony and Wyatt studying her. Tristan had his eyes lowered.

"You sure you didn't jump? Looked like the makings for a pretty sweet dive."

Riley closed her eyes, reliving the fall.

"Sorry," Tony said quickly.

"It's fine." Riley opened her eyes, forcing herself out of the memory.

"We need to figure out our escape plan, but I think everyone needs a little break first," Wyatt said.

Riley nodded and sat down against one of the

walls, wrapping her arms around her legs. It had been easy to push the fall to the back of her mind when they'd been attacked. Now was the difficult part: dealing with it.

Since she'd had her memories restored she'd been having nightmares, and every night she dreamed she was falling. The phoenix knew it was one of her greatest fears, and for whatever reason, it used their connection to plague her sleep with scenarios involving falling—whenever she wasn't having nightmares about losing her friends and family, that is. She felt drained. She wanted to sleep now, though she was scared that she would just have another nightmare. She could feel her eyes drooping and decided not to fight it. Maybe if she just took a cat nap, she would gain some energy back and avoid the nightmares.

She was happily surprised when she woke from a dreamless sleep. It couldn't have been more than half an hour. Her hair and clothes were still damp. But she definitely had more energy. She looked around the room, taking stock. Allyssa was dozing near the entrance, her head on Demetrius' shoulder. Wyatt and Tony were sitting across from her, Tony speaking in what he probably thought was a whisper, but barely qualified as one. Tristan sat near Riley, his head back against the wall.

If Riley was chilly, Allyssa probably was as

well. The building they were in didn't have furniture, but there was a spot in the far corner that looked like the remnants of a fire pit. Riley guessed guards used this as a shelter when they traveled nearby, stopping for the night. They probably didn't block the windows when they camped in here, though. That was just for Riley and her friends, to keep them contained. Still, the fire pit had been left decent. With the stone walls, a fire wouldn't catch and spread. She walked over to the fire pit and pushed together the bits of charred wood she could see. They ignited fairly quickly.

"Good idea," Tristan said when she returned to her spot.

"I should have made it right away."

"You needed time to process," he said. "Besides, we don't know how long they'll leave us in here. Now that we know it might be a little while, it makes sense to get as comfortable as possible."

It still amazed her how easily Tristan could make her feel better. "You need to stay away from cliff edges," she told him. She started to smile despite herself. "You clearly can't be trusted around them."

His lips tugged up as well, no doubt remembering the hiking trail incident last year. "Maybe I just like you coming to my rescue," he teased. His smile faded. "I would never have pulled you down the waterfall with me on purpose. I wasn't cautious enough, and I'm sorry."

"I grabbed you," Riley said firmly. "I knew there was a chance I would fall." She felt her cheeks warm. "Maybe I knew I already had."

His mouth opened in a tiny O, and it seemed like he was about to say something when Allyssa claimed their attention.

"Yes, fire!" Allyssa exclaimed. She rushed over to it and held her hands in front of the flames, and smiled at Riley. "This is perfect."

Riley studied her and decided Allyssa looked better than before. She didn't have to verbalize the question. Allyssa met her eyes and gave a tiny nod that let Riley know she was okay now.

"Why do you think they're holding us here?" Tony asked.

"Maybe they were told to keep us in one place, and Christopher's on his way," Tristan guessed.

Everyone looked to Demetrius. "I honestly don't know what he would have told them," he said. "I would say I doubt he would come here himself, but I can't be sure."

It was strange hearing Demetrius sound so uncertain. Wyatt spoke up immediately. Riley thought his immediacy was because he wanted to reassure Demetrius, or perhaps to overcome the awkward silence. "I don't think he would come this far from the castle unless he really had to. My guess is the guards are holding us while they wait for further instructions, or until they have a plan to move us. They know we'll fight back as soon as they open the door."

"I told Wyatt I can help," Tony said. "Maybe you guys can convince him. I want to Shift and fly out the window. I should be able to squeeze past the screen. Then I can get help." He scowled when no one agreed with his idea. "Let me help!"

"It could work," Tristan said. "Or it could get you hurt, and make the guards watch us so carefully we don't have another chance to escape. Wyatt's right to want you to stay here."

"So we sit and wait," Wyatt said. "It might help if we act weak and let them get close before we attack."

"I'm fine with that plan, but I do have another concern," Allyssa said. She looked towards the door. "Do you think Chitter is okay?"

Tristan had momentarily forgotten about their loyal chipmunk, and chided himself for it when Allyssa mentioned him. Then he reassured her, and a suddenly anxious Riley, that Chitter was probably fine. He ran or hid when there was trouble. They knew that from experience. He was safe.

Allyssa, Riley, Wyatt, and Demetrius stood near the fire, warming themselves and talking. Tristan went back to the spot he'd been in before, sitting with his back to the wall. No one had noticed that he'd spun his shirt around, and keeping his back to the wall would keep it that way. Maybe Wyatt had seen him do it, but he hadn't said anything, and Tristan didn't think he would. Tristan had wanted to get a new shirt from his bag, and wash the wound on his chest. Falling into the water hadn't qualified as rinsing the wound. Since he couldn't wash it now, and didn't have a new shirt, he'd settled for turning his shirt around, so solid fabric hid the wound from sight. The shredded section of the shirt now covered his back.

The scratches on his chest tingled, and he forced himself to think of something else. His most recent conversation with Riley popped into his head. Had she meant what he thought she had? Her blush indicated it, but she blushed easily.

Time seemed to pass slowly, and after what had to be an hour or two, they decided to try to get some real rest. Tristan volunteered to stay awake, and the others stretched out on the floor, Wyatt with a relief it took Tristan a second to understand. Of course. Wyatt didn't have to fear nightmares from the griffin anymore.

Tristan's gaze moved to Riley. As always,

she'd fallen asleep extremely quickly, but she wasn't safe from nightmares. When he heard her breathing pick up in pace and noticed how tense her expression was, he knew she was having another one. She wasn't getting enough sleep, and these nightmares were to blame. Tristan hated it. He hated being so unable to help.

But maybe he *could* help. He hadn't discovered a gift of the dragon's in the way Riley or Wyatt had, but maybe he did know a gift. Any dreams he had from the dragon related to feelings like calm and bravery. He felt them from the dragon. What if . . . ?

He partially Shifted, lightly touched Riley's arm, and focused on confidence and security, willing those feelings that naturally surged within him when he Shifted to flow into Riley. He kept it going, focusing and training his eyes on her, and after several seconds noticed a change in her breathing. It slowed. Almost at the same time her expression relaxed.

Tristan grinned, suddenly feeling much less helpless. He looked away when he heard movement and saw Tony sitting up. "What are you doing?" Tony asked.

"Helping Riley beat her nightmares."

Tony stood and stretched. "Didn't know you could do that."

"Neither did I, until like five minutes ago. I

guess it's a good thing I didn't plan on moving anytime soon, since now I can't."

Tony started doing jumping jacks, and Tristan pretended to scowl at him. That was something Noah would do. The reminder sent a pang of homesickness through him. Another thing to push to the back of his mind. At least he could honestly tell himself he was closer to getting home now. They'd reached the griffin.

Riley was surprised to find Tristan next to her with a partial Shift when she woke up, one hand over hers. She mostly seemed confused.

"I was starting to have a nightmare, but then it stopped. That was because of you?"

He dropped his Shift and half-smiled. "Figured out one of the dragon's gifts."

She leaned forward and hugged him. "Thank you."

As pleased as he was to have her hug him, the contact put pressure on the scratches on his chest, so he was relieved when she let him go.

The daylight coming through the small, netted windows became less as the day wore on, and around dusk, long after everyone had begun fidgeting and pacing and even longer after the tiny fire had burned away the wood scraps, there wasn't enough light to see everyone clearly from across the room. Riley brought a fire to her hand to help illuminate the rapidly darkening space.

"What are they waiting for?" Wyatt asked in a growl.

Wyatt seemed to go out of focus for a second, and Tristan blinked hard. Maybe he should have taken a nap himself.

"Maybe they're waiting for nightfall," Demetrius said. He leaned against the wall. "To make it harder for us to escape, so we can't see where we're going."

That would make sense. Tristan put a hand to the wall, lightheaded. He blinked hard again, but his vision didn't improve this time. The others seemed to be off as well. Riley's fire vanished in a flash. Tristan took a breath that didn't seem to replenish his breath at all, and saw the realization in the others' eyes.

"Shit," Allyssa said, as if personally offended. Tristan understood. It had to be a wind user that was thinning the air around them. Unfortunately, they realized it too late, and everyone dropped within seconds of Allyssa's exclamation.

Wyatt woke with a feeling of motion beneath him. He was on his horse. A rope circled Hermes' middle and went over Wyatt's legs. Another rope connected Wyatt's wrist to a guard that rode next to him. Without moving, he cast a quick look around. It was very hard to see more than their shapes, but he guessed that everyone was in a similar position. There were two people on horses immediately next to him. Allyssa was next to him, and he could see a rope around the hand farthest from him, so the other person had to be a guard. It seemed like the guards had formed a ring around them.

He decided there was nothing he could do without moving, and sat upright. As much as he hated it, he had to give the guards credit. It was a well-executed move, knocking them out so subtly and obtaining full control. He looked behind him and saw Riley and Demetrius. Tristan was in the back, still slumped on his horse's back.

Wyatt forced himself to look forward again, and around a minute later looked around, focusing his gaze on Demetrius and silently urging his friend to notice him.

You look like you have a plan, Demetrius said in his head. *How do you already have a plan, when you just woke up?*

Wyatt almost smiled. Times like this, when they needed to communicate without speaking, made him very thankful he had a friend that could read thoughts. They'd communicated like this many times. Now, as he sat on his horse and stared at the rope around his wrist, he loved that the guards had no idea they were planning. *I thought of it earlier, but I'm glad you think so highly of me. You're the key here, Demetrius. You can break through their mental shields.*

Demetrius hesitated. *I don't know if I can, Wyatt.*

Of course you can, Wyatt insisted. *Christopher made them their shields. You're stronger than him.* He didn't hear a response from Demetrius for several seconds, so he said it again. *You can do this. Just focus on one guard at a time. Slip past their defenses, destroy their shields, and convince them to help us. But tell the others what you're doing, so they don't try anything and ruin it.*

This might actually help them, he realized. If Demetrius could make the guards act as allies, they could ride back to the castle looking like prisoners, enter unopposed, and then attack.

Allyssa looked over at Wyatt. "Sorry," she muttered.

"This isn't your fault," he responded, just as quietly.

"If I'd been paying attention I would have noticed the air thinning. I can't believe they used wind against us!"

Allyssa jerked to the right, and Wyatt felt a sharp tug on the rope around his wrist. "No talking," the guard next to Allyssa said.

Wyatt tensed the hand the rope was connected to and set his gaze on Hermes' mane. He didn't have to speak aloud. He fully intended to keep talking, and waited patiently for Demetrius to reach out again.

CHAPTER 19

Fix You

Allyssa?

Allyssa startled when she heard Demetrius, but calmed immediately. *What's up?* she asked, confident he would read her thoughts.

I was just talking to Wyatt, and he had an idea.

He told her about the plan to sway the guards, but there was a reluctance to his voice. *You don't want to control them,* she guessed.

I've never wanted to control anyone, he admitted.

You don't really have to control these guards. We just need them to be willing to listen, and to work with us instead of against us.

She heard him breathe out in a tiny laugh. *I knew you'd say exactly what I needed to hear. I'll let you know when I break through each shield.*

He acted like she was always the one to re-assure him. As if he'd forgotten how he com-forted her earlier that day, when she'd been shell-shocked from being trapped in that bubble. No matter how she'd slashed with the wind, she hadn't been able to escape the bubble of water. The water Elementalist was incredibly strong.

All of these guards were strong. Allyssa guessed these Shifters and Elementalists were among the top fighters Christopher had em-ployed as guards. It made sense that he would have a special squadron with mental shields to go after them. Now, if Demetrius could really dismantle those shields and make these guards allies—which she was fully confident he could—they would have an even better chance of getting to the castle without issue.

Demetrius did as he'd promised and updated her each time he got through a guard's de-fenses. He gave her an overview of the process for each guard, explaining that Jerry, an earth user, seemed the kindest, and Amar, a Shifter, was most decidedly against them. He took extra time with Amar, working behind the scenes in his mind to persuade the man that they were the good guys. The others didn't have strong per-sonal opinions; they were just doing as they'd been instructed. Though the water user, Mia, was definitely more violently inclined.

It was early morning by the time Demetrius

finished with the last guard, and Allyssa could hear the strain in his voice when he told everyone it was done, this time speaking aloud.

They stopped and took care of the rope tying them to their horses and the guards, and decided to make a temporary camp while they made food. It had been about a day since they'd eaten. Allyssa went with Tristan, Tony, and Mia to the riverbank. That was when Allyssa noticed Tristan's shirt.

"Are you hurt?"

He jumped and kept his eyes on the river. "I got a little roughed up at the waterfall. Nothing to worry about."

Allyssa frowned but didn't pressure him. Mia manipulated the water to bring fish right to their hands when they reached the water. Tristan put water in a pot and asked Allyssa to bring it back. Mia and Tony started walking back to the others, a sphere of water with several frantic fish swimming inside it floating between them. Allyssa held the pot and looked at Tristan. "Aren't you coming?"

"I'll be there in a minute."

He looked at her until she turned and started walking. She walked several feet and then looked over her shoulder, to find him kneeling by the water's edge, his ruined shirt on the ground next to him. He reached into the water and brought a handful to his chest, and she saw his bare shoulders tense as if he were in pain.

She turned again and continued walking, giving him privacy, but decided she had to keep an eye on him. He'd definitely been hurt at the griffin's den. If he was keeping it secret, she guessed it was something the griffin had done. From the state of his shirt, probably a scratch. She understood wanting to keep it quiet. Wyatt would feel guilty. Riley would worry. Still, she was glad she knew now. She could keep an eye on him, and make sure he was healing.

It became apparent in the next few days that Tristan wasn't healing. He'd changed into an undamaged shirt when he'd gotten back from the river, and managed to keep his wound secret the rest of that day. He couldn't hide the pain he was in after that. He winced whenever he moved suddenly, or extended his arms, and he seemed weak. When Allyssa demanded to see the wound, he told them how the griffin had scratched him.

"You said it wasn't bad!" Wyatt said.

The griffin's talons had slashed deep marks across Tristan's chest, four angry gouges marked in red and tints of yellow.

"That qualifies as bad!" Wyatt continued.

"I didn't get to wash it out for a while," Tristan said. "I kept hoping it would just heal on its own, but I think it's getting infected."

"It's not getting infected," Allyssa told him. "It is infected. Maybe not fully, but it shouldn't look like that."

"Those cuts are deep," Tony said, leaning forward. "The griffin's claws must be like knives."

"I can't believe you didn't say anything," Riley fretted. "If I'd known you were hurt . . . ."

"We still would have done exactly what we've been doing. We need to get to the castle before the griffin, or at least at the same time. It'll go after Christopher without us if it thinks we're too far behind."

Wyatt inclined his head, silently agreeing that Tristan had a point.

Riley bit her lip, studying Tristan's wound. "Fine. But if you get worse, we're stopping. I don't care if it takes us an extra day or two to get back to Astrum."

Her voice was fully assertive, and Allyssa was proud of her. "I think that just about sums it up for all of us. We'll reassess in the morning."

Tristan wasn't any better the next morning. He was actually much, much worse.

He went to stand and swayed, and both Riley and Wyatt pushed him back down. He was too weak to fight them. His skin was clammy, his cheeks a bright pink, and inspection of his wound revealed the scratches to be a livid red, even compared to the inflamed skin around them. There was no way he was fit to travel.

"He needs to rest," Riley said.

"So we camp here for the day," Allyssa said.

Riley shook her head. "If you all stay, he'll only feel worse. He'll blame himself for keeping us back." She looked at Wyatt. "I know it seems silly, but I'm thinking of Tristan. He'll convince himself he's putting everyone in danger. Besides, you need to be there to meet the griffin and the phoenix."

She watched him consider what she was saying, and though he clearly didn't like it, he understood. Allyssa and Demetrius did too.

"We'll wait for you," Allyssa said. She held up a hand to stop Riley from disagreeing. "We'll keep going towards the castle, but we'll wait for you outside it."

Riley felt a rush of affection for her friend. Allyssa always knew how to help. Wyatt seemed to understand, and nodded once.

"What's going on?" Tristan was partially awake, looking at them. "Are we leaving?"

"The others are. I'm staying here with you," Riley said.

Tristan looked like he wanted to say something, but he closed his eyes, too tired. "Okay."

"Two of you, please stay with them," Demetrius said to the guards. "Keep them safe."

Jerry and Hannah were the guards that stayed with Tristan and Riley when the others reluctantly continued toward the castle. Hannah kept up watch from a distance. Jerry looked at Tristan and frowned. "I don't know if time will be enough to heal this."

Riley was worried about the same thing. The slashes from the griffin were long, deep wounds, and definitely infected. She didn't have any medicine other than the herbs Demetrius had left her, and none of those would heal an infection. She wasn't good with directions, but they'd passed by the village around the lake yesterday, probably an hour or two before they'd stopped here for the night. Her eyes snapped up to Jerry. "There has to be a doctor in the village we passed through last night. At least someone who will be able to help. You have to go back and get him medicine."

He was hesitating, looking at Hannah.

"I can't go," Riley said. "Please, he needs medicine!"

Jerry looked at Tristan again, then at Riley, and nodded forcefully. "Okay. I'll be back as soon as I can."

Riley checked on Tristan's cut, splashing a little water over it before re-wrapping it, and then sat down next to him. She brushed a hand across his cheek, a strange, protective feeling coming over her. But it was more than that. She'd never had to look after someone before, not like this. The fact that it was Tristan made her more determined to help him recover quickly. He had been there for her so many times—it was time for her to look after him.

She lost herself in her thoughts, thinking about freeing the Celestials and actually coming face to face with the phoenix. Thinking about going back home, and seeing her parents and brother, and Ash, Alice, and Noah. It was a long time, thinking of everything. She listened to Tristan's even breathing and let her thoughts take her whichever way they wanted, for what had to be a few hours.

She looked up when the rate of his breathing changed, the breaths becoming faster and shallower. His face had a sheen of sweat to it, his hair damp because of it, and his cheeks weren't pink anymore. Now they were red.

His eyes opened as he woke up, and this more than anything alarmed Riley. Tristan's eyes were always a clear, steady green, sharp and often humorous. The color was still the same, but muted by how glassy his eyes were. They were so dull, like a veil had been thrown over them.

"Tristan?" Riley asked. "Tristan, can you hear

me?"

He turned towards her, just a fraction of an inch. "Riley." His voice was weak, but she was glad he was responding.

"I'm right here," she said. "I'm going to clean off your wound, okay?"

He didn't respond. His head jerked to the side and he tensed, his breathing escalating. "The twins should be back by now." Tristan sat up and looked like he was about to stand. "Noah, where are you?" he called. He put his arms behind him to push himself up. Riley put her hands on his shoulders, gently pressing to make him sit again.

"Tristan, they're not here," Riley said in as steady a voice as she could. "You have a fever and its making you imagine things."

She couldn't tell if he even heard her, he was so agitated. He was delirious from the fever. He might not have even known where they were. He tensed again, his labored breath catching as he stared unseeing in front of him. "Jordan. No, don't turn away from her! She's going to kill you!" he shouted. He tore Riley's hands away and scrambled up. "Don't leave me!" he yelled.

Tears pricked at Riley's eyes. This wasn't a made up delusion. This was a memory: one of the worst ones she was sure both of them had. But if he thought he was experiencing it again . . . she had to get him calmed down.

"Tristan, please!" Riley said, stepping in front of him. If she could just make him see her, and realize his vision wasn't real. "Tristan!"

He turned his face to her and she saw the effort it took to focus on her face. "Riley," he said in a normal voice.

Relief bubbled inside her chest. "Yes, it's me!"

"Riley," he said again, and her relief flooded out of her in a second because of his tone. He sounded scared. "Riley, run!" he yelled, stepping forward. "Get out of here!" His chest heaved with his staggering breath, his eyes completely glassy again. "I won't let you touch her," he said in a low voice, his head down. He looked up, at the guard that had stayed with them. "I WON'T LET YOU TOUCH HER!" he exploded, running toward her. He Shifted, the brilliant emerald aura blazing around him.

"Tristan, stop!" Riley yelled, racing after him. Hannah shoved him back. Tristan moved to fight her, more fiercely than Riley would have thought possible in his state. Riley grabbed his arm as he drew it back, holding it tightly. "Tristan, you have to stop!" she shouted, trying to get through to him. "PLEASE!" she begged. *It's not real!*

He looked at the ground, closing his eyes for a second. When he swayed slightly Riley gripped his arm even tighter, but he kept himself righted. "Riley," Tristan said, looking at the ground. His teeth were clenched as he tried to calm down. "Need to keep you safe."

"You did," she promised him, her voice catching. "You saved me, Tristan."

He dropped his Shift. The guard kept her grip on his arm. Tristan didn't look up, and Riley acted fast, running to the bag Demetrius had left for her. There was a flower for sleep somewhere in there. There was one for energy too. She hesitated for a few more seconds before grabbing the one she thought was right and opening another bag to dig up a cup and their canteen of water. With slightly shaky hands she filled the small cup with water and set it down in front of her, picking up the flower. She crushed the dried petals in her hands, making it into a powder, and dropped it into the cup, then hastily brought it over to Tristan. He was trying to walk away, murmuring something. Hannah just pulled him back after two steps.

Riley stood in front of Tristan, holding the cup tightly. "I got you some water," she said to him, hoping he still heard her. She put a finger under his chin to make him lift his face, and carefully brought the cup against his lips, tilting it back as his mouth opened. She watched him swallow, and realized he was looking at her as she made him drink, his eyes cloudy but warm.

The effect was immediate. As soon as he finished the cup Tristan's legs buckled. Riley went to her knees next to him, hovering anxiously as he fell on his back. He looked at her with heavily-lidded eyes, blinking slowly.

"It's okay," she told him softly. "You're just going to sleep."

He blinked for the longest time yet, and when he opened his eyes a tiny bit he looked at her again. "You're safe?" he murmured loosely.

"Completely," she promised, taking his hand.

A hint of a smile played at his lips as his eyes closed. Riley held his hand and felt her lip tremble.

"You're going to be okay," she said in a choked voice.

Jerry appeared not long after Tristan fell into the drug-induced sleep, and jumped off his horse and ran to them. "I got something," he panted. He held up a small clay jar. "Honey. Apparently it's good at drawing out infections if you use it like ointment. They mixed it with a few other things that should do a thorough job healing him."

Riley reached out with shaking hands to remove the bandage over Tristan's chest, and then accepted the jar from Jerry. She reached one hand in, scooping up some of the gel-like mixture, and lightly rubbed it along the scratches. She let it sit for a few minutes and then replaced the bandage, and looked at Jerry.

"Thank you."

It was hours before Tristan started to wake up. Half of the day, really. The sun would be going down soon. Riley had slept for some time, in short bursts that kept her from having nightmares, and had been watching Tristan since waking up fully. Occasionally she had wiped his brow with a wet cloth, careful not to wake him. She'd put more of the honey mixture on his chest twice. She didn't want to be overly optimistic, but his fever seemed less each time she felt his forehead. It seemed like the gel, and rest, was working.

Around midafternoon something happened that made Riley smile. She heard a tiny chittering sound, and their little chipmunk ran into view. He scampered to Tristan's side, sniffed him, and curled up against his leg. Riley reached out to stroke Chitter, and was pleased when he let her rub a finger on his head. Tristan would be relieved to see him when he woke up. They'd both been a bit worried about the chipmunk. Apparently he'd just needed a day to catch up.

When Tristan started to stir Riley leaned closer with bated breath. His eyes would tell her how he was recovering. He exhaled slowly and then his eyelids crinkled before parting slightly. He blinked a few times before leaving his eyes open, and Riley looked at them carefully. The eyes that stared back at her were the ever steady green she joyed to see, without any trace of the veil or glassiness. She let out a sobbing kind of laugh in relief, and he looked at her quizzically.

"What's wrong?" he asked.

"Nothing," she told him, still smiling. "You're so much better now!"

His lips curved up when he spotted Chitter. "He found us!" He petted the chipmunk and sat up slowly. "I still feel tired. I slept all day, right?"

"Mostly. There was one time when you woke up."

He heard the hesitancy in her voice and looked at her. "Riley, what happened?"

She bit her lip. "You were seeing things, trying to be a hero. You thought people were in danger. Ash, Alice, Noah, Jordan." Her eyes flicked to the ground. "Me."

His mouth was open, his eyes distant as he tried to remember. A few seconds later he looked back to her, his shock fading. "It wasn't a dream. I tried to save you?"

"You were pretty convinced I was in danger."

"I must have been so out of it. I barely remember."

"You were definitely out of it," she told him.

"But still so clearly *you*. You wanted to protect everyone. You couldn't stand even the thought of us being in danger. You even Shifted."

"The dragon can be pretty headstrong," he said sheepishly.

She met his eyes. "The dragon can be pretty loyal, and compassionate. And so much more."

They were moving closer to each other, his lips slowly traveling toward her own. A spark went through all her nerves, starting a burning sensation that caught and spread, the heat of the fire reaching her cheeks as their lips met. He was so gentle, but she felt the insistence as his lips moved over hers, feeling their shape. She moved hers in response, learning the shape of his mouth, the way it puckered in the center and curved around the edges. His hand moved up her arm, fingers trailing over her skin and making goose bumps appear—tiny spots that, instead of shivering, burned with a lovely energy. They were creatures of fire: burning was in their nature.

Riley put one hand around his neck and kissed him more fully, more urgently. He crashed against her eagerly and followed her lead, his hand moving from her arm to her back, holding her closer. Riley couldn't believe she had been scared earlier, since she was in a state of bliss right now. Tristan drew his head back so that their lips were inches apart and breathed. His face was flushed, from both remnants of the fever and kissing, and she thought it was amazing how that splash of color only seemed to make his eyes brighter. They were looking at her so openly that she slid her hand down his neck and lightly placed it against his chest, feeling his heart beating fast as she looked at him.

"I was so worried," she said breathlessly. "Your fever was so high."

"You nursed me back to health. No need to worry anymore." He leaned forward and kissed her again. Riley surrendered herself to it immediately. He stopped after a few minutes, breathless. "You have no idea how long I've wanted to do that. To be this close to you."

She smiled. A cozy fire crackled inside her wherever he touched her. "Me too," she said honestly. She saw the jar in her periphery and picked it up. "I should put more of this on you. I might be overdoing it, but I'm not going to do it too infrequently." She told him how Jerry had gone to get this remedy. "It's working."

Jerry had gone to sit next to Hannah. Tristan looked in their direction. "I'll have to thank him later."

Tristan watched Riley put more of the gel onto his wound and replace the bandage, and she felt herself blush again. "You need to eat and then rest more," she told him. "Get as much sleep as you can, and we can leave in the morning. We'll only be a day behind the others. But if you're not well-rested, we'll stay here another day."

He half-smiled. "Yes, Dr."

CHAPTER 20

Joint Effort

Ash jumped on the opportunity Matt's theory presented. He needed his brother back.

They had a family meeting the night they got back to the Saratoga Temple, and Matt told everyone his theory. He said a local fire user, Heather, had agreed to help. Emily told them that Sergeant Spades, a lion Shifter, would be coming soon, and that he would look for a dragon-type Shifter. Ash didn't want to leave it up to Spades. He wanted to be able to go to the portal site right away, which meant having all the people they needed identified and present.

"Call Havier," he said to Alice.

Her eyebrows shot up. "Why?"

"Ask if he knows any dragon-type Shifters. If he looks, and Sergeant Spades looks, someone is bound to find one."

Emily nodded encouragement, so Alice went to call him. Emily then turned to Ash, Noah, Matt, and Derek. "I spoke with Detective Fords, at the local barracks. He's only allowing those directly involved with the attempt to go to the portal site." She held up a hand. "I'm supposed to tell you that. I'm going to be honest with you, though, and say I plan on disregarding that. I'm going. If he makes me stand back a little ways, fine, but I'll be at that park when we try to open the portal."

"Me too," Ash and Noah said.

Emily didn't try to dissuade them. On the contrary, she seemed pleased with their response.

Alice walked back in a few minutes later. "Havier doesn't know any dragon-type Shifters personally, but he's telling Pat and the others, and they're going to try to find one."

Ash looked at everyone, trying to figure out if there was anything else he could do. Not that he'd done much yet.

"Unfortunately, we've got time, guys," Emily said. "We need to wait and hope to hear from Sergeant Spades or Havier and Pat."

Everyone was silent.

"We haven't had a normal night in a while,"

Emily continued. "Let's play some games and throw on a movie."

It wasn't what any of them really wanted to do, but Ash knew they needed a distraction. Fixating on Matt's theory and waiting by the phone for news wouldn't do them any good. He was sure Emily had her phone turned all the way up, and on her. He knew Alice had her phone nearby too.

"So," Matt said. "Are we starting with the video games, or the board games? Cause I'd really like to beat you all at racing."

They spent the next two and a half days keeping busy, taking turns choosing movies and music and games, separating, and coming back to do it over again. In the afternoon of the third day they got a phone call from Sergeant Spades. He'd found a bearded dragon Shifter and convinced the man, named Joey, to help them, and would arrive late that night.

They would be able to attempt to open the portal the next morning.

Everyone went to the park. Detective Fords wasn't happy to see the car full of people, but Emily told him they only wanted to be nearby, and he relented. Emily, Derek, Noah, Ash, and Alice stayed just outside the park. Matt, Sergeant Spades, Detective Fords, Heather, and Joey walked in, straight to the portal site.

Matt didn't waste any time. Everyone knew what they had to do. He would guide them.

"Okay, Shifters first," Matt said. He adopted a partial Shift, and saw Sergeant Spades and Joey do the same. Matt took the lead, placing his palm on the rocky wall. They followed suit. The rocks seemed to give beneath Matt's hand, more malleable than before. "Now add fire."

Heather stepped up next to them, confidently placed a hand on the wall, and summoned a flame. It burned between her hand and the rock. She kept it going for several seconds, then looked to Matt. He stepped back, drawing back his hand. The others followed suit, Heather last.

Nothing happened for a long moment. Matt didn't dare to speak, watching for any slight change.

It wasn't slight. The rocks started vibrating, though they didn't make a sound. The crack in the stone wall glowed a pale orange color. Matt heard several sharp intakes of breath, and felt his heart start hammering faster.

The rocks stopped moving. The crack dimmed its pale orange glow.

Then the portal site seemed to explode.

It didn't really explode. The rocky wall remained intact. A concussive blast emanated from it, though, a blast that was immediately preceded by a flash of pale orange. The force launched Matt off his feet, sending him flying off the trail and into the stream.

"Ow," he muttered, rubbing a hand on his lower back. The stream wasn't that deep, and there were a fair amount of lumpy and/or jagged rocks. He was too focused on the portal to care much about the fall, or the fact that he was now dripping wet. He Shifted and flew back up to the crack in the rocky wall, and dropped his Shift again just as quickly.

"Why didn't it work?" Heather asked. She'd been knocked down, but not into the stream. No, Matt had been the only one to go that far.

"It didn't open, but it did something," Matt said. He observed the pale glow that still followed the crack in the rocky wall, and reached out a hand to touch it. He wasn't positive, but he thought it felt warm. "Let's try it again."

Detective Fords shook his head. "Sorry, son. It's too dangerous."

Matt turned to the man with incredulous eyes. "If it doesn't work, we'll be thrown back again. That's not dangerous."

"You don't know that it won't react more violently with a second attempt," Detective Fords insisted. "It was a good effort."

Matt wanted to shout, to curse at the man. He knew that wouldn't help his case.

"Sorry," Sergeant Spades said.

Matt looked back to the rocky wall. "Tell my mom what happened. And tell her I'm staying here."

"I really don't think that's a good—"

"Let him stay," Spades said, interrupting Detective Fords. "I'll stay with him."

Detective Fords muttered something but walked away, saying he would deliver Matt's message on his way out. Heather and Joey walked behind him. Matt glanced at Spades once they were gone.

"Thanks."

Spades was watching him closely. "You think it might do something else on its own."

Matt touched the wall again. It still had more give to it than it had before they'd done anything. "Yeah."

"I thought it was going to work," Spades continued. "It looked like it was going to work."

It wasn't the right fire, Matt thought. His mom had been right. Maybe the combination of Shifter types would equate to the Celestials being partially Shifted, but if Riley had her own fire . . . "It still might," Matt said. It was doubtful, but something was still happening with the portal site. Why else would it be glowing with that faint orange light? "I'm staying until it stops, or Riley comes through."

He was looking at the wall, but he could see Spades move in his periphery, as the man leaned against it. "How did you come up with this theory?"

Matt filled him in, not really caring if it got him in trouble.

"You've been working this case from the start, by yourself," Spades said a few minutes after Matt finished. His tone was thoughtful. "And you found the most promising lead we've seen, when countless others have been working on the same case, with better resources." He looked at Matt again. "You know what you want to do for a living, kid?"

Matt hadn't really thought about it, which must have been clear on his face.

"You should consider the police academy," Spades said. "You'd make a pretty good detective."

There was some immediate appeal in that, but Matt's focus remained primarily on the portal site. "I'll think about it."

Spades smiled as if Matt had just agreed. "I'll put in a good word for you with the Nation. You'll have to convince your mom it's a good fit."

Matt chuckled. He had a feeling Emily would be harder to convince. He also had a feeling she would be most supportive, once she got past the worry about him potentially being in danger. He sat down on the trail, facing the rocky wall, and for the first time in a long time, did some serious thinking about his long-term future.

CHAPTER 21

Plan and Attack

Wyatt hated having twine around his wrists again. Granted, it was extremely loose so he could remove it at a moment's notice, but it was still an inconvenience.

Traveling like this did keep them from attracting negative attention. The ring of guards around Wyatt, Tony, Allyssa, and Demetrius kept others from attacking them. Others thought they'd already been captured. At one point, when they reached Kin Woods, several guards offered to help transport them to Astrum. The allied guards politely refused, and since they were Christopher's elite squadron, the others didn't press the issue. They'd been able to dawdle in Kin Woods for about half a day before moving forward. Combined with their slow travel, Wyatt hoped Tristan and Riley would only be a few hours behind them, rather than a full day.

They were approaching Astrum now, and Wyatt kept focusing all his attention inward. He needed to sense the griffin. He shared its impulsivity, and knew that if it had gotten here before them, it wouldn't have wanted to wait for them. Hopefully the fact that it had needed to find the phoenix first meant it would reach Astrum around the same time. If not, there was a real chance it had already moved against Christopher.

"We should stop here," Demetrius said. He looked to the guards. "If you could set up a perimeter and turn back others."

"You're sure we should wait?" Wyatt asked.

Allyssa slid off Demetrius' horse and pulled her hands free of twine. "We need to give Riley and Tristan a chance to catch up. We also need to wait for the griffin and phoenix."

Wyatt got off his own horse. "What if they're already here?"

Allyssa crossed her arms. "We need to give it a little time."

Tony perked up. "I can fly closer and see if anything's going on. Be back in a jiff!"

He Shifted and flew off before anyone could really react, and Demetrius sighed. "I guess he does have the best chance of getting close without being spotted."

Wyatt was itching to go to the castle, and relieved his tense energy by pacing. He took out the obsidian blade he'd been wearing on his belt since just before getting his identity back and turned it over in his hand to have something to do. He'd taken it for defense. They'd ended up using it to cook. Now that he could Shift again, he didn't anticipate needing it, but he slipped it back into its sheath anyway. He'd grown accustomed to its weight.

It had to be almost half an hour before Tony came back. "Everything seems normal," he reported. "I flew right up to the castle. No signs of a fight. Not even many guards in sight."

And they once again had to hurry up and wait. Wyatt had always hated the expression, but he understood it now. He perked up when he felt something in his gut. He waited a second, to be sure, and then his adrenaline surged. "Here comes the griffin."

The others looked in the direction Wyatt faced, and moments later the griffin appeared. Its tufted ears were pricked, and its gaze was set upward, a slow kaleidoscope turning in its eyes. Wyatt looked up and saw the phoenix flying overhead. As he looked up the phoenix began to coast to the ground.

It was larger than Wyatt always imagined it

to be, resembling a giant eagle. He could have ridden on its back without difficulty, barring the fire that constantly covered its body. It just seemed so small compared to the dragon and griffin. Sunset orange and molten red blended effortlessly in the flames that crackled along its wingspan. Its ribbon-like tail flew behind it in a streamer as it flew closer and landed in front of them. When it landed on the ground, some of the flames faded. It tucked its wings close to its body and turned expectantly to the griffin.

"Have you had to use your gift on the phoenix the whole time?" Allyssa asked.

I was able to stop when it slept, but otherwise, yes. It's been getting harder as we get closer to Christopher.

Its ears drooped when it finished speaking, and its legs buckled underneath it. The phoenix jerked.

I can't hold it, the griffin warned.

Wyatt saw Demetrius snap his eyes on the phoenix in the same instant the griffin stopped using its gift, and knew it was too late. The phoenix sprang up with a cry of alarm, spreading its wings and ascending rapidly. Allyssa thrust her arms out, and the phoenix seemed to struggle to keep climbing.

"Keep it contained!" Wyatt cried.

The griffin staggered to a standing position and began its kaleidoscopic attack. The phoenix didn't look in its direction. Allyssa ripped her hands toward her, generating a stiff breeze Wyatt felt rush by him, blowing back his hair. It made the phoenix stagger as well, closer to the ground and right next to Allyssa.

Then the phoenix let out a cry and flared out its fire. The air burned. Allyssa shrank back, holding her arms in front of her face. The breeze reversed, wind pushing away from them to keep the flames out of reach. The phoenix rode the surge of wind and climbed into the air, flying in the direction of Astrum.

"Damn it!" Wyatt growled.

Demetrius inspected Allyssa's forearms, which were a bright pink. "I'm fine," she said. "Sorry."

"You deflected a fire attack," Demetrius said. "From very close range."

"It was instinctive," Allyssa said, "but it let the phoenix get away."

We have to get it back, the griffin said.

Wyatt shared a look with the Celestial and knew they were thinking the same thing. It dipped its head, and Wyatt moved to sit on its back. "Tell Tristan and Riley I tried to wait."

The griffin was running before Demetrius

and Allyssa could do more than say Wyatt's name, moving rapidly to Astrum.

Riley, Tristan, Jerry, and Hannah traveled at a brisk pace starting the morning after Tristan's fever spiked. He slept through that first night and seemed to have a normal temperature when he woke the next morning. He wasn't fully healed, but the worst was over, and he could finish recovering atop a horse. Riley felt bad pushing the horses to carry them for so long each day, and promised herself to treat the horses when this was over, with all the grooming, attention, food, and rest they wanted. She'd learned all about horses when she'd thought she was Jane, and knew they weren't really pushing them too hard, but it was still a long day for everyone.

Tristan's wound looked so much better by the time they reached Kin Woods. Riley had used the last of the honey mixture earlier that day, and was relieved to find the scratches no longer had a red and yellow outline. They seemed a bit smaller, actually. And Tristan was back to his normal self. Better, in some ways, because now he seemed to smile so much more.

Riley understood. She was smiling more herself. Especially when he held her close at night, partially Shifting until she fell asleep so she could keep the nightmares away. And waking up in the morning and being able to brush her hands across his cheeks, or kiss his temple to wake him? That definitely helped her smile as well.

Stress was returning now, as they left Kin Woods and moved toward Astrum. Stolen moments with Tristan while they'd been traveling were wonderful, but reality was setting back in. They had to face the phoenix, and Christopher.

"Don't worry," Tristan told her.

She thought he was doing a little worrying as well, but still found herself slightly comforted. Until they found Allyssa, Demetrius, Tony, and the rest of the guards.

"Where's Wyatt?" Tristan asked after immediately getting off his horse.

"He and the griffin went ahead, to follow the phoenix," Demetrius said.

Tristan swore. Riley followed Demetrius' eyes, her throat closing. Wyatt had gone ahead. Why would he do that? Even if the phoenix fled, he couldn't do it alone!

"It was a baller move," Tony said. "Wyatt jumped on the griffin's back and they ran so fast we didn't even have time to stop them."

"Are you okay now?" Allyssa asked Tristan.

"Great," Tristan told her. He reached into his bag and pulled his hand out seconds later, Chitter quivering in his palm. "You're going to want to stay here," he said in a softer voice, crouching and laying the hand flat on the ground. "Go on. We'll come back for you, or maybe you'll find us first."

The chipmunk scampered off.

Tristan took a deep breath. "Let's get going."

Demetrius and Allyssa got onto their horse. "Do we have a specific plan?" Allyssa asked. Riley looked at each of them and saw that they didn't. Allyssa nodded. "Well I made a checklist. Storm the castle. Save Wyatt's butt. Free the phoenix. Give Christopher a wedgie. Among other things. Anyone wanna add something?"

Tristan chuckled. "Sounds good to me."

The griffin moved incredibly quickly, even with Wyatt on its back.

The phoenix told me Christopher has the dragon as its prisoner, restrained in the castle, the griffin said. *Until recently the dragon was free to roam. When the shadow user freed my mind, Christopher surprised the dragon and captured it, and transported it here.*

"How'd they capture the dragon?"

It may be impervious to the shadow users' powers, but it has its weaknesses. My guess would be brute force, followed by natural methods of seda-

tion.

"Think the phoenix went right to Christopher?"

The griffin hesitated. *It's likely.*

That was what Wyatt was thinking. "Then our first goal is to free the dragon."

Wyatt adjusted his grip on the griffin, leaning forward. The castle was in sight now. "They're gonna try to stop us," he said.

The griffin scoffed, and despite how tired Wyatt knew it had to be, he could hear an undercurrent of energy in its voice. *They will try.*

The griffin ran past the small cottages that lined the path to the castle, one of which had apparently housed Allyssa. There were a few people walking around, and one, maybe two guards in the immediate area. Wyatt and the griffin blew past them and toward the castle. Once they passed the cottages and the villagers' area, there was a noticeable change. They went through the gates and saw multiple guards stationed at intervals.

"The griffin!" one yelled.

The two closest to the gate rushed at them. Wyatt leapt from the griffin's back, adopted a partial Shift, and rolled to keep his momentum when he hit the ground. He sprang upright in time to meet the Shifter guard, bowling him over. In his periphery he could see the griffin knock its attacker away in the same fashion.

A sort of haze filled Wyatt's mind when his adrenaline surged, and he ran and hit and blocked on instinct, working his way through guards and to the entrance. His partial Shift made him faster, stronger. More agile. Better, in every way.

"Can you feel the dragon?" Wyatt asked just after running into the castle.

This way, the griffin said.

Wyatt had never been in the castle before. He wasn't sure if the griffin had. He imagined it was like every other castle, but he had no point of reference. The floors and walls were stone. Lanterns at intervals mixed with the daylight in the narrow windows along the outer wall, making the lighting fairly consistent. That was about all Wyatt observed, jogging behind the griffin. He was too busy looking around for guards to appreciate much.

They didn't encounter as many people as Wyatt expected, and his wariness rose. It seemed too easy.

He realized when they found the dungeon why it seemed so easy. You didn't need a plethora of guards outside a cell when the structure was enough to keep a dragon both hidden and restrained. The wooden door the griffin stopped in front of had to be almost a foot thick, and it took Wyatt and the griffin both knocking against it a few times to break it open. Inside was a large stone room with a tremendous cage at its center. The far wall looked like it had a draw-bridge drawn up, a different material than the smooth, cold walls. Probably another absurdly heavy sheet of wood. It would explain how they got the dragon inside.

A tarp covered the cage.

"Dragon?" Wyatt called. "Dragon, can you hear me?"

I can hear you.

It was strange hearing a different voice in his head than the griffin and Demetrius. The dragon's voice seemed deeper than the griffin's. Warmer.

Wyatt pulled the tarp down and looked at the dragon. It was a horrible sight. A huge steel clamp stretched over its mouth and around its head. Heavy metal boots covered its feet, and chains crossing over its back restrained its wings.

"Can you move at all?" Wyatt asked.

The dragon fixed extremely familiar green eyes on him, and there was pain in their gaze. *My tail.*

That wouldn't be much help. Rage made the

aura around Wyatt burn brighter. No creature should be treated like this, but especially not a dragon. "I'll get you out."

Wyatt slashed a hand across the bars immediately in front of him. It didn't hurt him, but it didn't do much to the bars either. On a whim he took out his obsidian blade. That did nothing to the bars, and he sheathed it again quickly. The griffin was raking its claws over the bars in front of it, each motion making a sharp scratching sound. Wyatt could do the same, and the bars might eventually weaken, but he guessed it would take several minutes. He was sure Christopher or one of his guards would be here in that time. He looked at the griffin, silently communicating with it. He thought it understood, because it stopped attacking the cage.

Wyatt turned to face the dragon and made his eyes go kaleidoscopic.

The dragon's eyes narrowed. *What are you doing?*

Wyatt stepped closer, willing the swirl to intensify. Next to him, the griffin stared at the dragon with its own kaleidoscopic gaze. The dragon's pupils dilated under the weight of two griffins' stares.

Wyatt focused more energy on his gift, and slammed a hand against one of the bars, never taking his eyes from the dragon. The sudden movement seemed to help. The dragon strained against its bonds, thrashing from side to side. Wyatt raised the hand that didn't clutch one of the bars threateningly. The dragon spasmed and twitched in its restraints, and then renewed its desperate thrashing.

Until a chain broke.

Then another.

The dragon ripped itself free of the chains that had covered its body. They fell to the floor with a hollow ring. The dragon's chest heaved from the effort and pain, and probably from the fear, and Wyatt backed away and dropped his Shift. The griffin kept pace with Wyatt, stopping the use of its gift.

The dragon whipped its head side to side, then picked up each foot high enough to slip it from its metal boot. With the chains gone, the dragon was free of everything but the clamp around its jaw. It unfurled its wings, stamped its front feet, and raised burning green eyes to Wyatt.

He could sense about a dozen things the dragon wanted to say to him. He heard only one.

I understand.

Wyatt swallowed with difficulty. It had worked, but it had been almost unbearable to watch. The dragon was only free because it had been so completely terrified that its strength flared, and its raw power was enough to rip through the chains tied around it so tight. Wyatt, and the griffin, had done that. It disgusted him. It amazed him. He took in the dragon's angry, uneven tone and felt the disgust fade. There was something forgiving in those words. Something that said it knew why he'd done it without warning and maybe even appreciated it, now that it was over. It was the fastest way to set it free.

"Are you okay?" he asked.

Fine.

Can you break the cage now? the griffin asked.

Stand back, the dragon warned. Wyatt backed up to the wall, tense, and the dragon backed up as much as it could in its cage before ramming forward. The bars bent, curving outward so much that Wyatt couldn't believe they didn't snap off. A second assault from the dragon took care of that. They flew outward with tremendous force. One bar fragment hit the wall near Wyatt's cheek. A short piece hit the griffin on the top of the head, and though it glared, it remained silent.

The dragon stepped out of the remnants of its cage, and it was no longer a horrible sight. It stood proudly, wings spread, steel in its eyes. Even with the clamp still keeping its jaw shut, it was a beacon of power.

"Let me get the clamp," Wyatt said.

The dragon lowered its head. The clamp itself was the same thick metal the boots had been, but the straps that kept it tight were a sturdy leather. Wyatt didn't want to slash at the straps, fearing he might catch the dragon's scales. He plucked the obsidian blade from its sheath and sawed through the strap as carefully as he could.

He'd finally used it for something other than food.

The clamp fell to the floor with finality, and the dragon whipped around, stretched open its jaw, and drew in a huge breath. The column of fire that issued from its mouth startled Wyatt, sudden and forceful as it was. His partial Shift reappeared. The fire decimated the wooden slab, burning a hole through the center that left the drawbridge so unstable it fell open.

The dragon stopped breathing fire. *That felt good. Now to get the phoenix freed as well.*

Wyatt?

Wyatt recoiled when he heard Tristan's probing voice in his mind. "What the—?"

Tristan, the dragon rumbled, turning.

Wyatt frowned. *Can you hear me?* he thought.

Tristan's reply was immediate. *Loud and clear. And I can feel the dragon. Stay put. We're coming to you.*

"How can he do that?" Wyatt asked.

Both the dragon and the griffin seemed amused, which sent a current of annoyance through Wyatt. It was the griffin that explained. *As long as the distance isn't too great, Celestials can speak to each other telepathically. When our Shifters use their powers, they share the ability, though slightly less effectively. Your friends discovered it months ago.*

"They could have mentioned it," Wyatt muttered.

It took a few minutes, but Tristan and Riley appeared in the busted doorway. "You're bleeding," Riley said, her brows pressing close together.

Wyatt frowned, thinking it through, and put a hand to his cheek. His fingertips came back with droplets of blood. Apparently the piece of the bar from the cage had hit him. He still didn't feel it. "Just a scrape," he reassured Riley. "What took you so long?" he asked Tristan.

The boy had a partial Shift. "Ran into a few enemies on the way."

"You guys really must have made a scene, then. I didn't face any once I got in the castle."

"You made the scene, outside, so they were waiting for us!"

"Really not important," Riley reminded them.

It was great to see them, and to see Tristan so much better. Riley was right, though. "Can you feel the phoenix?" Wyatt asked her.

She nodded. "It's close."

CHAPTER 22

Rage . . . Rage

Allyssa watched Tristan and Riley run into the castle with mixed feelings. She was partially glad that they didn't have to fight the mass of soldiers that had been waiting for them. They were going after the Celestials, though, heading right to Christopher, so it wasn't like they were doing anything much safer. At least Tony was out of harm's way; Demetrius had seen to that at Tristan's urging, knocking the boy out and asking a guard to stay behind with him. He would be incredibly upset later, but Allyssa was fine with that.

She'd rather he wasn't caught in the midst of a battle, and this certainly qualified as a battle. There had to be thirty people waiting for them outside the castle. She made as clear a path for Tristan and Riley as she could, sending gales of wind in columns alongside them as they ran. They made it into the castle without much issue, and then Allyssa had to turn her attention to everything immediately around her. Several people had partial Shifts around them. Some had completely Shifted, so a moose, bull, lion, and hawk were in the melee. There were Elemental-ists of all types, and the evidence was in the air. Sparks from fire users crackled. Visibility re-duced due to bits of earth. The air became humid as water users condensed the moisture. And a breeze picked up around it all.

"Stay by my side," Allyssa told Demetrius.

"I was going to tell you the same thing."

Allyssa flicked her hand to make a wall of wind redirect the stones that had been sailing towards her head, and with a sweeping motion, sent the gust and the earthy ammunition back at the Elementalist that had tried to attack her. She sliced across with her other hand, sending a blade of wind against the lion that was rapidly approaching. Demetrius stood at her back, his hands held up to guard his face.

"My father must have spent days arming these guards with mental shields," Demetrius said. "They're not nearly as strong as those the guards that captured us had, but they're sturdy enough that I can't easily knock anyone out."

Allyssa thrust her hands up and watched the

vortex she'd just made buoy the lion into the air, spinning him around. "Can you work around them? Don't try to knock them out; make them aim with less precision, or cut off their powers."

He leaned his head back so she could see his face. He was smiling. "Your brain obviously works much better than mine in a battle."

The jerk in her gut that came from using her powers tightened when she made a whip of air grab a water user around the waist, hoist them into the air, and yank them to the ground. "Your brain works better than mine the rest of the time, so I'll take it."

"I would argue that isn't true, but not now. I'm really not good at multitasking."

Allyssa made a whirlwind and flicked her hand to send it near a cluster of Elementalists. She tensed before finishing the motion, as a different kind of tug pulled at her. Someone was trying to commandeer her whirlwind. She kept her hand out, flexing her fingers to tighten her hold on the rapid, and scanned the courtyard to find the thief. A tendril of air closed around her wrist and yanked her forward as a gust of wind pressed against her back, making her stumble. She kept control over her still swirling whirlwind and glared in the direction the air tendril had pulled her. She'd been shown up by a wind user at the waterfall. She wasn't about to let it happen again.

She saw the likely culprit and fed more wind into her whirlwind, giving it greater power and speed. She used both hands to shape it, feeling the jerk in her gut become more distinct, like a punch. It wanted to tear free of her control. She let it build a moment longer and drew her arms back before shoving them forward, launching the whirlwind in the direction of the other wind user. As soon as she sent it hurtling toward them she followed up by jerking her hands close to her, summoning a wave of wind to come from behind the enemy wind user.

It worked to destabilize the woman, so when the whirlwind reached her, she was too off-balance to control it and became caught in its current. Allyssa felt her mouth tug up in a smile.

The punched feeling Allyssa felt in her gut was spreading through her abdomen the more she used her powers. She ignored it and scooped up a blast of fire from nearby, redirecting it. She entered a hyper-focused state, her eyes jumping from person to person, her hands constantly moving.

Her focus broke when someone shoved her from behind. She caught herself with a blast of wind, righting herself and spinning to face the threat, and faltered when she saw Demetrius on the ground where she had just been standing.

The bull Shifter was next to him.

Her arms rested at her side, and she bent her fingers with her palms facing out before she could even think, her powers exploding. Hurricane force gales of wind formed around her as she ripped the air closer and bent it to her will. It tore against the bull, carrying with it fragments of rock and sparks of fire, crashing into the bull from all angles. It snorted and backed away in a panic, running into a water user who had been rushing to help it. Allyssa's arms burned and her hands shook. Her eyes streamed from the pain stabbing through her. She kept the hurricane going, and started to widen its range. She needed to check on Demetrius. It should have had enough energy to keep going for a minute or two.

She let her arms relax and dropped to her knees next to him, only to find him already sitting up. Her hands went to his face. "You're okay?"

He nodded. "One horn scraped my side, but it's just a scratch."

She looked at his abdomen and saw some blood on his shirt, but she thought he was right. It wasn't actively bleeding, because no blood was pooling. He moved the edge of his shirt to show her the wound and she nodded, satisfied. Black spots swam in front of her eyes at the sudden movement, and she felt Demetrius' hands grip her arms.

"Whoa, take a minute," he told her. "You just made a hurricane on command."

"Didn't mean to," she admitted. It had been instinctive. She'd had to get the bull away from Demetrius. She frowned now when she realized she still felt a tug in her gut. She wasn't actively using her powers. She shouldn't feel that.

She snapped her head up, closed her eyes for a second to keep from passing out, and focused. The air churned around her. The pressure she felt was her body's response to the air around her. "It's too much," she murmured.

Demetrius' expression changed to a more direct concern. "What's wrong?"

"There's too much energy. It's not dissipating, and my hurricane made it much worse." The gales of wind she'd expected to continue for seconds, maybe a minute or two, were growing stronger. They whipped around her. She'd given the wind a focal point, and now it was spiraling out of control—and taking the other elements inside it. The humidity was definitely rising, making the sparks from the fire users less like fire, and more like . . . lightning.

"I need to dissipate it," she said, putting a hand behind her to help herself stand. The world spun for a moment, and she leaned against

Demetrius.

"Use my energy," he told her. The wind stole most of his words, raging around them. He grasped one of her hands firmly, and she felt his consciousness brush against hers. *Take everything you need,* he said silently.

Her vision cleared, and strength flowed through her. His strength. He'd told her when they first met that he could act as a support, and she only now appreciated what it truly meant. Where a moment before she'd been drained, she could feel his body steady behind her, his hand tightly clasped with hers, and it was as if the energy were arching from his body to hers. She'd never felt so connected, so full of energy. She could still feel the wind churning around her, making her insides tighten, but it wasn't bad anymore.

Pace yourself, he warned. *It seems like your energy is full, but it's not.*

She set to work, extending her senses. Lightning flashed above them. She had to make a protective air bubble around the storm, before it grew too large. She reached beyond the churning air around her to the calm air in the distance, drawing it closer and visualizing it forming a dome. As soon as she made some progress, the hurricane battered against it, and she doubled the protective layer so that while it still collided, there was no danger of the storm breaking through.

Whenever the energy clashed against the bubble, she felt it as if it were her own body. Pieces of dirt and rock hit her body, and wind assailed her viciously from all sides, making her hair fly in different directions. She ignored it and expanded her air bubble, reaching for the other side of the courtyard once she had one contained.

Once she had the storm full of elemental energy contained, she sent a few quick bursts of wind to slice through the largest collections and break them up, and steered them to the edges of the air bubble. While she moved them she opened a small pocket. When the energy she wasn't controlling sensed the opening it surged toward it, slamming into it with incredible force and making her body feel like it was hit by a tree.

Allyssa steeled herself and grabbed hold of all the energy. A rush went through her, making her hair stand on end. It was so much power! For a moment she almost lost herself in it, and she felt Demetrius' hand jerk in hers. She held the wind steady as it raged, waiting for the worst of it to calm; the sparks began to die, airborne debris dropped to the ground, and the roar that had taken over her hearing faded to a hum. She made the air coil and snake into a line leading to the small openings she had created. She forced it to disperse slowly, keeping it restrained until the last possible moment, when she released it outside, to return to the way it was before the fighting started.

She let the air bubble pop, and was amazed to find that there was still fighting going on around them. She was equally amazed to feel her energy drain out of her as though punctured, fast and fully and all at once. She dropped to her knees, and then to all fours, bracing herself on trembling arms just to stay upright. Demetrius fell to his knees next to her in the same instant, his hand falling from hers, his mouth open as he took in heavy breaths.

"So that's what it feels like to control the wind."

Allyssa peeked at him from behind a tangled curtain of hair, and chuckled. It sounded more unhinged than she would have liked. She felt more unhinged than she would have liked, though if she was honest, she wasn't sure exactly what she was feeling. Except drained. Overwhelmed, maybe? Exhausted.

She didn't think she was in danger of passing out, though, and took that as a win. She might not be able to move beyond the effort of staying even remotely upright, but she would not pass out.

"I think I need to tag out of the battle now,"

she said weakly.

Shoes appeared in front of Allyssa. She knew she couldn't support herself if she tried to rest solely on her knees, and didn't risk moving more than her head. Her eyes moved up.

Christopher stood in front of her. "I appreciate your willingness to surrender," he said, a slight upturn to his lips. "You must have used every drop of power you have. Poor planning on your part. Though it was an impressive display."

Allyssa stared at him defiantly, wishing she had just an ounce of energy left to wipe that stupid smile off his face. Demetrius went to stand and Christopher snapped his fingers. Two of the guards that had been fighting nearby left the fight and grabbed Demetrius by the arms, hoisting him upright. One restrained him. The other picked Allyssa up and threw her over his shoulder. She tried hitting his back, but it was one of the weakest punches in history.

"Don't even try it," Christopher said, and Allyssa was certain Demetrius had just tried to use his powers on the man. "Let's go settle the terms of your surrender."

Riley ran through the castle, following the gentle pull she could feel that connected her to the phoenix. She knew the griffin and dragon could feel it as well, but they let her lead. The dragon had to make itself as small as it could to navigate the halls, meaning it was about the size of the phoenix. It hadn't been happy to shrink, but its determination was discernable. It wanted the phoenix freed.

The griffin wanted it as well, but she knew it also wanted Christopher. The thought that they would find both together made them all look for the phoenix.

She stopped in front of a rounded door near the base of one of the two towers. "It's in here."

Her hand was held up by the door handle, but she couldn't seem to open it. Wyatt reached past her and pulled it open, touching her arm in a reassuring way as he did. He had a partial Shift around him, yellow and brown and white and gold. The griffin rushed past as soon as the door opened enough. Wyatt followed, and then Riley braced herself and ran after him.

She needn't have worried, though. Christopher wasn't here. The phoenix was. It was stretched out on the floor in the middle of the room. The flames that always flickered on its wings burned low, and Riley's heart jumped into her throat. That she could feel her connection to it told her it wasn't dead, but could it be seriously hurt?

It's all right, the griffin said. *No external damage. Christopher must have made it lose conscious-*

ness.

The dragon walked in and placed a paw on one of the phoenix's wings, and hummed. Riley felt energy fill the room. The dragon was giving off feelings of alertness and anticipation, and though it was focused on the phoenix, Riley felt herself stand straighter because of it. The feeling in her chest grew as well, as the phoenix stirred. She'd thought it was muted, but assumed it was because of Christopher's spell. Now she knew it was because it had been unconscious.

"Why did he do this?" Tristan asked.

Riley turned to him. "What do you mean?"

Tristan's eyebrows were pressed together. "So the phoenix rushed back, and he knocked it out and left it in a room? Was he just trying to hide it? Or did he want it to be found?"

The phoenix sprang upright, flaring its fire.

"Again? Seriously?" Wyatt yelped, shielding his face with his arms.

Riley pushed out with her hands and the flames responded, bending away from her friends and the other Celestials.

"Phoenix, stop!" she cried.

The firebird acted like it didn't hear her. It seemed to be in a frenzy, whirling and sending out fire as it flew around them.

Phoenix, listen to reason! the dragon commanded.

The phoenix stood still for a heartbeat and then bolted towards the door, barreling into Tristan in the process. Tristan fell against the wall, his clothes smoking. The phoenix flew out the door and disappeared down the hall.

"That was rude," Tristan muttered, standing and raking a hand over his shirt to stop the sparks.

Riley stared at him for a second, determined he was fine, and ran after the phoenix. She followed the feeling in her chest, and instinct, both of which led her outside. If Christopher had left the phoenix with instructions to go on a rampage when it woke, it made sense for it to go outside, where plenty of people were gathered.

When she and Tristan had run past on their way into the castle, fighting had been starting around them. When she ran back out of the castle, fighting was still happening, though it seemed less intense than it had been. Though now there was a phoenix in the mix. As Riley stepped into the courtyard the phoenix's fire drew her eye, and she saw it dive toward Jerry and the woman he was fighting.

Jerry tried to put a wall of earth between him and the phoenix. He didn't have time, and the phoenix clipped him. He flew several feet before landing hard. Riley's pulse quickened. She ran to the man feeling like she was choking on a scream. She didn't know him well, but he was the reason Tristan was here today. And now he was burning.

She reached him and slapped her hands on his shoulder, trying to tamp out the flames, before common sense returned to her and she maneuvered the flames off of him and extinguished them. He wasn't conscious, but he was breathing.

She stood and looked up at the phoenix, circling back overhead. "You have to stop this!" she yelled. She could hear the edge in her voice.

A shape blocked the sun for an instant. The dragon. It climbed upward, its form expanding, and met the phoenix in the air, swiping at it with a massive paw. The dragon was strong. The phoenix was fast. It swerved around the dragon's extended paw and dove, and with a strangely beautiful cry, made the fire around it surge so it resembled a comet. It moved in tight circles as it dove, and the flames retained the circular pattern. A vortex of fire extended toward the ground.

"Whoa!" Wyatt exclaimed, suddenly on Riley's left.

Allyssa would be able to slash the fire tornado to pieces. Riley shook out her hands and ran forward. There wasn't time to over-analyze. She could tear the fire tornado apart too, if she got closer. The phoenix's flames wouldn't burn her.

She seized some of her mounting adrenaline and channeled it into the energy she needed to grab onto the fire tornado. She had to keep it steady, to prevent it from hurting anyone. Once it was relatively contained she started at the top, separating one section and diminishing the flames, and worked her way down to the base. It demanded her entire focus, and all of her control. The fire had a lot of force behind it.

Wyatt stood behind her, deflecting any attacks that came close while she worked on the fire tornado. She could feel him standing close, and knew Tristan was nearby as well, though she couldn't see him. The dragon and the phoenix were circling high above in a dance, with whirling green and red and gold and spurts of flames as accompaniment.

"We need it to be closer," Riley said. She couldn't get to the phoenix from here.

"I'll tell Tristan," Wyatt said, and dashed off. Riley followed his progress between tracking the battle around her and the battle in the sky. Tristan and Wyatt partially Shifted, and both looked up. Riley couldn't hear it herself, but she knew they were both calling to the dragon. If the dragon could lure the phoenix closer to ground level, everything would be easier. Riley felt she just needed to be in direct contact with the Celestial to help calm it down.

The way the dragon angled its head made Riley think it agreed, and the dragon and phoenix both started moving lower in the sky. The phoenix seemed to become suspicious when the dragon swooped over it to prevent it from flying back up. It coated itself in fire again and made as if to dart beneath the dragon's wings, and the dragon reacted instantly. The dragon blew its own column of fire toward the phoenix, then reached out two paws and trapped the firebird there, tucking it close to its body and diving. It leveled off just before it would have hit the ground and shoved the phoenix away.

The phoenix landed roughly and rolled to its feet. The dragon completed a tight turn. They faced each other again in a second, the dragon with a mouthful of high intensity flames, the phoenix with a wingspan of the same sort.

Realization struck Riley, and she raced toward them. Wyatt and Tristan started running forward as well. "No, don't!"

She sent her own fire toward them, aiming between the two Celestials in the hopes their attacks wouldn't meet. Their attacks had met in the air, but not from this close together. They would have a much different reaction like this. Her column of flame wasn't enough. Their flames collided with an audible crash as the waves of power knocked against each other, and everything surged outward with a boom. Riley was almost next to them, and saw the flames rushing toward her with an angry, powerful roar.

Hands grabbed her arms and yanked backward. White and brown light on the left. Emerald, green light on the right. Both boys grabbed her and pulled her back. Tristan pulled her closer to him, trying to curve his body around hers. Wyatt stepped in front of her.

There wasn't time to think, let alone react, before the flames and force reached them.

There wasn't time to think about it, yet it still seemed like slow motion, as she and Tristan fell to the ground. The flames reached Wyatt first. Wyatt, who was still standing, completely facing the coming attack with no means of defense. Wyatt, the only one of them who could be damaged by the flames. Tristan had pulled Riley aside enough that when the force knocked Wyatt off his feet, and the blast threw him backward, he didn't run into anyone. His shirt caught fire. He caught fire. His face was a mess of shock and pain, his eyebrows lifted in surprise, his mouth open in a soundless scream.

Riley's scream wasn't soundless. It tore from

her, piercing as it released.

"WYATT!"

Her collision with the ground stole the breath from her body, and the wave of force and heat swept past her. Riley replenished her air and scrambled upright, running to Wyatt's side.

He was gasping in pain, his eyes wide as saucers, a tight grimace on his face. His shirt hung in tattered scraps on his back. What had been the front of it was completely gone, vaporized by the flames. His skin . . . his skin shone a vicious red that bordered on black, charred and blistered. The burn covered his abdomen and climbed up part of his neck. As bad as it looked on the outside, Riley worried more of the damage was internal.

"Why would you do that?" Riley wanted to sound angry, but knew the only thing she conveyed was fear. Her heart pounded frantically in her chest.

"Go finish this," Wyatt urged.

"We need to heal you!" Tristan said.

"After," Wyatt said, "I'll be fine."

Some sort of understanding seemed to pass between the boys when they locked eyes. Tristan gripped Wyatt's hand, then stood and gently steered Riley away. "Dragon!" Tristan called.

Riley tried to push her emotions aside. The

sooner she focused and got through to the phoenix, the sooner she could figure out how to help Wyatt. She blinked back the tears she felt coming, and followed Tristan over to the dragon. It lowered itself to allow them to climb on, then climbed into the sky, where the phoenix had resumed its chaotic attack.

It flew closer to the dragon almost immediately.

An idea was forming in Riley's head, and though it filled her with terror, she thought it was the best chance she had. "I need to be alone with it. Can we fly higher?"

The dragon heard and started angling itself up, tilting its wings to gain altitude. "Riley, if I didn't know how scared you are of heights I'd say you wanted to jump off the dragon," Tristan said, turning to look at her. She looked at her lap, and when she glanced at him she saw his eyes were wide. "You can't do that! It's dangerous!"

She looked at him fully, with complete urgency. "Tristan, I have to do something. Wyatt was the one to get through to the griffin. I can get through to the phoenix."

"But like this?"

"It's the only way I can think to be completely alone with the phoenix, in contact with it and demanding its focus." Her voice was climbing, and she took a deep breath to try to calm her skyrocketing nerves. Pushing aside her emotions clearly wasn't working. At least she wasn't paralyzed by them. She would be if she let herself stop, though, and spoke quickly. "I really don't want to do this, but if I don't do it now I know I won't be able to. I over analyze, remember? Please don't make me more scared than I already am by saying it's dangerous." She swallowed and looked down at the ground, far below them. "I know that."

She saw the way he looked at her, his body tensed, his expression solemn. He grabbed her hand and blinked slowly, partially Shifting. *I know you're scared,* he said, *but you can do this. It's a good plan, and it'll work. I'll catch you at the bottom, if you need me.*

It wasn't just the confidence in his tone that Riley felt. There was a warm feeling spreading through her from his hands, and she realized she wasn't terrified anymore. She was scared, but it was a much healthier kind of scared than before. Fear put into perspective. She genuinely felt confident. Maybe even brave.

Riley looked over her shoulder at the phoenix, which was trying to attack the dragon's exposed belly. She sent a blast of fire at it to catch its attention, and it turned on her, flying out of reach of the dragon as it circled back towards her. Riley tensed, starting to stand. Tristan squeezed her hand and she mentally counted down as the phoenix got closer. Three, two . . . she skipped one on an impulse.

She jumped.

CHAPTER 23

Love and War

The guards dragged Demetrius and Allyssa to the throne room, near the top of the castle. Demetrius didn't resist while he walked. He was too focused on reinforcing the mental shield he'd given Allyssa. Wyatt, Allyssa, and Riley all had them now. It had been one of the first things Demetrius did after he recovered his energy from swaying the guards to help them. What he'd just done, though, sharing his strength with Allyssa, had required him to break her shield down. He'd made it to defend against his powers as well as his father's, in a moment of self-doubt. Stupid! He hastened to rebuild it now, knowing Christopher would go after her. Unfortunately, Christopher seemed to have already guessed Demetrius' plan. The man kept casually countering Demetrius' efforts.

The guard carrying Allyssa dropped her to the floor. Tobias, the head guard who held Demetrius' arms behind his back, tightened his grip when Demetrius moved to help her.

"Leave her alone!" Demetrius said, a snarl in his voice. He looked at his father with a burning hatred.

"And what would you do if I left her alone?" Christopher asked. He sat on the edge of his throne and looked at Demetrius carefully. "Would you swear loyalty to me? Be the son I was so convinced I had raised?"

"Yes."

Christopher met his eyes for a second before smiling. "It seems some of my lessons sank in. You would say anything for me to free her."

"I would do anything, if it saves her," Demetrius said. "If you believe nothing else, believe that."

Christopher's attention went to Allyssa, who was struggling to sit up. "I do." His dark eyes fixed on Allyssa, and Demetrius flinched as she screamed in pain. She sank back to the floor.

"Stop!" he yelled.

"What's this?" Christopher said quietly. "You're scared of water now?"

Demetrius saw the shard of fear in Allyssa's eyes and looked around, wondering which of the guards was the water user. He had to stop them before they started attacking her. But to his surprise, no one had to move for Allyssa to start thrashing and crying out.

"Wonderful," Christopher said.

"It's not real," Demetrius said, understanding.

"You seem to think I only want to hurt her. You don't understand I'm doing this for more than that. I know you think you love her. So by breaking her, physically, emotionally, and mentally, I teach you the consequences of betraying me. Though you've done a good job of draining her physically on your own."

Demetrius looked over at Allyssa as she made a strangled gasping sound, her eyes facing him but seeing whatever Christopher was making her see. Demetrius tried reaching out to her, to give her a shield against his father, but as soon as Christopher felt Demetrius he kicked him out brutally.

Allyssa stopped thrashing and looked straight at Demetrius, and he could tell she actually saw him now. "You're stronger than him," she said in a low voice.

He didn't have time to respond. Her eyes went distant again, her limbs shaking as Christopher started another mental attack.

Demetrius found new strength. He threw Tobias off him and ran at his father with a yell. Christopher seemed shocked to see Demetrius rushing at him, but not concerned. Unlike Demetrius, Christopher liked practicing his physical strength as well as his mental. He blocked Demetrius' attack and threw him backwards, sending Demetrius skidding across the floor. He held up a hand to stop Tobias from grabbing Demetrius again.

"Try it again and you'll regret it," Christopher promised in a low tone. Demetrius could hear the anger in his voice, and was hurt but not surprised when Allyssa cried out again from another mental attack. Demetrius picked himself up and took a step towards Christopher, reaching out with his mind. He had to disarm Christopher mentally, since he couldn't physically, and he had to do it fast, so Allyssa didn't suffer any more.

He aimed at Christopher's mental defense like a rocket and pushed against it. Wyatt believed he was stronger. So did Allyssa. And Christopher had even said it before, though he probably never thought it would be used against him. Demetrius was halfway through when he heard Allyssa suck in her breath in a sharp, ragged way, and knew something was seriously wrong. He drew his power back into himself in a heartbeat and turned to her, going to his knees next to her. She was staring blankly at the ceiling, her lips slightly parted. Demetrius hurried to check her pulse, and saw that her chest continued to rise and fall as she drew breath.

"She's alive," Christopher said. "Not that she knows it anymore."

"What did you do?" Demetrius asked slowly, his voice shaking.

"Disconnected her from her senses. She can't hear or see anything. Feel anything. But she is alive; something I've allowed for your benefit." Christopher stared at him. "I don't approve of your feelings for her, but I'm not unreasonable. Her talents with the wind are truly remarkable, and it would be a shame to kill her."

"Restore her senses!" Demetrius demanded, extending his powers.

Christopher shook his head and shut down Demetrius' powers. "Not until you've listened. I kept her close so you could see her, even if you didn't realize it."

"You made her a servant so you could gloat!"

Christopher barely reacted. "I did take some satisfaction from her role, and in being able to reinforce it when her mind broke down the spell each month. Between keeping her spellbound and containing the dragon Shifter, I had full security in my position here. I also kept them here for you, though. Eventually, you would have come around. I was lessening the amount of the neurotoxin concoction I created every few weeks, weaning you off of it. I never gave you enough to cause permanent damage; only enough to slowly change your thought process for the better. As it settled, you needed less of the neurotoxin, because your mind was adjusting and becoming accustomed to questioning less. If you'd stayed put, you would have returned to your senses a true prince. We could have had a long conversation, and I could have restored your true memories."

The words drifted into Demetrius' head as he stared at Allyssa, swirling around his mind. "What are you saying?"

Christopher stepped closer. "I need you to understand what I've done for you, and how you've repaid my kindness."

Demetrius could hear his pulse thundering in his ears. "Kindness? Is that what you call everything you've done, Father? It was a kindness to manipulate the Celestials, and take over their world? It was a kindness to erase my friends' identities and imprison them? It was a kindness to use your powers on *me*?" He realized he was shouting. At some point he'd stood.

The tension in Christopher's jawline revealed the anger he was clearly trying to restrain. "I gave you everything—"

"You *took* everything! And I won't let you take

anything else!"

He whipped around, facing Christopher, and sent a wave of power over him. As it did with Shifting, emotions made elemental powers stronger. With the grief and rage pounding through Demetrius now, his powers had a tremendous surge of strength. The power knocked Christopher off his feet, sending him reeling into the edge of his throne. Demetrius stalked towards him. The guards in the room started moving to apprehend him, and he waved a hand to send out another batch of power. They dropped like stones.

Demetrius barreled his way into his father's mind, slamming through the mental barriers he'd broken through only once before, when they hadn't been close to this fortified. He heard the final barrier shatter, felt Christopher flinch with pain. He didn't stop. He pressed into Christopher's consciousness, relentless.

You took away her senses, Father? Demetrius asked in a dangerously soft voice. *Allow me to take away yours.* He disabled Christopher's hearing first, and then his sight. And he heightened his pain receptors before launching a complete mental attack, punishing his father the same way he had been punished, countless times since his mother died. Christopher screamed in agony. Demetrius felt nothing but a vindictive pleasure.

You always said I'm the strongest Dark Elementalist in the world. I guess you're right.

Demetrius heard Christopher start to say something in his mind, but acted before he could get it out. He lowered Christopher's awareness, sending the man into a sleep comparable to a coma. "Sleep well, Father."

He stood over his father's comatose form, shaking, swaying as the crest of energy that had swept him forward slammed down and left him, and a second later turned and staggered to Allyssa's side, sliding to his knees. He brushed the hair back from her face, bringing her head to his lap, and forced himself to breathe deeply. He couldn't afford to lose control now. He needed to be precise with his powers. He reached out with some hesitance and latched onto Allyssa's consciousness. It was there, strong as ever. It was just shrouded. He focused and removed the blocks Christopher had implanted, one at a time; he connected her back to her senses of sight, touch, smell, sound. When it seemed there was nothing else for him to do he retreated from her mind, and stared down at her, waiting with bated breath for her to awaken.

It was as sudden as her reaction to being cut off from her senses had been. She took in a terrified breath. Her eyes opened wide, eyebrows shooting up. Her spine arched and she began hyperventilating.

Demetrius tightened his arm around her and smoothed back her hair, making calming noises before he realized what he was doing. Noises that didn't have set words, but clearly said *It's okay. You're okay. You're safe. No one's going to hurt you.* Maybe he said some of them aloud. He wasn't sure.

Her warm brown eyes locked on him, more vulnerable than he'd ever seen them, and she lifted her arms to his neck. He understood. He repositioned and helped her sit upright, and she buried herself against his chest, locking her arms tight around his shoulders and scrunching the fabric of his shirt in her hands.

He didn't think she was crying, but he could feel her body shaking. He might have been shaking. Holding her like this, it was hard to tell where her trembling stopped and his began. He held her close and murmured reassurances. The feeling of another body pressed close to his elicited a primal comfort in him; a sense of warmth and security that was achieved merely from physical contact. Gradually, the shaking that encompassed them both faded.

"Stop apologizing," Allyssa said. Her voice was quiet but strong, her breath warm against his neck.

Demetrius hadn't even realized. So the words in his head had slipped out of his mouth. *I'm so sorry. This is all my fault. I'm sorry.*

"Don't close yourself off. Don't punish yourself." One of her hands remained fisted in the material of his shirt. The other went to the back of his neck, her fingers skirting along his skin and rifling through his hair. "I need you." Her breath warmed his cheek as she pulled herself upright. He could feel her lips move against his cheek when she spoke again. "Demetrius, I need you."

Her lips met his in a hot, desperate rush, and everything but Allyssa, her body pressed close to his, her hand carding through his hair, her mouth firm on his, disappeared. His doubts, his pain, his shock—gone. There was only this moment, wrapped in an embrace he never wanted to end. Being told with each beat of his racing heart that he wasn't alone; that he would never have to be alone, because she trusted him, all of him, with every fiber of her being.

He touched his forehead to hers when he had to stop to breathe. "I thought I lost you," he admitted.

"I thought I lost you before, with the bull Shifter. I guess we're even." There was no humor in her voice. "Let's make sure it stays that way. No more thinking we've lost each other, or anyone else."

"No more," he agreed. "Which means it's time to finish this. Do you think you can stand?"

Allyssa nodded, and he helped her rise to her feet. She clung to him but did remain standing.

They began walking slowly but steadily out of the room, down to the entrance of the castle.

The first two seconds Riley was in the air were okay. Then she collided with the phoenix, landing on its back and wrapping her arms and legs around it as tightly as she could. It started thrashing and scratching, but she clung on to it as they started falling. Something inside her changed when she came into full contact with the phoenix. She felt a chaotic buzz fill her brain. She wanted to soar; to use her fire. To cause destruction.

The wind sent her hair flying behind her and made the phoenix's flames ripple. Warm, vibrant flames. She focused on those flames to keep herself from losing it, and pushed past the chaotic spell. No wonder the phoenix was on a rampage. Christopher had absolutely enraged it.

"Look at me!" she demanded. "Focus, and remember yourself!"

It continued thrashing, trying to flap its wings. The way Riley was holding on prevented it from controlling their fall with its wings, but it was more than capable of twisting.

"Phoenix!" She tightened her grip as it tried to

buck her off, and a trill of fear went through her as she realized how fast they were falling, so that her next plea was a scream. *"Phoenix!"*

The phoenix stopped fighting and they kept falling. Riley didn't know if it was stunned, but it wasn't even trying to fly anymore. She closed her eyes as they got close enough to see the faces of the people fighting, bracing herself for a very hard fall.

But it wasn't so bad. It felt very light, actually. Too light. And when she heard a warm chuckle she opened her eyes. Tristan was leaning over her. She was on the dragon's back, the phoenix next to her.

"Told you not to worry," Tristan said.

Riley practically jumped on him. He held her close to his chest while the dragon coasted to the ground. "I almost lost control," she said. "Christopher's spell was so strong that I felt its influence."

"Is the phoenix okay?"

The phoenix hadn't moved, but at Tristan's question it fixed its gaze on them. It still didn't say anything, but Riley thought she saw more of a struggle in its eyes than she had before. It was actively fighting Christopher's influence.

The dragon roared. Below them, all straggling attempts at fighting stopped.

Where is the shadow user? the dragon asked.

"They shouldn't be far," Tristan said.

They landed on the ground and Riley and Tristan slid off the dragon's back. Riley couldn't see Demetrius or Allyssa. She *could* see Wyatt. Her heart started pounding so fast again she thought she might pass out. He was incredibly pale, and horribly, horribly still.

Riley and Tristan yelled at the same time. "Wyatt!"

He's alive, the griffin told them, *but he's fading.*

The griffin sat next to him, pressed against his side. Riley reached them and grabbed at Wyatt's wrist with one hand and put the other on his neck, taking his pulse whichever way she could. He opened his eyes a crack.

Tristan was on his knees next to Riley, an emerald light burning around him. "What can we do?"

Wyatt moved his head slowly from side to side. "Nothing . . . to . . . do." Each word was labored.

Riley abandoned her efforts to measure his weak pulse. "There must be some sort of medicine we can find. Something we can do."

Wyatt took in a large breath, and a partial Shift appeared around him. It flickered before going out. He didn't have the energy to hold it.

"Sorry," he managed, his eyes squinting almost completely closed.

"Wyatt, no, you have to stay awake!" Riley cried. She realized red and orange light rippled around her, though she didn't know how long it had been there. She didn't care.

"Hold on!" Tristan ordered. "You're not dying on us!"

It seemed like Wyatt started to smile, and then his eyes closed. Tristan shook Wyatt's shoulder. Riley placed her hands on Wyatt's arms and leaned forward. "Wyatt, please!"

He didn't respond. His breathing was so slow, and now that he'd lost consciousness . . . .

"No," Riley said. Tears obscured her vision. "Wyatt, you aren't dying! You're not! Not after everything!" She choked on a sob and could barely get the words out. She blinked fast, and the tears broke through when she tried to say his name. Tried. She couldn't get any more words past the block in her throat. She couldn't see clearly, and her breathing hitched with a gasping effort to contain her sobbing.

She heard Tristan suck in a breath, and through her blurred vision saw Tristan's hand leave Wyatt's shoulder. Then she felt it cover hers.

"Riley, look," Tristan said.

She pressed her lips together when her breathing hitched again, squinted her eyes shut tight, and opened them forcefully. It helped clear her vision. She drew her hands back and wiped at her eyes to make it even clearer, and to make sure she wasn't seeing things. There were golden drops on Wyatt's chest.

"Your tears," Tristan said.

Riley watched the tears seep through the tattered fabric of Wyatt's shirt and absorb through his burned, damaged skin. She glanced at Tristan and then locked her gaze on Wyatt again. The pallor faded from his face as a healthy color returned. The worst of the external damage healed, the charred skin lightening and many of the blisters disappearing. His breathing evened. He opened his eyes a crack, and with a blink, opened them fully, and then looked between Riley and Tristan with focused but confused hazel eyes.

Riley laughed in a hysterical/still kind of sobbing way. "You're—okay!"

"How?" Wyatt asked.

Phoenix tears, the griffin said.

They all looked at Riley, and she couldn't maintain her fragile attempt to keep it together. She fell forward with a renewed sob she didn't really understand, gripping herself around the middle to keep from falling on Wyatt.

"Riley, I'm okay," Wyatt said.

She wanted to respond, to tell him she just needed a minute, but she couldn't make herself do anything, at the moment.

"She's processing," Tristan said for her. "A lot just happened in a really short time."

"You sound a little choked up too," Wyatt teased.

Tristan paused. "Yeah," he admitted.

Riley cried a little harder at that.

She must have passed out, because the next thing she knew she was flat on her back and both boys were leaning over her with worried expressions. It couldn't have been more than a minute or two.

"Riley?" Tristan questioned.

"I'm okay," she told them. Her voice was relatively normal. Her emotions were under control. Riley understood what had happened. Between the adrenaline surges and emotional spikes, her brain had done the only thing it could to regain control. It shut her down for a moment so she could wake in a more level state.

"We need to go over what 'okay' means," Wyatt said.

"I don't think any of us are okay right now."

Riley sat up to see Allyssa and Demetrius

walking over, Allyssa leaning heavily on Demetrius. Both looked absolutely exhausted. It was Allyssa who had spoken. Relief speared through Riley at the sight of her best friend.

"The phoenix is back to normal," Demetrius said. His eyes narrowed as he looked at Riley, Tristan, and Wyatt more closely. "What happened?"

"Wyatt took a hit for Riley that almost killed him," Tristan said.

"Riley discovered another gift from the phoenix that saved me."

Allyssa and Demetrius stared at them, and then Allyssa sat down. "Okay. Try that again, with a lot more detail. We've got plenty of time."

So they explained everything they'd gone through since running into the castle, and then listened when Allyssa and Demetrius filled them in on what they had missed. Demetrius mostly filled them in, but he was vague in describing one crucial part.

"What exactly happened with Christopher?" Allyssa asked.

Demetrius couldn't seem to meet any of their eyes. "I disconnected him from his senses, like he did to Allyssa, and basically put him in a coma." He swallowed heavily. "I didn't know what else to do. I couldn't kill him."

Allyssa squeezed his arm. "You would never have forgiven yourself if you had."

"I'm fine with the idea of you not killing anyone," Wyatt said. "Though Christopher deserves worse than a coma."

"If his powers weren't so strong, maybe there would be other options," Tristan said, "but this seems like the safest bet. Trust me, I'd love to put him in a cell for months on end."

"We still could," Allyssa said darkly.

Riley stayed silent not because she didn't want to participate, but because she didn't have anything to add that hadn't already been said. She agreed with them. She even agreed with Allyssa's thought of shoving Christopher in a cell somewhere, comatose or not. The thought should bother her, but she actually found herself wanting it. Just a bit more than she was comfortable with. She pushed her own analysis to the back of her mind.

Most of the fighters in front of the castle had left. Those that remained were either unconscious or too wounded to move on their own, and several doctors from the village were making rounds to attend to them. One of the doctors walked up to the group now.

"Everyone else has been looked at, and you clearly need medical attention," she said sternly.

She really hadn't liked it when Wyatt sent her away several minutes ago.

Look after all of them, the phoenix said. *Give them something for pain and rest, whether they want it or not.*

Especially if they don't want it, the dragon said.

If they give you trouble, we can help, the griffin said.

The woman seemed awed to hear the Celestials, and equally intimidated and amused. She nodded and began examining Wyatt's burns.

We will oversee things for the night, the phoenix said, looking at the group. *In the morning we can talk.*

CHAPTER 24

Taking Stock

The herbal drink one of the doctors gave Allyssa made it very difficult to stay awake, as did her own physical and mental exhaustion. The mattresses they'd pulled from a few rooms in the castle, when they'd unanimously decided to stay together overnight, were surprisingly comfortable. That made it hard to avoid sleep too. She kept finding her head drooping onto her chest, her eyes slipping closed, and put herself in increasingly uncomfortable positions to stay awake.

"Keep fidgeting and the Celestials will come and force you to sleep," a warm, sleepy voice whispered next to her. She turned to see Demetrius propping himself up on his elbows. "Why are you fighting so hard to stay awake?"

Allyssa listened to the deep, even breathing of Wyatt, Tristan, Riley, and Tony—they'd asked the dragon to go and get him, which had seemed to make up for the fact that they'd knocked him out, in his mind—and swallowed a lump in her throat. "I'm terrified to sleep," she admitted.

She felt Demetrius' eyes on her. "Because of what my father did."

She nodded.

"It was my fault. I couldn't put your shield back up in time."

"It wasn't your fault," she said quickly, with a bit of force. She'd known he would feel guilty if she brought it up. All blame belonged to Christopher. That wasn't what was bothering her now. "It was like I was in a dark room. A vacuum. There was just . . . nothing, but I couldn't realize it at the time. I realized it when you reconnected me to my senses."

It was like coming back from the effects of the neurotoxin those three Shifters had used on her last year. It wasn't the experience itself that was terrifying. It was realizing what she'd lost after the fact, when she'd gotten it back.

"You're scared of it happening again."

She didn't respond, and Demetrius moved closer to her.

"You need to sleep. It will actually make you feel better. I promise you, nothing bad will happen."

She knew it was a foolish fear, but she couldn't help it. "How can you be sure?"

He opened his arms and she nestled against him. "I won't let it," he said.

Her shoulders hitched in a silent laugh. That sounded like something she would say. "Thank you."

Demetrius tightened his arms around her for an instant, enveloping her in warmth. "'*No sooner met but they looked, no sooner looked but they loved.*'"

She interlaced one of her hands with his. "What's that?"

"A quote by William Shakespeare, which I think applies to us. To me, at the very least." His hand found its way to her hair, twisting a strand between his fingers in a way she found extremely soothing. "I need to tell you how much you mean to me. I know that everything has been so dangerous and edgy lately, feelings have been heightened, but the way I feel about you hasn't changed in the slightest. I've been falling in love with you since the moment we met, Allyssa."

She forgot how to breathe for a second. Then she sat up straight so she could see his face. "I love you too," she whispered. His face lit up, and she knew he wanted to kiss her. She wanted to kiss him too, but kept it to a very short, light press of her lips to his. She couldn't contain her laughter beyond that, and didn't want to hurt his feelings. She definitely wasn't laughing about the kiss, or the sentiment. "I know I'm completely ruining this sweet, romantic moment, but," she giggled, "I can't believe you just said 'edgy!'"

She rested her head on his chest again and felt his laugh as he lay back. "That did ruin the moment, but we should get to sleep anyway. I'll take your amusement as a sign you're completely exhausted."

She closed her eyes and smiled, knowing she was giddy but pretending she wasn't. "Maybe. Don't let that make you think I didn't mean what I said."

His voice was low when he responded. He seemed close to sleep himself. "I know you meant it. Your honesty is part of the reason I love you."

Her giddiness faded, and she hummed in contentment at how casual, and right, those words sounded. "I'm not afraid to go to sleep anymore."

He kissed the top of her head, and drowsy butterflies went through her. "Sweet dreams."

"With a little 'edge,'" she murmured with a partial smile.

She felt the vibrations as he chuckled again before she fell asleep.

It seemed like minutes later that she woke,

still cuddled against Demetrius. She felt remarkably changed, though, and knew it had been hours of restful, restorative sleep. She still felt she could sleep another day without issue, but it was with a rush of energy that she stood and stretched.

Tristan sat on the edge of his mattress, leaning down, and Allyssa grinned. Chitter the chipmunk stood on his back feet, looking at Tristan and munching on a berry. "I don't care what anyone says, we have to bring him home with us," Allyssa said.

Tristan grinned. "Fine by me."

"You seriously want to keep the chipmunk?" Wyatt asked. He was still sprawled out on his mattress, facedown, so his words were slightly muffled.

"I think he's proven he wants to stay with us," Riley said in a quiet voice.

"I say if he follows us through the portal, he gets to stay," Tristan declared. He looked at Wyatt. "Your burns are mostly on the front of your body. Why did you sleep on your stomach?"

Wyatt slowly rose to his feet, wincing. "I didn't start out that way, and you can't really control how you sleep."

It was better that he'd passed out, even if his front hurt a bit now. It meant he'd gotten meaningful rest. Riley's phoenix tears had fixed the deadly internal damage Wyatt had sustained, and some of the external, but the burns on the surface of his skin were still bad. It would take a while to heal, and definitely scar. The burns were focused on his abdomen, though part of the burns were visible on his neck. Allyssa volunteered to help him put more of the burn medicine on, since she wasn't squeamish—you couldn't want to be a vet if you were squeamish. The doctor reappeared before she could help, though, and Allyssa let the trained professional tend to Wyatt.

Allyssa didn't know where the Celestials had slept. She guessed they'd stayed close, because they appeared within minutes of everyone waking and walking out to the courtyard. Tony got so excited he Shifted and flew around their heads before taking off, potentially for a flight around the village.

"I'm sorry," Riley said right away.

All three Celestials seemed confused. The phoenix stepped forward. *Why? If anything, we need to apologize to you.*

Riley had her eyes set on the castle. "If we hadn't opened the doorway, none of this would have happened."

We wanted you to open it, the dragon said. *We sent you dreams to prepare you.*

I've never given part of my fire to a Shifter, the phoenix said. *We knew it would be the signal to your world that we were ready to return, if you were ready for us. That things were ready to change.*

Of course we'd forgotten no one would know what the fire meant, the griffin pointed out. *And you didn't really tell anyone about it.*

We all agreed it was time for our worlds to interact again, the phoenix said, ignoring the griffin's comment. *We pressured you to open the doorway on your side. You had noble intentions as well, with the war.*

"Christopher never cared about the war," Wyatt said.

Demetrius shook his head. "He didn't plan to let the Celestials come back to talk to the Shifter and Elemental governments, but that doesn't mean it wasn't a good idea. That's why you all agreed to do this. He said it to convince you. You did it because you believed it would work. And it still could."

"You said you wanted us to open the door so you could come back to Earth," Tristan said. "Do you still want to come back with us?"

Yes.

They spoke together, and there was so much power in the one word when their three voices overlapped that Allyssa was dazzled for a moment.

We'll go along with your plan, the griffin said. *We'll speak with your leaders and urge them to make peace, if they haven't already. Then we'll have to discuss the barrier between the worlds.*

"People have made new lives here," Demetrius said. "You plan to discuss that with the Nation and the Council."

The griffin nodded.

"We should go through the portal first," Tristan said. "We need to see our families before we do anything else, and then we can tell the Nation and the Council you're coming, so no one's startled."

The mention of their families had them all longing to go through the portal, Allyssa was sure. Except for Demetrius.

"The four of you should go now," Demetrius said. "No one is waiting for me over there, and someone should really stay and make sure things here don't become too chaotic after yesterday. I'll stay in Astrum for now, and tell people the king has been dethroned. They'll need an explanation of yesterday's events."

And they already see you as an authority figure, Allyssa thought. Their prince, though she knew he wouldn't introduce himself that way. "Do you want me to stay?" she asked.

He smiled. "I won't make your family wait any longer to see you. I'll be fine."

Tony appeared next to them, flying in at a high speed and dropping to the ground as a human. "What's going on?"

Allyssa explained how they would be leaving.

"I'll stay with Demetrius," Tony said. "I don't have anyone waiting for me, either."

"Are you sure about that?" Tristan asked.

Tony didn't meet his eyes, and Allyssa knew he wouldn't answer.

Before you go, we should discuss your gifts, the griffin said. *We've never had a direct conversation with our Shifters before, so we should take every advantage it offers. And taking a minute now to make sure you understand your gifts could help you as you approach your governments.*

If you practice, you will find your emotional gift is very valuable, the dragon said, looking to Tristan. *Your dragon steel can strike paralyzing fear into the hearts of any you see as enemies, while giving those you call allies a true sense of confidence and bravery. You will be able to project it beyond those you touch, and carry it as far as your roar can be heard.*

"Sweet," Tristan said.

Riley, you discovered your gift last night, when you saved Wyatt's life, the phoenix said. *Phoenix tears are pure expressions of the heart. Tears of love, in any form, will heal. Tears of hate will burn.*

Riley absently touched her cheek.

The griffin sat tall. *Wyatt, you've learned how to use the persuasion spell wonderfully. You've realized its full potential.*

Allyssa listened to the Celestials carefully, but tried to step back slightly. If they didn't want her to hear what they were saying, she knew she wouldn't be hearing it, but it still felt kind of private. Between the Celestials and their Shifters.

"I do have one question. Please don't think it's rude," Wyatt said to the griffin. "Aren't griffins usually drawn with wings? Why can't you fly like the others?"

Allyssa heard a chortling kind of laugh coming from the Celestials. *That's because of you*, the griffin answered.

They all looked at the Celestials in confusion. The dragon elaborated for them.

When we first chose humans to embody us in your world, we made an incredibly powerful bond. We gave part of ourselves, our abilities, to you, and in return, you shaped us. Every Shifter we bond with has our values and strengths, but there are many different cultures and types of people. The three of us have had Shifters who were male, female, and different colors and sizes. You transform to reflect our current image, but that is partly determined by your upbringing and appearance. Tristan, your green eyes tie you to me. They're the reason I am this color. My shape will change if my next human has a more serpentine image of dragons.

Allyssa blinked. It kind of made sense, but . . . .

"What about me?" Wyatt asked.

You're a male, the griffin said. *When I made the bond with my first human, a male, I surrendered my wings. As a male, you have more of a natural predatory power, giving your persuasion spell additional force. You can realistically control someone with either fear or attraction in equal capacity. To fly and be able to so completely control another would make you too strong. So to keep my Shifter balanced with the other Celestials, I only have wings when they are female.*

They were all quiet as they thought about this. Allyssa found amusement watching Wyatt's puzzled expression, and smiled at him. She saw Demetrius absorbing the information, memorizing it as best he could. "The power of your bond is overwhelming," he said.

It is a living, breathing union, the dragon agreed. *Now, we should go. We can reach the portal site in minutes if you ride on my back.*

That was how Allyssa ended up riding a dragon. She felt the wind all around her, and the solidity of the dragon beneath her, and felt confident enough to extend her arms to either side and bask in the experience. She didn't think she'd ever feel so free again.

The others seemed to feel it too, though Wyatt wasn't moving more than necessary due to his burns. The light in his eyes showed the thrill he felt. Tristan extended his arms as Allyssa had, and laughed. A trembling bulge in his pocket was all that could be seen of Chitter, who had stayed on Tristan when they climbed onto the dragon. Riley wasn't laughing, but she had her eyes closed and her face tilted up, with a tiny smile, so Allyssa knew she was enjoying the experience.

Tristan ran to the portal as if physically drawn to it once they landed. It wasn't active. The dragon placed a paw against the spot and hummed, and the portal activated as it had when Riley, Tristan, and Wyatt had first opened it so long ago.

"We'll be back as soon as we can," Tristan said.

I know. Now go.

Tristan didn't have to be told twice. He glanced at the others to make sure they were ready, then walked through, Riley and Wyatt just a step behind.

Allyssa went to go through, but paused when she realized the dragon was looking at her as if it wanted to say something. It seemed amused. *If nature weren't so strong in your blood, I would have had a very difficult time selecting my Shifter.*

Her mouth opened. "You would have thought of me?"

The dragon hummed. *It's rare to have two people to choose from, but yes. If you were a Shifter, it's possible you would have been mine.*

Allyssa thought about it. "I guess it's good I'm a wind user then. I'd be honored to be your Shifter, don't get me wrong, but Tristan is the dragon. He just is." She couldn't picture him as anything else.

The dragon chuckled, a deep, throaty sound. *That he is.*

She walked with a little extra bounce in her step after that. She could have been a dragon. She wouldn't trade being a wind user for anything, but it was awesome to imagine transforming into a dragon. She wondered if the dragon's scales were always determined by eye color, or if hers would be something different. Purple would be neat . . . .

She walked through the portal to join her friends, wondering if they'd heard any of that brief conversation, and unsure if she wanted them to have heard it or not. It was enough that she'd heard it.

CHAPTER 25

Family First

Tristan was the first one to step through the portal. He turned immediately to help Riley and Wyatt through, and had reached a hand out to each of them when he realized he wasn't the only one standing near the rocky wall.

"Matt?" he asked.

Riley stopped just past the portal and turned with a start at Tristan's question. Tristan turned as well. It was Riley's brother, all right, along with a man in a police uniform.

"Riles," Matt said, his tone stunned.

He strode forward, so by the time Riley took one step he was already next to her, and in the next instant they were holding onto each other, Matt asking a flurry of questions.

"Welcome back!" the other man said, looking

at Tristan and Wyatt.

"What are you doing here?" Riley asked Matt.

"We tried to open the portal ourselves yesterday. I'll explain later." He grinned at her, and then at Tristan and Wyatt. "Where's—?"

Allyssa walked through the portal, and Matt trapped her in a hug too. He staggered back when a powerful breeze blew against him. Tristan saw Allyssa tense, then realize she wasn't in danger, and end her wind attack with a sheepish grin.

"Sorry," she said.

Matt didn't seem to care about the wind attack. He touched Tristan's shoulder, and Wyatt's, and then hugged Riley again. "I can't believe you're all back! Come on, let's get away from the portal."

"Are the others here?" Tristan asked. He felt movement in his pocket, and Chitter peeked his head out, sniffing the air curiously. Tristan automatically let the chipmunk climb onto his hand and lowered him to the ground. He wouldn't force the chipmunk to stay with them here, even if he did worry slightly about releasing him in a new location. Chitter tensed and sniffed the air more intensely when he stood on the ground, and made his namesake sound.

"I don't know," Matt said, leading the way out. He clearly saw Chitter, but apparently decided not to ask. He was practically walking backward, he kept turning his head so much. As if he didn't want to lose sight of them. "I've been here for a few hours. If they're not at the park entrance, they're back at the Temple."

Tristan had to resist the urge to Shift and fly out. It would only take them a few minutes to reach the park entrance. If they weren't there, he was definitely flying to the Temple. The knowledge that he was back on Earth made the longing he'd felt for his family these past months feel like a physical void in his chest, that would only fill when he'd found them.

"Everyone's okay?" Tristan demanded.

"They will be when they see you," Matt said. "Yeah, everyone's safe."

"Looks like your family stayed close," the man in the police uniform said. He might have said more. Tristan was already past him. At the sight of Ash, Alice, and Noah, sitting at the park entrance, he lost all control, and sprinted the remainder of the distance between them. He shouted their names and saw them jump and turn to him. Partial Shifts blazed into existence around them.

In an instant he took in the differences he saw in them. Noah's increased muscle mass. Alice's longer hair. Ash's broader shoulders. All of them were taller. All of them were also safe, before his eyes, and he didn't stop to analyze them further.

The twins collided with him with enough force to steal his breath. Tristan pulled them as tightly against his body as he could, dimly aware that he was saying their names aloud. He reached out for Noah to come over, and was momentarily surprised when a huge brown bear stood on its back legs and wrapped its arms around the three or them.

Ash laughed. Tristan might have laughed too. He really wasn't sure what he was doing, beyond clinging to his siblings. He did find it hard to see, which made him think he was crying.

"I was so worried about you," Tristan said when he found control of his voice.

Alice's eyes were reddened, but she had a harsh glint in them. "We didn't know what happened to you. Then, we had no idea how to get you back, or if you were even okay on the other side of that portal."

"She means we were really worried, too," Ash said, giving Tristan a watery smile.

Noah grunted, then dropped his Shift. The multi-hued brown aura continued to burn around him, though he stared at them as a human. "You're never going to Christopher's house again," he growled.

Tristan pulled him close. "Not a problem."

Riley and Allyssa were surrounded by Emily, Derek, and Matt. Emily had a partial Shift around her, like Noah and the twins. She had tears running down her face, but there was nothing sad about her expression. She looked as happy as Tristan had ever seen her, as she embraced Riley and then Allyssa.

Wyatt stood somewhat awkwardly to the side. Tristan went to bring him over. Emily reached Wyatt first. She said something. Wyatt nodded. Then Emily gingerly wrapped her arms around him.

Derek came and touched Tristan's arm, smiling and saying he was so glad they were back. Emily walked over with Wyatt, and the twins and Noah addressed him. Emily pulled Tristan close and trapped him in a warm, tight embrace that made Tristan feel like he might start crying, it felt so good.

He didn't know how long they all stood there, but before long Derek suggested they go back to the Temple. Most went into Emily's mini-van. A few went in Sergeant Spades' car. It was a short trip, and Tristan sat with Ash and Alice on either side, so it was free of stress. Chitter climbed back into Tristan's pocket, trembling a bit more than usual but seeming to have decided to stay with him.

Wyatt hesitated at the steps of the Temple.

Tristan stopped next to him, watching everyone else ascend. "You still have a place here," he said quietly. "You always have."

"Thanks." Wyatt looked at him without a trace of animosity. Tristan realized it had probably been his own unrecognized sense of betrayal that had let bitterness color their relationship. Since recognizing it, and reconciling, there was no lasting negativity between them. If anything, their bond was stronger than it had ever been. That was how Tristan felt, and he was pretty sure Wyatt felt the same way. "I need to go see my own family," Wyatt said, "but I'll be back later."

There was a promise in those words, and sincerity in his gaze. Tristan nodded. Wyatt looked toward the Temple, and Tristan followed his eyes to see Riley standing halfway up the steps, watching the two of them.

"I'll be back later," Wyatt said again, louder.

"Wait here for a second," Riley said. She turned and ran up the remaining steps and into the Temple, and came back less than a minute later with a small piece of paper in her grip. She handed the paper to Wyatt, and Tristan saw that it had a phone number on it. "Let us know when you get home," Riley said. "That's my mom's cell phone, since we don't have ours."

"I wonder if Christopher stowed those somewhere," Tristan muttered.

417

Wyatt pocketed the phone number. "I'll text right when I get home," he assured Riley. She bit her lip and then darted forward to hug him. He smiled at her, and then at Tristan, and turned to walk to his house.

"Are you coming?" Noah called.

Tristan reached for Riley's hand and walked up the steps.

Riley had rarely seen the Temple as crowded as it was hours later. Apparently her mom, dad, and Matt had basically moved into the Temple, since Emily was officially the legal guardian of Ash, Alice, and Noah, and Guardian of the Temple. They'd been there in the weeks preceding the portal being opened, so Riley didn't consider them a crowd. It was the addition of Allyssa and her parents, Wyatt and his mom, step-dad, and sister, and Sergeant Spades and Detective Fords, that made the familiar setting seem crowded.

They all gathered in the common room, those that didn't have a seat at the table either standing nearby or sitting in the more comfortable chairs in the middle of the room. Riley, Wyatt, Tristan, and Allyssa all had positions around the table. They were the ones doing most of the talking.

Tristan took the lead, explaining everything from deciding to open the portal to the effort to find and free the Celestials. Wyatt and Allyssa volunteered information periodically, as did Riley, though Riley mainly listened.

She'd asked for a little time, right when they got back, and Tristan had echoed the sentiment. He'd wanted to build Chitter a little nest inside the Temple, so he could stay close. So while Allyssa called her parents and Tristan worked on making Chitter comfortable outside of his pocket, Riley ran upstairs to shower and change her clothes. She didn't need to shower immediately, but it was more of an excuse to get away. She'd still felt the burning in her eyes and her throat, from crying when she'd first hugged her mother. She had at best a tenuous grasp over her emotions, and knew in telling everyone about the last ten months, she would break down when she saw Emily's reaction. By taking a few minutes to calm herself in the shower, Riley was more confident she could keep it together, regardless of Emily's expressions.

She sat at the table in the common room now, her hair almost completely dry, it had been so long since they started. There was a lot more to tell, but the basics were revealed. There were some things she knew her friends had edited, in this larger group. Tristan had skimmed over his months being imprisoned, for the twins' benefit. Wyatt had made his life-threatening injury sound serious, but not fatal. Allyssa hadn't said much about her final confrontation with

Christopher. Riley had barely mentioned how real her foster family had felt, and how thoroughly she'd forgotten her real one. She had to make sure Demetrius restored her foster family's true memories, so they didn't think they'd lost a daughter they'd never really had. These were things that could be shared later, with certain people.

"So where's Christopher now?" Matt asked.

"Still in the castle in Terraria," Allyssa said. "We're going back after, so we'll bring him over then."

"You are not going back," Allyssa's mom said. She wasn't the only one to bristle at the words.

"Not to stay," Allyssa said, "but there are still things that need to be figured out. And I need to find Demetrius."

Allyssa's mom looked like she wanted to argue, but Emily stood up. "Let's talk about this more later," she said. Riley felt a rush of gratitude for her mother's peace-keeping ability. "I'm sure everyone's hungry, so we should get some food."

"And you can fill us in on what *we* missed," Tristan said, looking to Noah.

"Until recently, not much," Noah said. "These last few weeks are a different story."

A very stressful story, which had Riley hugging her mother even more tightly than before and Tristan looking at the twins like he'd never let them out of his sight again.

"I'm glad Michael is finally being held accountable for everything he did, but . . ." Tristan trailed off. "I'm sorry I wasn't there to help."

"Shadow users," Allyssa murmured. She looked surprised when everyone looked at her, and Riley was sure she hadn't meant to speak out loud. "Demetrius said he was a Dark Elementalist. That was what Christopher taught him. The griffin called him a shadow user, though, and Mrs. Madison said that's how the one she met referred to herself. I need to tell Demetrius."

It seemed like a small thing, but Riley knew why it seemed so important to her. Riley didn't know Demetrius as well as Allyssa, but it was clear he was becoming more and more uncomfortable with his powers. A large part of this was probably because he thought they were inherently bad. Being raised thinking the powers related only to darkness, seeing how his father used his powers so willingly to cause harm and further his own plans . . . maybe if he knew others didn't see the same powers as pure darkness, it would help him reclaim his confidence in using them.

Allyssa's mom's mouth was turned down in a small frown. "You really trust that boy, knowing what he can do?"

A spark of rage appeared in Allyssa's eyes. "We wouldn't be back here if it weren't for Demetrius."

"It also sounds like you wouldn't have been gone if it weren't for him."

Allyssa stood, and Riley felt the air in the room start pulling toward Allyssa. "Christopher was the one who couldn't be trusted, Mom. He was the one to convince us to go, and he was the one to trap us there. Demetrius has done nothing wrong, and I won't let anyone say he has." Allyssa breathed out low, and the air in the room relaxed.

Allyssa's mom seemed shocked by Allyssa's reaction, and more than a little suspicious, but not suspicious of Demetrius' character, Riley thought. More about why Allyssa was so defensive of him. They would surely be having a conversation about that soon.

It was late at this point, long past dark. Everyone had been so caught up in sharing their stories that it didn't feel that late to Riley, which surprised her. Things were winding down, though, and after Allyssa's brief standoff with her mother, the gathering was breaking up.

Detective Fords said he would be in touch with Emily if he needed more information, but he thought they were set for the immediate future. Sergeant Spades would stay the night and leave for North Carolina the next day. Allyssa left with her parents. Wyatt left with his family.

"Alice, you better tell Havier Tristan's back," Ash said.

"I already did," she said. Was that a tinge of pink in her cheeks?

"I'm glad he was there to help you," Tristan told her.

"Oh, he was there for her all right," Ash said.

Alice scowled at him. Tristan seemed confused. "What—?"

"Nothing," Alice said.

Noah shook his head. "Worry about it another time," he said to Tristan.

"Why do I have to worry about it? *What* am I worrying about?"

"I think Alice has a little crush on Havier," Emily said after Ash, Alice, and Noah walked out, whispering to each other. Riley thought she saw Alice playfully shove Ash. "It seems like Havier has a crush on her too."

Tristan blinked like his brain had just short-circuited. Then he sighed. "Noah's right. I can worry about that another time."

Riley looked at Tristan with amusement, and a silent question. She wasn't nearly ready to sleep, despite the late hour. She was too keyed up to try. She thought he was as well, when he gave her the tiniest of nods. He walked upstairs after Noah and the twins. She saw him partially Shift before he turned to the stairs and walked out of view.

Meet in the common room in half an hour.

Emily, Derek, and Matt were all looking at Riley, and before she could say anything, Derek was giving her another hug.

"I'm so glad you're home," he said.

Riley smiled. "Me too."

"Get a good night's sleep," Derek said. "I don't know what, but we'll do something big tomorrow, to celebrate."

"I'm sure I could come up with a few ideas," Matt said. He ruffled Riley's hair and said goodnight, walking out with Derek and talking about finding go-carts.

Emily was still leaning on the edge of the table, looking at Riley. There was something off.

"Are you okay?" Riley asked.

Emily breathed in like she'd been caught off guard and offered a tiny smile. "I'm fine. Just taking in how much you've grown. How much I've missed."

"I don't think I grew very much," Riley said lightly, gesturing to the space from the top of her head to Emily's. Still about the same height difference.

Emily wasn't joking, though. She walked over to Riley and reached out to slowly tuck a strand of hair behind Riley's ear. "I am so *proud* of you, sweetheart. Hearing what you went through, and how incredibly strong you are . . ." Tears formed in Emily's eyes, and Riley felt her own eyes start to burn. There was something about her mother showing fear or grief that made those same feelings take hold in Riley. "I didn't mean to make you cry," Emily said with the hint of a smile, brushing her hand across Riley's cheek even though no tears had yet been shed.

"I was about to say the same thing," Riley said quietly, guilt blossoming inside her.

Emily took in a slow breath and regained her composure. "No more tears," she promised. "Though if there is anything to cry for, it's this. Getting you back." She pulled Riley close to her, and Riley sank into the embrace. "I love you, my kind, brave phoenix."

Riley closed her eyes and let her mother's warmth envelop her. "Love you too, Mom."

Emily sighed and drew back. "We can talk about contacting the Nation and Council tomorrow, before whatever plan your father and brother are trying to make a reality." She studied Riley. "Is there anything you want me to do right now?"

Riley shook her head. Part of her didn't want to be alone, but she knew she wouldn't be alone for long. Tristan would be down shortly. Emily gave her a soft smile and walked out of the common room. Riley found herself walking to the library, looking at the familiar shelves. It had been so long since she'd read. She abruptly missed the feel of the pages beneath her fingers. She walked over to a specific section of the shelves, where she'd housed her favorite books in that period after her first time Shifting. When she'd hidden in those books to avoid reality.

She wasn't avoiding reality now, she thought. She just wanted to read something she saw as an old friend. She retrieved the first *Harry Potter* book and went to her favorite armchair, very carefully opening to page one.

Tristan followed Noah, Ash, and Alice up the stairs and to the room Ash and Alice still sometimes shared. He wondered how much they'd used this room while he'd been gone. Starting when they turned ten, it had been their refuge whenever they were mad or scared or sad and didn't want to be alone. One night together usually calmed them.

"Go get ready for bed," he told the three of them. "I'll wait in here."

"You don't need to," Alice said.

He could hear in her voice that part of her wanted him to. "Humor me."

So the twins went to their separate bedrooms, and Noah to his, and a few minutes later they all came back dressed in pajamas. Tristan had dimmed the lights and taken a seat on one of the twin beds, and stood when the others returned. Ash took one bed, Alice the other. Noah leaned against the wall, facing them.

A pang went through him when he realized how grown up they all were. Ash and Alice still looked younger than their actual age, but only just. They didn't look like kids anymore. Noah was taller than Tristan by almost an inch. They were too old to be tucked in. Tristan didn't care. He needed this, tonight. He needed to take care of them.

Tristan partially Shifted, and watched their reactions. Ash had a look of wonder. Noah had a slight smile. Alice was looking at Tristan carefully.

Tristan focused on the dragon's gift, harnessing all the security, warmth, and contentment he could, and breathed out as he imagined it extending to Ash, Alice, and Noah. The effect was almost instantaneous. Noah slouched a little more against the wall. Ash's shoulders drooped and he reclined on the bed. Alice sighed and stopped her scrutiny, instead simply looking at

Tristan.

"I know we have a lot more catching up to do," Tristan said. "I know you don't think you're tired." He almost smiled, seeing how Ash's eyes were looking heavier. They would realize how exhausted they were any minute. "I'm right here," Tristan said, a little more softly. "I'm right here, and I promise you, I won't leave you like that again." He reached out and touched Alice's shoulder, gently pushing. She let him, and laid down.

Tristan started humming. He had to gauge their reactions. If this was too painful, he would stop immediately.

They did stiffen when they heard the theme. Tristan heard Alice draw in a sharp breath. Then they relaxed, one by one, seeming calmer than before he'd started, and Tristan felt confident the words wouldn't hurt them.

"*Mm-hmm I want to linger, mm-hmm a little longer, mm-hmm a little longer here with you. Mm-hmm it's such a perfect night, mm-hmm don't want to leave your side. Mm-hmm but it's just goodnight and not goodbye.*"

The Scouts song Jordan had always sung to them as children. Tristan didn't know more than the one verse, and repeated the melody a few times without defined words, hoping the familiar tune would have the same result. He saw Ash's eyes slide closed, and heard his breathing deepen. He felt Alice's hand find his, and felt it go limp when she fell asleep as well. He sang the verse he knew one more time, after that, to make sure they were really asleep, and then gently drew his hand away and stood. He walked out the door, closely followed by Noah, and fully turned off the light and drew the door closed.

Noah was staring at the floor in the hallway. His eyes seemed a little red, so Tristan didn't press him. Noah put a hand on Tristan's shoulder and then walked to his room and shut the door behind him. Tristan dropped his Shift and walked downstairs, feeling more himself than he had in a very long time.

CHAPTER 26

Two Worlds

"I thought I'd find you here," Tristan said.

Riley looked up from her book, slow to surface from the fictional world she adored. It was easier to do so when the one calling her attention was the boy she adored. She put a bookmark in and set the book on the arm of her chair. "I didn't know how long you'd be. I thought the twins might take longer to fall asleep."

He chuckled. "You know me as well as I know you." He sat down in the chair next to her. "I used my gift to help make them drowsy."

"Bet you wish you'd been able to do that for years."

"It definitely would have come in handy at times."

He rested fully against the chair, his posture

relaxed, no sign of strain in his features. "You can go to bed if you want," she said.

"I've been dreaming about being back for so long, getting to sleep in my own bed. I know I'm tired enough to try to sleep. But . . . ."

"It doesn't seem right?" she guessed. He nodded. "That's exactly how I'm feeling. It was one thing to be back with everyone, talking and feeling like I was doing something. Now I'm . . . restless? Even though I'm not? It's so contradictory. I keep wondering where Wyatt, Allyssa, and Demetrius are, thinking they should be right next to us all the time."

"Getting home was everything I needed it to be, but now . . ." he trailed off, but he didn't need to finish. She didn't know how to fully describe it either, but it was clear he was feeling the same thing she was. Relief at being home, mixed with an anxiety about how to act and feel moving forward.

He stood and held out a hand. Riley rose and took it, following as he led her out of the library and toward the front door. "Where are we going?" she asked.

He looked at her with his clear green eyes. "We could use some fresh air."

Riley glanced over her shoulder, up the staircase. "Should we tell someone?"

"Do you think they'd let us go?" he asked. "I'm sure they're all sleeping, anyway. We won't be long."

Riley only hesitated a heartbeat longer, and then smiled. Tristan unlocked the front door and drew it open, and they stepped outside. Riley felt some of the tension leave her when the fresh night air surrounded her.

"Ready?" Tristan asked after closing the door.

"Where do you want to walk?"

"Who said anything about walking?" He partially Shifted.

It had been so long . . . Riley partially Shifted, and then focused and Shifted completely, transforming into the form of the phoenix. Warmth emanated from her core. A fierce joy filled her entire being, with a sense of rightness and wonderful, exhilarating energy. Partially Shifting made her feel good. Fully Shifting let her feel amazing.

Tristan was stretching his wings next to her. Riley stretched hers out as well, and pushed off the ground. She climbed into the air, Tristan beside her, straight up. The flames rippling along her wingspan offered a weak illumination in the darkness, once they left the lamp that covered the entrance of the Temple.

The last time they'd flown from the Temple, it had been an anxiety-fueled dash to find the twins. There was no anxiety now. No pressure. Riley found an air current and followed it, moving her wings in steady strokes. Tristan did a circle around her, and she laughed in the musical trill of the phoenix before darting in close and circling around him.

It became a game, trying to prevent each other from circling while still trying to loop each other. The temperature changed, the late night becoming cool, but between the constant motion and the warmth inside her, Riley barely noticed.

We should probably land soon, Tristan thought to her, what had to be two hours after they'd Shifted.

I guess you're right. She realized she hadn't kept track of where they'd flown. *Do you know where we are?*

Somewhere above the park.

She didn't want to go back yet, though she knew it was the middle of the night. *Let's land here for a bit.*

She sensed his eagerness when he started coasting to the ground. She took her time, angled only slightly downward, flying in large loops that gradually brought her to the grass. She landed not far from a lamp post, touching down on the outer edge of the light that pooled from it. Tristan had reached the ground before her, and smiled at her as a human. Riley dropped her Shift and smiled back.

"This was a really good idea," she said.

"I do get those occasionally."

Riley sat down on the grass and then lowered herself fully to the ground, looking up. Tristan mimicked her, lying close, and Riley reached out and intertwined her hand with his.

"The skies are different."

Tristan angled his head toward her, waiting for her to continue.

"I knew when we were in Terraria that they were different, but I didn't realize how much clearer it is there."

"It's nature at its finest," Tristan murmured. "Nothing can rival that. Though I do think it looks beautiful right here."

He wasn't looking at the sky. Riley felt her cheeks warm, and angled her head to look at Tristan. "It's wonderful right here."

He leaned forward so their foreheads touched. "We might need to do this every night."

Riley moved her body closer to him. "Don't talk like this night's over. I'm not ready to go back yet."

Tristan pushed himself up, taking care to maintain his hold on Riley's hand, and leaned over her, bringing his lips to her forehead. Riley sighed at the gentle, intimate gesture, feeling like her heart was swelling. Then he laid back down. "We don't have to go anywhere," he said in a soft, warm voice. "For right now, we're exactly where we need to be."

Emily was surprised when Riley was still asleep after eight o'clock the next morning. Surprised, but somewhat pleased. They'd gone to bed late, and she'd been through so much, that she deserved to sleep in. The surprise was that she was able to. Riley definitely took after her in sleep habits.

Emily had to wait until nine or so to reach out to President Summers, though she was ready to call by seven-thirty. The majority of the world wasn't usually as eager to start work so soon after getting up. Honestly, the majority probably didn't get up so early without a particular reason.

She had her phone in her hand at nine, and dialed the number Summers had given her. She'd only called once, right before they'd left D.C., to accept the position as Shifter advisor. Summers had told her to reach out whenever she needed to.

"Hello?"

Emily smiled. "Hi. Hope I didn't call too early."

"Not at all. What's going on?"

"My daughter and the others are back. They came through the portal yesterday."

"That's wonderful!"

"They spent a long time yesterday telling us what they'd been through, and now they want to tell the Shifter and Elemental governments. I was hoping you could schedule a meeting here in Saratoga, with you and Madame Neer, as soon as possible."

Summers was quiet for a few seconds. Emily thought she heard a click of a pen. "I can absolutely schedule a meeting, but if you don't mind my asking, why the rush?"

She pictured the young man she'd met only once, who bore a striking resemblance to his father. Purple eyes, she remembered. And another, younger boy she'd never met, though Riley wasn't sure he wanted to return through the portal. Emily didn't mention him, just in case he wanted to stay. "One of their friends stayed in the parallel world, to look after the population there until a decision is made about the two worlds. I don't want him to be alone for long. The Celestials are also waiting for them to bring back news."

Emily definitely heard the sound of pen on paper. "I'll call Neer now, and get back to you."

"Thank you."

Emily set down the phone and sighed. She really hated that hurry up and wait feeling. She hoped everyone got up soon, so they could go do whatever Matt and Derek had planned—or something everyone actually wanted to do.

She jumped when her phone rang twenty minutes later, almost ripping a coupon she was in the process of cutting out from a weekly flyer, and sprang to answer it. "Hello?"

"Emily Madison?"

She hadn't looked at the caller ID, and recognized the voice of Detective Fords with slight surprise. "Hi. Can I help you?"

"I thought you should know the portal is still open. The detail we've had on it for months is still guarding it. I hope the Celestials have a plan to close it again?"

"I'm sure they do," she said, with more confidence than she felt. She had a feeling he wouldn't like hearing that they needed it to stay open for the foreseeable future. Riley, Tristan, and Wyatt didn't know how to close it, and weren't looking to do so.

He paused. "Whichever officers are standing guard have been told to assist you and the Celestials in any way they can, but I'd appreciate it if you'd let me know when the portal is being closed."

"I can do that."

Detective Fords thanked her and hung up.

While she continued clipping coupons and waiting for a return call from Summers, a few people walked into and out of the kitchen. Derek had gotten up just after Emily, and came in to check on her progress before saying he had to go arrange something. Highly suspicious, especially when Emily heard Matt's voice in the entryway and saw both Matt and Derek leaving. Matt, up before Riley?

Sergeant Spades was the next appearance, coming in to have a cup of coffee before he left for North Carolina. "Are you sure you want to leave today?" Emily asked, while he waited for the coffee to brew. "You're welcome to stay longer. I hate feeling like you drove all this way for nothing."

"It wasn't for nothing. Your boy had a really good idea, which almost worked. I was glad I could be a part of it. Joey took the offered trip home right away. I should get home too. My offer still stands, though. You helped me more than you know, even if you don't think you did anything. I can make a much bigger difference in my current position than I could before. Anytime you need my help, just call."

Emily nodded and thanked him again, and he poured his coffee into his travel mug and left.

She realized it was really getting late in the morning now, and a flash of worry overtook her. She grabbed the phone and slipped it into her pocket before she went upstairs to Riley's room. She gave a tiny knock and inched the door open, peering inside. She wasn't there. Emily was just opening the door fully when she heard steps behind her, and turned to see Riley.

"Morning," Riley said with a relaxed smile.

Emily sighed and hugged her. "Morning, sweetie."

"I can't believe I slept so late!"

"I guess you needed it." Emily was about to offer to make a big brunch for everyone, if she could have Riley's help waking the others up, but stopped before she could when her phone rang. She reached for it and answered quickly, noticing Riley's puzzled expression.

"Emily?" Summers asked when the call connected. "Sorry it took so long. Neer and I can meet with you tomorrow at one o'clock."

"That's great!" Emily said.

"Did you have a preferred location?"

Emily looked at Riley. "The portal site."

She thought she could hear the smile in Summers' voice. "Okay. We'll see you tomorrow."

Emily put her phone away. "I called President

439

Summers a little while ago," she informed Riley. "She was just getting back to tell me she arranged a meeting for us all tomorrow."

Riley's face lit up. "I was worried it would take ages for that to happen. I have to tell Wyatt and Allyssa." Her smile faltered. "Can I borrow your phone?"

Emily handed it to her. "I'll go make some pancakes," she said. "We might need them to convince the others to get up."

"Chocolate chip?" Riley asked hopefully.

Emily grinned over her shoulder. "Of course!"

"I'm a Celestial, Mom, I have to go," Wyatt said for the tenth time. "And I'm going alone. The others will meet me there."

Wyatt's mom crossed her arms and huffed. "I don't like it."

"It's just a meeting." This was another thing he'd said several times, and he was pleasantly surprised when she didn't retort with the real root of her anger, as she had before: *it was just another day when you were training with the Thranes, and look what happened then.*

Wyatt looked her in the eye, called out a goodbye to his sister, and walked out. He knew his mom had been worried while he'd been gone. He couldn't stand how she was blaming Demetrius, and not trusting that Wyatt could take care of himself.

She had no idea he planned on going back through the portal today, to bring Demetrius home. They all did. They'd planned it the day before, when Riley's mom had invited he and Allyssa to join all of them for a picnic trip followed by bowling and laser tag. Riley's mom had agreed to it, provided she got to go through the portal with them. Since they planned on bringing Summers and Neer through as well, this only made sense.

Wyatt walked toward Spa Park with a quick stride. It was one of those spring days where the morning had been chilly, but the afternoon felt almost like summer, with the bright sun and minimal wind. He'd actually changed into shorts when he'd gotten home this morning. Then again, it was early May. This wide range of temperature was normal for upstate. He didn't like the added warmth of the bandage that crept onto his neck, covering his burn. A few more days and he should be able to take the bandage off, and see how much of a scar he would be left with.

It had been nice to escape early this morning, to go to Congress Park with his sketchpad like he had hundreds of mornings. He hadn't sketched since before they'd opened the portal. He was rusty. After about half an hour of mindlessly sketching, though, getting his fingers used to the grip of the pencil again, practicing the heaviness of the lines and the angles, he felt something inside him slip back into place. He saw a duck in the water and started translating the sight onto the paper. He was pretty pleased with the result. He'd given it to Jill when he'd returned home.

He reached the other park now to find a barrier set up near the entrance, and a group of people gathered around it: Riley, Tristan, Allyssa, Riley's mom, and two people he'd never met, facing two people in police uniforms.

Allyssa saw him first, and a gust of wind made Wyatt pick up his speed moving forward. He almost laughed. Yep, Allyssa was definitely eager to get this meeting done so they could go get Demetrius.

"Wyatt!" Riley greeted.

He dipped his head in greeting, looking at the two women he didn't know. Summers and Neer. "You must be the griffin," one of the women said. She looked to be in her fifties, with a serious expression. "I'm Rita Neer. President of the Nation."

Wyatt shook her hand, and then the hand of the other woman. "Elaine Summers. President of the Council." Summers looked much younger than Neer.

"Wyatt Rider," he told them. "Pleased to meet you."

"Let's get started, shall we?" Neer said. The officers moved the barrier aside to let the group through. Wyatt forced himself to walk in the back. He really wanted to go through the portal. He hated that Demetrius had been alone the last two and a half days. Being in the back of the group meant there would be a little more distance between himself and the portal, and therefore a little less guilt at knowing they probably had an hour or so before they went through. They had a lot to discuss even before the true Celestials were brought into the conversation.

He didn't have to worry about the guilt at being so near the portal but not going through it. They stopped before the start of the trail that led to the cracked, rocky wall, where they had more room, and sat down there.

"So," Summers said, looking between Riley, Tristan, Wyatt, and Allyssa. "What happened over there?"

They told Summers and Neer all of the big things, taking time to describe how Terraria had been their home when they'd had false identities. Christopher had really done his research, figuring out how to make the parallel world a thriving civilization, without overly harming the environment. Wyatt had to make sure they realized that. If they decided to let those who lived in Terraria stay, he would press for them to keep it similar to the way it was now, with minimal damage.

The presidents listened to everything with total concentration, and when they'd finished, the women shared a look. "Could we see it?" Summers asked.

Tristan stood. "We were hoping you'd say that. The Celestials wanted to speak to you themselves."

Neer's eyebrows shot up. Summers had a similar expression. Wyatt jumped to his feet. "They wanted us to make sure you were okay with what we had to say before they talked to you. I know it probably seems even more daunting now, but they earnestly want to meet you, if you're willing to meet with them."

Riley's mom looked at him with a somewhat proud expression.

"Willing?" Neer said. "I'd consider it an honor."

Summers nodded. "Lead the way."

Wyatt went in the front of the group this time, jogging ahead. He heard questions behind him, but they would see in a minute. He reached the portal site, which had someone stationed in front of it, said hello, and Shifted.

He closed his eyes and focused on his connection with the griffin. *We're coming through the portal now,* he said.

Then he dropped his Shift, just as the others reached the portal site. He had no idea if that had worked, but he'd tried. Hopefully, the Celestials would be nearby when they went through. Wyatt looked at the portal, surprised it was still open. Had they been supposed to close it, and then reopen it? Clearly it could be opened and closed multiple times, since Christopher had made the Celestials close it once he had his little world established. He looked at the others and walked through the rippling doorway, emerging onto the grass in Terraria.

Tristan came next, then Neer, Summers, Allyssa, Riley, and Emily. The adults were all looking around in amazement, and Wyatt shared a look with his friends at their childlike expressions. Had they looked like that when they'd first come through the portal? It *was* pretty amazing.

"Think they're coming to us?" Tristan asked.

"It didn't take long for the phoenix to come the first time," Riley said.

"I tried to reach the griffin, so we should give them a minute."

Neer turned to the teenagers. "How far are the settlements?"

"The closest one is Astrum, where Christopher built his castle," Allyssa said. "It took fifteen minutes or so to cross the distance flying on the dragon's back, so I'm not sure how long it would take to walk there."

"He probably didn't want his fortress to be immediately next to the portal site, but wanted to make sure it was accessible enough to easily move people and materials," Neer said, nodding to herself.

"Look!" Summers said.

Wyatt looked expectantly in the direction Summers was looking and found the phoenix and dragon soaring toward them. He moved his gaze lower, searching for the griffin that would no doubt be racing toward them on the ground, and felt his lips curve up when he saw it. Within a minute the three Celestials stood before the group.

Welcome, the dragon said.

You returned faster than we'd expected, the griffin told them.

The adults were looking at the Celestials with varying expressions of shock. Riley's mom kept looking from one Celestial and back to Tristan, Wyatt, or Riley, as if noting all the similarities between the matched pairs.

"It's incredible to meet you," Summers said. She introduced herself, Neer, and Riley's mom.

So have you concluded your war? the griffin asked.

The phoenix and dragon turned to the griffin

with force. *That's how you decided to ask?* the dragon said.

It's a simple question, the griffin defended.

Neer looked at Summers, as if for help in answering. Wyatt waited for a response too. "We're actively calling for peace," Neer said. "No one really knows this yet . . ."

Summers picked up where Neer left off. "We've drawn up terms that address some of the main issues for both sides, with our current best plans to resolve them. The terms are being analyzed by representatives in both governments as we speak, and if they're approved, we can officially conclude the conflict."

"It might not stop all the conflict, but it will make any continuing violence or aggression after the resolution scarcer," Neer said. "People like having the 'protection' of a state of war to act on hateful desires. Without that sense of protection, they're less likely to act in such despicable ways."

Riley's mom was looking at Summers. "You've been working on this non-stop since the last time I saw you, haven't you?" she asked.

Summers smiled. "Since a bit before that meeting, but yes, Neer and I have been working together for the last week to make a treaty we're both satisfied with. Our chambers are reviewing it, and we're hopeful everyone will sign it by the end of the week. We'll be the last to sign it, on a live stream broadcast to all Temples and Guilds."

"And then we can begin to move forward," Neer said.

The phoenix straightened. *I'm glad to hear it. If you've already made such significant progress in your efforts toward peace, we only have one course of discussion left: the connection of our two worlds.*

Let us take you to Astrum, the dragon said, crouching and extending its wings. The phoenix and griffin also lowered themselves.

Wyatt climbed onto the griffin. Neer, Summers, Emily, and Tristan went onto the dragon. Riley went onto the phoenix. Wyatt looked at the griffin and motioned for Allyssa to come with him, but she shook her head. "I haven't used my powers for anything significant since that final battle. I want to test myself." She spread her hands and held them facing the ground, and lifted inches into the air.

"Are you sure you're recovered enough?" Riley worried.

Allyssa met her eyes and nodded. "It's been a few days. I'm back to full energy."

We won't let you fall, the phoenix said.

You won't fall, the dragon said.

Allyssa seemed to like that comment better, and they left. Allyssa ranged between flying near the dragon and phoenix and soaring close to the ground, right next to Wyatt and the griffin. Soaring like Icarus, though propelled by the wind she could control, there was no danger of losing her wings. Wyatt didn't think she'd ever been able to do anything like this before. No, he knew she hadn't. It was obvious she was enjoying every second. It was somewhat windy, so he thought she might be coasting along the natural breeze for parts of the flight, and boosting herself when she needed more. Needless to say he was impressed, and a little jealous that he was the only one unable to fly.

The griffin was the fastest on land, though. It could have beat the others to Astrum if it had wanted to. Wyatt relished in the feeling of the wind rifling through his hair and the scent of the grass and flowers that surrounded him.

They went straight to the castle, landing/ stopping in the courtyard. A bluebird flitted around them excitedly. Demetrius stood near the castle's front door. He started walking toward them as soon as they touched the ground. Allyssa dropped down close to him and ran to his side, throwing her arms around him. Tony buzzed around Wyatt and the others again before dropping his Shift and grinning at them.

"Hi guys!" Tony said.

"How's it been?" Tristan asked him.

"Pretty quiet. Demetrius called a bunch of people here to explain what had happened, and told them to spread the word."

Demetrius and Allyssa reached them, and Wyatt put a hand on Demetrius' shoulder in greeting.

"Demetrius Thrane," Neer said evenly. She scrutinized him for a moment. "Your father caused a lot of trouble."

Wyatt saw some of the tension in Demetrius' shoulders lessen immediately after this comment. "Madame Neer." His gaze moved to Summers. "President Summers." He looked over his shoulder. "My father is still in the castle, in the throne room. I haven't moved him. He's comatose, and arrangements should be made to hold him. I'll let you decide what to do with him, but I suggest you keep him this way and lock him away somewhere he'll never be found."

Riley's mom walked right up to Demetrius.

"Mrs. Madison," Demetrius said, looking at the ground, "I'm so sorry for the pain my father and I—"

Riley's mom hesitantly wrapped her arms around him, and Demetrius stopped. She stepped back, and Wyatt was confused when he saw that she was fighting back tears. "You didn't know. And I can see he put you through a lot of pain himself, so don't take on more now, okay?"

Another shock. Demetrius seemed at a loss for words. He merely nodded, and gave a tiny smile.

Wyatt grinned at Riley, very glad her mother had come along.

"I can take you on a tour of Astrum, if you'd like," Demetrius offered. He started walking toward the castle with the presidents, explaining the planning that had gone into making this world a new home. Riley's mom seemed to debate, but a nod from Riley seemed to tell her the teens would be fine for a little while, and she joined Demetrius, Neer, and Summers. Wyatt wasn't sure if he should follow or not. He had a feeling no big decisions would be made in the next few hours. The presidents needed information, and they had to communicate with a list of people on Earth before they made a decision. The regular human governments had to be involved as well. He imagined it would work out fine, but anticipated it being a headache in the meantime, and he wanted to enjoy another day in this beautiful world without that strain.

"Let's go for a ride," he said, turning to Riley, Tristan, Allyssa, and Tony. "Our horses should still be in the stable. Tony, you can pick one out for yourself."

Tony fist-pumped and ran toward the stables. "Awesome!"

Riley didn't move immediately. She was looking after Tony. "Do you think he'll come back with us?"

Wyatt doubted it, but could tell Riley was worried about Tony, and softened his answer. "I think he'll go where he feels most at home. That might be here, now."

She nodded and took in a small breath. "Right."

"Everything will work out fine," Tristan said. "Talk of peace is in the air. The Celestials are free. I'm pretty sure the people who live here will get to stay." He looked at each of them. "We deserve to enjoy ourselves here for a little while, with no worries."

Wyatt smiled. He couldn't have said it better himself.

The time between Riley and the others going through the portal and coming back was quiet for Demetrius. He spoke to a large group of people who lived in the village, and guards from the castle, explaining that they no longer had to follow a king. That took a little time. The Celestials helped, explaining that there were no immediate plans for anything to change and insisting everyone go about their usual business. Once that was done, Demetrius walked into the village and found Riley's foster family, and

Wyatt's, and erased the false memories his father had given them. He spoke with them for a short while, apologizing several times for the worry they'd experienced recently. Riley's foster family was angry, the little boy confused. Wyatt's foster family seemed to take it better.

Demetrius didn't need them to forgive him. He was just glad they finally knew the truth. The deception on the part of his father had been in the back of his mind since the day they'd rescued Riley and Wyatt.

He spent the rest of that first day wandering the village and going for a long ride on Perseus, but as the day drew to a close, he knew he couldn't avoid going back to the castle much longer. He had one other task he had to do, and putting it off would only make it harder.

He returned and took his time giving Perseus and the other horses plenty of water and feed before going into the castle. His heart quickened in his chest when he approached the throne room. He paused outside the door when he realized he could hear a voice inside. Panic made him rush into the room, fearing Christopher had somehow awoken. It hadn't been a masculine voice, though. It was Madaleine.

The woman sat on the floor, Christopher's head cradled in her lap. She startled when Demetrius entered and stopped her low murmur.

"Demetrius."

He'd stopped just inside, and found he couldn't move any closer. He'd known Madaleine was still here somewhere. He'd planned to find her at some point. He hadn't expected her to be here, now. It seemed she'd been here at least once before, because she had a goblet of water next to her and was wiping a cloth across Christopher's forehead.

"What did you do to him?" Madaleine demanded.

It was her tone that unlocked Demetrius' voice. "I made it so he can't hurt anyone again."

Madaleine looked at him sternly. "You just left him here. He'll die without proper care."

Demetrius almost showed her the canteen he had. The only reason he'd come in here was to trickle some water into Christopher's mouth. He wouldn't let the man wither away in here, though he deserved it. He knew Riley and the others wouldn't be gone horribly long, and Christopher could be attached to fluids and whatever else comatose people needed when they brought him back to Earth. The man would be fine until then with even minimal water. Demetrius' hand twitched toward the canteen now, but he didn't reach for it. Madaleine could think what she wanted.

He had nothing to say to her. He did have

something to do to her. He placed an unconscious command in her mind, to keep close. She
wouldn't even realize it wasn't her idea, but it
would deter her from slipping away and avoiding
questioning by the Shifter and Elemental governments. He would make sure she was held accountable for her role in all of this.

Madaleine held his gaze, still waiting for him
to say something. He turned and strode from
the room, angry but also distinctly . . . relieved.
He wouldn't have to go near his father until the
others were back. He didn't have any other pressing tasks at the moment, so he could take his
time to process and think.

His mind was definitely busy in the days his
friends were gone, and after he gave the tour to
the presidents and Mrs. Madison, when everyone
was preparing to go through the portal again, he
thought again of what had been churning within
his mind.

For the first time in his life, Demetrius didn't
have a plan.

He didn't know what to do, really. His father
was out of the picture. He assumed his old house
had been sold, and even if it hadn't, he found
he didn't really want to go back there. Some of
his best memories had taken place there. So had
some of his worst. It didn't feel like he belonged
there anymore. It was too big for him on his own,

anyway.

He could get an apartment in Saratoga. He could go to college. He had plenty of funds in his account . . . assuming it was still in his name. He could just take his time to figure out what was next. He was twenty years old. He imagined many people his age were just figuring out what they wanted to do with their lives.

He couldn't ignore another thought inside him. A desire, really. Part of him wanted to stay here.

He could make a new life here, in one of the settlements. Learn a trade. Teach in a school, perhaps. There was some appeal in the thought of having a little cottage in this beautiful place.

It was a foolish longing. He'd imagined this world for so long, and in the last month, traveling with his friends, he'd truly gotten to experience it.

That thought was equally responsible for his desire to stay and his desire to leave. He'd started to bond with this world because he'd traveled part of it with his friends. They would all be going back through the portal, permanently. Would this world hold as much wonder if he were alone? Could he even bear to be alone?

He knew that answer immediately. Two faces flashed across his mind: one with messy, dirty blond hair and a crooked smile, the other with long brown hair and loving brown eyes. His best friend, and the one he loved.

No, he couldn't bear to be alone.

Wyatt and Allyssa would never let him be alone, either. The knowledge made it tempting to smile.

"I'm allowed to be happy," he murmured.

He heard footsteps behind him. "Of course you're allowed to be happy," Allyssa said. She circled her arms around him. "What's wrong?" she asked in a softer voice.

He sighed and put his hands over hers. "Nothing now."

"But something was bothering you," she insisted.

"Just thinking about the immediate future. Where I'll go."

She slipped her arms back and walked in front of him. "And about what would make you happy?"

"Yes. And I decided that's being around the people I care about. Even if they deserve better."

It seemed like she wanted to combat the last part. He saw the flicker of anger in her eyes. "None of us are letting you go away," she said. "We choose you. I choose you. Got it?"

His smile broke through. "Got it."

He knew she could see that he still worried he was bad for them. He hoped she could also see that, thanks to her and Wyatt, he was starting to realize he wasn't. Starting to. It would be a little while before he could confidently say he wasn't endangering them, or causing them harm. But he would take the small steps to get there, to firmly step out of his father's shadow.

Allyssa held out her hand. "Mrs. Madison will let you stay at the Temple while we figure things out."

"I'm a little scared," he admitted.

Allyssa moved closer and took his hand. "I'd be a little concerned if you weren't. I am too. Everything's changing again." She met his eyes. "It's a good kind of change, though. We'll go through it together."

He tightened his hold on her hand and imagined some of her confidence transferred to him with the contact. "I'm not that scared anymore."

She grinned. "Neither am I."

"You two coming?" Wyatt called from the entrance of the courtyard. He already sat astride the griffin. Riley was with him this time. The adults were on the dragon's back, Christopher's still form between them. Tristan was on the phoenix. "Are you sure you can support me too?" Demetrius asked Allyssa. "I can ride Perseus to the portal."

She raised one hand and he felt his feet leave the ground. "I don't have a magic carpet or anything, but I can show you the world this way."

He felt his eyebrows press together. "That's a reference to something, isn't it?"

She laughed and started making them both climb into the air. "We're definitely watching a Disney movie tonight. And making s'mores. I've got a lot to teach you from my childhood."

And then she was singing in her high, sweet voice, apparently the song from the Disney movie she was thinking of, and they were flying. It was terrifying. It was exhilarating. Allyssa took his hand, and Demetrius couldn't do anything but smile.

When they reached the portal site, she took his other hand and they faced each other as she gently lowered them to the ground.

"That was incredible," he told her.

"And about all the flying I can do today," she admitted. Her shoulders slumped. "That took more energy than I thought."

"Then next time we fly, use some of my energy."

Her eyebrow quirked. "Next time?"

"How else can we completely escape our lives

for a time?"

Her energy seemed to replenish in an instant. She motioned with her hand, and Christopher was lifted off the dragon's back. He dropped to the ground, and Allyssa said, "oops," before buoying him back up. She also 'accidentally' hit his head on the stone at the top of the portal before she made the wind shove him through.

Everyone turned to look at the Celestials. No decision had been made yet, which to Demetrius, said that a decision had been made. Both Summers and Neer seemed supportive of the settlements. Terraria would remain open to humans, with the Celestials ensuring that their world wasn't damaged. The people who had made their lives here would be allowed to stay.

A bluebird hovered near them, its entire body shaking, and Demetrius knew that was Tony's way of waving goodbye. He made a trilling sound and fluttered around each of them for a few seconds. He'd been a little emotional just before they left the castle, and Shifted and flown off. Demetrius was glad to see he'd followed them. They hadn't been able to convince him to go through the portal with them. He would be staying here, at least for the time being. Mrs. Madison didn't seem to like that very much, and Demetrius had a feeling she would ask after him from now on. The Celestials had promised to look after Tony. Wyatt's foster family had expressed interest in meeting with him, so Demetrius was optimistic things would work out for the boy. He would certainly be looked after.

The portal would have to close, only opening periodically, so both sides could keep track of who passed through it, but it could be opened from either side now. Realistically, they could return whenever they wanted. It made it easier to leave, knowing he could come back from time to time. He would miss parts of this world.

Thank you, the Celestials said together.

"Thank *you*," Neer and Summers said.

"You said we'll still be able to communicate, right?" Riley asked.

I heard Wyatt when he said you were on your way, the griffin confirmed.

Since we've come into physical contact, our bond is stronger than it has been with our Shifters in the past, the dragon said. *When you fully Shift in your world, we will hear you if you reach out to us.*

Don't worry, the phoenix said, looking mostly at Riley. *We're sure we'll see each other again soon.*

"We will," Tristan said. "We'll make sure of it."

The dragon hummed, and a calm washed over Demetrius, along with a sense of confidence.

Demetrius looked at everyone, and together, they walked through the portal.

Epilogue

It amazed Riley how quickly things could change —and how wonderful those changes could be.

She'd been torn between attending the school she'd always gone to and being homeschooled with Tristan, Noah, Ash, and Alice. After missing most of the last school year, she found the decision wasn't difficult. Emily had quit her part-time job and become Noah, Ash, and Alice's teacher when the academic year began last fall, and began teaching Tristan and Riley soon after they returned. She actually ended up teaching Allyssa as well, so the three could catch up on their learning together. Riley did miss Terrace High a little, but liked this arrangement a lot.

This time last year, she hadn't known her spirit animal. She'd only come to the Temple once, maybe twice a week. Allyssa had been her only true friend. Now she regularly Shifted into her phoenix form, going on moonlit flights with

Tristan almost every night. She practically lived in the Temple. She had a larger family, with Ash, Alice, and Noah filling the role of younger siblings. She had Wyatt and Demetrius as friends, in addition to Allyssa. She had Tristan as a friend and much, much more.

Riley missed seeing the group each day, and was thrilled when Allyssa made a group message for them. They met at the park frequently. About a week after closing the portal, and after learning the Nation and the Council had signed the peace treaty and celebrating *a lot*, Riley put a message in the chat that she wanted to meet at the Temple, in the gym.

She didn't even tell Tristan why, though it wasn't a big secret. It wasn't even anything overly important. She just wanted to train. She wanted to spar with them in a way they still didn't really dare to do in the middle of the park, despite knowing that the world of Shifters and Elementalists was no longer secret: partially Shifted, Riley sometimes using her fire, and Allyssa using her powers. Riley had gotten used to training with them in the evenings when they'd been searching for the Celestials. She missed it.

She told the others to walk right in, and went with Tristan to feed Chitter while they waited. The chipmunk seemed to love the forest-like bed and jungle gym Tristan had made for him in the far corner of the gym, though Riley knew the chipmunk slept at Tristan's side many nights. She helped Tristan hand the chipmunk berries and nuts and watched him stuff his tiny cheeks before rushing onto one of the branches Tristan had strategically mounted. She was glad the chipmunk had stayed with them.

Tristan was looking at Chitter with undisguised affection. "I was worried he might not want to stay with us, but I think he's happy here."

Riley took his hand and circled the back of his palm with her thumb. "You made him a home. Of course he's happy here."

Tristan looked at her with his steady green eyes, and Riley felt heat rush to her cheeks. He pulled her closer and tucked her hair behind her ear, letting his hand trail down her cheek. "You're happy here too, right?" he asked.

She leaned into his warm hand. "You made it my home too, Tristan. You, and Ash and Alice and Noah. But mostly you. All of *you.* I'm right where I belong."

His lips curved up, and she leaned forward to meet them with her own for a brief moment. Then Tristan stepped back, looking reluctantly at the door. Riley understood. In this moment, all she wanted to do was hold onto Tristan, but the others would be here any minute. There would be time to be alone later. She satisfied herself with standing close to him, his body brushing against hers, their hands loosely linked between them, as they waited for their friends.

"Welcome back, brother," Tristan said when Wyatt stepped into the gym. Riley remembered the last time Wyatt had come into the gym, and how standoffish Tristan had become. He'd been in the Temple a lot recently, but this was the first time he'd come up to the gym with them in ages, and Riley was glad Tristan was overwriting the last time.

Wyatt's eyebrows lifted in shock, and then a delighted, impish smile transformed his face. "What did you want to do?" he asked.

Riley partially Shifted. *That's simple,* she thought to them. *Let's have some fun.*

Both boys adopted their own partial Shifts, and smiled. For a moment, a star shone in both of their eyes.

The rippling, colorful auras burned around them, and Riley thought the colors started to bleed together in the space between them, curling around each other, combining and merging to make a different display of energy than any could make on their own. More beautiful. More powerful.

Riley felt a laugh build inside her as they started mock sparring.

The three Celestials, in the same age group, in the same geographic area, at the same time. A dragon, a griffin, and a phoenix.

The world had changed.

Riley guessed it would continue to change, at least partially due to them.

She dodged a high kick from Wyatt, ducked around Tristan, and pinned his arm behind his back, and the laugh escaped her.

Wyatt went to retaliate, and a strong breeze rushed past Riley, buoying Wyatt into the air. Allyssa stood in the doorway, one hand extended, one eyebrow raised. "You wouldn't have started without me, would you?"

"Wouldn't dream of it," Tristan said.

Allyssa scoffed and ran in. Demetrius walked in behind her, going to the sidelines and leaning against the wall to watch with a content expression.

"Ready?" Wyatt asked after Allyssa had set him down.

They all looked to Riley, and she grinned. "Let's go."

The End

Afterword

That concludes the Celestials series! I hope you enjoyed it.

Please consider leaving a review on Amazon, Goodreads, or both. Reviews are everything to independently published authors, as they help other readers find our works.

Acknowledgement

Thank you to my best friend, HC, for helping me brainstorm several sections of this novel. You may think I merely bounced ideas off of you, but you provided more help and support than you realize.

Thank you to SaphireYing on Fiverr, the artist who drew Riley on the cover of each book in this series. Your work is phenomenal.

And lastly, thank you to my readers. I hope you enjoyed Riley and the others' journey as much as I did.

BOOKS BY THIS AUTHOR

Stars Begin To Burn

Book 1 in the Celestials series

Stars, Hide Your Fires

Book 2 in the Celestials series

Shifter Stories

A novella in the Celestials series.
When you have the power to turn into your spirit animal, there's a lot of fun to be had - and a lot of trouble. Featured in this novella are three stories about some of the Shifters in the Celestials series: Matt's adventure flying over the Canadian border as an eagle, Ash's daredevil experience at an Imagine Dragons concert, and how Noah came to be part of the family at the Temple. Full of humor and heart, these stories give you an in-depth look at some of the characters who didn't play as ac-

tive a role in Stars Begin To Burn (book one of the series).

ABOUT THE AUTHOR

Shelby Elizabeth

Shelby Elizabeth lives in Upstate New York, surrounded by family. She is an English teacher, a cat lover, and a major geek (some of her favorite book series include Harry Potter and Percy Jackson). Celestials is her first series.

Printed in Great Britain
by Amazon